DATE DUE

Praise for

CAROLE MATTHEWS

and her novels

"It's a big five points for humor."
—Kelly Ripa, *Live with Regis and Kelly* on FOR BETTER, FOR WORSE

"Matthews…scores again with this charming comedy."
—*Booklist* on A MINOR INDISCRETION

"A natural for the beach, it will charm Bridget Jones
fans on both sides of the Atlantic."
—*Library Journal* on FOR BETTER, FOR WORSE

"Matthews delivers a realistic and unflinching look at love, marriage and
infidelity and still manages to inject some light humor."
—*Romantic Times BOOKclub* on LET'S MEET ON PLATFORM 8

"She entertains her readers with serendipitous trysts and near misses."
—*Publishers Weekly* on FOR BETTER, FOR WORSE

"Her humorous storytelling resurrects the power of
romance to conquer all."
—*Booklist* on FOR BETTER, FOR WORSE

Also by Carole Matthews

CAROLE MATTHEWS

*Welcome
to the
Real World*

**RED
DRESS
INK**™

WELCOME TO THE REAL WORLD

A Red Dress Ink novel

ISBN-13: 978-0-373-89590-8
ISBN-10:   0-373-89590-9

First U.S. Edition © 2006 by Carole Matthews

www.RedDressInk.com

Printed in U.S.A.

This book was great fun to write and, while it is entirely fictitious, I have to thank everyone at Welsh National Opera for their invaluable input and allowing me access to their company. To Caroline Leech, Catriona Chatterley and Hazel Hardy, for helping out a woman who didn't know her *La Traviata* from her *Turandot*. It's been lovely to work with you. Also, thanks to Simon Rees, Dramaturg at WNO, for kindly allowing me to use his translation of *La Traviata*—very much appreciated. To Christopher Purves—a huge talent and generous man—for giving me an insight into the life of an opera star. To Gareth Rhys-Davies, for letting me see him with *and* without his makeup. To Julia, Liz and Katie, for looking after me backstage. And to all the lovely members of the company who have tirelessly answered my inane questions. The only complaint I have is that I've had to make up all the diva moments and tantrums myself—you are all far too nice to be opera singers! Thank you all so much for taking the time to allow me to have an insight into your wonderful world—you have left me with some cherished memories. With kind thanks also to English National Opera and War Memorial Opera House in San Francisco, for helping me with additional material. All the mistakes and terrible liberties taken in the name of opera are entirely mine.

One

'I need more money.' Tilting the glass in my hand, I pull yet another pint of beer.

'Don't we all, man.' My dear friend Carl looks at me through the fog of his cigarette smoke, eyes barely slits. He's propping up the bar opposite me and I smile across at him, mainly because the hubbub of noise in the pub makes it difficult to be heard and I want to save my voice.

Carl is a man out of his time—I'm sure he would have been much happier as a 1970s rock god. His battered denim jacket, shoulder-length hair and tendency to say, 'Yeah, man,' don't sit comfortably with current ideas of personal styling. But Carl and I go back a long way. A long, long way.

'No. I *really* need money,' I say. 'This time it's bad.'

'It always is,' Carl remarks.

'Joe's swimming in a sea of unpaid bills. I have to do some-thing.' Joe is my older brother, but somehow I've become responsible for him. I don't mind at all. He needs all the help he can get.

'You work two jobs already, Fern.'

'Tell me something I don't know.' The till does its digital equivalent of *ker-ching* again and, grinning insanely at the next punter, I reach for another glass.

'How much more can you do?'

Win the lottery? Put on my shortest skirt, strike a pose outside King's Cross station and hope for a bit of business? Get a third job that requires minimum effort, yet doles out maximum pay? I'll fill you in quickly on what I like to call my 'situation'.

Bro' Joe lives on benefits and is constantly robbing Peter to pay Paul. Now Peter has been robbed so much he has nothing left. My brother isn't, however, the media version of a person living on the dole—work-shy, feckless or lazy. Joe can't work because he has a sick son, Nathan. My beloved nephew is a five-year-old blond-haired heartbreaker and has severe asthma—and when I say severe, I mean *severe*. He needs constant attention. Constant attention that his mother—the beautiful and brittle Carolyn—wasn't prepared to give him as she left my lovely brother and their only child when Nathan was barely a year old. And, call me a bitter old bat, but I don't think that could be considered as giving it a fair crack of the whip.

If anyone thinks it's easy to manage on measly government handouts, then think again. If anyone thinks it's easy being the single parent of a sickly child, then ditto. Joe had a promising career in a bank—okay, he wasn't setting the world alight. My brother was never destined to appear on *Newsnight* in a pinstripe suit giving his opinion on the world money market, but he was getting great appraisals, regular promotions, small pay rises—and a pension to die for. He gave it all up the moment Carolyn departed to stay at home and care for Nathan. And, for that alone, he deserves all the support I can give him.

'You're on in a minute,' Ken the Landlord shouts over at me, giving a pointed glance at the clock.

As well as pulling pints behind the beer-stained bar of the King's Head public house, I am also 'the turn'. I do two half-hour sets every evening Monday through Saturday—Sunday is quiz night—singing middle-of-the-road pop songs for a terminally disinterested crowd. I finish serving the round of drinks and then nod my head towards Carl. 'Ready?'

Carl is my pianist. Again, I think he'd be happier as lead guitarist—which he also plays brilliantly—for Deep Purple or someone of that ilk, leaping around the stage, doing ten-minute solos, head-banging to his heart's content. But Carl has bills to pay, too. He jumps down off his bar stool and we head for the small, raised platform that is our stage. A once-spangly curtain is attached by a row of drawing pins to the wall behind us. Despite Carl's rebel, dropout appearance he is the most reliable person I've ever met. He's very low-key rock 'n' roll, really. Okay, he smokes the occasional joint and puts 'Jedi Knight' as his religion on Electoral Roll forms, but I don't think he's ever been moved to bite the head off a live chicken on stage or any such thing. And he's never smashed up a guitar as a display of artistic expression, because he's far too aware of how much they cost. He is also patience personified, spending every evening on that bar stool waiting for our two brief periods of respite when we can do what we truly love doing.

'We could do a couple of extra hours busking in the Tube,' my friend suggests as we make our way to the stage. 'That usually pulls in a few quid.'

I grab Carl's hand and squeeze it.

He looks at me in surprise. 'What's that for?'

'I love you,' I say.

'Cupboard love,' he replies. 'Would you still love me if I wasn't the world's best ivory tinkler?'

'Yes.'

This is a confession now. Carl and I used to be an 'item'. We never did the horizontal tango together—something for which I'm truly grateful. But we used to spend hours necking and I used to let him feel my top parts—occasionally even under my jumper. In my defence, however, this was when I was fifteen and we were at school together. And it was a much more innocent era.

Now that I'm thirty-two, I have no boyfriend and no time for one. Not even Carl, who I think still holds a torch for me. Well, not just a torch, a bloody great flashlight, a beacon, whatever type of light it is they have on lighthouses. I feel sorry that I don't love Carl in the way that he loves me, but I got him out of my system years ago and, basically, he's still sporting the same jacket and hairdo that he wore then. Need I say more?

We take our places on the stage, Carl behind his keyboard, me at the temperamental microphone. I wish I had more presence, more va-va-voom, but I always feel so insignificant on stage—partly because I'm only fractionally taller than the microphone stand. There's a slight hiatus in the hullabaloo of conversation and a smattering of disjointed clapping. Without preamble—no 'one, two, one, two' as I test the mike, no shout of 'Good evening, London!'—we launch into our performance. As this is a predominantly Irish pub, U2 hits feature heavily in our repertoire, as do those of The Corrs and Sinead

O'Connor. We usually also knock out a few 1960s favourites and some classic ballads at the end to keep the maudlin drunks happy.

I spill my heart and soul, sliding flawlessly from one song to another, and at the end I take my bow and, in return, receive some muted applause. Is this what I do it for? For a few meagre crumbs of appreciation and an equally few extra quid in my pay packet at the end of the week?

When I'm back at the bar and serving pints again, one of the customers leans towards me and says with beery breath, 'You've got a great voice, darlin'. It's bloody wasted here.'

'Thanks.'

'You want to get on that *Fame Game* programme. You'd beat the pants off most of them.'

This isn't the first time I've been told that. Usually by men with beery breath and no knowledge whatsoever of the music industry.

'That's a great idea!' I don't point out to him that to take part in any of these talent-spotting fiascos, you need to be under the age of twenty-two and possess a belly flatter than your average pancake—neither of which applies to me.

My admirer lurches away clutching his drink.

I give Carl another pint of lager. 'That went well,' he says. 'I thought "With or Without You" was really heavy, man.'

'Yes.'

'I'll come round tomorrow and we can go through the running order. Maybe try out a few new songs.'

'Sure.' We analyse all our performances as if we've just come off the stage at Wembley Arena and, sometimes, it makes my heart break.

Once I was asked for my autograph at the end of the night by a young guy, but I'm not sure if he was taking the piss. All his friends laughed when he showed them the beer mat with my name scrawled on it in marker pen. It still made me walk on air for a week afterwards. I stifle a sigh. Don't think I don't have ambitions beyond being a badly paid barmaid–cum–pub singer. I, too, would like to be Joss Stone, Jamelia and Janet Jackson rolled into one. But, tell me, how on earth do I get my big break when all my days and nights are spent just trying to earn a crust?

Two

When you roll into bed at about one o'clock every morning, the next day comes around very quickly, I find. I force my eyes to open. Eventually the blurry mist settles and I think about getting up. Slipping my feet into my cow-patterned slippers, I try to pretend that my flat is not the skankiest place imaginable. Even Shrek would turn up his nose at living here—and that guy's at home in a swamp. My rising damp hit the ceiling years ago and, as is hugely beneficial for someone partly reliant on their voice for their earnings, I have developed a slight asthmatic cough due to the number of spores that live here with me. But it's cheap. I bet you couldn't guess that.

Shuffling into the bathroom, I stand in the bath while the warmish trickle of water from what I laughingly call my shower does its darnedest to revive me. My poor throat. Every morning, I feel as if I've swallowed a dozen razor blades. I put it down to the effects of passive smoking in the pub and spend the day drinking gallons of water to try to counteract it. I rub the scrag end of a bar of soap over my weary body.

My sense of smell is the next thing to wake up. The flat is situated above an Indian restaurant—The Spice Emporium. Their advertising says, As Featured On BBC Television, but what it fails to mention is that the only time it hit the TV screens was when it made the local news programme because of a salmonella outbreak when thirty of its diners went down with food poisoning. The owner, Ali, obviously hopes that his customers have very short memories. My main problem with The Spice Emporium is that the chef there has the frying pan on the go at about six in the morning. Everything I do during my waking hours at home is accompanied by the smell of cooking spices. My tummy constantly growls from the minute I'm awake, as it's convinced that onion bhajis are *the* thing to have for breakfast—whereas I am not.

I stay here because Ali, also my landlord, is lovely. The flat may not be a shrine to domestic elegance or even pass any basic health and safety regulations, but Ali takes a relaxed attitude when it comes to paying my rent. If I'm really strapped, he'll let me work a few shifts washing up in the restaurant until I've paid off my debt. That's the sort of landlord I need, not some ogre with a slobbering Rottweiler.

I'm still getting dressed when the doorbell rings, and I know that it can only be Carl. He will have brought me something wonderful to eat because he knows that I never have enough money to buy food. I often wonder if I'd simply cease to exist if Carl ever abandoned me. My friend has a degree in Social Anthropology—whatever that is—from Oxford, no less. I'm not sure how useful that is for swindling the Department of Health and Society Security, but it means that Carl is able to live on benefits and work most of the week cash-in-hand, so he's relatively flush—particularly when compared to me. I pull on my jeans and rush to the door while dragging my sweater over my head.

'Peace,' he says as I open the door, and does the accompanying sign.

'You are so seventies,' I tell him as I eye his bag of goodies.

'Bagels,' he says. 'From the new deli down the road. I thought we'd road test it.'

'Groovy.'

'Now who's being seventies?'

'I was being ironic,' I say as I relieve him of his delicious-smelling package.

'How's Blonde Ambition this morning?'

'I'm fine—if you discount the fact that I'm tired, broke and my voice has been destroyed by passive inhalation of eight thousand Benson & Hedges. And you?'

Carl smiles. 'Groovy.'

In the kitchen, complete with its one cupboard and death-trap gas boiler, I dole a couple of spoonfuls of cheap instant coffee into our cups while the kettle takes an aeon to boil. Carl starts to spread the bagels with the cream cheese that he also brought from the deli. It pains me to see how much care and attention he puts into preparing my breakfast. Life would be so much easier if I could love Carl as he loves me.

'Don't forget to do a bit for Squeaky.'

Carl rolls his eyes heavenward.

'Apart from you,' I say, 'he's the only friend I have in the world.'

'He's a mouse who's eaten through your baseboard and the wire of your toaster. I'm not sure I'm happy to share the same category as him.'

'He's my pet.' I don't share everyone else's view that Squeaky is a dirty, feral mouse who should be exterminated as soon as possible. He's fun and he's feisty and he doesn't cost much to feed. What I would really like is a cat—yes, I'm at that stage in my life—but I don't have the wherewithal to keep one. Despite being an excellent companion, it would simply be another drain on my meagre resources. Anyway, I console myself with the fact that it might not help my asthmatic cough or Nathan's.

Carl passes me a tiny bit of bagel spread with cheese, which I lovingly place beside the mouse bolt-hole in my kitchen. Squeaky used to dash out, steal everything I put down for him and rush away with it into his lair. Now when he appears, he just sits in the kitchen and nibbles away happily. If he could chat, I'm sure he'd join in with the conversation, such as it is. The downside of this is that I have to clean up more mouse poo. The upside is that Squeaky has stopped chewing through my box of breakfast cereal. Or maybe he doesn't like this brand. It was horribly cheap, and perhaps even mice have their limits.

Carl sits on the work surface, which makes me frown; nothing to do with hygiene, I just don't think it will hold his weight. 'I had an idea that might help your financial situation,' my friend tells me as he tucks into his breakfast.

'Rob a bank?'

'More legal,' he says. 'My sister's working at a temp agency at the moment. She could get you some regular work during the day.'

'Cool.' I'm up for anything. I've even been cutting ads out of the paper with a view to doing phone-sex. I know. I'm desperate. But I can pant and talk dirty if required.

'Can you type?'

'No.'

'Okay. We won't tell her that.' Carl rubs his chin thoughtfully. 'What other skills do you have?'

'None.'

'We'll miss that bit out, too.' He pulls out his mobile phone. 'Shall I call her?'

Before I have a chance to answer, Carl says, 'Hey, Julia. Yo. Bro.' And then they talk to each other for a bit in this gibberish sibling language that only they understand. 'I'm trying to help out Fern,' he continues when he reverts to English. 'Do you have any great jobs on your books that pay shitloads of cash?'

I can hear a faint muttering from the other end.

Carl turns to me. 'Do you know anything about opera?'

I shake my head. 'No.'

'Yes,' Carl says into his phone. 'She's a big, big fan.'

'I am not!'

'Shut up,' he tells me, hand protecting his sister's sensibilities again. 'Do you want to work or not?'

'I want to work.'

'We'll rent some DVDs of operas,' he says.

'Neither of us has a DVD player,' I remind him.

'Pen. Pen,' Carl orders. I duly pass him one, and he scribbles down an address. 'I owe you,' he says to his sister. 'Ciao, baby.' Then he hangs up and turns to me. 'You have an interview this afternoon.'

'Wow.'

'Personal assistant to some opera bod.'

I take the piece of paper from him. Looks like I'm going to be headed for an apartment in the Docklands later today. 'I'll never get it,' I say. 'I can't do anything.'

'You're a very resourceful woman.'

'I am.'

'And you need the money.'

'I do.'

'So go for it.'

'I will.'

'Now,' Carl instructs, 'eat those bagels, then you've got some serious singing to do.'

Squeaky comes out to join us for breakfast, turning his tiny piece of bagel and cream cheese delicately as he nibbles. Carl has long since lost the urge to scream every time my pet appears, but inches casually away from him.

'I want to put a few new songs in the act,' my friend tells me between chews.

'For the ever-demanding audience at the King's Head?'

'We won't always be playing pub venues,' Carl assures me.

'Oh. I keep forgetting the booking at Carnegie Hall,' I say.

'Sarcasm is the lowest form of wit, Fern.'

Laughing, we take our coffee through to the lounge, and I kiss Carl on the cheek. 'Thanks,' I say. 'You're a pal.'

'Does this qualify me for a sympathy shag?'

'No.' I slip the piece of paper with the address on it into the pocket of my jeans. 'But I promise I'll buy the bagels from my first pay cheque.'

I try not to think how tight my finances are and how much

I need this extra money. Personal assistant to an opera singer? That's got to be well-paid, hasn't it? Sounds as if it might be fun, too. I can't imagine that it would involve an awful lot of graft. I am a resourceful woman. I am a desperate woman. Joe needs my help, I mustn't forget that. If I don't want to be washing up at The Spice Emporium, I have to get this job. How hard can it be?

Three

Evan David paced through the apartment, his feet tapping out an impatient rhythm on the bleached oak floor. He stared out of the double-height glass windows and over the slate-grey thread of the Thames.

'I fixed up the interviews for this afternoon.'

Massaging his temples, Evan turned towards his agent, Rupert Dawson. 'If Erin can't be here, then I'll manage without an assistant.'

'You can't manage without an assistant, darling. Have you looked at your schedule yet?'

Evan held out his hands. 'If I'm so busy, Rup, then I don't have time to interview for a new assistant.'

'We need someone to help out temporarily. Until Erin is back on her feet.'

'How long does it take to recover from chicken pox?'

Rupert shrugged. 'I have no idea. But I don't think she'll

make it over here from the States.' A worried frown crossed his face. 'Have you come out in any funny spots?'

'No.'

'Itching?'

Itching to kill his agent but nothing more. 'No. No itching.'

'How's the voice?'

'The voice is fine.'

Rupert let out a relieved sigh. 'You're lucky. *We're* lucky.'

Evan was opening at the Albert Hall with the British National Opera in the next week or so as Pinkerton, the lead male role in Puccini's *Madame Butterfly.* Not exactly a taxing role for someone of his status. But it wouldn't do for the principal artist—*Il Divo,* The Divine Performer, The Voice—to miss his first performance. Tickets had sold out over a year ago. And the one thing Evan never did was let his public down.

'Have we sent Erin flowers to her San Francisco sickbed?' he asked.

'Your new assistant will.'

Evan hid a smile. He'd been with Rupert a long time, since he first started out in this business. His agent knew how to play him. And he had to face it, Rupert was the closest person he had to a friend these days. Evan stretched. There was tension in his neck. That would never do—it could strain his voice. Good job he had a massage booked for later in the day. And who would take care of all the small details and the administration for him if he didn't have an assistant?

He stroked his fingers over his throat distractedly. There was no doubt that the constant touring was starting to take its toll. For a youngish man, supposedly in his prime, there were days when his weary bones were very reluctant to leave his bed.

He'd been too many years on the road; it was time he put roots down in one city for a while. As soon as this trip was over and he was back in San Francisco, he wasn't moving for months, he'd decided. He'd had Rupert clear the diary—which had brought tears in the shape of dollar signs to his agent's eyes. Evan needed a break though, whatever the cost. There had been too many opera houses, too many rented apartments, too many hours spent on a jet—even if it was his own private Lear.

He looked around at the apartment. This place was fabulous—at the top of a high-rise block with amazing views across the capital city. It was sleek, modern and spacious, all painted white with glass staircases and balconies off every room. It was also a far cry from his home on the West Coast, which was a turn-of-the-century former archbishop's home filled with antiques and exotic carpets, surrounded by sprawling grounds. But this place served his purpose. There was no way he could become attached to living here; it was simply somewhere that required little maintenance and offered no distractions from his work. That was the way he liked it. Erin had found it for him—as she always did—and it suited him just fine. She knew that the less there was of other people in a place, the less he was likely to catch any of their leftover germs. Nursing his voice on a strenuous tour like this was all-important.

Rupert edged farther towards the desk, as if doing that would encourage Evan to do so, too. The agent was well over fifty now, more than ten years older than Evan. His skin was tanned like leather and he sported the bouffant hairdo preferred by game-show hosts and shopping channel presenters. He smoked back-to-back cigarillos when Evan wasn't around, wore sharp suits and a perpetually pained expression. It was clear, even to the casual observer, that there was a strong affinity between the two men. His agent had come into Evan's life when he was a callow youth and they had grown older together, if not necessarily wiser.

Rupert glanced at his watch. 'The first one is due here soon.'

'We need to be quick, Anton is coming over for a run-through.' Anton was Evan's voice coach and French tutor. If Erin was like his right arm, then Anton was the left. Evan tried out a few scales, filling the apartment with his rich voice.

'We have some great candidates,' Rupert said. 'All opera buffs.'

'Marvellous.'

The buzzer sounded and Rupert hurried to answer it. 'The first one's here,' he told Evan. 'Try to be nice.'

'I'll be divine.' He blew Rupert a kiss.

'You're a very intimidating person.'

'I'm a pussy cat,' Evan insisted.

'Don't scare them off. Please. We just need someone who can put up with you for a few short weeks.'

'What's this?' Evan picked up a piece of paper.

'Her résumé.'

'University degree... Love of opera... Personable and flexible... I want her to file a few papers and answer the phone, Rupert. I don't want to marry the damn woman.'

'No one in their right mind would have you.'

Rupert scuttled over to the door. Evan sat down behind the desk, humming to himself, perfectly manicured fingers joined in a contemplative steeple. His agent ushered in the first victim.

She edged nervously into the room, taking in her surroundings with wide-eyed awe. Evan followed her gaze.

'Wow,' she gasped. 'This is some place.'

Evan stood up and politely extended his hand. 'Welcome,' he boomed.

The woman jumped. Then tentatively took his hand. Her palm was clammy. Evan wanted to wipe his fingers on his trousers.

Rupert flashed him a warning glance. 'Sit down, sit down,' he said, putting on his most winning smile while pulling out a chair.

The woman sat down. There was an awkward silence.

'I'm Evan David,' Evan began.

She nodded. 'I've seen you on the telly.'

Heavens preserve us, Evan thought. This one was as nervy as Bambi. She looked like some sort of Boho hippy chick. Her embroidered jeans were a stark contrast to the tailored business suits Erin favoured. She had a mess of wild blond hair and a suede handbag with fringes. Fringes? Evan shook his head— it was a step too ethnic for him. Normally when people met him they praised him, for his Cavaradossi in *Tosca* or his Alfredo in *La Traviata*. And she'd 'seen him on the telly'. He tried not to sigh. So this was one of Rupert's opera buffs? There was no way he could do this all afternoon.

'And you are?' he prompted.

'Fern.' She licked her lips. 'Fern Kendal.'

'Do you have chicken pox?'

The woman looked puzzled. 'No.'

'No itching?'

'No.'

'Good. When can you start?'

Fern Kendal looked at Rupert for some sort of explanation. The agent's face was suitably blank, too, although he looked like he might be about to fall off his chair.

'Anytime,' she said with forced brightness. 'Today. Now.'

She had all her limbs, most of her faculties and no communicable diseases. As far as Evan was concerned, she'd do just fine. He stood up and shook her hand again having forgotten that it was unpleasantly clammy. 'You've got the job.'

'I have?' Her eyes widened farther, if that were possible. 'Thank you. Thanks. That's great. You won't regret this.'

Evan smiled tightly. He suspected that he might. Rupert looked to be in a state of stunned acceptance. 'Good. I'll leave you to it.' He headed towards the music room before adding, 'I guess your first task will be to tell all the other applicants that they didn't get the position.'

Four

Well, you've really done it this time, Fern! I slump back into the huge cream leather chair and close my eyes. I have spent the last hour or more telling ten disgruntled and very well-dressed wannabe personal assistants that the role has already been filled. I didn't dare to mention that it had been filled by me, as most of them looked at me as if I was a bit of doggy doo. And *all* of them looked as if they would have been a darn sight better at the job than I'm destined to be.

I can feel my lip wobbling. I want tea and I want chocolate. Both in large quantities. I want Carl to talk to me and tell me that I actually have a hope in hell of doing this damn job. My skills will certainly have to involve better clothing. I wish I'd put a suit on. I wish I *had* a suit to put on. There have been very few occasions in my life that have called for suit-wearing, and I realise that my existence has been very casual up to now. I wonder if I'll get a clothing allowance? In fact, I wonder what my pay is and what hours I'll be expected to work and what I'll have to do while I'm doing it.

After my interview—such as it was—the great Evan David and the other weird-looking guy with the big hair had simply grinned at me and left. They're now closeted in the next room with the door firmly shut. I've taken two dozen telephone messages from people who all insist the matter is of *utmost* urgency—not just normal urgency—but I haven't dared to disturb them.

Glancing around me, I try to gather my scattered wits. This place is amazing. It's like something you see in…in…well, I've never seen anything like it before. It's certainly a far cry from my own mouse-infested hovel (apologies to Squeaky). My entire flat would fit into this one room and still have space left over for a football pitch.

I can hear a few soaring notes drifting from the other room. Did I really say to the great Evan David that I'd seen him on the telly? Yes, I believe I did. I want to bang my head on the desk. What a lamebrain. I try to think what my duties might involve. There's nothing on the desk except a phone, a diary, a notebook and a laptop, so I guess that should give me a clue. My eyes are drawn to the direction of the singing. He sounds as if he's only warming up, but his voice is amazing. And I have to say that in the flesh, so to speak, Evan David is a lot more attractive than he looks on the television. I've never really taken much notice of him before, but that's mainly because I turn off opera the minute it comes on. I'm beginning to wish I'd paid more attention to it now. I'm an artist, too, I should cultivate a broader view of world music, not just diss opera as stuff for posh gits.

The apartment buzzer sounds and I go over to answer it.

'It's Anton,' the disembodied voice says.

Anton is Mr David's voice coach. I learned that much from the diary, so I let him in. While he's coming up in the lift, I knock on the closed door. Evan David opens it.

'Your voice coach is here.'

'Thank you,' he says. 'I'll be out in a few minutes.'

When he arrives, Anton turns out to be slight with shoulder-length curly hair, and he wears a red velvet scarf.

Evan David breezes out a moment later and they hug each other warmly, batting French greetings between them. Anton takes off his scarf and goes over to the piano, which is at the other side of the room, set in a bay by one of the huge windows and angled to catch the best light, I would guess.

Mr David strides towards me and my knees set up an involuntary knocking. He brings me a list, which he slaps down on the desk. 'Journalists,' he says. 'Can you fix up interviews for the end of the week? And send a bouquet to my permanent assistant, Erin. She has chicken pox.'

I nod.

He tries a smile, which doesn't seem to come easy. 'Settling in?'

I nod again.

'You might have taken your coat off.'

'I feel rather underdressed,' I explain.

'You're fine.'

Everything he's wearing probably came from Armani or Versace or somewhere like that. What he paid for his watch would probably feed my entire family for five years. He has dark, cropped hair and deep grey eyes. His features are sharp and stern.

'I have an appointment tonight.' I'm not about to tell him that I work in a pub. 'Is it okay if I leave soon?'

'Yes,' he says.

'What time do you want me in the morning?'

Mr David shrugs. 'Not early. Eight o'clock.'

'Eight o'clock.' That will give me nearly five hours' sleep. Fab. 'Fine. Fine.'

He leaves me and goes over to the piano. There's such a presence to him that when he moves away, he leaves a vacuum in his wake. That's my excuse for being a quivering wreck, anyway.

Anton already has some music set up on the stand. Without preamble, he starts to play and Evan launches into the most beautiful song I've ever heard. All the hairs on the back of my neck stand up and the power of his voice almost takes my breath away. If I had any idea what this song might be then I'd tell you, but I haven't a clue. I try to drag my brain back to the list of journalists and the appointments that I'm supposed to be making, but it's impossible. Evan David's voice commands attention. All my senses have sharpened. My ears are pinned back, my scalp is tingling and even my nipples are standing to attention. I feel as if I've been slammed back into my seat and paralysed by pleasure.

And I have to go. I have to tear myself away from this onslaught of sensation. I have to pick up my handbag and make my feet walk out in the middle of this to leave and pull pints and do my measly set with scraggy Carl at the King's Head. And I can't imagine that my audience will be quite so enraptured.

Five

I sit reeling on the Tube, still humming that song to myself—which is enough to create a large space around you in London. All things considered, it has been quite a successful afternoon. And then, in my blissed-out haze, I make the mistake of calling into my parents' flat on the way to the pub for five minutes to tell them about my great new job.

When I open the door, they're in the middle of World War Three. In the kitchen, my mum is flicking Dad on the head with the tea towel in a vicious manner. Not an easy feat as she is a good deal shorter than him, even in heels. Two bulging suitcases stand in the hall.

'Hey. Hey!' I call out. 'What's happening here?'

Mum snaps the tea towel at Dad again. She looks as if she's about to start foaming at the mouth. 'Your father's leaving me.'

'What? Leaving? What for?'

'I'm not leaving,' my dad insists, sheltering from the blows under the umbrella of his hands. 'Your mother's throwing me out.'

I turn to Mum. 'Throwing him out?'

'I've had it,' she snaps, both verbally and with her dish-drying weapon.

'I've had it with the years of drinking, gambling and womanising.'

My eyes pop out on stalks. Drinking and gambling, yes. But womanising? This is news to me. I know that my old man likes to look, but I don't think he's ever touched.

'He's a no-good, fit-for-nothing old git,' my mum elucidates.

'But he's been like that for the thirty-odd years that I've been around,' I remind my mother. 'Why are you throwing him out now?'

'I want to be my own person.' Oh, no. My mother had been taking advice from *Richard & Judy* again.

'Think about this,' I say, trying to introduce a note of calm into the storm. 'You've been married for forty-odd years. You wouldn't survive without each other.'

'I'd like to give it a try,' Mum mutters darkly.

'You'll laugh about this in the morning.'

'The only reason I'll be laughing in the morning is if I turn over and find *he's* not here.' She jabs a finger in Dad's chest, and he puts on a mortally wounded face.

'Fern's right,' Dad says. 'You'd be lost without me.'

'Ha!' Mum trills. 'I've had to manage this family all of my life. Exactly what couldn't I do without you?'

Dad pauses. For way, way too long. We all do. There is a look of triumph on my mum's face.

'I came to tell you that I've got a great new job,' I say.

'Wonderful.' My mother heads towards the cases. Dad and I exchange a glance.

'Amy, don't,' he begs. 'You know you don't mean it.'

Mum has the cases in her hands. They're well past their best, stickers for Spain, Portugal and Ibiza all tattered and torn.

'I'll change,' Dad tries.

Even I've heard this speech too many times before to be convinced.

'Amy, please.' Dad looks stricken.

Mum's heart must have turned to stone since, as small as she is, she heaves the cases to the door and throws them out into the concrete corridor that overlooks the rest of the flats. 'Get out,' she says.

Now *I'm* panicking. 'Where's he going to go?'

'Back to that whooore!'

'What whooore? Whore.'

Dad shakes his head. 'There's no whore, Amy. There never has been.'

My five-foot, two-inch mother manhandles my six-foot father out of the hall and after his bags.

'I want to stay and sort this out,' I say. 'But I'm going to be late for work.'

Mum folds her arms across her chest. 'As far as I'm concerned, it's sorted out.'

'I'm coming round tomorrow.' Then I wonder how, when my days as well as my nights are now no longer my own.

I follow Dad out of the door and Mum slams it behind me. Dad is leaning on the brick balcony, puffing furiously on a cigarette.

'It's bad for you,' I tell him.

'That woman will be the death of me first,' he retorts.

'Would you like to tell me what this is all about?'

'I didn't come home last night,' he admits.

I give him an Oh-Dad look.

'But I wasn't with another woman. I definitely wasn't with another woman.'

'So where were you?'

'Playing cards at Mickey's. I was on a winning streak,' he says. 'How could I walk out?'

'It looks like your winning streak has ended. I suggest you get in there and tell Mum the truth.'

'How can I? She'd only throw me out for that, too. I'd promised her that I wouldn't play poker anymore. Best to give her some time to cool off.'

'Well,' I say, eyeing my dad's baggage, 'what now?'

'I'll be no trouble.' Dad picks up his cases.

So my dad is moving in with me. Fantastic.

'I wouldn't dream of you giving up your bed for your poor old dad,' he says magnanimously. 'I'll have the sofa.'

I take one of the cases from him and sigh. 'Too right you will.'

Six

I rush into the King's Head, stripping my coat off as I go. Ken the Landlord gives me a glare. In response, I flick my thumb at Dad, trailing in my wake. 'Family crisis.'

'Again?'

'She's never actually thrown him out before.'

With a glance, Ken takes in my dad's cases. 'Brilliant.' My boss rubs his hands together. 'My profits always go up when your old man's around.'

Yeah. And the meagre amount in my bank account always goes down.

Carl is in his usual place, propping up the bar and my dad goes and sits down next to him. 'Hello, son,' Dad says, clapping him on the back.

'Mr Kendal. Man,' Carl responds, giving him a peace sign.

'Let me buy you a drink,' Dad says, full of bonhomie.

'It's cool.' Carl shakes his head. 'My round, Mr Kendal.'

'Don't mind if I do,' Dad says. 'And it's Derek to you, young man. A double whiskey,' he shouts to Ken.

'Make it a single,' I instruct as I get myself together behind the bar. 'You can have a double when you pay for it yourself.'

'I'm not sure I like the implication implicit in that statement,' Dad says haughtily.

'Tough.' I reach for a glass. 'If you're going to be my house guest, you play by my rules.'

'I have no need to question whose daughter you are,' my father mutters.

So while I catch my breath, let me fill you in on the details about my parents. Derek and Amy Kendal have been married, mostly unhappily, for about forty years. My mum has worked full-time in the same newsagent's shop at the end of their street for the last thirty of them. The benefit of this when Joe and I were kids was that we occasionally—if we'd been better behaved than the angels above us—were slipped free sweets. My dad is a cabbie on the verge of retirement. And I'd hate to be a fare in Dad's taxi, as he's one of these cabbies who'd natter your ears off, giving his opinion on everything from the state of world politics, global warming, the Royal family, *Celebrity Big Brother* and the size of Jordan's chest. My parents have lived in the same flat on the same council estate just behind Euston station for all of their married life, in the days when it used to be a good, old-fashioned London community and not the graffitied, drug den that it now is. The flat is clean, cramped and everything in it looks slightly threadbare—and that includes my mother.

Amy Kendal is a woman who is best described as careworn.

She has been the rock of our family throughout our lives, and she does more than her fair share of caring for her grandson, Nathan, too. Derek 'Del' Kendal, on the other hand, hasn't a care in the world. My father is undoubtedly adorable. He's the sort of bloke who's the life and soul of the party and also the sort of bloke who makes you want to kill him after an hour in his company. He lives on Planet Derek—population: one. It's governed by a benign dictatorship, and there's no room for anyone else on it. He drinks too much, talks too much and gambles or gives most of his money away. And he does have an eye for the ladies, but that's all there is to it. There were times when he used to stay out all night and my mum would be hollow-eyed and worried sick in the kitchen in the morning when he'd come waltzing in singing at the top of his voice. The tea towel would see some action once again, and he'd retire to bed to sleep it off, repentant. But I'm sure that his dalliances with the opposite sex have never been anything more than platonic, no matter what Mum's current opinion is.

I'm not really surprised that her patience with him has worn out, I'm just surprised that it has taken so long. You tend to take certain things for granted, and if your parents have lasted together for forty-odd years, then you can't really envisage anything upsetting the status quo.

It just goes to show how wrong you can be.

'Now sit there and try to behave,' I instruct my dad.

'Will do,' he says meekly as he concentrates on his whiskey, and I know from past experience that his penitence won't last.

'How did the job interview go?' Carl asks in the gap between my thoughts.

'Great,' I say. 'I started this afternoon. And don't say groovy.'

Carl closes his mouth again. 'So who's the opera guy? Some bald, bearded salad-dodger?'

'Quite the opposite. It's Evan David. Handsome and with a full head of hair. Far from being overweight, he's as fit as a butcher's dog, as my old Nan used to say. Not an excess calorie in sight.' I turn my head so that Dad can't hear me and whisper, 'Very shaggable.'

Carl looks distinctly put out. Perhaps he thinks that my mind doesn't turn to such base thoughts these days. And, quite frankly, it doesn't. Not that often. My sex life involves infrequent intimacy with a piece of 'soft-feel' plastic. Which I must remember to hide before my dad moves in.

'So what does this job involve?' Carl goes on.

'Not much,' I say. 'Answering the phone, that sort of thing. Should be a piece of cake.' How can I confess to him that I'm frozen with fear at the very thought of it?

'I'll let you have my bill for commission,' Carl says.

I lean over the bar and kiss him. 'Thanks for fixing me up with this.' And I really do mean that.

'Don't let me down,' Carl warns me, 'or my sister will kill me.'

'I won't. It seems I just have to sit there and make appointments and let people into the apartment.'

'Like who?'

'His voice coach…'

Carl raises an eyebrow approvingly.

'And he has a beauty therapist.'

This generates a horrified frown. 'A what?'

'A beauty therapist. He has massages and facials.'

My friend is stunned. 'Men have facials?'

'Yes.' I laugh at him. 'This isn't the Dark Ages, my dear Carlos. Some men care about how they look.'

He's unconvinced.

'Some men even believe they can change their socks more than once a month.'

Now Carl looks very sceptical. 'No way.'

But I can tell you that he's joking. Carl might want to give the impression that he and water have a very on-off relationship and his sole attempt at style seems to be to make Bob Geldof look like a vain dandy; however, he is—despite his outwardly scruffy appearance—one of the most fastidious people I know. I don't think he even enjoys smoking, he just does it to be antiestablishment.

Carl stubs out his cigarette and downs his drink. 'Nearly time for our set.'

A lump comes to my throat and tears prickle my eyes. 'Evan David lives in a very different world from ours, Carl.'

Looking across at the tatty stage and our equally ragged audience, I realise that more than ever, I want a piece of it for myself.

Seven

My dad is lying on my sofa in his underpants and vest, which is a sight I don't want to see at the best of times, let alone at seven o'clock in the morning. I head straight for the kitchen. We both look the worse for wear. Dad because he's been drinking—double whiskies on Carl's account—and me because, at my age, four hours of beauty sleep is nowhere near enough.

My dear friend Carl isn't coming round this morning because he doesn't realise there *is* any time before ten in the morning. He is blissfully unaware that life occurs before then—as, usually, am I. So no tasty bagels or treats today. There's no milk in the fridge—or food, come to think of it—so I'm going to have to go to work on black coffee and the inhaled vapours of onion bhajis from the restaurant below.

Braving the vision of my father's underwear, I stick my head round the door to the lounge. On the sofa, Dad stirs. He does cartoon rubbing his eyes and overexaggerated stretching. This is my father pretending that my couch is every bit as comfortable as his marital bed. But I'm not fooled. I have, in the past, spent an uncomfortable night or two on that sofa and, believe me, there are springs where you do not require springs to be.

'Make a cup of tea for your old dad, sweetheart,' he pleads.

This 'old dad' act is going to wear off very rapidly, too. My patience is already hanging by a thread.

'We've no milk,' I say, at which he frowns. The thread frays a bit more and I sound defensive when I explain, 'I wasn't expecting company.'

'I'll get some things in for you later,' he promises.

'Later,' I tell him, 'you're going to go home and beg Mum to take you back. She always does.' Although I skirt round the fact that she's never physically and forcibly evicted him from their home before now. 'You might just have to work a bit harder at it this time.'

Dad grunts.

'Are you going to tell me exactly what you've been up to?' I'm not sure I buy this story about playing cards at Mickey's. Mum has had to put up with that for years and has never cracked in this way.

He folds his arms across his chest, indignantly. 'Nothing more to tell. Swear to God, I haven't done a thing. I'm just the same as I've always been.'

That's just cause for divorce on the grounds of emotional cruelty *and* unreasonable behaviour.

I turn to go into the kitchen and Dad follows me, sheet wrapped round his waist—which does nothing to disguise the fact that he's slept in his socks. I shake my head. No wonder

Mum has had enough of him. One night with my dad and already I feel like stabbing him.

'Bloody hell,' Dad shrieks as he comes into the kitchen. 'There's a mouse in here.'

'Calm down,' I say. 'It's Squeaky.'

'It's vermin!'

'Don't be rude. He's family.'

'I'm not sharing a flat with a bloody mouse.'

'Fine. Get your complaining backside home then.'

Squeaky comes out to say hello.

'Do you know that mice can't control their bladders? They leave a constant trail of wee everywhere they go.'

'A bit like ageing parents, then.'

'You are just like your mother,' my dad tells me crisply. 'As a family we have saved a fortune on encyclopaedias over the years because you both know everything there is to know about anything.'

'I'm going to be late for work,' I say. 'Make your own tea.'

'What time will you be back?'

'I don't know. I might have to go straight from this job to the King's Head again. It depends how my high-flying day unfolds.' I get a buzz when I think that this might well be a real, exciting opportunity for me. 'What time are you working?'

Dad looks rueful. 'I might not go in today. Feeling a bit under the weather. Stress,' he says. 'And the back's feeling a bit dodgy.'

I refrain from telling my father that everything about him is dodgy.

He rubs at his back, wincing theatrically. 'I'll probably catch up with you at the King's later.'

I snatch up my bag and coat, heading for the front door. 'If you've got any sense—' which is always doubtful with Derek Kendal '—you'll be taking Mum out tonight to make up for whatever it is you haven't done.'

And with that relaxing little exchange, I launch myself into my day, wishing that I had the energy to sashay down the street like someone in a hairspray advert.

Eight

On the Tube, I sing along to Maroon 5 on my iPod all the way to work, which I know is deeply irritating to other passengers and that makes me feel so much better. As I trundle past the usual busking pitch that Carl and I nab, I see there's a saxophonist there and wonder if he's making more money than we usually do. His open case contains a pile of scattered change, and I try to do a rough calculation.

Bizarrely, I quite like playing in the Underground. The acoustics are good, and it gives us a chance to practise while earning a bit of spare change. We also throw in one or two of our own songs because we're less likely to be lynched than we are in the King's Head. There are legal pitches now controlled by London Underground, but we choose to tread the well-worn path of starving artists and still do it on the fly.

Eventually, I get off the Tube and skip over to the Docklands Light Railway at Bank, whizzing out to Canary Wharf hemmed in by City boys and girls in their sharp suits and even sharper shoes, arriving just before eight. Announcing myself at Evan David's apartment, I'm buzzed in and then I realise that I meant to make more effort with my appearance and, in my haste to depart, forgot.

'Hi,' the guy opening the door says. 'I'm Dermuid, the chef.'

'Chef?'

'*Il Divo* has to eat.'

'Of course. I'm Fern.' I shake his hand. 'I'm his... I'm not sure what I am. His assistant? I only started yesterday.'

'And you've come back for more? That's brave.'

I slip off my coat and then have no idea where to put it that won't make the place look messy, so I hide it behind the desk. This joint still makes me want to gape. There are no curtains to obscure the view, and the morning sun floods the room. I wonder how on earth anyone can earn enough money to afford somewhere like this. A lifetime of busking in the Underground wouldn't even pay for one of the rooms. There's nothing on the desk that looks like it's meant for my attention, so—not really knowing what else to do—I follow Dermuid to the kitchen, which is, of course, a state-of-the-art stainless-steel affair replete with the very latest in gadgetry.

The front door bursts open again and this time it's the man himself, Evan David. He's looking hunky, if a little sweaty, in shorts and a muscle top. And I notice that he has a good pair of legs; a healthy flush stains my cheeks even though I appear to be the only one who hasn't been exercising. Behind him is an equally handsome man—without a bead of sweat on his shaved head—who looks like he's just come straight from running a boot camp.

'Hi. Felicity,' Evan says.

I try a smile. 'Fern.'

'Fern.' He shrugs an apology. 'Good morning. This is Jacob, my personal trainer.'

A huge man-mountain of a black guy follows them both in. He looks like one of the baddies in a James Bond film. He's wearing dark shades in a menacing way and is clutching a walkie-talkie. The mountain, too, hasn't broken sweat.

'And this is Izak,' Evan tells me. 'My security manager.'

Chef? Personal trainer? Security manager? Agent? Voice coach? Massage therapist? Whatever I am? How many people does this man need to help him through his day? Does he float through life on a raft of minions?

No wonder I can't get out of my rut. Carl is the only person who supports me. Other than that I have a layer of people crushing me from above and keeping me down. No, that's unfair. I shouldn't feel like that about either my brother or my lovely nephew, Nathan. They haven't orchestrated their current situation on purpose. Thinking of them reminds me that I must call in to see them as soon as I can—otherwise they'll think that I've been abducted, as rarely a day goes by without me popping in on them.

'Have you had breakfast?'

I realise that Mr David is speaking to me. 'Er…' Does aroma of Indian food count? 'No,' I confess. Frankly, I'm too hungry to pretend otherwise.

'Get Chef to rustle you something up.' He glances back at the personal trainer. 'Join us, Jacob?'

Jacob holds up a hand. 'I have to fly. I have an eight-thirty at Lloyd's.' And then he takes up his holdall and flies.

'I'll shower and be with you in five, Chef.'

Chef nods his acquiescence, then turns to me. 'Your order, madam?'

I shrug. 'What's he having?'

'Fresh fruit. Egg-white omelette. Mango and blueberry smoothie and this shite.' Dermuid holds up a glass of green gloop.

'Yuch.'

'It's supposed to be equivalent to eating five portions of raw vegetables.'

'Nice.'

'He doesn't eat meat or dairy products or carbs.'

'Doesn't that leave fresh air?'

Dermuid grins. 'Or anything out of a packet.'

Trying not to think about how many times Pot Noodles feature in my diet, I reach for the kettle. 'Caffeine?'

'Definitely off the menu.'

'Why doesn't that surprise me?'

'These are all the vitamins he takes every day.'

There is an array of pills and potions set out on the counter like a window display in a pharmacy. 'He must rattle.'

'Complete hypochondriac,' Dermuid says. 'Don't sneeze anywhere near him or you'll be out on your ear in five minutes.'

'Why's he so neurotic?'

'His voice.' Dermuid goes about the business of separating the tasty part of the eggs from the whites. 'He thinks that a lot of these things encourage mucus production.'

'That is too much information.'

'I guess if your voice was your fortune, you'd look after it, too.'

I'm so not tempted to tell him about my smoke-filled nights in the King's Head belting out popular hit tunes. I look at the slimy egg whites. Perhaps I should start taking my health more seriously for when Simon Cowell comes knocking on my door.

'Evan David is a lean, mean singing machine,' Dermuid tells me. 'He runs, meditates, practices martial arts and works out.'

'You're making me hungry just thinking about it.' To confirm it my stomach groans. 'So what am I allowed?'

'Bacon sarnie?'

A bacon sandwich sounds quite appealing. 'Now you're talking.' I sit down on the stool next to him.

'Better eat it quick before he comes in though.'

'I'll bolt it,' I promise. 'I don't care if it gives me indigestion. Just so long as I don't have to drink any of that stuff.' I eye the green gloop warily.

'It's good for you.'

'I'll take your word for it.'

As Dermuid flings two rashers of bacon in the pan with a flourish, I ask, 'How long have you worked for the great Evan David? Is this a temporary gig for you, too?'

Chef shakes his head. 'I'm on the permanent payroll and have been for two years,' he tells me as he continues to prepare Evan David's healthy feast. 'I travel with him when he's on tour. Which is always. He never stays in hotels. Hates them. Too many nasties. We always hire a place like this. Palatial, minimalist and Erin has it practically fumigated before he arrives. I trail all my own stuff with me in three great trunks.'

'He doesn't believe in travelling light then?'

'The only thing he believes in is getting exactly what he

wants exactly when he wants it.' The wonderful smell of bacon fills the kitchen. 'He's a great bloke, really. Underneath it all,' he adds darkly.

'What do you mean?'

'He likes to shout,' Dermuid expands. 'Except on the days when he's performing, and then he might not speak at all.'

'Must make it fun for his wife.'

'He isn't married. I don't think that anyone would have him. His relationships always seem to be troubled. Evan reckons that the three worst karmas you can have are to be beautiful, successful and wealthy. He says they play havoc with your personal life.'

'Yeah?' I try not to laugh. 'This is from a man who's never tried poverty, crap jobs and doesn't exactly look like the back end of a bus.'

Dermuid looks slighted. 'I didn't say I bought into it.' He slaps my bacon sarnie onto a white, Japanese-style plate and decorates it with flat-leafed parsley and some sort of cherry tomato salsa.

It's difficult to stop myself from slavering, and I remember that last night's dinner was a packet of cheese and onion crisps. 'I don't suppose there's any ketchup anywhere?'

'No, there certainly isn't!' Evan David's voice booms out behind me.

I have no idea how to disguise the fact that I have a bacon sarnie in front of me and resort to flushing guiltily.

'So,' he says, rubbing a towel over his damp hair, 'I can't persuade you to join me in my healthy living plan while you're here?'

'Er...'

'Don't mind me,' Mr David says. 'Tuck into it. Enjoy.'

I smile weakly and lift the wonderful-smelling concoction to my lips. 'Even though it will shorten your life by five years,' he adds.

He sits down opposite me and studies me, which tends to reduce the enjoyment of my cholesterol overload. The jogging gear has been replaced by casual black linen, but the perpetual frown that he wears is still in place.

I'd say that Evan David was about forty-four or forty-five years old. There are a few crinkle lines around his eyes—which he can't have got from smiling—and a fine weave of grey in his dark hair. He raises an eyebrow at me and I realise that I've been studying him, too—and he knows it.

Dermuid hands him his breakfast, which does looks sickeningly healthy compared to mine. 'So, Fern,' he says after he swigs down his gloop. 'You're an opera buff.'

'Er... Well... I...' We exchange a glance and I can't help but laugh. 'Did I really say that?'

'You did.'

'Then I'm a liar,' I say. 'I've never been to an opera in my life. I'd probably be hard pushed to even name one. The only time I've ever seen you is in the *Royal Variety Performance* or interviewed on *Parkinson*.'

'Then you have a lot to learn,' Evan David tells me crisply. He finishes his breakfast and dabs at his mouth with a linen napkin. 'You might as well start today. I have a Sitzprobe rehearsal.'

I try to put an intelligent look on my face.

'A run-through with the full orchestra,' he explains. My intelligent look has clearly translated as completely blank. 'Come with me.' He glances at his watch. 'Get the laptop. We'll do some work in the breaks.'

'Right,' I say, jumping up. *'Right.'*

'You have bacon grease on your chin,' Evan David tells me. He points at the place with a slight grimace.

'Oh.' I rub frantically at it. 'Sorry. Sorry.'

He laughs and walks out of the room.

'Bloody hell,' Dermuid says, staring after him in astonishment.

'What?'

'Someone must have slipped him some happy pills,' he says as he clears away the plates. 'I've never ever seen him laugh at breakfast.'

Nine

Derek Kendal put the key in the lock and gingerly eased open his own front door. 'Hello, darlin',' he shouted tentatively.

The saucepan hit the wood frame and bounced at his feet. Derek flinched. He raised his voice slightly. 'It's only me.'

One of Amy's best teacups followed the same trajectory as the saucepan. As Derek ducked behind the door, there was an unhealthy thunk, and shards of china showered the hall carpet. He was stunned. It was years since his wife had last thrown crockery at him.

Derek put his arm up to protect himself. He didn't really want to be here at all. Amy clearly needed a few more days to calm down, but there'd be hell to pay if he had to tell Fern that he hadn't been home and tried to put things right today. It was hard to tell who he was most afraid of—his wife or his daughter. Derek shook his head. He'd spent his entire life surrounded by stroppy women who bossed him around. No wonder he needed to take a strong drink every now and again. Steeling himself, he risked another peep into his home. 'I just want to talk.'

'That's all you ever want to do,' Amy spat in return. 'What I want to see now is some action, Del. That's what speaks louder than words.'

Amy's action was to hurl another cup at him, which Derek barely managed to dodge. If only the England cricket team had such a good fast bowler, he thought, then they might not be in the trouble they were.

She was standing in the kitchen, arms folded, another domestic missile clutched in her in hand, all five feet of her looking as ferocious as Queen Boadicea. His heart squeezed at the sight of his red-faced, tight-lipped wife. She'd been a good woman over the years, and even he had to admit that he'd been a less-than-perfect husband. His indiscretions, to his mind, had all been small scale—too many hours spent in the pub, too many pounds spent on useless gee-gees, too many meaningless flirtations that required him to stay out all night.

They'd had their difficulties over the years. In fact, most of their marriage had been conducted in some sort of adversity. So why had she decided to throw him out now? If anything, he'd mellowed over the last few years, or at least, not got any worse. So why now? Why on earth now? What had been the straw that broke the camel's back? He'd better not ask Amy that—she wouldn't like being compared to a camel. She'd been through the menopause, he was sure. She was long finished with all that HRT stuff, so it couldn't be blamed on that.

They'd celebrated their fortieth anniversary last year—in style, with two weeks in Marbella. Had a great time. Barely an argument. Shouldn't they now be looking forward to growing old together? He was due to retire in a couple of years. Then they could have some fun—days out and the like. Take Nathan, too. Brighton was always nice—she'd like that. And what would happen after that, when they were too ancient to go trotting round the country on picnics, if they were to split up? Who'd look after him in his old age if it wasn't Amy?

Neighbours were starting to gather on the landing. Derek waved at them, genially. Bloody nosy parkers. Mrs Leeson was always the first out for an eyeful if there was any sort of conflagration going on. Her cigarette quivered with excitement on her lip and she leaned towards him. Derek shuffled farther inside the door.

'Can't I come in, love?' he pleaded. 'People are starting to look.'

'Let them look.'

'What is it I'm supposed to have done?'

'If you don't know that, then it's pointless us having this conversation.'

He banged his head on the door frame. 'Let me in. I'll make it up to you, I swear. Whatever you want me to do, I'll do it.'

'Clear off, then,' Amy said. 'And stop bothering me.'

'I'm your husband.'

'Pah!'

'We've had forty years together, Amy. Forty good years. Doesn't that count for anything?'

'They might have been good for you, but who said they were good for me?'

'Think of the kids,' Derek begged. 'You don't want them to come from a broken home.'

'They're all grown-up,' she said. 'They don't need us. I've given the best years of my life to you and those children. Now it is time to do something for me.'

'What?' Derek said. 'What can you do by yourself that you can't do with me?'

Amy refused to be drawn on that one.

'Come on, darlin',' he wheedled. 'What's the point of splitting up now? We've got a nice home.' Admittedly still owned by the council. 'Neither of us are getting any younger.'

Amy's expression darkened. Perhaps that wasn't the best thing to point out. His wife was no longer in her first flush of youth as she had been when he'd first set eyes on her. Her golden hair now owed more to the products of Clairol than any genetic material. They had met when Amy was just twenty-one at one of the dance halls in the West End—she was the most beautiful girl he'd ever seen and one of the most ac-commodating. They'd had a wild time back at his digs and she was pregnant within weeks of them meeting. The wedding was already arranged and paid for when Amy lost the baby, but they decided to make a go of it and got married anyway. It had been a great party and he'd never regretted it. Not for a moment. There were two more miscarriages before she finally gave birth to Joseph, and then another two years later before they could eventually afford to have Fern. They might not have had the most passionate relationship—they were no Burton and Tay-lor—but they'd rubbed along well enough all these years. Hadn't they?

Derek thought he'd try another tack. Amy had always been frugal. 'Have you any idea how expensive it is to get divorced?'

'No,' Amy snapped. 'Have you?'

'No, but...' Derek sighed. 'The worst years are behind us now. All the struggling's over. Think of the days when the children were young and we hardly had two pennies to rub together. Those were the tough times.'

'They were,' she replied. 'I had to work all day at the newsagent's and take in other people's ironing at night just to put food in our mouths.'

'I know,' he agreed. 'You've always been a worker.'

'But no matter how hard it got, it never meant you had to go without your booze or your little flutters, did it?'

That made him hang his head. There were times when he hadn't treated her right, but those days were behind them. Largely. 'We'll soon be able to sit back and enjoy ourselves a bit.'

'Perhaps I want to enjoy myself without you.'

'We've not got much longer to go, Amy. We're in the twilight of our years. Shouldn't we stick together now more than ever?'

'And that's the best you can offer?' Her hands went to her hips. 'It's better to be married to you than to be dead?'

It didn't sound right when she put it like that. 'Well...'

'Some of us might not agree with that,' she said.

He had a horrible feeling that he was losing this battle, and he didn't even know what had started the skirmish. She couldn't really mean that it was over between them? That would be madness. 'I know I've not been perfect, but I've tried, Amy. I've really tried.'

His wife sighed and he could see that there was a tear in her eye. 'I've tried, too, Del.' She wiped the tear away. 'And I just can't do it any longer.'

Ten

'**I**'ve been in a limousine like this before,' Fern said, running her hand over the walnut door panels.

Evan had been humming gently to himself and staring out of the window onto the elegance of Park Lane as they swept towards the rehearsal rooms near the Albert Hall. Now he turned towards her. 'Excuse me?'

'On Jemma MacKenzie's hen night. Well, not quite like this. We're not sitting in the back listening to Abba hits at full blast or swigging cheap Cava and pretending it's champagne.' She fiddled with her hair, twining it round her finger. 'And there are no disco lights.'

'So what you're trying to tell me is that this limousine experience is distinctly more sedate.'

'Yes.' Fern twiddled with her thumbs and tried to sit nicely. She pulled her floral skirt over her knees.

Evan thought she might have smartened herself up today, but

she still looked like a hippy. A cute hippy, but a hippy neverthe-less. He wondered why he'd wanted to bring her to the rehear-sal. And he *had* wanted to, even though the invitation was out of his mouth before he had a chance to consider it. His assis-tant, Erin, accompanied him everywhere—of course—but this was different. Fern certainly wasn't Erin. Despite Rupert's pro-testations to the contrary, Evan was sure that he could have managed without a temp for the time being. As it was, he was quite pleased that he'd chosen Fern—if 'chosen' was the right word. But this woman was here for a matter of weeks. All she had to do was open the post and make some appointments, and yet here he was, for reasons best known to himself, trying to form some sort of bond with her.

Perhaps he was simply tired of spending all his time with Rupert. He was, after all, a good agent but a pretty awful com-panion. Evan took in Fern's appearance once again. There was no doubting she was a pretty little thing. And a good few years younger than him. Nothing wrong with that, these days. She was certainly a breath of fresh air. Everyone else he knew seemed to be in the same business, and here was Fern not knowing her *Turandot* from her *La Traviata*. Somehow that was quite appealing. Maybe it would be fun to mix business with pleasure for once. It was certainly a long time since he'd en-joyed a woman's company.

Before he could think of a thousand reasons why he should-n't ask the next question, he leaned towards her and said, 'Would you like to have dinner with me tonight?'

Her eyes widened in shock. 'No,' she said, backing away from him. 'No. No. I can't. I've got a commitment tonight. I've got commitments *every* night.'

Evan felt himself tighten up. Well, she couldn't put it any plainer than that. An unexpected feeling of disappointment washed over him. 'I wanted to fill you in on some of your duties,' he said briskly. 'Nothing more. I thought it would be a good opportunity.'

'It's not that I don't want to,' she said, blushing. 'It's just that I can't. I've got…'

'Commitments.'

Fern fell silent.

With perfect timing to save him from further humiliation, they pulled up outside the rehearsal room.

'Okay, governor?' the chauffeur said.

'Fine. I'll call when I need you to come back for us, Frank.'

If he hadn't been so embarrassed, Evan might have smiled to himself. Normally, he had trouble fobbing females off. There was a queue of women at the Stage Door every night—women who were only too willing to share dinner and a lot more with him. And yet he'd very nearly been in danger of making a fool of himself with his young assistant.

Fern gathered her bag and the laptop to her, giving him a rueful smile as she clambered out of the car. 'I can't wait to hear you sing though,' she said.

He shook his head as he followed her. She was certainly different, this one.

Eleven

Sometimes I am the biggest jerk you can imagine. I follow Evan David into the rehearsal room with a heavy heart. Do you think—to use a musical term—that he was making overtures to me? It's so long since I've been asked out to dinner that I'm not sure whether he did mean it to be purely work-related or not. The only experience I've had with men in recent years is with Carl, and dinner with my dear friend would involve stopping for a kebab or some chips on the way home from the pub.

Evan David is so sophisticated, while I must appear so gauche. Fancy blabbing about being in a limousine at Jemma MacKenzie's hen night. As if he was interested when it's his everyday mode of transport. Good job I had the sense not to tell him about the male stripper we kidnapped and bundled into the car. The lovely Jemma never did end up getting married. Hee, hee.

Evan David strides ahead of me and I notice that the crush of waiting people part as he approaches, rather like the Red Sea when Moses turned up. I'm not sure what I expected of the other opera singers, but I didn't think they'd look like common or garden people who'd just come out of Tescos. I thought they'd have an air to them—like Evan David—but they don't. They're all wearing jeans and T-shirts that have seen better days, and I blend in perfectly.

I suddenly realise that I don't even know what opera my new boss is here to rehearse. What a great assistant I am. So I scuttle after him, trying to catch up. 'What part are you playing?' I ask his left shoulder, hoping this is the right terminology.

'Pinkerton.' He stops and turns round, then smiles at my blank expression. 'In *Madame Butterfly*. By Puccini. The story of Cio-Cio-San.'

I clearly look none the wiser as he adds, 'It's a tale of tragically unrequited love.'

I'm not sure if he's putting me on, but I get no time for further questions as he marches on.

The rest of us mortals shuffle after Mr David and into the rehearsal room which looks rather like a branch of Homebase with all the garden furniture and tins of paint removed. It's a big steel hangar with a jolly red frame, lined with a barrage of mushroom-shaped pads which I assume are there to enhance the acoustics. There are rows of tiered plastic seats at the back with the mass of people filing into them.

'Sit here,' Evan tells me. Rather too loudly, I think. 'With the chorus.'

And, of course, I do as I'm told, slinking into a seat on the end of a row, hoping that I'm not in anyone's way and trying to avoid the enquiring glances. The orchestra are crammed in the middle of the vast building—strings at the front, wood-wind, brass section and percussion behind. There are two sep-arate rows of chairs and music stands marked Principal Artists, and Evan takes up his position there. A tiny Japanese woman stretches to kiss him warmly on both cheeks. If I had inher-ited my dad's love of gambling, I'd bet a week's wages that this is Madame Butterfly, herself.

She's extraordinarily pretty, with porcelain skin and a skein of glossy black hair that reaches down to her waist. And I get a pang of…what? Plain old-fashioned jealousy, that's what. I sigh and settle into my seat.

A tall, skinny man comes into the room carrying a baton, and everyone stands and claps. Not knowing what else to do, I join in.

Evan claps him on the back and they hug each other warmly. 'Maestro!' Evan says in his booming tones.

'*Il Divo,*' the maestro returns, and they exchange small talk in what sounds like French from this distance. Then the maestro takes his place on the raised podium at the front of the orchestra.

'Good morning, ladies and gentlemen,' he says. Then he taps the podium, finds his place in the score and announces to the assembly, 'We will run through once and then stop for notes.'

He takes up his baton and the orchestra commences. And I'm transfixed, from the very first note. I've never been in such close proximity to an orchestra before, and I can feel the sound vibrating through my body, speeding through my blood, re-verberating in my chest. Time and place melt away—even my uncomfortable plastic chair ceases to exist as I'm transported to another world.

When Evan starts to sing, my mouth goes dry. I thought I knew a bit about singing, but I've never heard anything quite like this before. The pure tones stir up emotions I didn't even know I had. My heart is pounding like a hammer drill and I hardly dare to breathe in case I miss anything.

Nearly two hours later, when Cio-Cio-San sings her sorrowful lament, I'm reduced to a blubbering wreck. I have no idea what she's singing because it's all in Italian, but I know instinctively that this is the unrequited-love bit and it has moved me more than any other piece of music ever has. I sniff too loudly into my handkerchief and some of the chorus smile indulgently at me.

When the session has finished, the maestro taps his podium again. 'Thank you, ladies and gentlemen. We'll take a half-hour break now. Come back in fine voice.'

Chatter breaks out and everyone heads towards the cafeteria. I hang back and wait for Evan. I try to stop crying, but the tears stream from my eyes.

A few moments later, he comes towards me, a look of surprise on his face. 'You're crying.'

Nothing gets past this man.

'What's wrong?'

'I'm happy,' I manage to blub.

He's clearly taken aback. 'You enjoyed your first experience of opera?'

I can hardly bring myself to speak as there's still a lump lodged in my throat. I'm weak at the knees and quivering like a jelly. Nothing British will sum this up and I have to borrow an American phrase. 'Totally awesome,' I sob out loud. My mascara is halfway down my cheeks and, no doubt, my face is all red and blotchy. I'd like to be a contained and appreciative audience, perhaps make some intelligent observations. Instead I'm crying like a baby. 'That was totally awesome.'

Evan David looks quite shaken and then he does something that I really don't expect. He takes me in his arms and holds me tight.

Twelve

I have a big, fat hour all to myself to fritter away before starting my shift at the pub and, therefore, have a choice between visiting my brother and my sweetie-pie nephew, Nathan, or my mum on the way. I'm still feeling absolutely wrung out after listening to the Sitzprobe rehearsal today. Even when they were going over and over the songs during the afternoon, I was close to tears each time. Inside I'm trembling as if I'm coming down with flu, and this has absolutely nothing whatsoever to do with the fact that I can still feel the strength in Evan's arms as he held me, or that if I close my eyes, I can still capture the scent of his skin. Pulling my coat around me, I have a pleasant little shiver to myself.

I wonder what it feels like to perform at that level. Does it shake you to the core as it has shaken me? I have to say that I've never been moved to the depths of this emotion when bashing out a few tunes on stage at the King's Head, and it makes me realise that there's a world of difference between what I'm trying to do and what Evan David has achieved.

As I rattle along on the Tube, I come to my decision. I'm not sure that I can face the next instalment of my parents' marital shenanigans, so opt to see my brother and Nathan instead. Normally, I see them every day, and they must be wondering what has happened to me. I can grab a quick cup of tea with Joe and have a freshen-up before my shift. Jumping off the Central Line at Lancaster Gate, I enjoy the cold evening air as I walk up Westbourne Terrace.

Joe lives in a flat just along here. It's quite a salubrious area, near Bayswater, but the endless, meandering road has an eclectic mix of high-end places, squats and properties that definitely should be condemned. My brother's flat seems quite nice inside, if you don't inspect it too closely. Joe keeps it clean and tidy—he has to because of Nathan's condition. But the building is crumbling, the management company don't care and there's way too much damp for someone with a severe medical condition to be living there. The rent that Joe pays is horrendous—although it's covered by housing benefit at the moment—and my dearest wish is that one day I will earn enough to be able to get them both out of there. The smart terraced house in Cricklewood that was previously his marital home had to be sold to pay off his dearly beloved ex-wife and her not inconsiderable debts.

Joe will be delighted to hear that I've got another job—particularly as the job, at the moment, doesn't seem to involve anything other than eating a nice breakfast and listening to music all day. I think Evan David was still miffed that I left after the rehearsals this afternoon, especially as I turned down a lift in his limo, but he didn't mention dinner again. I'm going to have to get an advance on my wages from Ken the Landlord as I'm currently spending all my income on Tube fares.

The front door of Joe's building is broken, so I push inside and, as the lift is in a similar state of disrepair, climb the stairs. Some of the doors have black rubbish bags outside and there's a general air of neglect. Had my parents dreamed of my brother and I going to university and getting great jobs and living in four-bedroom detached houses in suburbia, then they must be sorely disappointed. My clutch of middle-range GCSEs proved to be three quarters of useless when it came to getting a good job, but my two-year foundation course in Fashion and Textiles means that I do very tidy hems on curtains when required. And, as I've already explained, my poor brother's steady job in the bank went out of the window when he was forced to become a full-time caregiver.

I know that Mum worries that both of her children are living in homes that are one step up from slums, but house prices in London are so expensive that I'd have to move miles away from my family to ever have any hope of buying a place of my own and I couldn't bear that. I want to be where I've grown up, with all my friends and loved ones around me. That's surely more important than having your own pile of bricks and mortar. I wouldn't want to be in, say, Northampton or Norfolk or Nottingham, when everyone else was here. Besides, I'm not sure that Joe and Nathan could manage without me. Wherever I went, I'd have to take them, too.

I knock on the door of their flat and, moments later, Joe lets me in. 'Hi, sis.' He pulls me to him in a nonchalant hug. 'Haven't seen you for days. Thought you'd run off with a rich Arab sheik.'

'I did consider it,' I say, 'but they couldn't cope without me at the King's. Betty's on holiday and we're short-staffed.'

'Ah. Same old story,' my brother commiserates.

Nathan is sitting upright on the sofa, breathing rhythmically through his asthma inhaler. The big clear plastic globe that he uses as a spacer for the drugs nearly obscures his tiny face. I go over and subject him to a kiss, which he tolerates graciously as it's only on his forehead. 'How's my favourite nephew?'

He pulls his inhaler out. The tube has a smiley clown's face on it. 'I'm your *only* nephew.'

His voice is always slightly husky due to his medication and is punctuated by a breathless wheeze.

I hug him to me. 'That's why you're my favourite.'

Nathan giggles and, abandoning his inhaler, flops back onto a cushion. My nephew is possibly the nicest-natured child in the world. He has a mop of blond hair, blue eyes. Nathan looks and behaves like an angel. Despite the difficulties his illness brings, he's never been one of these tantrum-y children that you see being dragged through supermarkets screaming— probably because he's been aware from a very young age that any overexertion brings on an asthma attack. He's borne all his troubles with stoicism beyond his tender years and my heart breaks for him. When all his friends are running round like things possessed, Nathan sits quietly on the sidelines waiting until they remember to come back to him.

I ruffle his hair. 'I love you.'

'Yuck,' Nathan says.

'Finish your medicine.' Obediently, he takes up his puffer again.

Following Joe back into the kitchen, I jerk my head back towards Nath. 'How is he?'

'Good,' Joe tells me brightly. 'Not bad.' Some of the light goes out. He shrugs with a certain hopelessness and says dully, 'You know how it is.'

Only too well. Next to Joe on the work surface is the size-able stash of drugs that follow him and my nephew wherever they go.

'Has he been to school today?'

'No.' My brother shakes his head. 'Not today.'

My nephew misses a lot of school. Not through any fault of his own. The overstretched teachers at the school he attends have too much to do to keep their eyes permanently trained on him and his care is sometimes erratic. When he's bad, Joe has no choice but to keep him at home. I wonder whether the hospital will ever be able to get his condition under control and whether he'll be able to enjoy normal schooling one day. I do worry so much for what his future holds. I'm hanging on to the hope that he might suddenly and miraculously grow out of it.

Nathan has been asthmatic since he was a baby. The so-called Wheezing Baby Syndrome he developed while still in his pram was rapidly diagnosed as something more serious. For a time it was thought he might have cystic fibrosis, and the stress of having a sick baby and spending too much of their time on hos-pital wards took its toll on my brother's marriage. There was more than one argument about the fact that Carolyn had smoked twenty cigarettes a day throughout her pregnancy and continued to do so even when their child sounded like he was coughing his little life away. Joe might not feel the same but, personally, I was delighted when the selfish cow cleared off. I never knew what my brother saw in her—she might have had model girl looks but she was a right royal pain in the arse from day one. Mother material she was not. Confirmed by the fact that she has had no contact whatsoever with Nathan since she left, not even a birthday or Christmas card. How could anyone be so callous? Still, her loss is our gain.

The only downside is that not having a permanent partner makes life so hard for them both and they really don't deserve it. I've offered a million times for Joe and me to throw in our lot together, pool our meagre resources and for me to move in with them. But Joe is under the illusion that one or both of us will, at some point, find suitable partners and that we should keep our options open. I like his optimism and I never say anything to bring him down—believe me, he has enough on his plate—but my options closed down years ago.

'Do you want to join us for beans on toast?' Joe asks, reaching for a pan.

'You're a lifesaver.' I sit down at the small table. These are organic, sugar-free, additive-free beans, as Nathan is allergic to practically every convenience food known to man. Anything from cleaning products to strong scents to peanuts can cause him to go into dreadful and sudden bronchial spasm. He has regular, long courses of steroids and he doesn't sleep or eat well—all of which have combined to make him small for his age. He has 'vulnerable' written all over him—though not in felt pen, to which he's also allergic.

I wonder whether if we moved out of London and went to live, say, in the Caribbean, life would be easier for him.

'So,' my brother says. 'What have you been up to, sis?'

'I got a new job yesterday. That's why I couldn't come round.'

'Cool.'

My heart not only breaks for Nathan, but it tears into shreds for Joe, too. Caring for a sick child 24/7 is no fun. I'm sure that Joe would love to go out to work—even part-time would help him to get a break—but such is our benefits system that he'd be so much worse off if he even earned a few quid legitimately.

Very rarely, Joe might do a cash job for a friend which helps him out—but most of the time he's barely above the breadline. How wonderful it must be, not to have to continually worry about money and to be able to rent huge penthouse apartments at the drop of a hat, and have chefs to rustle up whatever your heart or your stomach desires, and to be chauffeured around in limos wherever you go.

'What are you doing?'

'Working for an opera singer.'

'What, like Pavarotti?'

'He's even bigger than Pavarotti.'

'No one's bigger than Pavarotti.'

Joe has a point, even though Evan is as far removed from the stereotypical image of a portly opera singer than it is possible to be. 'It's Evan David.'

My brother looks at me blankly. He doesn't get out much. Particularly not to the opera.

'He's quite famous,' I say lamely.

'Fantastic. And what do you do?'

'Not much yet,' I admit, 'but it's a full-time job—for the next few weeks, at least. I haven't been paid yet, but it means that I can help you out a bit. Maybe I could pay for you both to go away for a week.'

'You do enough for us, sis.'

When I see them both here in this dump, I don't feel that I do anywhere near enough. 'You could get a cheap week in Spain, maybe. Some sun would do you both good.'

My brother slides his arm round me and says, 'For once, I'd like you to think about what would do *you* good, Fern.'

Thirteen

Carl is all ready and waiting on his bar stool by the time I get to the King's Head.

'Peace,' he says when I arrive and puts two fingers up—in the nice way.

'Whatever,' I reply as I strip off my coat and throw my bag down with a sigh.

'How did the job go today?'

'Fab,' I say. But for some reason I don't want to share my experience with Carl. I want to keep it private. And, besides, it would worry Carl. He'd think that I'd want to go off and become an opera singer. Or at the very least, slip *'Nessun Dorma'* or something into our set at the pub. 'Tell your sister thanks from me. I owe her one.'

'And you owe *me* one,' Carl points out.

'Yeah,' I say, taking up my place behind the bar. 'Send me your bill.'

Carl looks shifty.

'What?'

'There is something you could do for me.'

'Does it involve strange sexual practices?'

My friend looks offended. 'No.'

'Shoot then.'

'Don't dismiss this out of hand,' he says. Then he takes a deep breath. 'The *Fame Game* are holding auditions this weekend at Shepherd's Bush Empire. I think we should go along.'

I laugh out loud. 'No way! That's for fresh-faced, hopeful kids, not jaded cynics like you and me. They didn't have anyone over the age of twenty in the last series.'

'They're extending it,' he assures me. 'The upper age limit is thirty-five.'

'Wonderful. So we just about squeeze in.'

'It would be good for us.'

'How do you work that out?'

'It will stretch us as artists, and you never know…'

'I do know.'

'Someone's got to win,' Carl insists. 'It might as well be us.'

'No. No way.'

My friend frowns. 'You said you'd consider it.'

I stare at the ceiling for a moment. 'I have. And the answer's no. No way.'

'Fern,' Carl says. 'I ask you to do very little for me.'

This makes me feel ashamed. Carl is my prop, my life, my one true friend. And it's true, he asks for nothing in return. Well, that's not strictly accurate. He frequently asks for sympathy shags, but never gets them.

'Please do this for me.' He gives me his little-lost-boy look.

'I'll probably be working.'

'Can't you ask Pavarotti for the time off?'

'It's my first week,' I say. 'I don't want to piss him off.' And what I don't voice is that I'm reluctant to admit to Evan David that I have aspirations to become a singer. My attempts seem so feeble compared to his and, don't ask me why, but I wouldn't want him to laugh at me. And, believe me, I'm used to people scoffing at my ambitions.

'This could be our last big chance,' Carl says seriously. 'Do you really want to spend the rest of your life behind the bar in here?'

We take in the all-encompassing dreariness of our surroundings, the billowing smoke, the tar-coloured curtains and the sticky 1960s orange-and-brown carpet.

'No.' I indulge in a pout. 'But the *Fame Game…*' I rearrange my features into a suitably disdainful expression.

'If you won't do it,' he says, 'it'll have to be the strange sexual practices.'

'I'll do it.'

Carl reaches across the bar and squeezes my hand. 'Thank you.'

'I'll do it if I can get the time off,' I qualify.

'That's good enough for me,' Carl says. 'We could win this.' His eyes are bright with excitement. 'We could really win this.'

And then my dad comes in and I lose the will to humour Carl. Instead, my heart sinks. What is it about this man that makes me want to grab him warmly by the neck and shake him? 'Did you go and see Mum today?'

'Hello, darlin',' my dad says, pulling up a stool. 'I'm fine, thank you. How are you today?'

I ignore his jibe. 'Well, did you?'

'Yes.' He sighs.

Pouring a pint of beer, I put it down in front of him, noticing that he offers me no money in return. I also notice that this isn't his first drink of the evening.

'Hi, Mr Kendal,' Carl says. 'Derek.'

I don't like to tell Carl that my dad is only 'Derek' to him when he's being bought double whiskies.

'Hello, lad,' Dad returns in a slightly slurred voice, looking relieved to see at least one friendly face. My guess is that he's been in some other hostelry since lunchtime. So much for him changing his ways.

I'll not be swayed from my interrogation. 'And?'

He hangs his head. 'I'll be making use of your couch again tonight.'

I tut at him. 'You are hopeless.'

'Love, I tried my best. She's not a well woman,' he says after he's drained half of his drink. 'I can't understand what's wrong with her.'

I polish some glasses with a certain amount of venom. If only it was as easy to rub some sense into my most annoying parent. 'She's had enough of you, that's what's wrong.'

He tips the rest of his beer down his throat in two gulps and then slams his glass down onto the bar.

'Fuck,' my dad says suddenly and rather loudly. 'Fuck it all.' Both Carl and I jump. My father might be a lot of things, but he's not normally a potty mouth. We both look at him in astonishment.

'Dad.'

'I'm fucking sick of it,' he continues in the same vein. He's now starting to wave his arms in an aggressive manner. Ken the Landlord straightens up and pays attention. I give him the eye to say that everything will be okay—which I'm sincerely hoping it will be. He's used to closing-time fights in the King's Head, but it doesn't mean to say that he likes them any better. 'I've tried my naffing bloody best all my life and what for?'

I decide not to point out that Dad's best isn't really anything to shout about.

'Well, fuck her.' Dad is in full flow. 'Fucking, fuck her.'

His voice is rising with every 'fuck'. People are starting to look. Even people who normally make no distinction between this pub and the building site.

'I don't know what to do. So she can fuck off. She can fuck off and make her own life. Without me.'

'Dad,' I grumble. 'Lower your voice. And stop swearing. You sound like you've got Tourette's syndrome.'

'Tourette's?' Dad brightens. I can almost see the light-bulb ping on above his head. 'I wonder if she'd take me back if I was ill?'

Fourteen

'How's she working out?'

Evan turned to his agent, Rupert, as he fiddled with his tie in an effort to stop the knot from lying crookedly. 'Who?'

'Your new assistant. Fern.' Rupert had been waiting for him for ages.

'Oh. Fine,' he said dismissively.

'But she didn't remind you about the dinner tonight?'

'No,' Evan had to concede. Perhaps Fern *wasn't* working out too well. It had completely slipped his mind that he was attending a reception with the Blairs at Downing Street. That wouldn't have gone down too well if he'd missed an important party with the prime minister of England. If she'd done her job properly and jogged his memory, then he wouldn't have embarrassed himself by asking Fern out to dinner. 'I think I distracted her.'

'And would you like to tell me how?'

'Not really.'

The last thing Evan wanted his agent to know about was his rather gauche approach to his new assistant. Rupert usually had more than enough to worry about without Evan adding to it.

Evan was even less likely to confess that since this afternoon he hadn't been able to stop thinking about Fern. It had been a shock to him to see the way that she had responded so honestly to the music today, but rather a pleasant shock. Perhaps he'd been in this business too long, but the music somehow failed to move him like that any longer. It was clearly the first time she'd heard opera at close proximity, and it was a potent reminder of how it used to affect him, too. He remembered times when tears would stream down his face as he was singing—but only just. It was years and years since that had happened. Was it surprising that some of his enthusiasm had waned when his whole world had revolved around singing since he was parcelled off to choir school at the tender age of eleven? The passion and drama hadn't gone out of his performances, but they had in recent years gone out of his heart. It would be nice to think that he might recapture that through Fern's eyes. If she did that for him, then whatever they were paying her was worthwhile—he allowed himself a rueful smile—even though she forgot to tell him about important appointments.

To inject some new life into his creativity was part of the reason he had agreed to come to Britain in the first place. One of the projects on the cards was recording an album with some of the up-and-coming stars of the future. Rupert assured him that it was a marvellous thing to do. Evan felt it was more like the sort of publicity stunt someone like Tom Jones would be involved in. Not that he blamed Tom. To be hanging in there

in the entertainment business after all that time was something
of a miracle and, no doubt, you had to use every trick in the
book to do it. He just wasn't sure if he wanted that for himself. Already, he was criticised by the purists as being 'too commercial'. He wondered what they'd make of it if he started
recording with Keane or Athlete or some of the other bands
he'd only just heard of. What would it do for their street cred,
too? It had never hurt Freddie Mercury's career to sing with
Monserrat Caballé, he supposed. That, primarily, was why
he'd allowed Rupert to set up some 'exploratory' sessions for
him with a few new kids on the block—mainly acts that Rupert also represented. There was no harm in that, either. Over
the years Rupert had made him one of the most sought-after
and highly paid opera stars in the world—a long way from the
impoverished chorus member he'd once been. So what if Rupert wanted to exploit him a little every now and then. His
agent was always telling Evan that he had a unique talent that
he should fully embrace, and it was true, there were very few
people who were comfortable singing anything from contemporary songs to Broadway show tunes to Mozart arias. Perhaps
it was time to unleash that on the world. Evan smiled indulgently at the other man. He'd drawn the line when Rup mentioned hip-hop though.

'We'd better get a move on, Evan.' His agent tapped his
watch. 'If we want some money for the arts out of this
wretched government, then I suggest we don't start the evening by being late.'

Without argument, Evan followed Rupert to the door and
to the waiting limousine. The other reason that he was in Britain was to open the new National Welsh Opera House in Car-

diff in a few weeks' time. This evening was a formal celebration of the forthcoming event and an excuse to go cap in hand to the tightwads in the Treasury who controlled the funding for developing arts. It had long been a pet project of Evan's to try to get opera to a wider audience. His dream was that it wouldn't be seen as some expensive, elitist pastime and that he could bring it to inner cities and to kids in schools. The California Opera House provided free 'brown bag' opera performances every year, which were staged in Yerba Buena Gardens, and a huge annual feast at the Golden Gate Park, which celebrated the opening of the fall opera season. Both were open to all comers and were some of the most exciting events that Evan had been involved in—bringing opera to the masses—and he'd be taking part in another one later this year. That was something he'd certainly like to see over here, but when this country didn't even seem to have enough money to clean its hospitals anymore, it certainly felt like an uphill struggle. Did people really feel that their life was the poorer for never having seen a performance of *Turandot?* Evan sighed. And yet the way Fern had reacted today…it was moments like that which gave him hope.

As the long black car pushed its way slowly through the evening traffic Evan wondered where Fern might be now—and, once again, surprised himself by doing it. This woman was starting to occupy his thoughts far too often. Maybe she could have even come along with them tonight. That would have got Rupert's radar twitching.

There was already a long line of people waiting outside the imposing iron gates at the mouth of Downing Street, which barred the general public from the prime minister's official resi-

dence. The glossy black front door of Number Ten lay tantal-
isingly inside, the days when the general public could drive
straight up to it long gone in a frenzy of security clamp-downs.

'This is as far as we go,' Rupert muttered. 'Celebrity or not,
you've got to queue up with the hoi polloi and have your arm-
pits tickled by a policeman toting a machine gun.'

Evan stepped out of the limo after Rupert. There was the
flash of paparazzi cameras. Magnanimously, he gave them a
wave.

'Why couldn't you be a visiting head of state? They're the
only ones who get straight in without all this nonsense,' his
agent complained. 'There are times when being an opera singer
is absolutely no bloody use at all.'

And Evan really couldn't have agreed more with him.

Fifteen

This morning I'm regretting agreeing to go to the *Fame Game* auditions with Carl. Mainly because I'm now going to have to ask Evan David for some time off work to attend them, and that seems rather foolish after only a few days in the job. I'm not even sure that he's happy with me sloping off early every evening—but then he doesn't know about my second career in the leisure industry. Even I, who am not generally known as the world's most reliable employee, have the sense to realise that it's not a good idea.

Plus this job has the huge potential to be enjoyable, and I don't want to mess it up. For instance, this morning I've spent the time simply listening to Evan having another singing lesson. Now, I'm not sure if that's the technical term, because it seems to me that someone who can sing like he does has no need of lessons. I wonder if Madonna has a voice coach? Or J-Lo? I also wonder, miserably, if whether the only thing I will ever have in common with Jennifer Lopez is the not inconsiderable size of my arse.

Listening to Evan makes me feel overwhelmed by the things I know I will have to do in order to become a better singer. I think I have a good voice—I'm sure I do—but I've never had any coaching in my life. How could I be so stupid as to think that it involved nothing more than belting out a few tunes? Carl must be equally stupid to think that we have a chance of winning the *Fame Game*. Do I really want to put myself through this form of humiliation just to keep my dearest friend happy?

There's a fear in this because singing is the only thing that I've ever been any good at and, if we were to fail—which there's a very strong chance of us doing, as the odds are stacked against us—then it would simply go to prove that I'm absolutely useless at everything. It seems such a long time ago since Carl and I used to get together at our local youth club and put on impromptu shows to entertain our easily pleased friends. It was a quantum leap for me to go after paid gigs—Carl had to bully me even then—and now I'm not sure that I have the courage to stick my head above the parapet and say that I want to be taken seriously for doing this.

Evan was a little cool with me this morning. Breakfast was over and done with by the time I got here, even though I wasn't late, so I'm starving already. We exchanged a few pleasantries, then Evan pointed out that I nearly made him miss an appointment at Number Ten Downing Street—which made me want to shrivel up on the spot. How could I do that? And then he disappeared to another room in the apartment with Anton to get down to work. I think there's a piano in every room in the place, though I haven't checked it out that thoroughly. To be honest, I'm too frightened to move from my desk.

Now, accompanied by Anton on the piano, his wonderful voice is filling the apartment through the crack of the open door. I have no idea what the song is—perhaps I should start reading the reviews of operas in the daily newspaper to gen up a bit—but I've got goosepimples in places you wouldn't believe. On the one hand, this is cheering me up immensely but, on the other, it's very dispiriting as I realise that I'll never be anywhere near as good. Still, the wintry sun is shining through the windows and warming my cold toes—the heating is on the blink again in my flat—and I'm trying to look busy while drifting away with the soaring music. My tired soul is in seventh heaven, letting the melody wash over me. My body is also dog-tired because it took me ages to drag my drunken, ranting dad home last night and pin him down to the sofa. I've never heard language like it—at least not from my parents. I thought I was going to have to club him over the head with one of my shoes to get him to go to sleep. If my true and faithful friend, Carl, hadn't come along to help me, then I don't know what I would have done. Between us we managed to wrestle some of Dad's clothes from him and cover him with a blanket. Which is lucky, because I was considering putting a pillow over his face.

Evan starts to run through some exercises. His voice rises and falls, giving his tonsils a great workout, I'm sure. I start to hum along with him and surprise myself with some of the notes I can hit. Our voices sound good in harmony together. Another surprise. I stand up and throw my head back, imagining that I'm on the stage at the King's Head, giving my regular punters the shock of their lives. I'm getting quite into my stride, when suddenly the door swings wide, reverberating on its hinges, and Evan stamps in.

'Where's that noise coming from?' he demands to know.

'I...er...I...er...'

'Is there a radio on? I thought I heard singing.' His forehead is creased in an unhappy frown.

'I...er...I...er...' I have nowhere to hide.

'It's not a radio, is it?' He looks at me with something approaching horror. 'Was it you?'

I can feel myself blanching and flushing both at once. My goodness. I had no idea that he'd be able to hear me, but I was clearly getting more carried away than I thought. How much did he hear?

'Was it you?' he demands to know again.

I can see where he gets his reputation for being difficult from. This is my first glimpse of *Il Divo*. But no wonder he's furious. Fancy his assistant having the audacity to join in with his vocal exercises. I could curl up and die. Why will the floor never conveniently open up and swallow you when you want it to? Anton comes to stand in the doorway, too. He's also regarding me with a dark frown. I feel like a trapped animal. Maybe a lickle–ickle fluffy fox with a pack of nasty, snarling hounds bearing down on me. *Die,* I say to myself. *Just die, it would be so much easier.* 'Er...'

And then my mobile phone rings. We all look at each other in a startled way. Never has the sound of that irritating Crazy Frog mad motorbike ring tone been so welcome. I owe the universe one.

'Hello,' I say with a voice that has a lurking tremor.

I glance over and though Anton has made himself scarce,

Evan is now waiting, arms folded, one eyebrow raised in question. Obviously, he's not going to let this lie.

'Is that Ms Fern Kendal?' the voice on the other end of the phone asks.

'Yes,' I say. 'This is Fern Kendal.'

'This is Doctor Parry,' he tells me.

'Oh, hello.' Doctor Parry has been our family GP since time began. He has seen me without my clothes on more times than I care to remember—and not in a sexy way. In a way that involves rubber gloves and saying, 'Just relax'. I wonder if I'm overdue a smear test. Why else would he be calling me?

'I'm phoning about your father.' Which, I guess, answers my question.

'Dad?'

There's a sigh. 'We have him here. At the surgery.'

'Is he okay?' And, of course, he wouldn't be at the doctor's surgery if he was perfectly all right.

'No,' Doctor Parry says. 'He's not okay, Fern. Can you come down here right away?'

I risk a glance over at Evan David again. He's still doing a manly glower. 'I…er…' This might be a very good time for me to make a sharp exit. 'I'll come right away.'

Grabbing my handbag, hanging up and dashing towards the door all in one movement, I tell Evan David over my shoulder, 'I have to go.'

His mouth drops open slightly, but I have no time to worry about his reaction to my sudden departure. This is an emergency and he'll have to live with it. My dad is one of the most important people in my life, and if he needs me, I'll be there. Evan David can stuff his poxy job.

'Wait!' he shouts after me. 'Don't go like this. Tell me what's wrong.'

I stop momentarily in my dramatic exit. 'My dad's ill,' I say. 'Terribly ill.'

And I hope deep in my heart that this isn't true.

Sixteen

Half an hour later, I burst into the packed waiting room at the doctor's surgery. My dad is sitting on one of the plastic chairs, looking the picture of rude health. All the images I had of him with an oxygen mask on his face or possibly a limb missing, evaporate into the air.

He smiles when he sees me. 'Fuck off!'

There's an audible gasp in the waiting room. Mothers clamp their hands over their children's ears. Two women with blue rinses tut loudly. A toddler who is knocking seven bells out of a brightly-coloured play centre stops mid-hammer.

'We won't have that, Mr Kendal,' the receptionist shouts. 'I've told you.'

'Arse. Bum. Widdle,' my dad responds.

I edge in, hardly daring to admit that this flushed-faced, foaming man is my relative. If the woman behind the appointments desk hadn't already clocked me, I might have turned and run. I note that the receptionist sags with relief. 'I'll buzz through and tell Doctor you're here, Ms Kendal.'

'Dad?'

'You're a bagful of shite,' he tells me cheerfully.

'What?' I feel myself recoil. 'I'm your daughter. What's going on? Why are you saying that?'

He turns to the woman on the chair nearest to him. She's trying to put as much distance between them as possible, edging into the corner. 'Do you like big willies?' he asks her.

There's another gasp. The poor woman is about to pass out. She is an ageing spinster and looks, quite possibly, as if she's never seen a willy in her life, let alone a big one.

'We can't have this, Mr Kendal,' the receptionist says sharply. 'Apologise at once.'

'Poo. Fart.' My dad pauses while he chooses his next word. 'Testicles.'

'What's going on?' I spread my hands. 'What on earth is going on?'

Not a moment too soon, Doctor Parry opens his door, ushering out an elderly lady with a bandaged hand. 'Ah, Ms Kendal,' he says. 'Come straight in. And you.' He gestures towards my dad, who stands up and makes a very lewd gesture involving his hips to his audience in the waiting room.

Grabbing him by the arm, I snatch him into the doctor's office. Dad sits down on one of the chairs and grins happily.

'Have you lost your mind?' I shout.

For once he is silent. I flop in the chair next to him while our GP runs a hand through his hair in a weary manner.

I don't know whether to address the doctor or my dad. I try

both, but reserve my fierce look for my deranged parent. 'Do you want to give us an explanation for this?'

My dad folds his arms.

Doctor Parry huffs. 'Your father insists he has Tourette's syndrome,' he tells me.

I start to laugh.

'Fuck off,' my dad says again.

'And you shut up,' I tell him.

'He says he caught it at the King's Head.'

'You can't *catch* Tourette's syndrome.' At least I don't think you can. I look to Doctor Parry for confirmation. 'Can you?'

'No,' he assures me.

'Bog off.'

I think Doctor Parry is being patient beyond the call of duty. If I were him, I'd have strong-armed Dad out of the surgery within minutes. Or I'd have given him an armful of some powerful sedative reserved for violent lunatics or horses. 'He has *not* got Tourette's syndrome,' I hiss. I have to say that Doctor Parry doesn't look surprised.

'I bloody well have,' Dad insists.

'He's attention seeking,' I say to the GP. 'This is all because my mum has thrown him out.'

'Kiss my arse.'

'Shut *up!*' Is punching your own dad a criminal offence? I might be tempted to risk it. 'You never swear.' Well, only if he hits his thumb with a hammer or something. 'Stop it. Stop it at once.'

'I called your mother, Fern. Before I tried your phone.' Doctor Parry looks at his notes. 'She wouldn't come down here, I'm afraid.'

'He thinks if he's ill, she'll take him back.'

'Well, it doesn't seem to be working.'

'Stop pissing talking about me as if I'm not here!'

'Then stop *"pissing"* acting like a spoiled child!'

'I'm ill,' Dad insists.

'You are not. You have the constitution of an ox. The only time you're ever under the weather is if you've had too much beer.'

'Nellies. Knackers. Knockers,' is my dad's lovely rejoinder.

I feel like banging my head against the peeling paint on the wall in Doctor's Parry's jaded office. Why didn't I just hang up and face the music—or questions *about* the music—with Evan David?

'What can I do?' I make my plea to the GP.

'I'm very busy,' he says apologetically. 'I'll write him a prescription for some antidepressants.'

'He's not depressed.' This is ludicrous. 'He's as right as rain. Acting like this will only make my mum more determined to divorce him.' I turn to my Dad. 'Can't you see that?'

'Big dangly bollocks.'

He might be fit and well now, but he won't be if he carries this on for much longer. 'This is not funny, Dad. It's an insult to Mum, to me and to Doctor Parry.' Not to mention all the people who do genuinely have Tourette's syndrome. 'This sort of behaviour is ridiculous. Nathan is the only one who's ill in our family. Don't you think we have enough to worry about with him?'

'Your father clearly has some mental problems, Fern.'

'He hasn't. He's making this all up.'

'Are you happy to take him home?' Doctor Parry asks me. 'I can have him hospitalised.'

At the thought of this, Dad perks up even more.

'He's not going to hospital,' I tell Doctor Parry as I scowl at my dad. I won't have him taking up a bed, denying treatment to someone who really is ill. 'He's coming home with me.'

Dad's smile fades. Yes, I'll sort him out. Just wait until he gets a taste of my medicine.

Seventeen

On the Tube on the way home from Doctor Parry's surgery my dad said, 'Bottom,' in a lascivious manner to the woman seated next to him. She whacked him over the head with her copy of the *Guardian* newspaper three times and so he spent the rest of the journey in morose silence. Which just proved to me, as if there was ever any doubt, that he's simply making all this up. Now he's sitting at the kitchen table, chin on his hands, sulking.

Squeaky pops his head out of the skirting board. Rummaging in my bread bin, I find a crumb of cake for him and put it on the floor. I wish someone would give me the same sort of unconditional love that I lavish on this mouse, and then I remember that Carl does. Carl adores me and yet gets little more than a few crumbs of cake in return.

My dad sighs theatrically.

'Don't. I'm not in the mood. I have just walked out on my

new job for you,' I snap at him. 'For no good reason. A job that was very important to me.'

He opens his mouth.

'And don't even think about saying arse or bugger!'

He closes his mouth again.

'I don't know where you got this stupid idea from.'

Without realising it, my dad's eyes slide furtively towards the lounge and the site of my ancient computer. I stomp into the front room and log on. This is yet another gift from Carl; his sister's company was throwing them out to make space for whizzy replacements with flat LCD screens and more mega-bytes or gigabytes or whatever sort of bytes are important for computers, so he rescued one for me and one for himself. Ali, my landlord, lets me use his broadband line for free, so that I don't even have a bill for my e-mail—not that I ever get any. All I ever get is spam offering me dodgy American medications, a Russian bride or begging letters from African princes who have fallen on hard times. The theory behind the computer ac-quisition is that it will be easier for Carl and me to compose music together, although we've never quite worked out how this will benefit us in practice, and still sit on my sofa strum-ming away until the wee small hours, fuelled by cheap vodka.

When the computer has finished whirring, I check out the history of places that Dad has visited on the Internet and gnash my teeth at a government that provides free computer tuition for the over-55s. The government should have better things to do with the money, like putting more research into child asthma and affordable housing, so that Nathan doesn't have to spend every day wheezing in a damp flat. And the over-55s should have better things to do with their time, like gardening and playing bowls. The first thing they do when they get hold of a computer is buy Viagra and get themselves into all sorts of trouble in chat rooms. My dear parent hasn't been buying medication to enhance his sexual prowess, but sure enough, he's been onto a dozen different sites all discussing the symptoms of Tourette's syndrome. No wonder he now considers himself to be such an expert on it. I could kill him. Really I could. And guess what? You can't catch it in pubs. One vital flaw in his completely cock-and-bull story.

Back in the kitchen, I fold my arms and put on my most disappointed voice. 'I know what this is all about, Dad, but it won't help. It just won't help.'

'Go and see your mother,' he whines. 'Tell her I'm ill. Tell her your old dad needs her.'

'All this will do is make her more determined to keep you out of her life,' I tell him earnestly. 'Can't you see that? She needs you to be strong. She needs you to give up the booze and the gambling. She needs you to stop seeing diamond-patterned jumpers as a style item. And, most of all, she needs you to put her at the top of your list for once.'

Somehow, my dunderheaded dad still manages to look sceptical.

'No wonder she's had enough of you,' I say in exasperation. Two days and I've had *my* fill. Snatching up my handbag, I head for the door. 'I'm going to see Mum.'

My dad brightens.

'But not to plead your case.' Though, of course, in reality I'm going to beg her on bended knee to take him back so that I don't have to put up with him for a moment longer. 'I'm going to see how she's managing.'

'Tell her I love her,' Dad says.

'You should tell her yourself.'

'She won't listen to me.'

'Well, pretending that you've got Tourette's syndrome certainly isn't going to do anything to improve the situation.'

My dad hangs his head. 'Bloody bastard bugger,' he says with feeling.

Eighteen

Mum is working at the newsagent's shop today, so I head off there to speak to her. I decide to walk in the hope that not only will I get a bit of fresh air and exercise, but that it will give me time to calm down and put some distance between me and my darling daddy and all his foibles. I love my father dearly, but that doesn't mean that I like him all the time.

Also, I need to decide what I'm going to do about Evan David. I suppose I should phone to explain what has happened after my hasty departure this morning, but what can I say? 'My father has gone completely doolally, but other than that it was all a big hoax—sorry I skipped out unnecessarily.' I'm not sure that he'll want me back anyway. I've hardly proved myself to be the most efficient personal assistant. I've turned down the possibility of a dinner date with him. I've forgotten to tell him about a meeting with the most important man in Britain. And I've muscled in on his singing lesson. Not what you'd call a great start. Plus, there seems hardly any point in ringing up to grovel and then ask for tomorrow off to attend the *Fame Game* auditions. I'd have to explain about my singing aspirations, and that would be too, too embarrassing for words. It's a shame because I think I really would have enjoyed myself working there. If nothing else the view was great—and I'm not talking about the one out of the windows. Oh well.

This newsagent's shop has been here for as long as I can remember, and my mum, Mrs Amy Kendal, has been one of the fixtures for just as long. It's a tiny place, every spare inch crammed with sweets, birthday cards and magazines. The shop has a long history of loyal customers even though it has looked like it needed a good clear-out for the last twenty years. When I round the corner, I'm astonished to see that a man in overalls is painting the façade an attractive shade of blue. I'm astonished not because it isn't long overdue, but because someone is actually *doing* it. The man is whistling as he works and wishes me a good morning.

My mum is behind the counter when I swing into the shop, and something about her demeanour stops me in my tracks. Usually, she wears a work-weary expression, there's a permanent slump to her shoulders and a frown comes easier to her than a smile. Today, by contrast, she is looking positively sprightly. She's wearing make-up—something she saves for high days and holidays—and for some reason, this appears to be a blue eye shadow day. It looks as if she's been to the hairdresser's, too, as there are unnaturally tight curls in her freshly dyed hair. A red jumper that normally languishes at the back of her wardrobe—'for best'—has also been pressed into service on a weekday. All of this is very strange—nearly as strange as my father shouting obscenities every five seconds.

As I approach, my mum pats her hair self-consciously. 'Hello, darlin'.'

'Mum?' I can't help but blink in surprise. 'What's got into you?'

She looks around shiftily. 'I don't know what you mean.'

'You look great…not that you don't always look great,' I blunder on, 'but you don't normally look this great to go to work.'

'That's because I've got more time to spend on myself now that I'm not having to look after your lazy, good-for-nothing father.'

This is not a good set-up for me pleading a case for him to return to the marital bed.

'I thought I might even take myself off and have one of those facials,' she tells me with a rather defiant nod.

This is my mother who eschews all types of face cream—even Nivea—as a profligate waste of money. Then I look round the shop. Someone has definitely tidied it up. Dust no longer lurks in every corner. The magazines lining the racks somehow look more perky. The ancient birthday cards that rotated forlornly in a wire carousel have been swept away, and brightly coloured ones in protective plastic wrappings have taken their place. Gone is the cracked lino, giving way to that wood-effect laminate stuff.

'We've got new owners,' my mum says in answer to my questioning look. 'They're doing the place up. Mr Patel—Tariq—has big ideas.'

'Tariq?'

'My new boss.' Mum's face takes on a girly flush.

Oh, no. Oh, very no. My heart drops to my shoes and there's a bad, bad feeling in my bones. Tell me this is all a terrible dream. Not only has my dad developed an imaginary illness, but my mum now has a fancy man.

'Mum,' I say pointedly. 'I've come to talk to you about Dad.'

'I've nothing to say, darlin'.'

'He's in a terrible state.'

'That's his own fault,' she tells me with a startling lack of sympathy. My mum is one of life's carers—the Florence Nightingale of Frodsham Court flats. When did she get this sudden personality transplant?

'I'm sure he's having some sort of mental breakdown.'

Mum shakes her head, unmoved by my plight. 'All this rubbish about him being ill is just another one of his silly scams. I've given him enough chances over the years. He's used them all up.'

'I just wish you'd see him.'

'No,' she says in a voice that would be difficult to argue with. 'Look, darlin', I'm sorry that you've been landed with him. But me and your father, we're over. He's not coming home no matter what he does.'

At that moment, a stately Asian man comes out of the back room and stands next to my mother in a proprietorial manner. He has a look of Omar Sharif about him—eyes that are limpid brown pools, skin the colour of caffè latte, strong wavy hair flecked with silver—and even I, a good thirty years younger than him, can see the attraction.

'This is my daughter, Mr Patel.' My mum's voice has suddenly gone all breathy.

'Ah,' he says. 'Fern. I have heard a lot about you.' I wish I could say the same about him. My mum has been extraordinarily quiet about the subject of her new boss until now. This is the first I've heard about it, and yet normally she's so keen to share all the gossip from the shop.

He takes my hand and brushes it against his lips, but not in a smarmy way. Hmm. Charm personified. My mum giggles alarmingly. If only my dad could see this, he would let out a stream of blood-curdling expletives that he wouldn't have to put on.

Nineteen

When Rupert blew his nose for the third time. Evan stared at him, eyes narrowed. 'You're not getting a cold are you, Rup?'

'No. No.' His agent shook his head vehemently. 'Just a sniffle. Maybe a touch of hayfever.'

'In London? In winter?'

Rupert withered under his gaze. Evan pulled the neck of his black cashmere sweater round his throat and unconsciously massaged the muscles with his hand. His temperature had been perfect this morning when he'd taken it, as he did every morning. You could never be too careful. Catch a bug early enough and, with some judicious care, you could sometimes nip it in the bud. Did his throat feel sore at all? Evan did a test swallow and felt for any sign of swollen glands. No. All seemed fine.

The press were always keen to point out that he was completely paranoid about protecting his voice. But who wouldn't be when it was their fortune? It was only this talent that was keeping him out of the gutter and away from obscurity. You didn't take something like that lightly. It meant that he had to avoid dairy products and smoky atmospheres and anyone with germs or who might have come into contact with anyone with germs. He didn't touch alcohol, either, but other than that he lived a normal life. Didn't he? And it was the first question that Rupert asked him every morning—'How's the voice?' Not how was he as a person. Just the voice. The rest of him could go to hell in a handcart. The voice was everything.

'Just keep your distance,' Evan said. 'Take some vitamin C. Get some from Dermuid. Ask him to take your temperature, too.'

Rupert gave him a look of weary acquiescence.

Evan's chef had been with him for some time now and the arrangement was working out fine. Not only did he turn out great, nutritious meals, but Dermuid had taken an interest in Evan's general well-being and made sure that his vitamins and supplements were always on hand. He also tried, mostly in vain, to keep Rupert in line, too. Dermuid had never let him down, which meant all that Evan had to concentrate on were his performances. And he needed people around him whom he could trust. Evan hated to admit it, but he felt safe with regular staff around him who understood his ways. And speaking of staff…

'Have you heard anything from Fern?' Evan tried to sound casual as he asked Rupert.

'Who?'

'Fern,' he repeated, failing to keep the note of exasperation out of his voice. 'The new temp. She scuttled out of here yesterday and didn't come back.'

Rupert raised an eyebrow. 'Perhaps she's naively assuming that you give your staff weekends off.'

'Whatever gave her that impression?'

'I never had time to discuss terms and conditions with her,' Rupert said. 'I was going to do it today. Then she would have known that it's a full-time nanny you need, not a personal assistant.'

'Rupert…' he said in warning. His agent was the only person who could get away with teasing him, but sometimes even Rupert pushed it too far.

'Okay. Okay.' Rup held up his hands. 'If she doesn't turn up, I'll ring the next candidate on the list.'

'Can't you phone the woman yourself?'

Rupert looked puzzled. 'Yes. I've got her number. But…'

'I thought she was quite good.'

'She forgot to remind you of an important appointment and then scarpered without warning yesterday. How are you quantifying "good"?'

Evan had the grace to look sheepish. 'She was fun to have around.'

'Oh, dear,' Rupert sighed. 'Oh, dearie, dearie me.'

A frown darkened Evan's forehead. 'What?'

'Do we need someone whose sole qualification is being fun? I'm not sure that it will help your situation to go chasing after this woman.'

'I'm not chasing after her,' Evan scoffed, even though he felt he might be. How could he explain to Rupert that she'd sparked something in him that he hadn't even realised was long dead? That somehow she was the only person he'd met in a long time who didn't drain his creativity but added impetus to it. Fern was fun and she was funny. That was something that had been missing in his life for a long time. 'And exactly what "situation" are you referring to?'

'The "situation" where we've got an increasingly deranged woman chasing *you*.'

Evan sighed.

'Lana has been on the telephone a million times this week already,' Rupert expanded. 'I'm running out of excuses for you.'

'I'll call her back,' Evan said. 'I promise.'

'You said that last week.'

'I have to be in the mood for Lana. You know that.'

'I know that if you don't ring her, there'll be trouble. Big trouble.'

Lana was an opera singer, too. If Evan was nicknamed *Il Divo,* then Lana Rosina was definitely *La Diva Assoluta.* The fiery Italian was one of the most stunning and outspoken figures in the world of international opera stars today.

In a rave review of her last performance in England—*Tosca* in Puccini's opera of the same name—she was described in the *Independent* newspaper as having the vocal strength of Maria Callas, the dramatic delivery of Edith Piaf and the body of Angelina Jolie. A heady combination which made her—as a woman—very hard to handle. Her performances were always critically acclaimed as nothing less than perfect, her off-stage behaviour was legendary as less so. She was known as an outstanding singer and a mean left hook. Her favourite pastime seemed to be making the paparazzi eat pavement. Lana was also the most charismatic soprano that Evan had ever had the pleasure of sharing the stage with—and, subsequently, his bed. At best, she was wickedly funny and wilful. At worst, she was a neurotic witch with an inferiority complex. She needed to be adored and became demanding and difficult when she felt she wasn't. There were days when Evan definitely didn't adore Lana. To say that their relationship was mercurial was understating it. Her singing was always full-throated, her timbres loaded with variety and her glinting top register couldn't fail to move the audience—but have that voice turned on you in a torrent of Italian abuse and then it was a different matter altogether. It was something he'd been subjected to a number of times over the years. The hairs stood up on the back of Evan's neck just to think of it. Her voice was often described as colourful and fluent—it was never more so than when screaming invective.

They'd met a long time ago in San Francisco, at the California Opera House when she was singing Cassandre in Berlioz's opera *Les Troyens* at short notice—a performance which sent the critics into a frenzy of delight. And Lana had been wowing them ever since. Their own association, however, had been more erratic. She'd attended a closing night reception at his home over there and he'd been drawn to her passion and vibrant beauty. They were both classed as the hardest-working opera stars today, kept in demand on the international circuit more than either of them could ever have dreamed of at the start of their careers. The downside was that it meant relationships, even with the best will in the world, were sporadic. Lana made it clear, on many occasions, that she didn't think this was ideal. They hadn't spoken now in weeks, since their rehearsals for *La Traviata,* which they were due to perform in Wales together very soon.

'Call her,' Rupert urged. 'She's getting cross.'

That was never a good thing. Lana was like a pot of pasta left on the stove for too long—eventually everything would boil over and create a terrible mess everywhere. But Evan didn't want to speak to Lana now. If she was angry with him—and it was likely that she was—the whole experience would be draining. He'd need to psyche himself up to phone her.

'Later,' he said evasively. 'I've got things to do.' He was due on stage for a full dress rehearsal of *Madame Butterfly* in a few short hours and he needed to gather his thoughts, make preparations. As Evan went to leave the room, he saw Rupert muttering under his breath. 'Don't forget to call Fern,' he called out.

'Later,' Rupert echoed. 'I've got things to do, too.'

Twenty

'I can't accept this,' I say to Carl. 'It's too expensive.' It's also too sexy.

He blushes furiously beneath his mop of freshly washed hair. My friend is clearly taking this very seriously. His very best frayed blue jeans are in evidence and he's standing awkwardly in my kitchen—and Carl never stands awkwardly anywhere.

'When did you buy it?'

'Yesterday,' he mumbles. 'I thought it would suit you.'

'That's a fine piece of kit,' my dad says over his bacon sand-wich. The all-pervading smell of curry in the flat seems to have fuelled his appetite. He gives an approving nod. 'It'll knock them dead.'

'No one's asking you,' I tell him. His snoring from the sofa kept me awake all night—it was absolutely nothing to do with nerves about today's audition for the *Fame Game*.

'Just try it on,' Carl urges.

And, as I seem to be doing so much to please everyone else these days, I march through to the bedroom, strip off my T-shirt, which I thought looked absolutely fine, and put on the silky top that Carl has purchased.

Slipping it over my head, I wonder whether he's nicked it or gone without food all week to pay for it. Then I stare at myself in the mirror. My goodness, it's wonderful. If I didn't know me, I might fancy me.

It's a wisp of silver chiffony stuff, gathered in full folds over the bust, giving me the voluptuous breasts of a page three girl. Never a bad thing. The bodice is boned, tightly fitted and laces up the back like a corset. It flares enticingly over the black trousers I'm wearing, giving me a cinched waist and curvy hips. I would never have believed that a piece of clothing could transform my shape so much, and I wonder why I don't entrust my future wardrobe to Carl. That man definitely has hidden talents.

I dash back into the kitchen and shout, 'Da, da!' which sends Squeaky scurrying back to his hole in the skirting board.

Carl's eyes pop wide open and he looks like he might spit out his cup of tea. 'Wow!' he manages.

'It's fabulous.' I go over and kiss him on the cheek. 'You are a great mate. I don't know how to thank you.'

'If your dad wasn't here,' he murmurs, 'I might be able to come up with a suggestion or two...'

'Put your tea down and lace me up properly.' I proffer my back to him. He takes hold of the laces of my corset. His hands are warm and are shaking slightly. I hope that Carl isn't worried about today, because that truly would make me go to pieces. His fingers brush against my skin and give me very strange feelings. I move away from him.

'Are you okay?' Turning to look at him, I see his eyes are shining bright.

'I'm great,' he says huskily. 'You look wonderful.'

'We'd better get a move on,' I suggest. 'We don't want to be late.'

'Let me look at my little girl,' Dad says, breaking into Carl's mooning.

I give him a twirl.

'Lovely,' he says.

I take a bit of Dad's bacon sandwich, not caring that it will ruin my lipstick. 'What are you doing today, troublesome parent?'

'Oh, nothing much.' Dad adopts his shiftiest face. 'A little bit of this and a little bit of that.'

Sitting in the pub until he's pissed, then blowing the rest of his money on the horses before he finds some blowsy tart to fund him for the rest of the day. No wonder my mum has her eyes trained on Mr Patel with his movie-star looks and surfeit of charm.

'Wish us luck, Derek,' Carl says as he picks up his guitar.

'Ah, you won't need it,' my dad assures us. 'You'll be coming home with a contract in your hand. No one else will stand a snowball-in-hell's chance.'

I wish I had everyone else's confidence in our abilities. To me we're just another middle-of-the-road pub act.

I give my dad a kiss on his thinning hair and then wink at him as we head for the door. 'Notice that you've not got Tourette's syndrome today.'

My father folds his arms grumpily and frowns. 'Fuck off,' he says.

Twenty-one

The open auditions for the *Fame Game* are being held at Shepherd's Bush Empire, a wonderful old theatre turned music venue that still retains a lingering air of its original elegance. Carl and I turn up hours early only to find that the queue is already out of the door and is snaking—anaconda-size—down the road. By the time we get to the judges, they'll already be bored to tears and may possibly have lost the will to live. I let out an unhappy huff.

My dear friend is unperturbed. 'We always knew it was going to be manic, Fern.'

'Yes,' I capitulate. I also always knew that most of the auditioning hopefuls would be under twenty and would look like pop stars already. But it's still a shock to see quite how many of them there are—and quite how much flesh is on display. It's not exactly warm in London at the moment and they must be frozen. The fact that if it wasn't for Carl's prompting I'd have dressed for comfort and warmth above sex appeal also marks me out as someone fifteen years older than the average wannabe. I gaze along the constantly lengthening line and also note with horror that there's not an ounce of fat to spare anywhere.

Although I'm looking considerably sexier than I would have done left to my own devices, I'm bucking the trend by not having my midriff, my legs or my entire cleavage on display. 'Look at them,' I complain to Carl. 'They're all so young.'

'It just means that we're so much more experienced than they are.'

Sometimes I could batter my friend because he's so relentlessly optimistic. For some strange reason, he's convinced that one day our talent will win out. We will be 'discovered' by some fantastic pop impresario and our miserable little lives will be transformed into one of wealth and wonderment. For Carl, all that means is that he will buy designer jeans rather than ones from Matalan. But then he also buys a lottery ticket every Saturday and gaily assumes that one day his boat will come in if only he believes hard enough—despite the fact that he's not won so much as a tenner in the last three years, proving that the odds are very definitely piled against him.

There are boy bands, girl bands, too many Britney lookalikes to mention, but very few long-haired hippies accompanied by ageing barmaids. All the men look gay—apart from Carl—and none of them look as if they've wandered out of the line-up of Black Sabbath. This is a dreadful, dreadful mistake. We are people in the wrong place at the wrong time. I'd really like to go home now and have some hot chocolate and put my feet up and pretend that this never happened, but I know that Carl—having managed to get me here—won't be that easily dissuaded. He might look laid-back, but that man is blessed with a core of steel. I'm going to have to go through this whole unhappy ritual just to please him.

Despite my misgivings—and there are many of them—we join the back of the queue. A camera crew wanders up and down, recording our misery. Everyone else waves and pouts in a suitably hysterical manner. I can't be the only one who feels like giving them the finger. Even Carl gives them a peace sign and a goofy grin for heaven's sake! The only solace I can take is the fact that it isn't raining. Which is just as well, because an hour later than the auditions were due to start, a couple of harassed-looking assistants totter out on impossibly high heels and slap stickers bearing numbers on us all. Carl and I are, collectively, number 342. How long, I wonder, is it going to take to get through all the 341 acts before us? Darkness will surely have fallen. We'll have to take it in turns to go out of the queue to visit the loo in the Kentucky Fried Chicken place down the road and to get sustenance. I glance down at our number.

'We haven't got a name,' I say suddenly.

Carl looks shocked, while I panic. In the pub we're just known as Carl and Fern—not exactly cool. Shouldn't we have spent more time thinking about calling ourselves something suitably trendy and happening to grab the judges' attention?

'Bollocks,' Carl mutters.

'Not catchy enough.'

My friend gives me what I can only class as 'a look'.

'The Winning Couple?' I suggest, trying to bolster my rapidly failing bravado.

'"Just the Two of Us",' Carl says. 'That's what I feel it's always been like. Just the two of us against the world.'

114

Carole Matthews

I can see that he's serious, so I say, 'Okay. Just the Two of Us, it is.' Or do I mean Just the Two of Us, we are. And, rather late in the day, our duo is born. It doesn't sound very showbiz to me, but I say nothing.

And then, with nothing much else to do, we settle in for the long wait. Carl amuses himself throughout the day by smoking a dozen fags and strumming his guitar. I amuse myself by thinking of Evan David in faintly erotic situations until I realise that it is doing me absolutely no good at all. I wonder if he's noticed my absence today. Does he think that I'll be back on Monday as if nothing has happened? I have no idea, and I'm sure that he won't mark it down as a significant loss in his life when I'm not. Still, I can't help wondering what might have been. In my fantasy land, Evan David would have been so impressed by my personal assistant skills that he would have sacked the chicken-poxed Erin and would have given me her job instead, whisking me around the world in five-star comfort for the rest of my days. And we would have flirted endlessly and hopelessly, like James Bond and Miss Moneypenny.

After a while, when Carl and I are bored with each other, we chat to a couple of the other hopefuls in the queue, and it's fair to say that none of them are blessed with our wealth of experience, as Carl predicted. We've been singing in pubs for years. Too many years. For most of them, this is the first time they've ever auditioned for anything. And I can't help but admire their sheer optimism that all they need is a belief in themselves to carry them through. A lot of the people queuing for their five minutes in front of the judges seem to have no particular talent but are here fuelled only by blind ambition and a desire to grab fame in whatever shape they can get it. None of them seem to have my inhibitions despite the fact that I could probably—when I'm feeling confident—sing most of them under the table. But so many people want to achieve celebrity status these days without having to work for it and without doing anything of merit to warrant it.

The *Fame Game* phenomenon has gripped the nation and, whether we like it or not, the entire population of the UK is glued to the telly at six o'clock every Saturday night to watch the struggling pop artists of the future in their quest for fame. Sometimes it is a supportive and fun show. Sometimes it's positively gladiatorial. But I guess, as they say, that's entertainment! As long as it keeps pulling in the viewers, they'll keep running it.

A mere five hours have passed while we've been standing in the queue, and we're finally nearing the front. Carl has kept me going by nipping off to nearby cafés to ply me with regular supplies of hot tea and chocolate. I wish I'd let him bring a couple of joints and we could have smoked them. Or even a hip flask of booze might have helped for Dutch courage. To do this stoned would be infinitely preferable than doing it stoned-cold sober. Already a stream of weeping girls have been dispatched from the bowels of the Shepherd's Bush Empire. Some are begging the high-heeled assistants for another chance. Some are rejoining the queue at the end, probably in the hope that the judges will be so addled by the time they perform again that they won't realise they've already seen them three hours previously.

'Feeling okay?' Carl asks.

'No.' My hair has gone flat in the damp air. My feet hurt. Inside my coat, my lovely chiffon top is getting crumpled.

He puts his arm round me and squeezes me tight. I can feel the tingle of excitement running through him and wish I could share it. 'It'll be fine,' he says confidently. '*We'll* be fine.'

Will we? All I can do is wait.

Twenty-two

When we eventually reach the front of the queue, one of the Identikit assistants asks us our name, so I'm really glad that we remembered to make one up. 'Just the Two of Us,' Carl informs her.

She fails to swoon at our originality, but instead she hushes us lest we feel inclined to speak and then ushers us into a corridor, which takes us down to the backstage door. I hadn't considered that we might be required to perform on an actual stage. Apart from one summer when Ken the Landlord at the King's Head had a beer festival in a nearby park and Carl and I—Just the Two of Us—performed on a sort of open-sided trailer from a lorry that formed a makeshift arena, this is the first time I've been on a real stage. My knees tremble with anticipation. Why on earth did I wait until today to make my debut?

I can't feel nervous anymore, because I can't feel anything. We stand in the wings and watch the act before ours. It's a frighteningly young girl—number 341—also known as Amber who we've been chatting to for most of the day. Carl bought her a couple of cups of tea and they swapped a few ciggies, but not in a chatty-up way because she's only seventeen. I think he just felt sorry for her. Amber is a truly awful singer and my heart breaks for her. Even her mother wouldn't come along with her today because she thought she was wasting her time. Sometimes it's worth remembering that Mum is so often right. She strangles some Shania Twain number for a few bars until a voice from the darkened auditorium says, 'Thanks,' with a degree of boredom that must be very difficult to achieve.

And then we're shoved in the back by the lovely assistant onto the waiting stage. I follow Carl's footsteps in a kind of trance, listening to my feet clonk on the wooden boards. Foot-lights blind me, but I can just make out the vast empty space of the theatre. The seats are long gone and, instead, there is a makeshift table behind which are the judges, seated on three chairs. Some minions wander round in the background.

The assistant has followed us onto the stage. 'Three hundred and forty two,' she announces. 'Just the Three of Us.'

Carl and I both look round for the other one of us. Perhaps they think we're being ironic. We should have stuck to plain old 342.

'Just the *Two* of Us,' I correct and I hear a returning sigh out of the gloom for my pains.

'Okay,' one of the judges says. 'When you're ready.'

Fame Game speak for 'get on with it.'

I can't make out the judges too clearly. The main man is usu-ally one of the well-known pop impresarios—people whose manufactured groups have topped the charts for a number of years. There's usually some sort of fashion pundit, too, and I wonder what he or she will make of Carl's retro-style. To make up the three judges, there's more often than not a media rent-a-quote presenter from one of the youth programmes. Three people who can break a person's spirits or help them fulfil their dreams. What a position of power to be in! They all look slightly bored by the weight of it.

Carl takes up position with his acoustic guitar and gives me an encouraging look. My heart suddenly shoots out of the doldrums. I have to do this for my friend. For him alone, I have to give this my best shot.

We went through a million different songs before we settled on one that would be suitable. It's an old Prefab Sprout number 'Couldn't Bear to Be Special', a bit of a melancholy ballad which I'm hoping will stand out amid the hundreds of ear-splitting renditions of Britney's 'Toxic'. The lyrics of the song really reach out to me and I can only hope that they reach out to the judges, too. I suddenly wish that I'd spent some of the time in the queue doing vocal exercises. How would Evan David have prepared for this? At the thought of him, my mind goes into a tailspin again and I have to force myself back into the present.

Carl plays the first chord and I call on whatever inner strength that I might, unknowingly, possess and give my performance all that I can summon. My mouth is dry and my palms are clammy. Sweat trickles between my breasts. The first note comes out strong and clear, then the music takes over and I lose myself in it.

Just when I'm starting to relax and even venture to think, 'This could be my moment', a voice out of the darkness says,

'Thank you', in that same bored-to-death fashion I heard for the previous act. Which seems so unfair as I'm so, so much better than her—even though I'm the only person who seems to think so.

My singing grinds to a halt. Carl strums what sounds like an annoyed riff.

'We'll be in touch,' a disembodied voice says.

'Thanks,' I mutter feebly, sounding pathetically grateful. 'Thanks.'

Thanks for what? Humiliating us completely? Getting our hopes up and dashing them against the rocks? I want to shout and stamp my feet and say that they should have listened to the whole of the song. Wouldn't that be common courtesy? And then I think of the hundreds and hundreds of other hopefuls waiting for their turn in the spotlight, and I shuffle off the stage in Carl's wake.

Outside, in the harsh daylight, I can see him shaking. With fear or excitement, I don't know.

'That wasn't too bad, was it?' he says.

'No.' I have no idea how to class that experience. Nerve-wracking. Terrifying. Exhilarating. Mind-blowing. My body feels electrified. Adrenaline is galloping round my blood like a wild horse charging inside me. I've never felt like this before and I only know that it's a drug I want more of.

Carl wraps his arms round me. I wonder if he's going to cry. I feel like I might join him. 'You were sensational,' he says.

'You weren't too shabby yourself.' We hug each other some more and then we become aware of the people on the street and the traffic and reality hitting home once more. I stand away from Carl.

His arms hang limply by his side. 'So what do we do now?'

'We could get some food before I start my shift at the King's.'

'I meant about the audition.'

'There's nothing else we can do,' I say. 'We gave it all we'd got.' And I really believe that we did—for our one brief moment of glory. 'If they liked us, they'll be in touch.'

I shrug as if I really don't care. How can I sound so nonchalant, when at this moment I would sell my very soul to the devil for a chance to appear on the *Fame Game* show? And, to be honest, I'd sell Carl's, too.

Twenty-three

My shift at the King's Head drags interminably. Every time a phone rings—*anyone's* phone—my nerves turn me into a jangling wreck. The good people at *Fame Game* didn't say exactly how long it would be before they would call if they wanted us back to go through to the next round and audition again. My stomach has turned into a swirling maelstrom, but that could be due to the dodgy-looking Chinese takeaway that Carl and I consumed in great haste after our ordeal. I can't even think how I'll feel if they don't call us at all.

Even Carl is subdued this evening. After the high, here comes the low. Mind you, Carl *is* sitting next to my rather inebriated father—and that's enough to make anyone depressed. Dad is rambling on incoherently about love gone wrong. As far as I can ascertain, he hasn't done anything remotely useful or constructive towards putting his own particular 'love gone wrong' right again. Neither has he forgotten that he's pretending to have Tourette's syndrome and tosses out the occasional torrent of abuse at a passing punter—a very dangerous occupation at the King's Head, which is known locally as something of a pugilist's paradise.

'Nellies. Knockers. Knackers,' he mumbles at a large and much-tattooed man, who glares at him.

'He's not well,' I tell the man, making a politically incorrect this-is-a-loony circle against my temple with my finger.

He gives me a glare, too, but continues on his way to the dartboard without thumping my dad into the ground. Which I view as a result.

'Dad!' I snarl at my extremely annoying parent. 'Stop it.'

'Nellies…'

His repertoire is wearing thin and I cut him off before he can repeat himself. 'You're going the best way about getting yourself flattened.'

Dad returns to staring into his beer.

Don't I have enough to worry about without adding my dad's self-inflicted mental illness to the list? I can't wait for our set to start tonight. I want to see if I can lose myself in the music again as I did this afternoon. That's not something that happens often to me—probably because I'm too concerned about someone throwing stuff at us while we're on stage at the King's.

At the allotted time, Carl slides down from his stool and we wander over to the little dais. Unusually, Ken the Landlord follows us. Before I can take up the microphone, he grabs it.

'Ladies and gentlemen,' he says, 'tonight we have our very own songbird…'

I give him a sideways glance. *Songbird?*

'…the lovely Fern Kendal, who's performing for you tonight straight from her fabulous audition for the *Fame Game!*'

I'm glad I didn't mention to Ken that we'd only managed to get half of our song out before we were unceremoniously ejected. Also, unusually, the crowd cheer up a bit and give us a round of perky applause. Ken hands me the microphone. I cover it. 'We'll be wanting a pay rise if you build us up too much,' I warn him.

His face falls and he slopes off to the bar to pour himself a stiff drink.

Carl and I launch into our first song and, I don't really know how to explain this, but I feel somehow more confident. I'm not exactly jumping around the stage in ecstasy; however, somewhere there's been a very subtle shift in my belief in myself. Self-aggrandisement isn't normally my forte, but I know that I could do this. I could do this in a big way. Given the chance.

We finish the set and again, it might be my dream-fuelled imagination, but I do think the reception is a little more rapturous than usual. Jumping down from the stage, I'm clapped on the back by some of the punters, faces smile widely at me—and not just the mad ones. Then my phone rings: I feel it vibrating in my jeans. I can hardly catch my breath. Could this be it—the call we're waiting for? Our destiny nestling impatiently in my pocket? Could our second performance have drifted to them through the ether of the universe, prompting the powers that be at *Fame Game* to contact us?

'This could be it,' I say to Carl. My mouth feels as if it's filled with sand. 'This could bloody well be it!'

Hurriedly, I snatch at my phone before it switches to voicemail. 'Hi,' I say, trying my hardest to hold on to the confidence I'd experienced just a moment or two ago.

'Hi.' It's a man's voice. One I don't recognise. 'It's Rupert Dawson,' he says smoothly. 'Evan David's agent.'

'Oh, hi.' The bubble of my jubilation is popped.

'I'm calling to check that everything is okay with you.'

'With me?'

'You left in a hurry yesterday and didn't turn in for work today. Evan was worried.'

'He was?'

'He wanted to know if he could expect you tomorrow.'

Tomorrow's Sunday. I was hoping to see Joe and Nathan, who I'm neglecting at the moment. I chew at my lip. If Evan wants me to go to work tomorrow though, it means that I still have my job. This, I should be thankful for.

'Are you still there?' Rupert enquires.

'Tomorrow's fine,' I say. 'And I'm sorry that I didn't make it today.' I didn't realise I had to work the weekend, too. I'll let them assume that I was absent due to my continuing crisis. They'll never find out I'd been skiving off to audition for *Fame Game*. Evan David might not have been so worried about me if he'd known where I was.

I hang up and turn to Carl. 'It wasn't fame and fortune knocking, but at least I have my job back.'

'I don't know whether to be disappointed or pleased,' Carl says.

'Me, neither.' We rejoin my dad at the bar. Call me shallow but I'm getting quite a buzz from knowing that Evan David was thinking about me at all. I cup my chin in my hands and stare wistfully into the middle distance.

'Fern!' Ken the Landlord shouts. 'You might have to take a pay *cut* if you don't serve your customers.'

I shake myself out of my reverie and adopt a smiley pose behind my beer pump. 'What can I get you?'

The tattooed man is back. He's at the front of the queue and is eyeing my dad with deep suspicion. 'A pint of Guinness.'

Oh, no. That will take ages to draw. Why couldn't he have had a Diet Coke and then I could have had him away from the bar in a thrice.

'La, la, la…' my dad starts.

'Shut up,' I say.

'Are you talking to me?' the tattooed man growls.

'No,' I tell him. 'I think my father's having one of his funny turns.'

I shoot Dad a glance that says, 'you dare!'

'La, la, la,' my dad continues tunefully. 'Lard arse.'

The tattooed man spins around. His face has gone very black and there's a throbbing pulse started up in his thick neck. This does nothing to thwart my dad, who is in full flow. 'La, la, la. You are a lard arse.'

'And you're a gobshite.'

I think I'm going to have a heart attack.

The tattooed man pushes my dad off his bar stool and onto the floor.

Dad looks up in surprise. 'Fuck me,' he says.

The punters of the King's Head need no further encouragement. Someone shouts, 'Fight!' Within seconds, fists are flailing, glasses are flying. My dad, the instigator of it all, is crawling towards the front door, head down, bottom up.

Ken the Landlord phones the police. He looks over towards me. 'Your dad's barred.'

I fume silently. That's not all he is.

Twenty-four

Dad and I aren't speaking this morning. I do moody banging and crashing round the kitchen while he sits glumly at the table. Having crawled, unscathed, out of the fracas he caused at the pub, he isn't sporting a black eye, but he jolly well deserves one if you ask me. How my mum has put up with him for so long, goodness only knows. If she doesn't take him back soon, *I* might be tempted to black his eye for him.

It takes me most of my Tube journey to calm down, and then I have an unexpected surge of joy as I'm let into Evan David's apartment. I can't believe how pleased I am to be back here. It's like stepping into an oasis of calm when all else around me is utter chaos. A waft of classical music greets me, and relief seeps out of me in an audible sigh. Evan is in black sweats and a T-shirt. He's towelling his crop of dark hair dry with lazy, rhythmic movements. When he sees me, he stops in his tracks.

'Hello,' he says with a tight smile, draping the towel around his neck. He starts towards me and I think for a moment that he's going to kiss me. Then he pulls up abruptly and we're suddenly shy with each other.

'Hi,' I say. 'Sorry about yesterday's misunderstanding.'

'I'm just glad everything's okay.'

I'm not sure I'll expand on my version of okay.

'Is your father better?'

'He's improving,' I reply somewhat cagily. I hope that by the time I get home this evening, my dad will have come to his senses and will have set about saving his marriage in a rational manner, rather than going down the imaginary mental-illness route. If not, I might have to drop into the conversation a few snippets of information about Mr 'Omar Sharif' Patel. 'It's good to be back.'

I feel as if I've been away from a treasured friend for weeks instead of having just returned after a couple of days AWOL from a new job.

'There's not much to do today,' Evan tells me.

I wonder why Rupert wanted me here then. Perhaps Evan is so incapable of functioning in the real world that he needs some form of attendant 24/7.

'Join me for breakfast?'

I shrug. My dad had eaten the last of the bread, so no toast for me or Squeaky the Hungry Mouse this morning. 'I'd love to.'

'I've had Dermuid set the table on the balcony.'

'Sounds great.' Why have none of my previous jobs been so civilised?

'I took the liberty of ordering breakfast for you,' he says.

Ah. So no bacon sarnie then.

Taking my arm, Evan leads me out onto the balcony. A table is set with a white linen cloth and proper linen napkins, not the crappy paper sort. Red roses fill a small glass bowl—the stamp of über-florist Jane Packer is all over them. I only know this because I'd seen a feature about her ages ago in a tattered magazine in the dentist's waiting room. She has a certain style that's instantly recognizable, and I wish that someday someone will be able to say the same thing about me.

The morning is still wearing its daybreak chill, but a giant patio heater is working full-time to dispel it. There's no sign of the winter sun and the sky is white, dappled with grey clouds like a piebald horse. I keep my jacket on as Evan picks up a cashmere sweater from the back of one of the chairs and slips it on. It strikes me again just how handsome he is with his angular cheekbones that look as if they've been fashioned by a sculptor and full sensuous lips that are terribly reluctant to come to a smile. Today his grey eyes reflect the colour of the River Thames as it slides beneath the balcony. There's an intensity to him, a contained power in his body waiting to be unleashed at any moment, as if it's a struggle to hold all the strength of his powerful voice inside. An alpha male of the highest order. I thought I was immune to all that macho rubbish—but, hey, I was wrong. This man is opera's answer to George Clooney.

We sit down, the warmth from the heater blowing over us, which, strangely, gives me goosepimples. Following an awkward moment of silence between Evan and me, Dermuid brings us breakfast.

'Hi, Fern. Good to see you.' He turns his face away from Evan David and winks at me. A lecherous comedy wink.

I smile back guilelessly. What did that mean? Is there a joke I'm missing out on? Dermuid drifts away, leaving us alone once more.

My attention is drawn to the feast laid out before us. Fresh berries and yoghurt to start. My word, I haven't eaten this healthily in years. This beats long-life white bread with green, furry edges.

Evan David lift his glass of freshly squeezed orange juice and clinks it against mine. 'Good to have you back.'

I'm already wading into my luscious strawberries. 'Good to be here,' I mumble.

I look around me, feeling overwhelmed by the setting. This is how movie stars take their breakfast or—it seems—opera stars. It makes my own harried life of constantly eating on the hoof look rather pathetic. Standing up stuffing a stale slice of toast into your face just can't compete. I look over at Evan David. He seems inordinately pleased to see me. Does he treat all his personal assistants like this, I wonder?

Evan's strawberries remain untouched. His wonderful eyes lock onto mine, his slow-burn smile widens and then the penny drops. It drops from a great height. And lands with a loud clatter on the floor. So that's what all this is about. I'm on the menu, too. My heart and my self-esteem plummet. He thinks once he's plied me with a healthy brekky that he's going to shag me! I sigh to myself. My goodness, I wish I'd got the details of this job sorted out before I started it. That will teach me to lurch into things unwittingly. Little did I realise that my duties would extend to keeping Evan David amused in all areas of his life. That smile suddenly takes on a new meaning.

My strawberry sticks in my throat. What am I going to do

now? I'm out of my depth in this glamorous sort of lifestyle. I had no idea that this would be expected of me. Perhaps if I'd been working for a rock legend, I'd have seen it coming, but I thought opera bods were more moral than that. Just because they sing posher songs I guess that doesn't make them any better than the rest of us. I somehow thought it would. It only goes to show I'm naive in the ways of the world. Or in the ways of *this* world. If someone behaved like this at the King's Head, I'd more than likely deck them.

'Are you okay?'

'Fine. Fine.' I start to cough. 'Lodged strawberry.'

I fancied the pants off him five minutes ago. Five minutes ago when we were both single, red-blooded people who might move forward with a mutual attraction and a bit of respect. Now that I know he sees me as some sort of paid-up plaything to use as and when he sees fit, this casts a very different light on it. Plus I haven't had sex in such a long time. There's never been anyone I've fancied that much or who's been prepared to give me some love or commitment. If I've held out for so long, I'm certainly not going to jump into bed with someone simply because it's expected of me—even though he's possibly the only person I have considered jumping into bed with in recent memory. What does he think I am, for goodness sake? Oh, God—what if he pounces on me? No wonder Dermuid was giving me that weird wink. He's clearly seen it all before.

I cough again. If I'm not careful I'm going to compound my embarrassment by spraying half-chewed strawberry everywhere. Good grief, why was I born with my sophistication gene missing?

Evan David dabs at his mouth with his napkin and goes to

stand up. There's a concerned look on his face. 'Do you want me to pat your back?'

'No. No!' Keep your damn hands off me, mate! 'Loo. I need to go to the loo.' Bolting for the patio doors, I slam them shut behind me.

'Bathroom!' I shout to Dermuid in panic and, without questioning my urgency, he points me in the right direction.

The nearest bathroom is a palatial marble room as big as my flat, of course. Grabbing a glass from the side of the double sinks, I fill it with water—once I manage to work out how the hi-tech taps work—and take a swig. My strawberry slips down smoothly out of harm's way.

Red-eyed and flushed, I stare at myself in the vast expanse of mirror. What should I do about this? Is another disappearing act on the cards? I could probably sneak straight out of here without being noticed at all. Sneak out and never come back. But do I want that? This was shaping up to be a nice job. If I could have walked away from it so easily, I wouldn't have come back here today. And, goodness only knows, I need the damn cash. But do I need it that much? I take a deep breath and realise that I'm probably overreacting. He's hardly going to try to ravish me over his egg-white omelette, is he? If I can handle the frisky punters at the King's Head, surely I can keep Evan David at arm's length for a few weeks.

While I'm struggling with my moral dilemma, my mobile phone rings. This is a bad, bad time. Which probably means that it's my dear old dad.

I snatch it up and snap, 'Hello?'

'Fern Kendal?'

At least it's not my dad. 'Yes.'

'This is Alana from the *Fame Game.*'

My knees go weak and I stagger back until I'm perched on the edge of the enormous marble bath. I can't remember who Alana was, but I'm sure she was one of the squad of polished PR people. 'Hi,' I breathe back. 'Hello. Hi. Hi.'

'We've got some news for you.'

My heart is racing, but I think my breathing has stopped.

'We want you to go through to the final selection,' she says brightly. 'If you get through this, then you'll be on the television show.'

Ohmigod. Ohmigod. Ohmigod. I think I say something banal into the phone but I'm not sure. We've done it. We've bloody well done it! Carl and I have done it. I can feel tears rolling down my cheeks. We've beaten all the Britney look-alikes with nonexistent bottoms and we're through to the next round. I have to phone Carl. I have to phone him right now! He won't believe it, either.

'Fern?' Alana is talking to me on the phone. 'Are you still there?'

'Yes. Yes,' I say. 'I'm just so…so…' So pleased to see a glimmer of hope that could bring an end to my miserable life of drudgery. 'I'm so thrilled.'

'There's just one thing,' she says.

My tears of joy halt sharply. Isn't there always 'just one thing'? My euphoria seeps away like water down a plughole.

'Go on,' I prompt.

'It's your partner.'

'Carl?'

'There's a bit of a problem,' she tells me. 'We think you should proceed as a solo artist.'

'A solo artist?'

Alana clears her throat. 'Carl has to go.'

I never expected this. Out of all the 'just one things' it might have been, I never thought they'd tell me that Carl and I couldn't go through together.

'We realise this will be difficult for you.'

'I can't,' I blurt out. 'I can't go through without Carl. We're a team. We've been together for years. He'd be devastated. What's so wrong with him?'

'At *Fame Game* we don't feel that he fits with your image,' Alana tells me coolly.

I don't even have an image. I have one smart top which I wore for the bloody audition. Is that now my image?

'We want to give you the best possible chance to succeed. Carl would only hold you back.'

My brain is whirring. Carl wouldn't hold me back. He's the one that bullied me and cajoled me into going for the audition. How can he be blamed for holding me back? Without him I'm a shambling wreck. Does this woman know that there are days when I wouldn't even eat if it wasn't for Carl? Of course she doesn't. She just sees him as another guitar-playing hippy who can easily be disposed of. But I don't see it like that. I don't see it like that at all.

I shake my head, trying to clear the fog that's settled in it. First I seemed to have my chance and now there are catches, there are always *bloody* catches. My voice sounds feeble when I say, 'I'm not sure that I could do it without him.'

There's a long silence at the other end.

'Well,' Alana says, and I hear a deep breath. 'One thing is for certain, you won't be able to go through with him.'

My tears start to roll again.

'There's no negotiation on this. We want you to perform on your own or not at all.'

A sob catches in my throat. What do I do now? 'I can't do this to him,' I tell her. 'I can't.'

'You can have some time to think about this.' Alana's voice has softened slightly. 'You must be absolutely sure that you want to pass up this chance. You have a great voice, Fern. Don't blow this. We could make a huge difference to your music career. Call me back on this number tomorrow.' She reels off a phone number. I have nothing to write it down on so rely on the fact that it will be logged in my phone's memory rather than mine.

'Thanks,' I say dully, and then she hangs up.

I lean my head against the cold marble tiles. *Music career.* The words reverberate in my head. She thinks I'm good enough to have a *music career.* But not with my dearest, darling friend, Carl. I can't get my brain around this. Is this the sort of ruthless world that I want to belong to? One that encourages you—no, *insists*—that you dump your closest friends, the people who have helped you most, without a second thought. Suddenly, fending off Evan David seems the least of my worries. If only I knew him well enough to be able to talk to him about this, I wonder what he'd advise me to do? Perhaps he wouldn't see it as a problem. To be the biggest and best star in the world, do you always have to trample on other people?

Carl will be crushed. I can't think of a worse thing that I'll ever have to tell him. Or perhaps I won't tell him at all. Perhaps I'll just pretend that the *Fame Game* judges thought that neither of us could make the grade. It would mean that I'd have to pass up my one slender chance of stardom, but if I have to sacrifice that, then so be it. I'd rather have my own dreams dashed than callously ditch Carl. I nibble nervously at my nail. That would be the best thing to do, I'm absolutely sure.

Twenty-five

I don't know how I'm going to get through the rest of the day—or even through breakfast, come to that. But I do. In a slight daze. But I get through it, somehow. Perhaps Evan David senses a change in my demeanour when I come back to the table because we both hurry through our food and he keeps the conversation to the banalities of his schedule—frantic as always—and then he disappears into the depths of the apartment for the rest of the morning.

I sit at the desk, open the laptop and stare at it, doing nothing remotely useful. All I can think of is the ultimatum, delivered by Alana, from the powers-that-be at *Fame Game*. Carl has to go. Hours pass and I still haven't come to a decision and I still haven't done any work, but the papers are all rearranged neatly on the desk. Eventually, Evan David comes out of his lair again and prowls around the room.

'I'm singing at the *Royal Variety Performance* tonight,' he tells me.

And if I'd been paying any attention to his diary at all then I would have realised that. It's the one time in the year when the Royal family are wheeled out to watch the cream of the British entertainment business be put through their paces. Millions watch it on television. It's probably one of the few times I've seen Evan David perform before. This must be a big night for him and yet he's as cool as a cucumber.

I realise that I'm staring blankly at him.

There's a questioning note in his voice when he adds, '"Nessun Dorma"?'

My goodness. That's the one Pavarotti always knocks out. And an opera song that I actually know. 'Yes. Yes,' I say, trying to sound intelligent.

'It's one of my favourite arias.'

'Oh, mine, too.' I nod furiously.

'Would you like to come along?'

'To the *Royal Variety Performance?*'

'You'd probably have to watch from the wings,' he says. 'Unless Rupert can magic up a spare ticket.'

I'm supposed to be working at the King's Head tonight. It's quiz night, which means it's madly busy, but at least Carl and I don't have a set to do. Ken the Landlord would be furious if I asked for the night off but the *Royal Variety Performance…* This is a once-in-a-lifetime chance, the nearest I'll ever get to seeing the queen—though I'll probably have to peep round a curtain to do it. I can feel my brain chewing this over. When am I ever going to get such a glamorous invitation again? Of course, there may well be strings attached.

I look up at Evan David. His face seems sincere enough. If all he was trying to do was get me into bed, then he's going quite a nice way about doing it. Before I think how I'm going to explain my absence to Ken at the pub, I say, 'I'd love to be there.'

'That's settled then,' he says, and I think there's a genuine note of pleasure in his words. 'Call Rup. See what he can rustle up.'

'Is there anything else you need me to do?'

'I have a rehearsal this afternoon with the orchestra and television technicians. I'll go to that alone. They're very tedious. You can organise with Frank to collect me and take me there. Then my clothes need packing for this evening. One of the dinner suits, shirt, bow tie, socks, underwear, shoes. And a fresh change of clothes for afterwards. Casual. I'll leave the selection to you. Everything goes in the black holdall.' Evan David does a mental calculation. 'I think that's all.'

'Right.'

'When you've done that you can go home and get ready, too,' he tells me. 'Leave your address and we'll swing by in the limo to collect you on the way back to the theatre this evening.'

'I'll come back here,' I say. There's no way I want Evan David 'swinging by' and finding out that I live in a poky hovel above The Spice Emporium—the botulism centre of Bloomsbury. I glance in the diary and, for the first time today, take note of the entries. 'I'll be back at five. Make-up call is six o'clock.'

He nods at me as he heads out of the room. 'See you later.'

So. Several minutes of scheming later and I've sorted out what I'm going to do. I'll quickly pack Evan's clothes. Then I'll phone Ken the Landlord and tell him I'm sick. I can't remember last when I faked an illness to skive off work, if I ever have. Clearly I'm becoming my father's daughter. But I'll tell him that I've got food poisoning rather than a case of insanity. Ken will just have to cope without me tonight. Then I'll phone Carl and tell him about *Fame Game.* I have to come clean. Lying to your employer is one thing, but lying to your best mate is another ball game entirely. Then I'll go home, have a run round the shower and put on the top Carl bought me. Who would have thought that it would get two airings in one weekend? Not me, that's for sure. If I've got time, I'll pop in to see Joe and Nathan, who I'm missing dreadfully. I haven't seen them in days. Won't they be stoked when I tell them that I'm off to the *Royal Variety Performance?* I can hardly believe it myself.

I'm so happy that I can even pretend that I've not got to have the worst conversation of my life with Carl later. I drift through the apartment, searching out Evan David's bedroom, which I manage to find after opening half a dozen doors onto rooms that contain nothing. I could move Joe and Nathan in here for the duration and no one would be any the wiser. I could move in myself, too. It would certainly be one way to get away from my dear old dad.

Evan David's bedroom contains the largest bed I've ever seen in my life. It's one of those American super-king-size jobs. Big enough to hold a rugby match on. The sheets are shimmering grey material and there's a teal cashmere throw, achingly soft to the touch, draped over the bottom of the bed. Full-length windows give another superb view over the Thames and I stand and imagine myself waking up somewhere like this. Though on my own, I'd like to add. That particularly fantasy doesn't involve Evan David. Not necessarily. And, although it's an impersonal room in many ways, I do feel as if I'm intruding into his inner sanctum. Beside the bed there's a music score and a little-thumbed Martin Amis novel. There's a dressing room with wall-to-wall walk-in wardrobes and, even though I've been instructed to do this, I slide furtively inside. Where on earth do I start?

Tentatively, I open one of the doors. A row of starched white dress shirts faces me. All neatly spaced. All on identical wooden hangers. No bent wire ones here. Beneath them is a row of identical black shirts. The wardrobe smells spicy and musky. The ghost of Evan David's aftershave. Hmm. Nice. I run my hand over the white shirts and then take one out, draping it over my arm. The next wardrobe contains a dozen black dinner suits. The styles differ only slightly, so I select the nearest one to me and slip it into the black leather suit holder that's hanging expectantly next to it. At the bottom of this cupboard is a soft, black leather holdall. I tug that out, fold the shirt and slip that in. The next wardrobe is just as maniacally tidy. It contains rows of spotless black and white T-shirts, continuing the monochrome theme. I'm getting the idea that you'll never see Evan David in shocking pink. I pick some black socks out of a drawer and then a pair of black, silky hipster undies from another. They're gossamer fabric, an Italian make I've never heard of and they're tiny. I hold them up against my hips.

'Hmm.' I admire them in the full-length mirror. 'Nice small bum.'

'Thanks.'

I spin round only to see—all my worst nightmares rolled into one—Evan David standing in the doorway behind me. My cheeks flame.

There's a hint of a smile at his lips. 'I came to see if you'd managed to put your hands on everything.'

'Yes,' I say, bunching his underwear into my fist. 'I certainly did.'

Twenty-six

Ken the Landlord is furious when I phone to tell him that I'm sick and can't come into work. In fact, I do *actually* feel sick while I'm phoning him—which is me getting my just deserts, I suppose. All that Ken is concerned about is who will dish out the greasy sausage rolls to the sparring quiz teams rather than my ill health. I want to tell him that I *so* don't care, but try to sound suitably mortified at his dilemma instead. If he paid better wages then he'd have a team of temporary barmaids on tap, ready to step into my shoes at a moment's notice. But he doesn't. And that's why I know I can afford to phone in sick once in a blue moon and not get the sack.

Then, when I can delay no longer, I call my dear friend. Carl is, as always, delighted to hear my voice. He tells me that he's working tonight at another job he somehow manages to fit into his busy schedule. His job at Peter's Pizza Place is somewhat sporadic, but pays well when it's available. He gets the use of a scooter to carry out his delivery duties, so he arranges to 'swing by' that afternoon and pick me up so that we can talk as he does his rounds. I don't mind Carl swinging by The Spice Emporium. My friend has seen me in all my moments of darkest despair. I have no façade to maintain with him. He knows that my curtains all have holes and that my knickers—also with holes—are likely to be drying over the bath. We have been through more than any couple I know—married or otherwise. He's been with me in sickness and in health, for better, for worse and for poorer—the richer has yet to materialise. He's witnessed too many boyfriends coming and, inevitably, going. Carl has been there to weld my broken heart back together on more than one occasion. And this is the first time in my life that I've dreaded seeing him.

I sit and worry at my fingernails—realising too late that it might be a good idea to paint them—until I hear the toot-toot of his horn outside my window. I grab my bag and rush down the stairs.

'Hey.' He gives me the peace sign.

'Likewise,' I say and jump on the back of his scooter, just in front of the big, insulated pizza box.

'No helmet?' he says.

'Funnily, I don't have a scooter helmet lying around.'

'This makes you illegal,' Carl tells me. See, I told you he was only a little bit rock 'n' roll. He still stresses about breaking traffic laws. I bet Ozzy Osbourne never did.

'It's the least of my worries,' I say. 'Drive on.' Or scoot on, if that's the right term.

Sliding my arms round Carl's waist, I lean into his back. We pull out into the Sunday teatime traffic and I snuggle into him. It's nice to hold someone without it feeling complicated.

'You're giving me a hard-on' Carl shouts over his shoulder.

'Live with it,' I yell back. 'I need a hug.'

My hair whips into my eyes, stinging them. I try to talk to him as we phutt-phutt along the busy roads heading towards Camden Town, but I can't make the words form the right sentences. And maybe I shouldn't tell him now, as he might crash.

'What was it you wanted to tell me?' he shouts again.

'Let's pull over somewhere. This is bad news.'

'You think I'll crash?'

'Yes.'

'This doesn't sound good.'

I shake my head even though he can't see it. The red brake lights on the cars in front of us start to blur together and I realise that I'm crying.

Carl squeezes my hand. 'We can go to Oakley Square,' he says. 'It's on the way to my delivery.'

Oakley Square is a familiar place to us. Just behind the heaving mass of Euston Road, it's the playground of our childhood. Happy hours have been spent sitting in the middle of its ragged grass deep in cigarette butts putting the world to rights—chatting about love, life and, for us girls, the latest shade of lipstick. It was one of our few refuges in this concrete jungle. This was a rough area not too long ago, but now we have a Starbucks and a Costa Coffee just around the corner—a sure sign that an area has 'arrived'. Property prices have soared and the surrounding streets are now the haunt of up-and-coming media companies and advertising agencies with their glass staircases and aluminium floors. Last year, a huge complex of offices, cafés and gyms was built slap bang in the middle of this rapidly fading urban decay, directly opposite the Square. In the summer, the grass here is now covered with young executives, basking in their Paul Smith suits drinking their low GI fruit smoothies and eating granary sandwiches stuffed with salad, fresh from their power workout. In the winter, however, it's still inhabited by a sprinkling of miserable dossers tied into their overcoats with string. And the drug dealers and daytime boozers are never too far away, so the regeneration isn't quite complete.

Carl pulls up outside the Square and chains the scooter to a post in a parking bay. My friend and I have had our moments in this park. This was the main venue for our teenage canoodling. We have loved here, laughed here and drunk cheap cider until we were senseless. Maybe this was the place where we first started to sing a few tentative songs together. We've been here many times before when the park is shut—it's a good place to come and talk through problems, and I'd consider this a major problem. As it's dusk the park has already been locked up for the night, so with a well-practised move Carl hoists me over the black wrought-iron railings and I drop down onto the grass. The light is fading and the street lamps have yet to illuminate the park.

'The pizza might get nicked,' he says, removing a zip-up bag from the box. 'I'll pass it over to you.'

As he does so, I get a wonderful waft of melted cheese and warm tomato from the pizza bag and remember that I haven't eaten since my posh, but hurried breakfast with Evan David. Without needing my assistance, Carl jumps over the railings after me.

'I'm starving,' I say.

'No.' Carl takes the pizza bag off me. 'Don't even think about it.'

We wander over to the climbing frame. There's a whole conglomeration of brightly painted recreational equipment that wasn't here when we frequented this place. I'm not sure we were the poorer for it. We made our own entertainment. And I'm not sure that the kids these days are easily wooed by a yellow slide and a couple of red swings. Cocaine and a couple of Es are more likely to make their eyes brighten now.

I eye Carl's pizza bag greedily as he clutches it to him. 'They'd never notice,' I cajole.

Carl sighs and hands over the bag as we sit down on a flat seat at the bottom of the climbing frame. Sometimes he's such a pushover. I unzip it and dig out the cardboard box inside. 'I'll just take one piece and then rearrange the others. Trust me—they'll be none the wiser.'

'If you say so.'

Unveiling the pizza, I set about carefully removing one slice, taking care to fill the resulting gap by shuffling the other triangles around a bit. It doesn't look too bad. I offer Carl the first bite, but he shakes his head.

'I don't want to be incriminated in your criminal activities.'

'Think of it as comfort food.' I lick my fingers, hungrily.

'Is it me,' Carl asks, 'or is everything you're doing tonight loaded with sexual tension?'

'It's you,' I tell him as I slurp tomato sauce from my lips.

'I thought Evan David might be stirring up your hormones.'

'He certainly isn't,' I say with as much indignation as my tired heart can muster.

'Go on then,' Carl prompts me with a nudge in the ribs. 'Tell me what the problem is.'

The wind is whipping litter round the park in cheerful little circles. Paper bags dance gaily with one another. And I wish I could find some other way to tell Carl this. Or some way to avoid doing it at all.

'Do I need to light a cigarette for this?' my friend asks.

'It might be a good idea.' And I buy myself some more time while Carl goes through the ritual of lighting up.

'The *Fame Game* phoned,' I eventually say.

Carl brightens and I can hardly bear to see it. 'When?'

'Earlier today.'

'And you're not whooping and hollering?'

'No.'

'Then they can't want us to go through to the next round.'

'No.'

Carl huffs and flops back onto the seat. If there were stars, he'd probably gaze up at them. 'It's not the end of the world,' he says in a tight voice. He drops his head to his hands. 'Yes, it is. I was so sure. So sure.' He looks over at me. 'I was so sure we'd done it. I was convinced that this was our moment. What did we do wrong?'

I say nothing. What is there to say? I've finished my slice of stolen pizza, so I slide my hands into the hot pizza bag for a bit of warmth.

Carl is silent for a moment, then he turns to me. 'That isn't all, is it? If they'd turned us down flat, you'd have been on the phone straight away in tears. You wouldn't have waited to see me. If you have to tell me face-to-face there's more to this.'

My friend is wiser than his denim jacket indicates. I still can't make the words come out and the tears rush to my eyes again.

'I've got it,' Carl says. He stands up and paces in front of the seat, running his hands through his hair. 'They want me to go through and not you. Oh, man. They said you just haven't got enough talent to cut it. And here you are, eaten up with jealousy.'

A tearful laughs escapes my lips. 'No!'

He sits down next to me again and slips his arm round my shoulders, pulling me into his embrace. 'Then it must be the other way round,' he whispers. And then I really start to cry at the indignity and injustice of it all.

'Hey. Hey.' He wipes his thumb across my cheeks. 'You've done it. You should be proud of yourself.'

'I'm not,' I sob. 'How can I carry on without you?'

'You will. Of course you will.' Carl makes me look at him. What a sight I must be, but I know that Carl doesn't care. He loves me just as I am, and I only wish I loved him the same way. How much easier life would be. His voice cracks when he says, 'I might have blown it, but you've still got your big chance to come. You have to do this, Fern.'

'No,' I say, sniffing loud enough to make one of the sleeping dossers look over at us. 'I won't do it without you.'

'Don't be stupid! You can't throw this away. You have a real chance here. Where else will you get this sort of opportunity?'

I let out a wobbly breath.

'Besides, if you make it big and become a rich bitch, then I might consider marrying you and you could keep me in the style I'd like to become accustomed to.'

I laugh again.

'I wasn't joking,' Carl says, pretending to be offended.

'You are a prat,' I tell him.

'All words of love.'

'You're my favourite prat.'

He leans against me. 'I bet you say that to all the boys.'

I wipe my nose on my sleeve. 'So you think I should phone back and tell them yes?'

'I wouldn't have it any other way.'

'I love you, Carlos. You're my best friend in the whole world.'

'*And* I'm a fantastic lover.'

'So you keep telling me.'

'Well, one day I might let you find out for yourself.'

Dusk has fallen over the Square and the wind is picking up, making me shiver. For some reason I don't want to tell Carl about my trip to the *Royal Variety Performance* with Evan David; that would be like rubbing salt into his wounds. I don't want him to think I'm going to fly up and away without him. So instead of explaining all this, I say, 'This pizza will be stone cold if we don't deliver it soon. And I will be, too.'

'Come on then.' Carl pulls me to my feet. 'If you're not going to ravish me on this bench, then we'll go and dish out carbohydrates to people who probably don't need them.'

We walk back towards the railings. 'I won't forget this, Carl.'

'I should think not,' he says. 'You owe me.'

I pull him close to me. 'Thank you for being you. You're so lovely. I'd never have the confidence to do this if you weren't behind me.'

'And you'd never get back over those railings, either.' He holds out his hands and I put a foot into them, while he hoists me over.

My friend puts the remaining pizza inside the box on the back of the scooter and we both climb on.

'Did they give any reason why?' Carl asks without looking at me. 'It wasn't my playing?'

'Of course not. You know you could give Eric Clapton a run for his money. It was your image,' I tell him. 'It didn't fit with my image.'

'Wow,' he breathes. 'I didn't know either of us had an image.'

'You mean that seventies-rocker look is an accident?'

Carl tuts ruefully. 'If I'd known they were going to be so shallow, maybe I would have had a haircut.'

'When you were buying me that knockout glittery top, maybe you should have got yourself one, too.'

'Nah,' Carl says. 'It wouldn't have suited me.' He pushes the scooter back from the kerb and glances over his shoulder at me. 'I know because I tried it on first.'

I punch him.

'If they'd ridiculed my talent, that really would have hurt.'

'Don't be silly. They just don't appreciate sheer genius when they see it. All they see is an outdated denim jacket and hair in need of gel.'

'This look will be back in fashion one day,' Carl advises me. 'And then who'll be laughing?'

Before I can comment further on his choice of clothing, we set off. Whizzing through the streets, I wish I knew what Carl is really thinking about this. I wish I could make sense of my own thoughts, too. And then I know that I have to do this. I have to do it for me. I have to do it for both of us. Carl is right. As he always is.

Minutes later, we pull up outside one of the few rundown

houses in among the posh terraced homes of Haverstock Hill, and Carl turns to me. 'You okay?'

I nod. Carl takes the pizza and rings the bell. Eventually a dishevelled young guy opens the door. Possibly a student. Definitely pissed. Carl hands over the pizza. The guy claps him on the back as if he's a long-lost brother. My friend wanders back to the scooter, a bemused look on his face.

'My, my,' he says, 'here we are. You've got the pop world at your feet and I've just been given a ten quid tip for a half-eaten pizza by a drunk. I think that makes us quits.'

He looks down at the crumpled ten pound note in his hand and gives me a brave smile. Which makes me break down and cry again.

Twenty-seven

Carl drops me off at my flat. Dad has gone out, thank goodness. Probably in search of a pub that won't refuse his custom. This, at least, means that I have the bathroom and the trickle of hot water from the shower to myself. Taking advantage of this, I luxuriate under it for the three minutes it takes for the water to turn icy cold again. Ali keeps promising to do something about the dodgy boiler, but, like most men, his well-intentioned promises lack a certain practical element.

Squeaky is sitting in the middle of the kitchen floor, emboldened by the absence of my dad's presence. Dad not only abuses my mouse with a stream of obscenities but has also taken to throwing inanimate objects at him whenever he appears, no matter how strongly I object. My dad, of course, blames this on his fake Tourette's syndrome. In return for Squeaky's continued loyalty as my ad-hoc pet mouse, I break off a square of my emergency bar of Cadbury's milk chocolate, hidden in the recesses of my cupboards, for him. Ignore everything you've ever seen in kids' cartoons, mice—or at least this one—don't give a fig for a triangular lump of cheddar cheese. Squeaky will, however, jump through hoops for a bit of Mars bar. Perhaps Squeaky's a female mouse, rather than a bloke, and it's that time of the month. Whichever sex he is, he now holds the chocolate possessively in his tiny claws and nibbles frantically, his dark eyes wide with apprehension. I worry about Squeaky. He isn't like one of those silky, pink-pawed, cutesy field mice with a perfect, twitching snout. No, he's a scrawny, battle-scarred, edgy city mouse who looks as if he's been chewed up and spat out by one too many cats. Danger waits for him at every turn. Relaxation is as alien a concept to Squeaky as it is to me. Perhaps that's why I have such an affinity with him. Both of us world-weary city-dwellers, scratching out a living. This is the only time I get to stop and think, when I'm watching this tiny mouse and his fight for survival in a harsh environment. I wonder where he sleeps. Not in a small comfy bed with a mouse-size duvet, as Jerry of *Tom and Jerry* would have us believe. I'm anxious about where Squeaky goes at night. Carl says I'm too soft, but he understands nevertheless.

Squeaky finishes his chocolate then disappears and I get on with my chores. There's a message on my phone to say that Joe and Nathan are at Mum's place, so if I get a scoot on, I'll still just about have time to see them before heading back to Evan's apartment. With trembling fingers, I call Alana at the *Fame Game* and tell her that I'm going to proceed to the next round all by myself. She sounds suitably delighted—having manipulated me so skilfully, she should give herself a pat on the back—and tells me that the next audition is the following Saturday. Yet another day to try to wangle off. I know that Carl will want me to practise every night, which will eat further into my rapidly dwindling time. It's going to have to be when I get back from the pub, as I currently don't have another spare minute to my name. I can't even bear the thought of failing at this now that he's put so much faith in me. I should also find time to pray to the god of pop stars to allow me to join their ranks.

Running round, I put some slap on and then the fab top that Carl bought me, together with my very smartest trousers. Hope this is an adequate outfit for a *Royal Variety Performance*. If it isn't, it's hard lines, because it's the only one I've got. I check myself out in the mirror. Once upon a time, I used to think that I looked young for my age—in fact, people used to regularly comment on it. Not anymore though. My age is definitely catching up with me. Too many late nights and too many early mornings are starting to take their toll on me. Apparently, if you earn a salary of more than £150,000 a year, it can add up to three years to the length of your life. Less than £15,000 and you're looking at shortening your time on this mortal coil by a good two years. I'm afraid I definitely fall into the latter category. And I'm sure if you have to work at three jobs to even earn *that* measly amount of money then the sums are even worse.

I put on my coat, wishing I had a posh one, pick up my bag and set off at a brisk pace for Frodsham Court. The warmth embraces me as Mum opens the door.

'Hello, darlin',' she says, and gives me a hug.

We've always been a close family and it breaks my heart to think that Dad is somewhere doing who knows what, outside of our cosy circle. I open my mouth to speak.

'If you're going to say anything about your father, then don't,' Mum warns. 'He's got no one to blame for this but himself.'

'I wasn't going to say anything about Dad.' The coat gets shrugged off. I was, but I hadn't bargained on my mum's mind-reading skills. 'But now that you've mentioned him, I think I should. He's struggling without you, Mum. Really struggling.'

'Good,' she says. 'Cup of tea?'

I give up the fight, realising that I'm never likely to win. 'Yeah. A quick one. I haven't got much time.'

In the lounge, Joe and Nathan are already tucking into chocolate biscuits.

'Hey.' I go over and kiss them both and then slide onto the rather threadbare sofa next to Nathan. He's looking pale and drawn. Rather than devouring the biscuit as most boys of his age would, he's nibbling at it listlessly. Nathan doesn't eat well because of his asthma. I don't know if it's the drugs or what, but I've yet to see him wolf down a plate of food like most boys his age do. I stroke his fringe from his forehead. There are dark shadows under his eyes. When his chest is bad, his sleep is disturbed, too. Come to think of it, Joe looks exhausted as well. 'How's my favourite boy?'

'Okay,' he says, with an effort.

I look over at Joe, who gives me a resigned shrug. Same old, same old, I imagine. 'Tired, tetchy, but not completely downtrodden,' my big brother tells me.

For whatever reason, the doctors at the hospital are still struggling to get Nathan's asthma under control. And, for once, it isn't a failing of the NHS—the staff at the asthma clinic are brilliant with Nath and have tried everything at their disposal. My poor nephew seems doomed to huff and puff his way through life no matter how many drugs they pump into him.

'I've got a favour to ask of you, sis.'

Joe knows that I never deny him anything and, consequently, he doesn't ask me to do too much for him unless it's important. 'Ask away.'

'I've got the chance of some work next week,' he tells me. 'Nice job. Cash in hand.'

'Great.'

'But I need you to collect Nath from school and look after him until I get home.'

'You know that I've got a daytime job myself at the moment,' I remind him. 'Can't Mum do it?'

Mum sweeps into the lounge carrying a tray bearing the tea pot. 'I'm away.'

'Away?'

'I'm off to Brighton for a few days.'

'Brighton,' I say. 'Why Brighton? What's there to do in Brighton?'

'Lots of things,' Mum says as she pours our tea. 'The nightlife's wonderful.'

Joe and I exchange a glance. *Nightlife?* Why would she be interested in nightlife?

'Who are you going with? How long for?'

'Now, Little Miss Nosy.' My mum gives me a look. Normally she would be gushing to tell us about any organised break, not see it as an infringement of her liberties to have to share the details. 'I'm going on my own. And I'm going for a three-day break.'

My mum has never, ever taken herself off for a three-day break before.

'Oh,' she says. 'I've forgotten the milk.'

When she pops back to the kitchen, I turn to Joe and lower my voice. 'Do you think she's acting strangely?'

'First she kicks out her husband of forty-odd years and then she takes off on a mini-break by herself?' My brother purses his lips. 'Oh, no, I don't think she's acting strangely at all.'

My dad going to pot is bad enough, I couldn't cope if my mum did, too. What's happened to the backbone of this family? The one that previously saw us through all manner of adversity. I hate it now that we've moved onto this shaky, shifting ground.

'Have you seen the new Mr Patel at the newsagent's?' I ask Joe.

'He was here when we arrived,' Joe whispers.

'Here?'

'Having tea. He ate the last of Mum's homemade cakes.'

That to me is damning evidence enough. No one gets their hands on my mother's butterfly fancies without good reason.

'I think there's something funny going on,' I say.

'Where?' Mum asks as she comes back in with the milk.

Joe and I fidget guiltily.

'At work.' I hope that Nathan doesn't spill the beans. 'Ask me where I'm going tonight,' I say to change the subject.

Now I have Mum's attention.

'To the *Royal Variety Performance!*' I announce.

'I wondered why you were looking so spruce,' she says.

'What's that?' Nathan asks.

What exactly do you have to do to impress a five-year-old these days? 'It's a concert where the queen goes along to watch.'

'Oh,' Nathan says. 'Will you sit next to her?'

'Probably not.'

'Oh.' My nephew's interest wanes now that he knows I'm unlikely to be in the royal box hobnobbing with our sovereign, and his eyes drift back to the television.

'You can watch it tonight, Mum,' I say. 'I'll try to park myself in front of a camera and give you a wave.'

Mum fusses with her hair. 'I can't do that, love. Not tonight.'

Joe and I give her a questioning look.

'I'm going out,' she says and then makes it clear she's not going to be drawn further. This is not looking good. Where is my mum skulking off to that she can't tell us? I'd like to bet that Mr Patel has had his hands on more than her fancies. It's hard to imagine my mum as a wanton sex kitten—she's more into bedsocks than bondage—but there's no doubt that she's up to something. Dad would be frantic if he had any idea of what was going on in his own home. I don't want to be the one to break it to him.

'Set the video,' I say crisply.

'That was always your dad's job,' she admits, slightly cowed. 'I don't know how to work it.'

Well, I'm not going to offer to do it. If she prefers to go out gallivanting with her bit of stuff rather than stay in and see if her only daughter pops up on television, then let her suffer.

'So what about Nathan?' Joe interrupts my thoughts. 'I don't want to let this guy down. If I do a good job, maybe he'll give me some more work.'

I'm torn. How can I let Evan David slip to the bottom of my list again? Yet if I don't help Joe then he won't be able to take this job, and I know how desperate he is for the cash. Plus

I love to spend time with Nathan. I've seen far too little of him during the last week.

'I'll be home in time for your shift at the King's Head,' he says. 'I swear. And I'll be for ever in your debt.'

I throw up my hands. 'Okay, sweet-talker. I'll ask if I can get away for a couple of hours,' I promise as another part of my brain tells me that I must be mad to agree to this. Will Evan David really understand why I'm having to skive off to collect my nephew? Do small children even exist in his world? 'I'll pick him up from school and take him home.' Home to that dismal, damp flat…

I realise that I've been so mixed up in worrying about everyone else that I've forgotten to tell them my other news. 'Hey,' I say, feeling a surge of excitement. 'I'm through to the next round on the *Fame Game*. They called to tell me today. One more hurdle and then I could be on the telly.'

Nathan cheers and throws his arms round me. 'You're very clever, Aunty Fern.'

'Cool,' Joe says. 'A rock chick for a sister. My street cred will go up no end. Carl must be pretty pleased with himself, too.'

And somehow, I can't find it in my heart to tell them that to do this, I've had to dump my dear Carl. I realise that Mum hasn't yet said anything. 'Mum?'

She is frowning. 'And when exactly are you going to find time to be a pop star, young lady?' she tuts.

And although I laugh, I wonder whether she might be right.

Twenty-eight

I make it to Evan David's apartment by the skin of my teeth—thanks to delays on the Tube due to signalling failures. These are the things that trouble people in my world and I now know why Evan David travels everywhere by limousine.

He's pacing the floor when I arrive. He gives my outfit the once-over but doesn't say anything about it, and I'm not sure whether this is a good sign or a bad one. His face is impassive.

'You made it here,' is all he says.

'Yes.' I'm still breathless and all my rehearsed apologies blaming the Tube for my lateness go completely out of my head.

'Come on, Rupert!' he shouts and his agent appears at his side.

Without further ado, we collect the pile of bags and Evan's suit-holder and head for the door. Then I'm whisked into the aforementioned waiting limo—the front one in a short convoy of two—and we're off to the London Pavilion Theatre where the *Royal Variety Performance* is being held this year. The Pavilion is the home of the British Opera Company and they're celebrating their centenary—one of the main reasons they're having Evan David headline the bill this year. As well as the fact that he's an international megastar, of course. Plus it's common knowledge that he's the queen's favourite tenor.

I don't know what to say to Evan on the journey, so say nothing—but I'm more than aware that we're alone together. The neo-classical facade of the theatre looms ahead of us and the limo swings soundlessly to a halt. We jump out at the stage door. I can't believe that this is the second time in a week that I'm arriving somewhere in a limo. Oh, how I could get used to this life! The pavement is lined with barriers, and crowds are screaming for Evan David. He gives them a cursory wave and one of his reluctant smiles. But all women like a man who plays hard to get, don't we? And, so, the women scream even louder. From the car behind, Izak, the man-mountain of a security manager, emerges and hustles us into the theatre. I scuttle behind Evan, clutching his bags. Rupert follows in our wake. Evan is greeted like royalty and then we're all shown through a maze of corridors to a door with a big star on it marked Mr David's Dressing Room. A security guard stands at the door; Izak ushers him away and takes over.

'Good to have you back here,' the theatre manager says.

'It's good to be back.' Evan clasps his hand and then turns to me. 'This is my assistant, Fern. I'd like her to watch the show from the wings.'

'That's fine, Mr David. Just let me know if there's anything else you require.'

How I wish people would speak to me like that. The manager doesn't even glance in my direction, I'm so below his radar. Evan sweeps into the dressing room with me in tow. I'd expected it to be more palatial, but it's clean, comfortable and functional. A chestnut-coloured leather sofa graces one wall. A small shower cubicle is slotted into the other side. It's a good job that Pavarotti isn't headlining, as he'd never fit into it. Hollywood-style lights surround a huge make-up mirror in front of which a make-up box waits patiently. There's a tiny television and a giant bouquet of lilies.

'Take those out,' Evan instructs me. 'The pollen affects my voice.'

I whip the lilies out quick-smart and find a place to put them in the corridor where no one will kick them over. By the time I open the door again, he's stripping off his clothes. His jacket and shirt have already gone and he's barefoot and undoing his belt. I freeze in the doorway. What am I supposed to do now?

'Come in, come in,' Evan barks. 'Close the damn door. I don't want the world to see me in my underwear.'

I'm not sure I want to see him in his underwear, either, at this particular moment in time. I slide into the room and close the door behind me. 'Sit down, sit down, for heaven's sake,' he says. 'We've got a while yet.'

He's getting very tetchy and I wonder whether this is usual before his performances. Is it at this time his famous short fuse will blow? I do as I'm told and sit down. If I could make myself invisible, I would.

'Hand me my trousers, Fern.'

I stand up again and take Evan's dinner suit out of the leather suit-holder and hand the trousers to him, which he slips on. At this distance I can't help but notice that he has a finely honed torso. Broad shoulders, toned pecs, bulging biceps. It's getting a bit hot in here. I wonder if Evan wants a window opened?

There's a knock at the door and I open it again. A pretty young woman bearing a workman's toolbox appears.

'Hi, Mr David.'

'Ah, Becks.' They exchange an air kiss.

'Becks does my make-up when I'm in Britain. We go back a long way,' he says to me over his shoulder. And I mentally add yet another minion to his ever-growing list. This guy probably employs more people than Marks & Spencer. 'This is my assistant, Fern. She's standing in until Erin can join me.'

Becks puts down her box of tricks and sets about her preparations. 'I heard that Erin was unwell.'

'She's got chicken pox.'

'Oh. Poor love.'

I don't know whether she means me for standing in or Erin with the chicken pox. 'Hi,' I say. We shake hands.

'Ready for some slap?' Becks asks Evan.

He sits down at the make-up mirror and she slips a white, wide-necked T-shirt over his head, then fusses with foundation and sponges which she pulls from her toolbox. I retreat to the sofa to watch the process of transformation.

Evan sits perfectly still with his eyes closed, hands in a relaxed steeple while Becks fusses and flirts with him. They're clearly comfortable in each other's company and she has a very soothing effect on him. I wish I could do the same. He makes me such a nervous wreck that I can't behave normally in his presence. She coos and cossets him while she takes her time turning him an alarming shade of orange.

'Switch the television on, Fern,' Evan tells me. 'The performance will be starting soon.' When Becks has finished, she air kisses him and takes her leave.

Evan comes to join me on the sofa. On the television, the crowds waiting on St Martin's Lane go wild as the royal Rolls-Royce pulls up outside the theatre. The queen and Prince Philip emerge, waving regally to their subjects. Our monarch is resplendent in white brocade and a glittering diamond tiara. They glide up the red carpet and into the theatre.

For the next hour we watch as the show unfolds, sitting in Evan's dressing room. It's a bit like watching it at home, except occasionally Evan will stand up, pace the room and run through a few scales or bars of his aria. Sharing the billing tonight are Michael Bublé, Donny Osmond, Gwen Stefani, Ozzy and Sharon Osbourne, the Cirque du Soleil, Katie Melua and sketches from hit shows *The Producers* and *Billy Elliot The Musical*. I sit transfixed that this is all going on outside our dressing room door. You cannot believe how much I want to be a part of this world. My stomach flutters with anxiety. The next act is the winner of last year's *Fame Game* competition—a cheeky Irish chappy called Thadeus, who captured the nation's heart. His single, 'I Can't Do This Without You', is currently at number one in the charts. There's a cheer from the audience. My heart leaps in my chest. I can hardly dare think this, but play my cards right at the *Fame Game* audition and this could be me.

'Talentless shit,' Evan David sighs next to me. 'Look at him.'

Thadeus is dancing about on the stage, looking a bit demented I have to admit.

'Why does everyone think they can be a singer these days?'

My mouth drops open, but before I'm required to speak,

Evan David continues, 'Do you know how long it took me to train as an opera singer?'

I shake my head, but it's clear that my input really isn't required.

'Eight years. Eight *long* years. Working my way up, being paid a pittance. Giving up all of my social life, sacrificing relationships to learn roles. Spending everything I ever earned on vocal coaching to learn my craft and improve my technique. The voice of a tenor is not born, it has to be moulded, sculpted, built into a great instrument. It takes hours and hours of endless work, refining, honing, to make it as perfect as humanly possible. I have studied and practised and *lived* the roles that suit my voice, making them mine. This is why I bring La Scala to a standing ovation. Do you know the things I've given up to be where I am today?' He sneers at Thadeus on the screen. 'And now they want to make it overnight. The women do nothing but flaunt themselves half-naked. The men think they can make up with hair gel what they lack in talent. What does it matter if they can't hit the right notes? They'll edit that out in the studio.' Evan David points a finger at the screen. 'He can't even sing live.'

Now that I look closely I can see that Thadeus is, as accused, miming to the music. His lips are going up and down not quite in time with the words on his backing track. I feel embarrassed for him. He fought so hard to get through to the end of the *Fame Game,* supposedly singing live every week to avoid being thrown off the show, and now he can't cut the mustard without faking it. I sink lower into the sofa. No wonder Evan David feels free to ridicule him.

'I don't blame the kids,' he says. 'It's these bloody facile talent shows. They give everyone the impression that they only have to wiggle their butts to be famous. No one wants to put in the hard work anymore. No one wants to bleed for it.'

I want to tell him that queuing up in the rain with thousands of other hopefuls just to get your one minute chance of fame isn't a barrel of laughs and that for people like me it might be the only opening we'll ever get. But then, I guess that isn't quite the same as eight years of relentless struggle when you're clearly gifted.

He looks at Thadeus again. 'Next year, no one will remember his name.'

It makes me want to cringe. And I try very hard to dredge out the name of the guy who won on the series before Thadeus, but I can't. His name has gone for ever. A one-hit wonder who's headed straight back to Oblivion City and a lifetime of, 'Didn't you used to be...?' I think of Carl struggling to make ends meet doing sets at the King's Head and dodging the traffic on a scooter to deliver pizza. That's real life. That's *my* life. Is the pursuit of this stupid dream the reason why I've sold my most important friendship down the river?

Thankfully, before I can dwell on this further, there's a knock on the door. 'Fifteen minutes to go, Mr David.'

He stands up and stretches. 'I'd better get dressed now, Fern.'

Evan slips off the white T-shirt and I go to get his wing-collared dress shirt. He's bare-chested again and I can feel myself gulp as I slip the soft material over his shoulders. He buttons it briskly and, with fingers that are more trembly than I'd like, I help him to fasten his cufflinks. I hand over his bow tie. Evan swivels it expertly until he produces a perfect knot and then I hold open his jacket for him while he shrugs it on.

'How do I look?'

Reaching up, I smooth down the shoulders of his jacket and check that the collar of his shirt is sitting properly. I give the bow tie a minuscule tweak to make sure it's absolutely perfectly in place. There are pin-tucks on the front of his shirt and, before I realise what I'm doing, I run my fingers over them so that they're all lying straight. I can feel the heat of Evan's body through the fabric and my hands stop abruptly in their journey, coming to rest on his chest.

'Please continue.' Evan gazes down at me. 'I was quite enjoying it.'

'I'm sorry,' I say. 'I was getting a bit carried away. Overdoing my duties. You look fine as you are. Wonderful.'

His dark eyes twinkle and I can tell why he's a pin-up on a million office walls across the globe. 'Thank you.'

'I hope it goes well tonight.'

'I'm sure it will.'

I know that Evan David has performed a million times before, but my hands are clammy with nerves for him. I feel exactly like I do when I have to take Nathan to the asthma clinic. I wish it was me that had to go through it, not him.

He tugs his shirt cuffs into place. 'We never did discuss whether that was you singing before you had to dash off.'

'Yes,' I confess. 'It was me.'

'Do you have aspirations to become a singer?'

I can feel myself burning up. After what he's just said about Thadeus, I'd be mad to admit to anything. He raises a questioning eyebrow at me.

'What? Like the sad muppets on the *Fame Game?*' My laugh is too loud and too shrill. 'No. No way. I save my singing for the shower. And maybe the odd family wedding if I've had enough to drink.'

'You have a good voice,' Evan says. 'It shows promise. We were harmonising perfectly.'

And now I know that he's spinning me a line. Oh, yes, me and Evan David in perfect harmony. Before I'm subjected to further humiliation, there's another knock. 'We're ready for you, Mr David.'

Evan David takes my hand and puts my fingers to his lips, kissing them softly. 'Wish me luck,' he murmurs.

And I would if I could only find my voice.

Twenty-nine

The spangly curtain goes up and the crowd roar their approval. They're on their feet applauding before he's uttered a note. He takes a bow before the royal box and then walks to the front of the stage. My insides are in a thousand knots.

The audience take their seats again and fall into a reverent hush. All the fidgeting stops—even the obligatory round of coughing has ceased. Rows and rows of the beautiful people have fallen under his spell. And they're not alone. I, too, am transfixed. Evan lets out his first soaring note and I suck in all my breath. His enraptured audience collectively hold theirs.

As the beautiful sounds of 'Nessun Dorma' fill the auditorium, you could hear a pin drop. Evan's control is perfect, he has the audience eating out of his hand and I'm not sure that a thousand singing lessons could ever produce something this good. What Evan has is star quality—the elusive X-factor that so few people possess and, yet, when you experience it you know that you truly are in the presence of something very special. That's something that you either have or you don't. No one on this earth can teach you how to be extraordinary.

Evan's aria reaches its haunting crescendo and the audience are on their feet again. Tears spring to my eyes and I join the tumultuous clapping. He looks towards the wings, and I'll swear that our eyes meet and he smiles just for me. Then he turns and takes a last long, low bow towards the royal box where the queen and the duke of Edinburgh are sitting. From here, I can see that even the queen has been moved by his performance. Although she hasn't jumped up like the hoi polloi, her hands are raised high in the air as she applauds him.

Every time he goes to leave the stage, the crowd cry for more. Evan is the last performer and his standing ovation lasts for a full five minutes before the curtain comes down for a final time.

He comes towards me and I can't help myself; without thinking what I'm doing, I rush to him and throw my arms around his neck. After a moment's hesitation, I feel his warm arms slide around my waist and he hugs me to him.

'That was fantastic,' I say. 'Truly fantastic. *You're* fantastic.'

Evan looks down at me. I can't read what is in his eyes, and then the stage manager comes for him, clipboard in hand.

'You're needed back on stage, Mr David.'

We break our embrace and Evan walks briskly back onto the stage where the other artists are assembling, ready to meet the queen. He joins his fellow performers, all of whom he has knocked into a cocked hat. And I'm not the only one who thinks that. A shimmering Elizabeth II is escorted onto the front of the stage by a dozen toadies. It takes an age for our monarch to move along the line of eager, waiting performers, offering each one a word of thanks or encouragement, pressing the flesh as the royals do so well. And then it's Evan's turn and the queen lingers to chat with him, clearly thrilled by his performance, and I guess it's never going to hurt to have a fan like that. Eventually, the queen takes her leave of the theatre and the audience claps as the string of completely hyper artists depart the stage in her wake.

Evan comes back to me. 'Let's get out of here,' he says, and he takes me by the arm as we retreat to the dressing room amid much back-slapping and praise. Despite his moving performance, he's a lot calmer than I am. I'm still shaking inside, and I wonder how people manage to come down after something which must take so much out of them. Perhaps that's why so many artists turn to drink and drugs and goodness only knows what else. I didn't see much evidence of booze in Evan David's dressing room. He seems to thrive on nothing more shocking than green algae drinks and water.

We close the door behind us, blocking out the frantic hubbub backstage. After the chaos, the silence in here is all-encompassing. I lean against the door and sigh heartily.

'Can you put my clothes out while I take a quick shower?'

I nod wordlessly. What happens now?

Evan starts to undress again. 'Perhaps we can go somewhere for dinner,' he says, as he undoes his bow tie. 'Are you hungry?'

I nod again.

'I know somewhere we can go. Somewhere quiet.' He slips off his jacket, and I busy myself with gathering up the clothes that he discarded earlier.

Suddenly, Evan comes to me and stills my fussing. He puts

his hands on my shoulders and turns me towards him. Then he clears his throat. 'Thank you for being there for me tonight, Fern,' he says. 'It meant a lot to me. I've never had anyone waiting for me before.' He hesitates again. 'I didn't realise that it makes a difference. Thank you.'

His mouth is close to mine. That beautiful, powerful mouth, and it frightens me. I'm not sure that I'm ready for this. He scares me as much as he enthralls me. My body is shaking beneath his hands, and I try a careless shrug to lighten the moment. 'It's my job.'

His face darkens and he recoils slightly. 'Yes,' he says, as his hands fall to his side. 'I'm sorry. I forget. You're here because I'm paying you to be.'

'I didn't mean that,' I mumble hurriedly. 'I mean that it's my pleasure. I wouldn't have missed it for the world.'

But I can tell from his tight lips and the sudden tension in his shoulders that I haven't lightened the moment, I've fucked it up completely. Bugger. Why am I not better at this relationship shit?

Evan briskly strips off his shirt. 'Maybe we'll skip dinner,' he says. 'I'm tired.' He glances towards me. 'And I need some privacy. Get Rupert to organise you some transport home.'

'I…' I start to speak, but I don't know what to say, so I shut my big fat stupid fuck-up mouth again.

'We've got a busy week ahead,' Evan continues crisply. 'I take it you've checked the schedule?'

I nod meekly. Of course I haven't checked the fucking schedule. I'm the most useless personal assistant known to mankind. I've got a gob the size of a bucket and a brain the size of a pea.

'Then you'll know that starting tomorrow I've got three performances of *Madame Butterfly* at the Royal Albert Hall. Then we're in Cardiff for the opening of the new National Welsh Opera House at the end of the week. There's a whole list of back-to-back press and PR appointments. Erin has organised it all, so I'm sure it will go smoothly, but I'll need you there. We'll leave Friday, stay for the weekend and come back perhaps Tuesday. Double check all the arrangements are in place.'

'C-Cardiff…' I stammer, sounding as if he's just asked me to visit another solar system.

'Yes. Is there a problem?'

'Er…' What do I say now? I was going to try to blag Saturday off to attend the *Fame Game* auditions. How on earth can I mention that now? Especially as I'm fully aware what high regard Evan David has for talent shows. It might be the one big chance in my life, but as Mr David has already let me know, he views this sort of thing as a complete waste of space. Well we can't all be bloody mega-bucks opera stars. I *have* to do this! I have to do this for me, for Carl, for my family and for every other bugger that might be depending on me.

Instead of unleashing my pent-up frustration and coming clean with Evan, I go down this route: 'As you know,' I say rather feebly, 'I do have other commitments. It may be difficult for me.' For that, read *nigh on impossible,* mate.

'Difficult.' Evan David makes a curt little humphing noise. 'Then may I remind you of something you said a moment or two ago. This is your job, Fern. Think about *that.*'

Then he turns his back on me and it's clear that I'm dismissed. So I really have little opportunity to do anything else.

Thirty

Evan David was pumping iron—with a little more venom than was strictly necessary.

'Who are you mad at this morning?' Jacob, his personal trainer, asked.

Evan kicked viciously at the leg-press machine.

'If you don't take it a little easier,' Jacob advised, 'our next visit will be to the physio.'

With an unhappy grunt, Evan gave up on his presses and wiped a towel over his face. The gym was set up in another one of the vast apartment's rooms, but he'd only just managed to stagger in there bleary-eyed today. He'd hardly slept a wink last night. After his performance he was still wired, and he'd done nothing useful to help himself come down. Dinner had been forgotten and his churning stomach had only served to keep him tossing and turning. Whether it was down to hunger or to something else entirely was another matter that he didn't want to dwell on. Then he'd lain awake until the early hours going over his fractious conversation with Fern. Not that it had done him much good, either. She was right—the reason she'd been so attentive and at his side last night was because he damn well paid her to be there. It was easy to labour under the mistaken belief, in a world where he was surrounded by people he paid for, that occasionally one of them might stick around because they actually enjoyed his company.

The truth was that he'd wanted her to stay and he'd hoped that she would because she wanted to be with him. Instead, she'd blown him out and, in turn, he had treated her to a display of his sparkling repartee and innate charm. He wanted to hang his head in his hands. This woman was starting to get under his skin, and that was a very bad place for any female to be.

He realised that Jacob was still watching him. 'Do you want to call it a day?' his trainer asked.

Evan nodded. It was ten o'clock and he hadn't yet been able to settle to anything. 'Sorry, Jacob,' he said. 'Just not in the mood today.'

'Don't punish yourself,' the other man replied. 'You can't put in a hundred and ten percent every day.'

But that's what he did, Evan thought. That's what he did with everything, and it pained him when he couldn't give of his best. He had built his name, his reputation, on being the best at everything, by going the extra mile. 'Come back later today and we'll go for a run.'

'Four o'clock?' Jacob asked.

'Four's fine.'

When his trainer left, Evan showered and changed, forcing

himself to stay out of the main living room of the apartment for as long as possible. Fern hadn't yet arrived last time he looked, and he wanted to appear casual, as if nothing unto-ward had passed between them last night. On the other hand, he wanted to see her as soon as possible to set things right be-tween them again. He'd spoken to her too harshly and that was unfair. This was ridiculous, she was supposed to be here to help him focus on his work, not distract him from it. Shaking his head, he finally emerged into the living room.

Rupert was sitting at the desk, leafing through the day's newspapers looking for reviews of last night's *Royal Variety Per-formance.* 'Good morning, Mr David,' his agent said with mock formality. 'How's the voice?'

'The voice is fine.' He sat down opposite Rup.

'Good performance last night.'

His agent was clearly referring to his talent on the stage and not to the fracas in the dressing room afterwards.

'A five-minute standing ovation,' he continued with a smug grin. 'That very nearly tops the time when you brought the house down at La Scala.' Rupert flicked over the pages. 'Great picture of you.' He held up the newspaper for Evan's approval. 'Great caption, too. "The Man Who's Making Opera Sexy." I like it. In fact, I love it!'

Evan tried to look as if he was unconcerned both by the re-views and the obvious absence of his assistant. 'No sign of Fern?'

'No,' Rupert said. 'I got the feeling that we wouldn't be see-ing her again after you dispatched her last night—rather un-ceremoniously, I have to say. She looked very downhearted.'

'Damn,' Evan muttered. 'Why don't you call her?'

'Why don't *you* call her?' Rupert wanted to know. He put his feet up on the desk and clasped his hands behind his head. 'Remind me. Haven't we been in this same place before with this particular young lady?'

'I seem to be messing it up all the time with her,' Evan confessed.

'That doesn't usually worry you unduly,' Rupert pointed out. 'You have a shouting match with Erin every other day and you both carry on as if nothing has happened.'

'I *never* shout at Erin,' Evan contradicted him. 'I have to take care of—'

'—the voice,' Rupert finished for him. 'And very sensible, too. I take it that this is more to do with pleasure than business then?'

Evan refused to be drawn. Truth to tell, he wasn't quite sure what the situation was himself anymore.

'You haven't yet phoned Lana,' Rupert reminded him. 'And she's still calling a dozen times a day. Let's do one lady at a time, please. Call Lana before we go down to Cardiff, or our beloved *Diva* will be hissing at you like a cornered alley cat. How will you manage to be Alfredo to her Violetta then? You're supposed to be in love on *and* off the stage. Remember?'

'We've worked together before when we haven't been speaking.'

'Yes,' Rup sighed. 'And didn't the press have a field day with *that*. This is an important performance…'

'They're all important.'

'…and it would be nice if it were all sweetness and light between you.'

Evan massaged his brow.

'For once,' Rupert added.

'I'll call her later.' And as his agent gave him a disbelieving look: 'I promise.'

'If we can turn to matters other than your tortured love life, I have a few proposals that I'd like to discuss with you.' Rupert put on his most placating tone. 'Come out onto the terrace. Do you want a drink? Let me get Chef to squeeze you some orange juice.'

'That would be fine,' Evan said. 'Get Dermuid to do some for you, too—or are you still only drinking fresh blood these days?'

'I'll ignore that comment,' Rupert grumbled. 'Go out. Take in the smog. I'll follow you in a minute.'

The air on the terrace wasn't smoggy, it was fresh and cool. The silver thread of the River Thames snaked by, heading into the heart of London. England was great, but Evan was beginning to pine for the long, hot summers of Tuscany. Maybe he could find time to go to his villa there. It had been over a year since he'd last visited it. His weary spirit could do with a few days lounging by the azure-blue swimming pool in the heat of the lavender-scented air. If he tried very hard, he could almost smell it. What was the point in owning a handful of mansions if you never got to spend any time in them?

Rupert followed him out, sat down and opened his laptop. Evan pulled himself away from the balcony and joined his agent at the table, just in time to be presented with a glass of freshly squeezed juice by his chef. Rupert had stuck to his usual tipple of extra-strength black coffee.

His agent flexed his hands and cracked his fingers, indicating that he was now in business mode. He launched into his pitch without preamble: 'The time is right for a new generation of the Three Tenors. Pavarotti has retired. The other two are over the hill.'

'They'd be pleased to hear you say that.'

Rupert shrugged. Sometimes his friend was more obviously an agent than others.

'It's time for some new blood to take their place. Do you know how many people bought that DVD worldwide?'

'I'm sure that doing another would swell your coffers considerably,' Evan said wryly.

'Hey,' Rupert said. 'Don't you want me to retire comfortably?'

'Luciano would never forgive me if I tried to usurp him.' The highlight of Evan's career had been when Pavarotti had first embraced him, telling him to nurture his God-given talent and saying that he'd never heard a young tenor with such clarity and brightness in his voice. It was a moment he had always cherished. Since then, he'd sung with the maestro many times over the years—usually at his annual *Pavarotti and Friends* concerts in the great man's home town of Modena.

'You wouldn't be usurping him,' Rupert said with a frown. 'You'd be carrying on his work for a new generation.'

'Agent-speak,' Evan sighed. 'We'd be ripping off his idea.'

'So you'll do it?' Rupert asked.

'Will you ever let me rest until I do?'

'I'll call Emilio Rizzi and Jacques Franz this afternoon. They should be the other two tenors, don't you agree?'

They were both shining stars on the opera circuit and Evan admired their considerable talent immensely. He waved a hand at his agent. 'Whatever.'

Rupert stroked his chin thoughtfully. 'Now,' he said warily, 'one other thing—and I don't want you to dismiss this out of hand. It would be very easy to be far too hasty and say no.'

'Which means you think I will.'

'Keep an open mind.'

'I want to say no before I've even heard this.'

'The *Fame Game* called me this morning.'

'No.'

'Hear me out,' Rupert pleaded.

'No.'

'They want you to be on their panel of judges for the television show.'

'No.'

'They say they've got some great acts for this series. It's not all blond bimbos and failed club singers. There are some kids with real talent out there. They've found some bird with a golden voice that they reckon could be the next Madonna.'

'How lovely for her.'

'They've got a boy band singing opera classics.'

'Marvellous.'

'Come on, Evan,' Rupert whined. 'At least think about it. They thought you'd give some weight to the show. Some maturity.'

'God only knows, they need it.'

'I said that you'd consider it. Very carefully.'

'I won't.'

'They're offering a lot of money.'

'You're thinking of that retirement place in Spain again.'

'A *lot* of money.'

'Money is something I don't need any more of.'

His agent looked affronted. 'How can you say that?' He leaned forward, elbows on the table, and put on his sincere face. 'Do it. Please. For me.'

'No,' Evan said. 'I can't do it. The programme's a pile of crap.'

'When did you last watch it? It got better. Really it did. They had Sharon Osbourne last time. Would she do crap? Don't answer that.'

'You're wasting your breath, Rupert.'

'It would be great for your profile. Prime-time Saturday-night television. It would blast your market wide open. You have a natural touch with the common people. Think of all the yummy mummies who would dash out and buy your latest CD. Please do this. Just for me.'

'No. No. No.' Evan shook his head emphatically. 'Nothing you say can persuade me. I won't do it.'

'Oh.' Rupert looked sheepish. 'That's a shame, Evan. A real shame.' His agent reached into his briefcase and pushed a contract across the table. 'Because I'd kind of agreed that you would.'

Thirty-one

I do not want to sing this bloody song ever again.

'One more time,' Carl says.

'No.'

'It's not quite perfect yet.'

'It's as good as it gets,' I tell my friend, as I flop back on the sofa. 'That will have to do.'

'Oh, man. That's not the attitude, Fern.' Carl tries to look stern, but he puts his guitar down nevertheless.

'If you make me sing any more I'll be hoarse by the time the audition comes around.'

Carl flutters his eyelashes. 'Just once more.'

'There is a very real phenomenon known as overrehearsing,' I say. 'I'm frightened that we're rapidly approaching that point.'

My tormentor only laughs. 'We could stop for a cup of tea,' he suggests.

If I have a cup of tea, it means that I'll have to go into the kitchen again and face my dad. He's sitting at the table with a rapidly diminishing bottle of whiskey and a miserable face. A three-day growth of grizzled, grey beard is covering his wavering chin. Plus he's still insisting that he's got Tourette's syndrome, so he may well tell me to go forth and multiply the minute I put my head round the door, and I don't think I can cope with that right now.

'A pizza and a couple of glasses of wine would be better.' I give Carl my most endearing smile, the one that he can never resist. His stern mask slips and I can see that he's weakening. This man will do anything for a bit of pepperoni. 'I'm starving.'

'Me, too,' he admits and reaches for the worn denim jacket that always graces his person.

'My treat,' I say even though I'm not going to be flush with money now that my glamorous job in the world of opera seems to have evaporated into thin air.

'Do you think we should have written our own song for this?' Carl asks, a worried frown crossing his brow.

Not in the mood I'm in. It would have been about driving very fast into a big tree, and all the judges would have felt like slitting their wrists by the time I'd finished with them. Not quite the impression I want to make. It's Monday morning and I haven't bothered to return to my job with Evan David after I was so summarily dismissed last night following the *Royal Variety Performance* and my tactless comments. I wonder what might have happened next if only I'd kept my mouth firmly zipped. Personally, I thought it was looking likely that a bit more than dinner was on the cards. I keep a heavy sigh to myself.

Unlike last time, I didn't get a call from Rupert asking me to return to my post. I'm sure that Evan David has found that he can manage perfectly well without me. And the other thing that I need to take into account to soothe my wounded heart is that Evan David was only ever going to be in my life for a few weeks. My loyalty should lie with Ken the Landlord at the King's Head, who will have the dubious pleasure of employing me long after the aforementioned opera superstar will have moved on to break other susceptible hearts with his rather obvious brand of charm in numerous countries around the globe. All these things I can rationalise, but it doesn't stop me from feeling like complete shite. Can you miss someone so much that your eyeballs ache? Or that your fingernails yearn for him? Sounds strange? Well, take it from me, it's something that's never happened to me before.

'I think it's safer to stick to a classic,' I say in answer to my friend's question.

Carl has chosen Roberta Flack's old hit, 'The First Time Ever I Saw Your Face' as my pièce de résistance and I'm so grateful for his input, even though I might not be demonstrating it at the moment. Although I'm going to be the one up on stage by myself, at least I don't feel as if I'm doing this alone.

'Come on,' I say. 'If you ply me with cheap Chianti, then you might be able to persuade me to do some more rehearsing later.'

'Could I persuade you to do anything else later?' he says with an evil wiggle of his eyebrows.

'One day I'll surprise you,' I warn him. 'I'll say yes and then you won't know what to do.'

'I'll give it my best shot,' Carl assures me earnestly.

I kiss him on the cheek. 'I value your friendship too much to want to spoil it by introducing condoms into the equation.'

'Playing hard to get is not attractive in a woman of your age,' he tells me as we head for the door.

'And greasy Italian food isn't normally considered an aphrodisiac,' I counter.

Then, out of the corner of my eye, I spy my morose—and possibly insane—parent sitting drowning his sorrows in the kitchen. It's on the tip of my tongue to invite him to come out with us, and then Carl gives me a warning look. He's right. It would only end up in a shouting match.

'We're off, Dad,' I tell him.

He lifts his head and glares at me. 'Lucky old you.'

'This won't do any good,' I say, casting a withering glance at his rapidly diminishing bottle of Jameson's.

'Arse. Bum. Tit,' he says, but with a certain lack of enthusiasm.

'Can't you try another illness?' I ask. 'This one is becoming rather tiresome.'

'I think I might be getting a touch of vertigo, too,' he confesses dourly, spreading his hands on the table as if to maintain his balance.

I can feel my teeth grinding involuntarily. 'What about rabies? There must be more mileage in that,' I suggest. 'You could use the washing-up liquid to create the foaming mouth effect.' Plus it might help to clean out all the rubbish that's been spewing forth from it this last week.

His red-rimmed eyes grow ever more doleful.

'None of this is working with Mum, either,' I remind him. 'She's not interested.' I decide not to inform him that she's much more interested in the attractive Asian gentleman who's now running the shop where she works and is disappearing on late-night and weekend assignations without telling her family where she's going. It might make my dad shape himself up a bit more if I did, but try as I might, I can't be the harbinger of doom. Perhaps Joe and I need to have a family conference about this with him when I have more evidence of our mum's infidelity.

Despite my more base instincts wanting to let him stew in his own juice, I go over to my dad and give him a hug. He's a solid, stocky bloke, but somehow he feels shrunken and small. 'We won't be long,' I say. 'Have a shower. Perk yourself up a bit.' *Try to rejoin the human race.* I give him a jocular nudge. 'Faint heart never won fair lady.'

'Fuck off,' he offers in return.

As steam starts to come out of my ears and I'm building up for a major eruption, Carl curls his fingers around mine and pulls me towards the door.

'I could batter him,' I say with a weary shake of my head. 'I really could.' Outside in the street, the cold evening air slaps my face.

'Faint heart never won fair lady, eh?' My friend gives me a quizzical look when he asks, 'Does that advice count for me, too?'

Thirty-two

This was Cardiff—the vibrant, cosmopolitan capital city of Wales. It was also the heart of Evan David Land—a place where his fame was fondly embraced as a son of this city. Millions of pounds of EU money had been pumped into its decaying landscape over the last ten years to transform it into a world-class tourist city and European centre of culture. Victorian shopping arcades stuffed with designer boutiques now rubbed shoulders with towering modern apartment blocks at prices that would make even the residents of the London Borough of Kensington and Chelsea shudder. A fairy-tale medieval castle in the city centre competed for visitors' attention with a museum holding a superb collection of Impressionist paintings—one of the best outside of Paris. Yet, every time Evan came home, the place seemed more and more alien to him. Another landmark had been flattened to make way for a new stainless-steel sculpture.

This time his visit was organised to coincide with the opening of the new National Welsh Opera House, a building dedicated to the furtherance of the art of opera and the home of the National Opera Company of Wales—the company that had given him his very first job as a professional singer in its chorus. Now, whenever they required his services, he'd try to make sure that his diary was clear for them. Wherever he went in the world, his reception was never as warm as in this big-hearted city. The Welsh—his kinsfolk—certainly knew how to celebrate.

Crafted in the finest, heather-coloured Welsh slate to resonate with the surrounding landscape, and topped with a curving stainless-steel roof, the theatre—known affectionately by locals as 'the armadillo'—stood proud on the edge of the stunning waterfront development of Cardiff Bay and was already firmly ensconced in the hearts of the nation. Six-foot-high poetry in the Welsh language emblazoned on the front offered words affirming artistic truth and inspiration: In these stones horizons sing. It would be a marvellous place to perform. A good time to renew old friendships.

While he surveyed the area, Rupert busied himself by lifting their bags from the limousine. Erin had organised for them to stay in the penthouse of one of the towering apartment blocks on the waterfront. The faint, salty scent of sea air clashed with the aroma of coffee from the myriad of bistros that were dotted about the area. He was here to star in a performance of *La Traviata* with the lovely Lana Rosina as his leading lady. As Rupert had muttered all the way down here from London, Evan had yet to call her.

Later today, there was a full list of media interviews to work through and a visit to the local BBC radio station to make pleasant noises. Tomorrow was the dress rehearsal, followed by another press frenzy the day after. The performance itself would be in two days' time—allowing a respite for the singers' voices. Evan fully expected that the last thing Lana would do when she saw him after so long was to give her voice a rest. The woman could talk for Britain—and Italy. No doubt there would be a lot she wanted to tell him. No doubt he wouldn't get a word in edgeways. He hadn't seen or spoken to Lana since the rehearsals for *La Traviata*. Where had she been since then? He could hardly remember what she'd told him. Was it San Francisco? Or maybe Rome? Or had she been performing at the Met in New York? Countries and cities had a tendency to blur together these days. And, it seemed in this case—for him, at least—absence didn't always make the heart grow fonder.

He'd unpack, he decided, and then go for a run with his trainer, Jacob, who had come along with them. One thing he found in this place was that memories became too keen and he needed to pound the pavements to even have a hope of keeping them at bay. The older he got, the harder it seemed. Wasn't that contrary to the way of nature? When you were older, weren't the memories supposed to fade to grey, become as insubstantial as cobwebs fluttering in the mind? To Evan they were still too clear, too sharp, too raw. Perhaps that's why he'd stayed away for so long. His last journey to Cardiff before the rehearsals had been several years ago, and only he knew the reasons why he was so anxious to avoid repeat visits. Evan kicked at the newly laid block paving at his feet.

Dermuid, as always, was here, too, and was currently unloading his portable kitchen, whistling quietly as he worked.

The only person missing from his entourage was Fern. Beautiful, feisty, frustrating Fern. He hadn't called her and had decided he wouldn't. His fingers had hovered over the buttons of his mobile phone, but he couldn't bring himself to press them. He had enough on his plate without the complication of trying to form a relationship. But hadn't that always been the way? What chance was there that he could ever devote enough time to finding himself a wife? Success always came at a price. There were sacrifices that needed to be made to fill cavernous auditoriums to capacity—goodness only knew, he was more aware of that than most. The few women who had been in his life had never appreciated that. Why should it be any different this time? Fern was on the outside of his world. How could he expect her to understand what made him tick? She knew nothing about opera—absolutely nothing—though her joy in discovering it was obvious. And she knew nothing about him, either. It looked as if it was destined to stay that way.

'Evan,' Rupert said at his side. 'Come inside. There are things we need to go over.'

Evan nodded at his agent, his manager, his only true friend in this world. 'I'll be right behind you.'

'Don't let your throat get cold,' Rupert said over his shoulder as he headed into the apartment block.

Evan looked out over the waterfront. He was constantly surrounded by people, yet so often in recent months he felt isolated. What had happened to him? Had the shell that he'd so carefully constructed around himself finally started to crumble? It was made of brittle material, glued together with pain. Perhaps it was inevitable that it wouldn't protect him for ever.

Why was it that the feel of Fern's touch, her arms sliding around his neck, the tears of joy she shed for him were playing over and over in the back of his mind, tormenting him? Perhaps because it seemed to him at the time that it had been the most sincere affection and emotion that he'd experienced for longer than he cared to remember. And he'd been wrong. The wind stung his eyes, bringing tears to them. Complaining gulls wheeled on the sharp air, sounding as pained as he felt. He had everything that money could buy, so why did he so often feel empty inside? Despite millions of adoring fans around the globe, could it possibly be that he was lonely?

Thirty-three

Rather than the fifty thousand who queued up for the original open auditions all over the country, this time we've been whittled down to about fifty acts. If my maths are correct, that means that 0.1 percent of us have got this far. Horrifying odds, which I've somehow managed to defy. But even vying for my place against forty-nine other very talented folks still seems like a scary amount of people to be competing with. And there's a tangible atmosphere of nervous tension in the air—apart from an occasional eruption of giggles that have a slightly hysterical edge.

We're all crammed into a conference suite in the sumptuous Savoy Hotel in the Strand. I have never been anywhere this posh in all my life. It's the sort of place that Evan David would frequent if he wasn't so neurotic about germs. I'm doing quite well, I think, because that's only the twenty-seventh time I've thought about him today. Still it is only ten o'clock, plenty of time to obsess yet.

The waiting around is a bit more civilised this time—we're being plied with tea and chocolate biscuits, although the tea is in flimsy plastic beakers rather than the bone china I'm sure they normally use. I'm not complaining, though. You can't believe how grateful I am to have made it this far.

One or two of the solo performers have brought companions with them. My dear friend, Carl, decided that he couldn't stand the strain and has set up camp to wait for me in the Starbucks opposite the Savoy. I can picture him fretting over his caffè latte and granola flapjack. Secretly, I think that he was worried about them marking me down if he was seen to be accompanying me to the audition. I told him he was talking rubbish, but he may be right. Stranger things can and do happen. We have television cameras trained on us the entire time, waiting to record our worst moments—and if you weren't nervous before you arrived here, you would be by now.

I covertly eye my fellow competitors and, quite frankly, they all look much, much better than me. Better dressed, better groomed, better prepared and, of course, better performers. They're younger, sexier and I bet half of them are sleeping with the judges. If I were a judge, I tell you, I'd be tempted. There are more breasts and bums on display than in a nudist colony. It might be to do with my age, but my breasts are the only ones that are firmly ensconced in my shirt—just over my heart, which is pounding against my ribs to get out. And while I realise that this isn't a great time to be developing an inferiority complex, mine is coming on in leaps and bounds.

The blond-haired bimbo presenter and television überbabe, Kiera Karson, comes to talk to me, hugging and squeezing me, treating me as her new best friend, pushing her microphone halfway down my throat as she asks me some inane questions. I can feel my smile freeze on my face as I gibber back some banal rubbish about this being my big chance—as if they don't know this. The torture seems to go on interminably—I have no idea what she asks me or what I say in response, but I know that it's this sort of thing that will have me awake and shaking at three o'clock in the morning. This day will be my recurrent nightmare for years to come. The camera crew don't even try to disguise how bored they are, yawning as they dream of me finishing my chirpy banter so they can get off to their next tea break. This truly is purgatory. Waiting, waiting, waiting. Pacing the floor between heaven and hell.

Then the next round of auditions starts and the team of Identikit PR women move into action, herding us nearer to the door ready to lead us up to the inner sanctum or lion's den. I just want to get my turn over and done with—preferably before I throw up—and then run back to Carl to lick my wounds.

Not a moment too soon, but far too soon—if you know what I mean—my name is called by one of the slender-hipped lovelies, who then escorts me out of the room, to the carefully filmed shouts of encouragement from my fellow contestants. I bet they're all wishing that I'll fall flat on my face.

This feels as if I'm going to the guillotine. It will be a very short time before my career is cut short, my poor head plopping bloodied and lifeless into the basket of almost-might-have-beens.

My legs are shaking and my feet slide on the plush carpet as we pass beneath chandeliers that glitter with the dazzling intensity of a million stars. I think of all the famous people who must have visited the hotel in the past, walking the same carpet as I am—people who have made it in the harsh world of showbusiness. My PR person opens a pair of glass double doors and before I have time to hightail it out of here, she marches me inside.

'Just the Two of Us,' she announces and I realise that I should have changed our name now that I'm no longer part of a duo.

At the very front of the vast airy room, there's a makeshift stage. Far too close to it, sit the row of judges. You'd know all their faces from the television series. There's pop impresario, Stephen Cauldwell, and next to him is Jackson, the boy band manager who's as famous as the pint-sized poppets that he manufactures. The other judge is Carly Thomas, one-time chart-topper who now spends her time penning the ultra-catchy hits for the likes of Kylie and Natasha Bedingfield.

'Hi, Fern,' Stephen says, casting me a cursory glance. He indicates the stage. 'When you're ready.'

And this is it. Somehow my legs manage to walk up to the microphone. As Carl was banned, I'm going to sing my song unaccompanied. With a quivering breath I then belt out 'The First Time Ever I Saw Your Face' as if my life depends on it. I close my eyes, blocking out my judges. Instead, I torture myself further by thinking of Evan while I sing and feel the notes deep in my chest. It's as though time itself stands still, but then as soon as I've started it's over. Looking up, I can see the panel conferring. There's much whispering, nodding and shaking of heads while I stand there waiting to be put out of my misery.

Eventually, Stephen Cauldwell looks up. 'Thank you,' he says flatly. 'You're through to the next round.'

If Stephen Cauldwell doesn't show any emotion as he announces my success, then my reaction certainly makes up for it. I collapse to my knees on the stage and I begin to cry and hyperventilate both at the same time. A television camera is pushed into my face. 'Thank you,' I sob. 'Thank you.'

Then Kiera, the blond-bimbo presenter, rushes in and scoops me into her arms, helping me to my feet. Elation kicks in and we dance round together laughing. Even the panel are smiling.

'We'll see you on television next week,' Stephen tells me and then Kiera rushes me out of the room. We dash back up the plush carpeted stairs, pursued by the camera crew, and burst into the room where all the other contestants are waiting.

'Fern's through to the next round!' Kiera shouts to the assembled performers, and immediately I'm engulfed by a cheering mob. If I was in the same situation, I'm not sure I'd be so magnanimous—wouldn't I be thinking that it meant one less place for me? If that's how any of them feel, they're certainly hiding it well.

'I must phone Carl,' I say. 'I must phone Carl.' With trembling fingers, I reach for my mobile phone and find his number. He answers instantly. 'I'm through,' I tell him breathlessly. 'I'm through.'

'I'll be right there,' he says and hangs up.

'Be quick,' I say to no one.

Moments later, the doors to the conference room crash open and my dear, dear friend is running in to meet me. His face is flushed with exertion, his grin jubilant. I start to cry again, and Carl grabs me by the waist and lifts me high into the air, twirling me round. I throw my arms round his neck.

'You did it!' he cries. 'You did it!'

'We did it,' I murmur into his hair. '*We* did it.'

He lowers me to the ground and now we both look embarrassed. The cameras move away from us, seeking new prey.

'I'm so pleased for you,' Carl tells me. 'What am I saying? I'm over the *fucking* moon!'

We both giggle self-consciously.

'What happens now?' I want to know.

Kiera Karson is by my side in a flash. 'Congratulations,' she says, more muted now that the cameras have departed. 'We look forward to seeing you in the studios next week. You'll spend the week doing media training and seeing an image consultant.' I'll swear she gives Carl a sideways glance at this point. 'There'll be sessions with a voice coach.'

I wonder how on earth I'm going to fit all this in. I shall have to beg some time off work from Ken the Landlord at the King's Head again. But surely the fact that I've been a finalist in the *Fame Game* will draw in the punters to listen to us, so he should view it as a business investment. I'll try to sell it to him that way.

'I'll hand you over to Melissa, she'll tell you all about it.'

Another one of the Identikit PR girls pops up next to us, clipboard in hand, grinning wildly. 'It'll be great,' she enthuses. 'And we have a special surprise for this series.'

I'm all ears. I'm beginning to like surprises.

'We have a *fantastic* guest judge who'll be joining the regular panel.' Kiera clasps her hands together with glee. 'Evan David,' she says. '*The* Evan David!'

And my bubble of joy goes pop right in my face.

Thirty-four

Lana Rosina, Evan was sure, had grown more beautiful since he last saw her. Her glossy black hair tumbled down her back in lazy waves, her red bee-stung mouth pouted more prominently than ever. And her voluptuous curves tightly bound into her costume—a scarlet leather corset—were, without a doubt, a sight to behold.

Evan's leading lady had arrived late—her plane held up for hours by a security scare in Los Angeles if you believed her account of the incident. Lana might be opera's most exciting female star, but she was also the most tempestuous.

The dress rehearsal had gone ahead with Lana's understudy assuming the main role, as *La Diva Assoluta* had taken straight to her bed with crippling jet lag and a sore throat. Evan wondered just how much of it was designed so that she could avoid him until opening night. She had refused to take his calls, her PA insisting that she wasn't allowed to speak even one word,

on doctor's orders, of course. And Lana knew Evan too well—
she knew that he wouldn't dare visit her for fear of the sore
throat being a real infection rather than an imagined one.

Was this her way of trying to put him under pressure, at a
disadvantage? It was a typical Lana trick. They'd been in this
situation before where she'd hidden herself away until opening night, refusing to calm the very real fears that the performance might well have to go ahead without her. It made
everyone else in the company, particularly the conductor and
the chorus, hysterical with nerves, but miraculously Lana always seemed to make a full recovery just in the nick of time.
He'd got past the point of feeling hysterical about anything that
Lana did. Evan now looked on all of her off-stage performances with much the same attitude as a tolerant parent would
view an indulged child. She demanded attention wherever she
went and, invariably, got it.

And here she was. Standing in his dressing room, looking
the very picture of rude health, sore throat apparently banished
until the next time it was needed. *La Diva's* understudy would
be disappointed once more.

Lana turned to Becks, who was currently applying Evan's
make-up. 'Can you leave us for a moment?'

Evan stood up, stifling a sigh as Becks left the room, giving
him a sympathetic look as she did so. Becks was only too aware
that it didn't do to cross Lana so near to a performance. She
was highly strung at the best of times, and two hours before
curtain up she was as wired as a stallion before a race and twice
as likely to kick out at the nearest object. Clearly Becks had
no intention of being that object.

When they were alone, Lana touched Evan's sleeve, eyelashes

lowered in an attempt to be coquettish. It was a look that Lana couldn't sustain for long. She was too fiery, too feisty and soon, with little provocation, there would be the usual fireworks.

'It's been a long time,' she said, stepping into Evan's embrace.

He kissed her on both cheeks, then Lana turned her head and found his mouth. Her lips were soft and searching against his. There was a stirring of old feelings. Had he loved her once? It was hard to tell. Their liaisons had always been brief, passionate and increasingly antagonistic. Was there ever any way that they could have sustained a normal relationship? Whatever that was. It wasn't something he wanted to explore right now. Evan held her away from him and asked: 'Ready for tonight's performance?'

She flounced her hair. 'Of course.'

This production of *La Traviata* was a reprisal of one they had performed together a few seasons ago in Paris—to sell-out houses and rave reviews. The same French directors they had worked with then had flown over to stage the show again. Due to Lana's commitments the main preparations and rehearsals for the production had been weeks ago, before she'd jetted off to fulfil other commitments. Rehearsing together in the run-up to the opening night would have been infinitely preferable—it was a witness to Lana's status that she could get away with the liberties she frequently liked to take—but they were both so familiar with the roles that they could perform them in a deep sleep if necessary.

This production was using a contemporary setting, in which the idea of *La Traviata*—the fallen woman—represented the modern obsession with celebrity. The irony wasn't lost on

Evan. Here was a woman, a singer hailed as an icon of the age, a celebrity adored by celebrities, playing a woman, Violetta Valéry, who abandons her hedonistic lifestyle to find true love. Would the real Lana ever do that? he wondered. It was unlikely. She loved to grace the covers of magazines, took unmitigated joy in her photograph being splashed across the gossip columns, flirted with the paparazzi who dogged her every move as much as she professed to loathe them. In the past she'd been on the front cover of American *Vogue* and pictures of her dressed from head to toe in black leather as a gangster's moll had appeared all over billboards in New York to promote a series of concerts she'd been giving in the city. No one would ever call Lana Rosina a shrinking Violetta.

How would she feel, Evan asked himself, when she grew older and the public, in turn, grew bored with her as they inevitably would, replacing her with a younger, fresher model? It was bound to happen, it was simply a matter of when. Lana wasn't immune to the fickleness of fame, and neither was he. She had a hit album at the top of the classic charts, which was the fastest-selling album since opera singer Maria Callas's phenomenal success. But however much she achieved, it was never enough for Lana. She'd been sorely stung by the critics saying that she'd sold out by 'putting on leather trousers and belting out her top ten arias.' His leading lady had never learned how to handle the occasional criticism she received—it was something they all found hard. Evan knew that it was one of Lana's biggest insecurities—that she would be nothing when her extraordinary voice started to fade. As it was, they had both been lucky to stay at the top of their chosen tree for so long.

What did he feel about his own celebrity lifestyle? Having

achieved more success than he could ever have imagined, did he still want to keep giving a piece of himself to every face in a crowd? How much longer would he want to be owned by the public who had made him what he was? Why was there such a void in people's lives that they wanted to fill it with crumbs of gossip from the shallow existence of celebrities? It was possible to become a celebrity these days by wearing a revealing dress or sleeping with a married footballer or appearing on one of those dreadful Saturday-night talent shows that were so popular now. Already he was bitterly regretting that he'd let Rupert talk him into appearing on the *Fame Game*. He was dreading it as much as he was dreading tonight's performance with Lana.

'You know that I'm still in love with you,' Lana said.

There was an uncomfortable pause when Evan didn't really know what to say.

'You could tell me that you love me, too,' she prompted.

His role tonight was that of Alfredo Germont, Violetta's lovelorn suitor, who pursues the woman he adores, a woman desired by so many other men, a woman who, despite his best efforts, stays steadfastly beyond his reach. The lyrics were emotionally loaded, the ending tragic.

'I'll be telling you a hundred times tonight,' he promised.

What a shame that *La Diva*'s sore throat hadn't lasted just a little while longer, he thought. There was no doubt that he'd rather be singing words of love to anyone other than Lana.

Thirty-five

I fly through the automatic doors of the hospital and then run all the way to the children's ward. After a dozen different security questions, I'm finally admitted. Getting into a kids' ward these days is like getting into Fort Knox, and I guess it's an indicator of the sad times we live in. I suppose I could have done it James Bond-style and abseiled down the building—that might have been easier. As it is, having jogged through the confusing maze of corridors, I'm completely out of puff.

The call from Joe came as Carl and I were still deciding whether or not it was pertinent to celebrate my success in the light of the new development. Carl was trying to be philosophical, but quite frankly, having Evan David sit in judgement on me is all my worst nightmares rolled into one, and nothing my friend could say would convince me otherwise. Still, all thoughts of fame and fortune or what might have been went straight out of my head when Joe rang and told me with shaking voice that Nathan had been admitted to hospital again. Carl paid for a cab to get me here in double-quick time. And now he's helpfully gone to tell Ken the Landlord that I'll be late in for work, yet again. I think Ken must secretly fancy me; otherwise, he'd have fired me long before now.

Nathan used to have this sort of asthma attack regularly. When he was younger, it could happen once, twice, sometimes three times a month, and I guess that we should be used to it by now. But asthma is a tricky illness, as you can so easily get lulled into a false sense of security by it—just when you think you've got it more or less under control, it has a habit of biting you on the bum. Nathan hasn't been in hospital now for ages, so the news comes as a shock. Everyone in the family tries to ignore the fact that today asthma is still one of the biggest killers of children in the UK. Sometimes my nephew doesn't tell us when he's feeling bad, either, because he hates to come into hospital and hates being different from his friends. It's tough for a kid to cope with all this stuff at such a young age and my heart goes out to him.

I see Joe and Nathan at the end of the ward in a bed just next to a six-foot-high Tigger. Nathan is propped up with a pile of pillows, there's an oxygen feed attached to his nose and his lips are slightly blue. Not a good sign. There's a probe on his finger which measures his haemoglobin levels, and a kindly, big-bottomed Jamaican nurse is fussing over him. She gives Nathan's hand a squeeze as she finishes her checks and says, 'You is doin' jus' fine, sugar.'

Joe sags visibly with relief.

Kissing Nathan on the forehead, I say to them both, 'What happened here?'

My nephew is wheezing and struggling to speak. He gives up and lies there looking wan.

My brother shakes his head as I give him a kiss, too. 'I let him go to a friend's birthday party. Sent along all his drugs with specific instructions…'

As Joe always has to do.

'He must have had some food additives or something that triggered it.' He gives Nathan a rueful smile. 'Although he's not fessing up.'

His son tries a weak smile again. Even strong smells can set Nathan off wheezing like a train—and this place stinks of cheap disinfectant. That can't help.

'Maybe he was just overexcited. Anyway, when he asked for his inhaler and aerochamber, the stupid woman was so flustered with two dozen kids around that she couldn't remember where she'd put the bloody thing.' Joe rolls his eyes in disbelief. 'Luckily, she did have the sense to ring for an ambulance when my laddo here started to turn a funny colour. Turns out his puffer had ended up in the bin along with all the paper plates. Don't ask me how. She's mortified.'

'So she should be.' This is what I mean. People just don't treat asthma as a serious condition. Didn't she realise that if Nathan couldn't get his breath, he could have croaked it? That would have been a memorable end to her kid's birthday party.

I feel so sorry for Joe. He constantly has to strike a balance, fighting a tendency never to let Nathan out of his sight or entrusting his kid's health to someone who doesn't understand the situation. Or he hangs around at the party and makes Nathan feel like a dork. Whatever he does it isn't right. I flop down in the plastic chair next to my brother. Joe looks pale and drawn. He rubs his hand across his forehead. 'When are we ever going to get this sorted out?' Joe sounds close to tears. 'I don't want Nathan going through life with this hanging round his neck.'

'I'll be all right, Dad,' my brave nephew gasps from his bed.

'Of course you'll be all right,' I say too brightly as I pat his hand. 'You'll both be fine.' And I wish, not for the first time, that I could win a million quid and get them out of their flat and out of the London pollution.

'You look pretty knackered, too,' Joe observes with typical brotherly concern.

'I had my final audition for the *Fame Game* today,' I remind him as a wave of exhaustion washes over me.

'Jeez, sis,' he says. 'I'd completely forgotten.'

'Well, you do have things on your mind other than my feeble quest for stardom.' We both cast an anxious glance at our boy.

'So, tell me. How did it go?'

'Fine,' I answer warily. 'I'm through to the next round, which is the television programme.'

'Wow!' Joe says. 'Hey, Nathan, your auntie's going to be a star!'

My nephew gives me a tired version of thumbs-up. I know that he's very poorly; otherwise, he'd be jumping up and running round the ward in jubilation. I give him the thumbs-up back.

'I still have a long way to go,' I say, 'and it's not all great news. One of the judges is the guy I was working for.'

'Isn't it usually an advantage if you know one of the judges?'

'The guy who I insulted and then left in the lurch...'

'Oh.'

'I wouldn't say that gives me a huge advantage.'

'You should have slept with him,' he mouths so that Nathan shouldn't hear.

The thought has occurred to me. 'What I *shouldn't* have done is told him lies about my unexplained absences. He has no idea that I hold secret ambitions to be a singer. I laughed it off when he told me I had a good voice. How could I tell the great Evan David that I thought I could pass muster with the likes of him?' I want to crawl into a very big hole and never come out again. 'He'll pass out when he sees me on that stage. Or I will.'

'Your life always seems so complicated.'

'Tell me about it.'

'Why don't you just give in and marry Carl?'

'Carl?' I laugh. 'Because he's never asked me.'

'That's only because he knows you'll say no.'

I shake my head. 'Carl wouldn't want to be fettered by a conventional arrangement. He likes being a little bit rock 'n' roll. He might not bite the heads off live bats, but he's still a free spirit.'

'You know that's rubbish, sis. Carl's not free. He never will be. He's hopelessly devoted to you.'

'I'm devoted to him, too,' I insist, 'but in a sisterly way. I couldn't get squishy with Carl. We just don't feel like that about each other.'

'I don't think Carl sees it that way. If you offered him a wedding ring, two tousle-haired kids and a house in the suburbs, he'd give up any ideas of a rock 'n' roll lifestyle like a shot.'

'Can we stop discussing my relationship dilemmas?' I say, and check my watch pointedly. 'When will our misbehaving parents get here?' Perhaps seeing their dear grandchild like this will bring them both to their senses. All else seems to be failing.

Joe looks grim. 'I've tried phoning Mum, but she's not at home and she never has her mobile with her—if she does, she never remembers to switch the damn thing on. She's the only person I know who can make a ten-pound credit last for two years.'

'I can't believe it,' I say with an exasperated sigh. 'I'd love to know where she keeps sloping off to.' I'd hate to think that she's blaming the breakdown of their marriage totally on my dad when all the time she's playing hooky with another bloke.

'Dad won't come down at all,' Joe continues, echoing my sigh. 'Selfish git. Says he doesn't like hospitals.'

'A fine comment from a man who's going the quickest way about getting *himself* hospitalised,' I snap. When I get home, I'm going to give him a piece of my mind, and not the piece that's nice and fluffy. He's going to get the stroppy piece.

'I'll have to give up that job I'd got lined up for next week,' Joe tells me. 'I can't leave Nathan when he's like this.'

'You must,' I say. 'They'll give Nathan some steroids and he'll be as right as rain by Monday. You wait and see.' We all marvel at Nathan's rate of recovery from these terrible bouts. And we all pray that it continues as he gets older. 'I'll look after him. I promised I would.'

'How can you now that you've got through to the *Fame Game?* You need to concentrate on that, Fern. This could be your big chance.'

'And it could be my biggest disaster,' I remind him. 'The odds are not looking good.'

'Someone has to win. I'd rather it was you.'

'I'll manage. As long as Nathan's fit enough to go back to school during the day, I'll manage just fine.'

'If you're sure,' Joe says reluctantly.

'Of course I'm sure.'

I can't let my brother down—I've promised him. Inside me is a deep weariness. Sometimes I feel there are so many balls in the air that I'm trying to juggle and that one day they'll all come crashing down on my head, leaving me thrashing about at thin air. Until then, I'll manage. I always do.

Thirty-six

Act One. The set was bright, contemporary. Glossy black-and-white photographs, twelve feet high, formed the backdrop and featured Lana, in her guise as Violetta, striking *Vogue*-style poses for her loving public. A party was in progress—much chatter and tinkling of glasses. The chorus, lounging on pink and orange sofas, were excelling themselves in their gaiety. Evan suspected that only half of it was down to superb acting; most of them were only too relieved that their *Diva* had finally made it on stage.

Lana, black hair flowing and in the revealing red leather corset, was holding centre stage. The audience were spellbound. Evan, as Alfredo, was wearing a black Armani suit and white shirt, looking every inch the sophisticated suitor. As he'd promised Lana in the dressing room, he was declaring undying love for Violetta, impervious to the fact that she was dying.

The story of *La Traviata* is simple and contains an eternal truth. Boy meets girl, boy persuades girl to fall in love with him, boy has no idea girl is dying, his interfering but well-meaning father keeps them apart, boy thinks it's all the girl's fault, boy and girl are reunited, boy finds out the truth just in time for girl to depart this mortal coil. An everyday story of ordinary folk.

Tonight, for some reason, the emotion of the words was reaching into Evan deeper than it had ever done before. There were tears in his eyes as he sang to Lana, embraced in his arms. The rich Italian lyrics filled the auditorium as Alfredo declared that he had loved Violetta since he first set eyes on her. 'I trembled with a love I had never known before. The love that is the heartbeat of the universe…'

And then Lana sang back, gazing at his face, 'Can I risk a real love? No man has yet made me fall in love. Oh joy, such as I have never known, to love and be loved.'

To love and be loved. Would he continue to go through life not knowing what it felt like to love and be loved in return? It suddenly seemed like a bleak prospect.

Lana pushed away from his arms, and it shocked him to realise that he wanted to feel the warmth of her again. 'Can I disdain such love in favour of the empty folly of my life?' she sang.

It was a question he was starting to ask himself every day. Over the years, he'd hardened his heart whenever there was a chance to throw caution to the wind and let himself fall in love. Look how he'd behaved with Fern. It was appalling. She was someone who'd got under his skin more than anyone before and yet he'd blown it. He'd always held back. Always protected himself.

'Let us grasp at pleasure,' Lana urged him, gripping his hands tightly. 'Since love is fleeting, short-lived joy. It's a flower that blooms and quickly dies…'

He, more than anyone, knew that love was often only a fleeting pleasure that could be ripped away from you at any moment. Was it worth risking the pain to taste the joy? He'd been there once and never wanted to experience that emotion again. That was why he put so much of himself into his performances, for which he was lauded the world over. It was simply that his love knew no other outpouring. And that suddenly seemed rather more pathetic than noble.

Thirty-seven

Cut to Act Three and a monochrome set. The partying was over. All was now grey and bleak. Violetta's hospital bed took centre stage and, in her death throes she appeared in her pure white nightgown, stripped of all her make-up, her finery, her glamour.

Tonight's performance had been exhausting. With all this talk of love and longing, Evan felt for the first time as if he'd bared his troubled soul on stage. The audience had lapped it up, sucking every ounce greedily from him, leaving him drained and needy. His heart had been torn open and put on display for all to see.

Lana's portrayal of the anguished Violetta had never been better, grasping at love before her life was taken from her. For Evan it was the performance of his life. They were no longer two overpaid celebrity opera stars singing from a well-worn sheet of music; they were speaking directly to each other's hearts. Telling each other, as they had never done before, exactly how they felt. The atmosphere was electric, the audience long-forgotten. How had he ignored the qualities in this woman for so long? How had he not seen how much she loved him?

On stage, this is their one last chance to be reconciled before Violetta dies. Alfredo is full of contrition for the way he has doubted Violetta's love, and once again the lovers dream of a happy future while knowing full well that Violetta only has a short time left. It's a heartbreaking scene, in stark contrast to the vibrant party images at the start of the opera. Violetta's celebrity friends have all abandoned her; the hedonistic lifestyle she once led cannot sustain her now.

As she dies, Violetta begs Alfredo not to spend the rest of his life alone. 'If a young girl, in the flower of youth, should give her heart to you, then marry her.'

And then, falling back onto her bed, she passes away.

When the curtain came down, there was rapturous applause. The house was on its feet.

Evan wept openly. Tears ran down Lana's cheeks.

'I don't want to be alone tonight,' she said in a quiet voice.

He nodded in acquiescence. He never wanted to be alone again.

The curtain was raised and they pulled themselves from the bed, both going to the front of the stage together, taking a long, grateful bow. Both Lana and he were trembling with emotion, and Evan wondered how he'd managed to get through to the end of the performance. Old wounds had been opened. Blood was let. In some ways it had been cathartic, and in other ways it had made him realise that there were still so many issues he had to address.

As in *La Traviata,* in opera when the female character dies at the end, as she so often does, it's normally done with great grace, fine strong voice and lots of fake blood. A superb and elegant death. Very rousing. But Evan knew that it wasn't like that in real life. It wasn't like that at all.

Thirty-eight

They'd left the theatre together in Evan's limousine pursued by a motley gang of paparazzi on scooters. And, by mutual agreement, they had gone straight to Lana's hotel instead of taking a circuitous route trying to shake off their unwanted entourage.

As they pulled up outside the magnificent five-star establishment, a landmark architectural splendour overlooking Cardiff Bay, another gaggle of press photographers were huddled round the entrance and snapped viciously at them as they emerged from the car, flashbulbs blinding them. Rupert had warned him against this when Evan had told his agent that he didn't intend returning to his apartment until morning. Their late-night liaison would, no doubt, be plastered all over the pages of the next issue of *Hello!* magazine, but after a night of high emotions, Evan had come to the decision that he didn't care anymore. He couldn't keep on living his life like a monk just to avoid the gossip columns. He was a red-blooded male, and sometimes he simply had to behave like one.

Now, in the cold light of day, the benefit of years of wisdom was slowly beginning to surface again, along with the rest of his body, and he wondered just what he'd done. He reached over and turned off the bedside lamp, pondering for a moment over the action. Light streamed in through the windows from Lana's private balcony, illuminating the plush penthouse suite in sharp relief. The place looked absolutely immaculate. There was no indication of their tempestuous night of passion. The side table that they'd knocked over had been righted. The clothes that had been strewn all over the floor as they undressed each other in a frenzy were neatly folded on a sofa in the corner of the room. Well, *his* clothes were there. Of Lana's there was no sign. Nor was there any sign of their owner. The space next to him in the enormous bed, though crumpled, was quite resolutely empty. There were no running-water sounds coming from the bathroom that might indicate that Lana was already up and showering.

He couldn't even blame his dull headache on an excess of alcohol. Lana might have downed the best part of a bottle of Bollinger but, as always, he'd only drunk mineral water. Some habits were harder to break than others.

Evan propped himself up on his elbow. 'Lana?' he called out. But there was no reply. He hauled himself out of bed—every part of him aching. After both of his performances as a lover, on and off the stage, he felt like he'd run a dozen marathons back-to-back. Lana was as demanding sexually as she was in every other aspect of her life. He shook his head and allowed himself a wry laugh. That woman never did anything by halves.

Perhaps he'd take himself along to the spa here and maybe have a steam and a swim. Let the water massage some life back into his battered body. And then he thought of how many other people he'd have to share the water with and changed his mind. He couldn't afford to risk an infection with the manic schedule he had ahead of him.

Taking advantage of one of the fluffy bathrobes in Lana's suite, he checked in the bathroom just in case she was hiding from him. 'Lana?' he tried again.

They'd promised each other all kinds of love and commitment last night while they were riding high on a tide of emotions. She, too, might well be having second thoughts this morning. But, amid the acreage of white mosaic tiles, there was still no Lana.

In the lounge, he found fresh juice and fruit on the glass coffee table. Evan stretched out on the peach leather sofa and helped himself to an apple while he mused on where his leading lady might have gone. Perhaps when she finally emerged they might spend some of the day together—at least share breakfast. He had no idea what her plans were, but they certainly wouldn't involve hanging around in Wales. This would be another of her famous fleeting visits.

Then he spotted a note addressed to him in wildly theatrical handwriting that could only belong to one person. He opened it and scanned the contents. 'Ciao, darling,' he read out loud. 'It was fun. Call you soon. Lana.'

Evan sighed. Oh well. At least there was a kiss on the bottom of the page. She was always destined to be more like the real Lana Rosina than her stage persona of Violetta. There was no way that Lana would ever give up her decadent, celebrity lifestyle for true love. So much for all her protestations of love in the heat of the night! When the time came to face Evan in the morning, she'd hightailed it out of here. It looked like their performance, both on stage and in the bedroom, had been strictly for one night only.

His mobile phone was on the table. He picked it up and rang Rupert. 'Hi, Rupert,' he said.

'She hasn't flayed you alive then?'

'Not quite.' Evan allowed himself a smile. 'Can you send the car over to collect me?'

'Straight away? You bet.' His agent sounded relieved. 'We've got a million things to go through. Last night was a tour de force. You were marvellous. Wonderful. All the reviews are sparkling.'

'Good. Good.' He wondered if he'd get a sparkling review from Lana, too.

'There's also lots of speculation about you and *La Diva*.'

'Less good.' Evan let out a long sigh.

'I'll see you in a few minutes,' Rupert said. 'We can decide how to handle it.'

'I'm not coming straight back,' Evan said. 'There are a few things I need to sort out first.'

'Would you like to let your agent know what you're up to?'

'No.'

There was a pause before Rupert asked, 'Would you like to tell your best friend what you're doing?'

Evan rubbed his hand through his hair. How did he start to explain this? There were feelings floating to the surface that he couldn't even identify himself. He decided that he wouldn't even try to convey that to Rupert. 'I'm doing something that I should have done a long time ago,' he said.

Thirty-nine

The small mining village of Llangolleth looked largely un-changed as Evan David's sleek black limousine manoeuvred its way painfully through the streets of tiny terraced houses. But looks could be deceptive.

Evan did a rough calculation. He hadn't visited this place in over twenty years. It wasn't that he hadn't wanted to. It was just that he couldn't bring himself to face the journey. The brief show from the sun this morning over Cardiff Bay had been woefully shortlived. Now that he was down in the valleys, a fine mist still hung over the village and the River Taff. A con-stant drizzle had started, and Evan shivered despite the fact that the heater in the car was blasting out. His driver, Frank, was red in the face and looked like he might faint with the heat. As soon as he had thawed out, Evan would get him to turn the temperature down.

The smart BMWs and Mercedes so often seen in Cardiff had

now, not more than half an hour from the city, given way to rusty old Fords and Vauxhalls. The sleek chrome–and–glass buildings were replaced by dilapidated Victorian homes displaying immaculately clean net curtains but with paint peeling off the window frames. The one social club in Llangolleth had been boarded up. The corner shop had closed down and the streets were empty but for a mangy-looking barking dog. Scars from the long-gone mining industry were still visible on the hills.

This was the place of his birth. The place that was filled with memories he tried to avoid. Once a close community hewn from generations of stoic miners and their families, nestling in the shadow of the local pit and the mountainous slag heaps that it produced. His own family were no different. His father, Geraint, had—since he was a teenager—earned his meagre living by breaking his back in the filthy black hole of the pit as was expected of him. It was a difficult life, fraught with danger, but it was *their* way of life—along with his fellow miners, he worked hard by day and sang in the pit's male voice choir three nights a week. The only thing that stood him apart from his colleagues was the fact that, despite being choked day after day by coal dust, his voice had the clear, pure power to make the women of the village weep. His talent was respected throughout the valleys, making the Llangolleth Colliery Male Voice Choir in high demand for performances. Men would doff their caps to Evan's father when they passed him in the street and say, with a note of awe: 'There goes Geraint David. He has a voice.'

His mother, Megan, stayed at home and, it seemed at the time, baked wonderful cakes and ironed clothes all day long.

In the evenings the rhythm of her clicking knitting needles filled the house as she knitted toys for underprivileged children accompanied by the sounds of Enrico Caruso and popular opera star Mario Lanza, long before Pavarotti took over the mantle. These were the recordings from which he'd first learned to love the rich, foreign tones of opera as his father did, when he had first risked trying out his own voice as he sang along to the scratchy music, encouraged to feel the notes in his belly by his Da. Everyone said that he was destined to be a chip off the old block—he was Geraint David's boy, all right: from the top of his dark mess of hair, down to his ability to transform an ordinary tune to make it sound like an angel was singing. Their home was a happy one. Evan and his sister, Glenys, were the only two children produced by the union.

'Stop here, Frank,' Evan instructed, and the limousine pulled up outside his old family home in Thomas Street. There was another family living there now. The door was a different colour—a brave red shining out in the general greyness. There was a Sky satellite dish at the front, but little else had altered. Evan settled back in his seat with a heavy sigh.

Glenys had been a superb sister. Not one of these scaredy-cat, wet-blanket girls. She was a tomboy, robust and sturdy. Full of life. Glenys, meaning 'pure and innocent', was named for her maternal grandmother. Two years older than Evan, she was the one who was always in trouble for climbing trees or falling in the river or coming back with the blackened face of a coal miner from playing on the slag heaps, which definitely wasn't allowed. His father was for ever pounding home how dangerous they were.

His sister was also the one who showed him how to play

rugby, fish for minnows in the River Taff and arm wrestle. During the summer holidays they'd disappear into the fields for the entire day while she found branches they could use as see-saws, instructed him in the art of making daisy chains and how to catch frogs. She knew where all the best birds' nests were and what times the local trains ran so that they could play down by the railways tracks in what they mistakenly believed was relative safety. When Dai Jenkins had started to bully Evan after school, Glenys was the one who punched his adversary to the ground. His mother despaired when all her frilled dresses returned from their outings dirty and in shreds.

Apart from the annual holiday to Tenby or Anglesey—when very occasionally his father might 'go casual', which involved rolling up his trouser legs or his shirt sleeves and they were allowed to eat enough ice cream to make themselves feel sick— their lives passed unremarkably.

But that was all to end one grey winter afternoon. Their father was rehearsing for a concert in the local village hall, and Evan had begged to be allowed to go along, too. There was a fine drizzle settled over the valleys, meaning that any outdoor play would be banned and Evan would be forced to kick around the house for the rest of the day. His only solace would be if Da would let him go with him to the rehearsals. After a suitable amount of begging had been completed, his father had relented, but Evan was allowed out only on condition that Glenys come along, too, to keep an eye on him. Evan didn't feel that he needed keeping an eye on, but he didn't voice that opinion. Rhys Williams would be at the hall, too—along with a smattering of other children whose fathers had been badgered into letting them tag along. Unusually, Glenys hadn't wanted to go. She'd wanted to stay home and play with her dolls. Evan didn't know what was wrong with her today—she always loved to hear Da sing, too. Her face lit up in rapture whenever she watched him perform. More begging ensued and, eventually, she'd given in, but only after being threatened with the smarting side of her mother's hand and told to buck her ideas up and to look after her younger brother. Evan had rushed to get his coat and Glenys had been belted into her raincoat by their mother while his father tapped his foot impatiently on the front doorstep. Both children knew that Da's reluctance to take them along was only halfhearted. He was proud of them both and, occasionally, coaxed Evan to sing for the other choir members so that they could see how his voice was improving.

Glenys had dragged her feet along Thomas Street, grumbling all the way. As a token protest, she'd brought along a pale, cross-eyed rag doll she called Molly Dolly which she cuddled ferociously to her, which was not the way Glenys usually was. Normally, they sang all the latest hits when they walked together on the way to and from school. They liked the Beatles best of all—the valley rang to the sounds of 'I Want To Hold Your Hand', 'Can't Buy Me Love' and 'She Loves You'. Paul McCartney was Glenys's favourite Beatle. She thought she might marry him when she grew up. Despite the heavy skies that the village regularly enjoyed, his sister was for ever in sunshine. Like today's weather, the cloud was hanging over the hills that afternoon, rain seeped through their clothes, plastering their hair to their heads as they plodded and dawdled their way to the village hall, Da chivvying them along.

The hall nestled like a child's toy at the foot of the mountainous slag heap that provided a dramatic backdrop to the community. Their father had left them at the back, with a warning to behave themselves, and went to join his fellow singers on the stage. The atmosphere always lifted when his father arrived in a room, and his friends slapped him on the back as if they hadn't seen him for a long time—when Evan knew for a fact that he'd been working with them all just yesterday.

Glenys had helped Evan—her useless eight-year-old brother—out of his coat, fussed trying to make some sense of his hair and then had dragged him into the hall, sneaking into the rows of chairs that were already set out in preparation for the concert that night. Evan's friends were already there—all come along to listen to their dads, too—Rhys Williams, Dylan Hughes and Idris Edwards, whose Da was known as Arwel Ham Arms because of the gargantuan size of his biceps.

'Let's sit with the gang,' Evan whispered, and Glenys tutted her disdain for the ragged row of boys who were already wriggling on their chairs. 'Please, Glenys.' He was asking a lot of favours of his sister today, and he knew that he'd have to pay them back. Maybe she'd make him kidnap Mrs Jones's cat again so that she could put the hissing and spitting animal in her pram.

'On Top of Tredegar Moor' was already in full flow, their father's voice soaring away over all the others, his eyes directed heavenwards, as they took their places. Evan slid into the seat next to Rhys, and they nudged each other in lieu of greeting.

It was hot in the hall and Evan took off his jumper—a bright red home-knitted affair lovingly fashioned for him by his mother—his favourite sweater even though it made him as hot as a greenhouse. He folded it on the back of his chair, as Glenys had shown him and tried, in vain, to smooth his hair down again. Glenys digged him in the ribs.

The choir moved on to 'Blackbird Will You Go' and Evan and his friends whispered to each other along the row. They were all high with unspent energy through being cooped up indoors all morning. Glenys had already been transported and was sitting gazing at her father in awe. Her face took on a glow of happiness and she looked just like she did when she'd been the angel in the nativity play last Christmas. Evan wanted to concentrate on the music, too, but it was so difficult when Rhys kept talking to him.

'Evan, look.' His friend opened his hand, and he had a clutch of shiny new marbles. He tipped them into Evan's hands with ill-judged timing and, just as the singing stopped, the marbles clattered noisily to the floor and scattered beneath the chairs.

Geraint David was down from the stage in a flash, jerking Evan out of his chair by his arm. Humiliated in front of his friends, he was unceremoniously dragged down the length of the hall and was dumped in the last row of chairs by the door. 'If you can't behave, you can sit at the back by yourself,' his father said crossly. 'Any more mischief and I'll get your sister to take you home.'

'But, Da!' Evan started to protest his innocence. 'It wasn't me...'

Before he could finish his plea, there was a loud explosion, which shook the room. Evan turned and looked out of the window. 'The pit,' someone said with a note of panic in his voice, and a few of the men raced off the stage towards the door, knocking over their music stands in their haste.

Forty

There was a roaring sound like a jet plane flying too low over-head. Evan heard his dad shout, 'Get out of here!' and there was a mad scramble to obey.

Evan thought it was a plane coming to land on their heads and huddled into a tight ball, forehead on his knees. The roar-ing increased, and Evan watched open-mouthed as before his very eyes a huge spinning boulder smashed through the win-dow, flattening two of the choir members—Mr Vaughn and Mr Boyce—who were in its path. Then all the world went black as they were hit with a wall of shale, slurry and mud as the six-hundred-foot mountain of waste coal that had stood silently behind the village for years slid, with devastating speed, down the valley and engulfed the tiny hall.

All the people here knew that there were risks that came from living in the shadow of a slag heap and being perilously near to the pit head, but it was the landscape they lived with every day. The slippery components of the towering black masses shifted regularly, resettling their immense weight, but it was the price you had to pay for keeping jobs in the community. And no one could have imagined quite how catastrophic the consequences of a major slippage would be or how easy it would be to trigger.

When the roaring stopped, Evan remembered, there was the most unearthly silence. You could hear no noise from the road outside and no birds singing. Idris Edwards had somehow ended up next to him, though his head was at a funny angle and there was dark blood running from his nose. They were both half-buried by a horrible, foul-smelling slurry. Evan shook his friend, but he didn't move even though icy, black water was running round their legs and it was really frightening.

'Come on. Come on,' a voice said by his ear. It was Dylan Hughes, standing looking shell-shocked with his shirt all ripped down the front. His mam would kill him when she saw the state of him. Evan scrambled from under his chair, urging Idris to come with him, but still he wouldn't move. Across the hall he could see the dirtied arm of his red jumper stuck out from the mud. Evan struggled to wade towards it and he pulled it out. It was ruined. Shredded beyond recognition. His mother would tan his backside for that later. He picked it up and clutched it to him. Megan David could work wonders with her knitting needles—maybe she could mend it.

He couldn't see his Da or Glenys anywhere. Tangled music stands stuck out of the muck, and Arwel Ham Arms, face filthy and bleeding, tore at the black mass with his bare hands like a man possessed. All the men who had stood side-by-side with his Da on the stage had disappeared.

'Da!' Evan shouted. 'Da. Where are you?'

'Get out!' Arwel Ham Arms yelled at Evan.

'What about Da?' Evan heard his voice shake. 'What about Glenys?' They were there just a moment ago, where had they gone? Had they left without telling him? Had he been so naughty that Da had left him behind? Evan felt himself wanting to cry. Then he spotted a ruined Molly Dolly abandoned on the slurry and knew that it was a bad thing. Glenys would never be parted from her favourite toy if she could help it.

'Get out!' Arwel sounded frantic. 'Get out, quickly. Go for help.'

Dylan Hughes tugged at his arm and then scrambled ahead of Evan, scaling the pile of waste coal and mud which had smashed through most of the windows, blocking their exit. Evan couldn't even see the door. He couldn't see any of their friends, either—not even Rhys Williams, who was his best friend—they always went everywhere together.

'I can't leave Rhys,' Evan gasped, coughing as the dust choked his throat.

'He's gone,' Dylan told him and, at the time, he'd assumed that Dylan meant his friend had already left.

Rhys would have been cross if he'd found out that Evan was going off with Dylan without him—he could be funny like that. There was one window right at the top of the hall which was still intact. Dylan climbed higher, and when he reached the window he started to kick.

'What are you doing?' Evan asked in shock.

'I'm going home to Mam,' Dylan told him flatly. 'She'll know what to do.' His hands and knees were black and bleeding from scaling the coal. 'I'm not staying in here.'

It seemed like a sensible plan. Though Da would be furious that Dylan had broken one of the few windows that seemed to have survived the impact from the tip. Evan hoped that he didn't get blamed for that, too.

Forty-one

The limousine swung into Stackpole Street, and Evan instructed Frank to slow down. The place where the village hall used to be was now a children's playground. There was still a gap in a row of terraced houses where the cataclysmic slippage of waste coal had taken out the homes, smashing the solid bricks and mortar to the ground like matchsticks. The street now looked like a rictus mouth with all of its front teeth knocked out. A small, immaculately maintained memorial garden marked the tragic event with a neat brass plaque declaring that the disaster had claimed the lives of fifty miners, including twenty men from the Llangolleth Male Voice Choir and five of their children. Evan ran his fingers over the cool metal. Among them his father, Geraint David, and Glenys, his beloved sister.

Bright yellow daffodils swayed bravely in the cold breeze, the weight of the rain bowing their heads. The Prince of Wales had attended the memorial service and had planted a tree. Evan David, to his lasting shame, had stayed away. He was too angry, too hurt, too outraged, to have been able to mumble platitudes to visiting dignitaries who had no idea how this community had suffered. The noisy laughter of the children now playing on the gaily painted swings and the slide seemed alien to him. For so long after the disaster a pall of hush had fallen over the village.

Evan leaned forward and spoke to Frank. 'Let's go up to the cemetery.'

On that fateful day, Dylan had helped Evan to struggle through the window and the first shock was breathing fresh air again after the dust-laden atmosphere of the village hall. He remembered gulping it greedily into his lungs.

The second shock had been that the village hall was gone, smothered under the shale, completely obliterated by the shifting mass. The towering tip looked as if it had exploded like a volcano, leaving a crater the like of which Evan would have only expected to see on the moon, not in this sleepy village. They found out later that over half a million tons of coal waste had been loosened by three days of continual rain and set on its tragic route by an underground explosion from the pit. A tiny spark from a coal-cutter had ignited a build-up of gas caused by a fault in the colliery's ventilation system. A fault that Geraint David had complained about for years to his foreman at work and had continued to complain about every night when he returned home from the depths of hell.

A group of miners straight from the pit, still blackened from work and reeling from the impact of the explosion, were already on the scene when Evan and Dylan kicked their way out of the village hall. They dug frantically at the heap that had brought down trees, bricks, cars and anything else that had been in its voracious path, knowing that their colleagues were trapped inside. Evan folded the tattered remains of his jumper and left it on a wall while he too ran to claw at the coal with his hands, trying to reach his sister, until a policeman came and lifted him gently away while he struggled ineffectually at the air.

'My da's in there,' Evan said to him stricken. 'And my sister.'

'Come away, son,' the policeman said softly. 'There's nothing you can do for them now.'

Some of the miners, blackened with filth, were crying. Of his father and Glenys, there was no sign.

Moments later though, his mother, in her carpet slippers and still tying her headscarf over her hair, ran towards the hall. She'd brought all the towels from the house with her and Evan didn't know why. When she saw him, she ran to him and hugged him briskly while Evan tried to hide the remains of his jumper.

'Where's Glenys?' she'd demanded of him, shaking his shoulders. 'Where's your sister?'

'I don't know,' he'd answered, but feared the worst.

'Where's your da?' His mother had left him before he could answer to run to the coal heap, pushing aside anyone who tried to stop her. Other mothers joined her—Idris Edwards's mam among them and Evan didn't like to tell her what he knew—and they'd scrabbled at the muck and silt with their fingers until they bled while he stood on the sidelines, forgotten, along with his rescuer, Dylan, not knowing what to do.

After an hour or more, his father was lifted out of a window by policemen. His limbs were floppy like Molly Dolly's. He was cut and bleeding, his hair was matted with mud, his clothes torn and dirty. His da was laid on the ground, and a policeman covered him with a sheet. Which Evan thought was strange—how would his da be able to see with that all over his eyes?

Megan David couldn't stand unaided after that. She leaned against Mrs Edwards, her knees buckling with the weight of her limp body. As darkness fell, Evan's mother was persuaded to leave the scene, and one of the ambulance men washed and bandaged her hands, which were nothing more than bloody strips of raw skin. She took Evan home, but forgot to give him anything to eat. He bathed himself, getting dried with a rough flannel as all the towels were gone, while Megan David cried in front of the fire, making a terrible keening noise the like of which Evan had never heard before and never wanted to again. Then he sat with her in his pyjamas in silence, not knowing what to say. Later that night, leaving Evan alone and scared, his mother went with a policeman to the little Baptist chapel, waiting in line for hours to perform the grisly task of searching through the bodies wrapped in blankets until they found Glenys.

Today, Frank swung the limousine round the tight bends as they climbed towards the village cemetery, a place that seemed disproportionately large for the size of the community. The church stone was blackened with age, and Frank pulled into the car park outside the wooden, studded front door.

'I won't be long,' he said to his driver.

The older man's face was creased with concern. 'I could come with you, governor.'

Evan shook his head. 'I prefer to be alone.'

'There's an umbrella in the boot of the car.' The rain was heavier now, weighing down the grey sky. 'Let me get it for you.'

'Thanks,' Evan said, 'but I'll be fine.'

He wanted to feel the discomfort of the rain on his head. He wanted to feel it soaking through this ridiculously extravagant cashmere coat. This shouldn't ever be a visit undertaken in the glare of the summer sun.

Evan left the car and walked up the steep path through the cemetery. The ancient gravestones were higgledy-piggledy and fallen, the grass overgrown. Stones that needed repairing were tied up with yellow and black tape like the stuff they use to mark the scenes of crime in American cop movies. It was a mess, and someone should do something about it. The memorial garden at the top of the hill looked too new and too immaculately kept by comparison. No one had forgotten these graves. The stark white stones stood out against the gloomy landscape—the last of the treacherous slag heaps flattened many years ago due to public pressure. After the disaster, there had been a mass burial service and the sounds of crying had carried along the valley to the next village.

Megan David, having just rescued her husband and her only daughter from being buried in the earth, was forced to return them to it once more. It was a torture that she never recovered from. Her hair had turned white almost overnight. She learned that Glenys had been found wrapped in her father's arms, but the fact gave her no comfort. Illogically, his mother blamed herself for the tragedy—she should never have allowed her children to go to the rehearsal, she should have found an excuse to keep her husband at home. But Evan knew that it wasn't really his mother's fault—it was his. The fault was all his.

To say that nothing had ever been the same again was an understatement of magnificent proportions. The village, when the residents should have been mourning together in peace, went into battle against the coal board—who they blamed for the disaster by ignoring the miners' worries about the problems with ventilation in the mineshaft. Evan's mother no longer knitted in the evenings; his ruined red jumper was the last she ever made for him and she never did mend it. There were no more luscious cakes. Dust lay unnoticed on the furniture. The wonderful opera recordings lay unplayed. The only sound was the clock ticking.

Back then, there was no counselling, no talking about it, crying was not 'the done thing'. You simply had to sit on your feelings, button them down, zip them up tight. No one talked to him in the street. No cheery greetings were called after him. People turned away from him as if he were too awful to look at. He never played with Dylan Hughes after that day. Whenever they met at school, they just looked at each other sheepishly, and Evan wondered if Dylan too felt guilty about surviving when so many others had died. He went to the chapel with his mother and they said the prayers and listened to the hymns and, though no one ever mentioned it, everyone knew that the strongest, purest voices in the village were missing. Only five members of the Llangolleth Male Voice Choir survived and, after the disaster, they never sang again. Evan couldn't sing the hymns, either, even though he wanted to, as they made a big lump come to his throat and the words wouldn't come out.

Nothing seemed to matter to his mother anymore. When his high standards of academic achievement started to slip, she didn't chide him as Da would have. Failing to complete homework went unpunished. He could leave his neck unwashed for weeks and his mother wouldn't notice. Dai Jenkins stopped bullying him even though Glenys was no longer around to protect him. And Evan didn't sing Beatles songs on the way to school anymore.

He went along the lines of gravestones—the names so familiar and so many of them—Rhys Williams, his best friend. Idris Edwards. Merfyn Davis, who'd been so good at running that he won all the medals every sports day. Hywel Owen, who could make all the class laugh with his bad jokes and clowning—a born actor if ever there was one. Short lives snuffed out too soon. The rows and rows of miners' graves stood to attention behind them—men who had lived their lives underground. Evan wondered if the confines of the earth held some peace from them now. He truly hoped so.

Evan reached the grave of his father and his much-loved sister, Glenys. He laid his hand on the marble stone. In his eyes she had never aged. To him she was always ten years old. It was hard to accept that his father had been younger than Evan was now when he'd died. They'd now been joined by his mother. 'Reunited,' Evan had put on the headstone, and he prayed that it was the case. It was the last time he'd come back to the village; to attend Megan's funeral. His mother had never regained the will to live after the loss of her husband and her daughter and had simply taken her time to fade away. Who could survive after that? From that day she was as lifeless, as dead as the loved ones she'd buried.

He looked out over the magnificent valley—shrouded in mist today as then—the tiny, proud houses hugging its contours and his soul filled with sadness. At the age of eleven, after enduring three years of hearing his mother cry at night, even though she had boxes and boxes of unopened antidepressants in the bathroom cabinet, and too many nights lying in his bed alone wishing instead that he was lying in the earth with his da and with Glenys, he'd tried in his own way to cheer her up after she'd taken to her bed with a headache, to try in some small way to bring some happiness back to the house. He could bear the oppressive quiet no longer, so he'd stood in the sitting room and sang 'Oh Pure Heart'—his mother's favourite song. In the months of enforced silence something strange had happened to his voice, and it was his father's rich tone that leaped forth from his throat. Megan David had careened down the stairs, swinging him round by his arm as she lashed out at his head in a frenzy. 'Never ever do that again, Evan. Never,' she said, and then collapsed sobbing on the floor.

A month later, without her ever looking him in the eye again, he'd been sent away without consultation to a school that had specialised in music at Oxford. Which was far enough away for him not to be able to go home regularly. After not being allowed to sing a note at home for all that time, Evan still wondered how he'd managed to gain one of the coveted scholarship places. Perhaps his da or Glenys were still protecting him and knew that he had to be taken away from that terrible place. This time he knew that the fault didn't lie with him.

He could understand his mother's agony, but he'd never been able to address it with her. Why hadn't she been able to find succour in her one surviving son? Megan had never rejoiced in his success; never watched him on television; never listened to his recordings. She'd been embarrassed by his stardom, so he'd stopped returning home to face her torment. To his mother he would always sound too much like his father, and nothing he could do would ever help her to bear that pain. Evan had never been reconciled with her, and she died with too many unspoken issues lying unresolved between them. Too many other mothers had also joined their husbands and their children in their graves prematurely. It was heartbreaking to see. There were always fresh flowers on the Davids' family graves—Evan paid the mother of Rhys Williams, monthly by direct debit, to maintain it perfectly as she did her own husband and son's memorial. And it very nearly helped to assuage Evan's conscience.

Every single person from the village had been marked by the legacy of the disaster. Many of his friends took jobs at the colliery that had blighted their lives, that had robbed them of fathers, uncles and brothers. They went down into the darkness of the pit every day even though their hands shook. They married local girls and settled down to build the next generation of villagers, the next generation of miners, the next generation of sacrifice. Evan had done it differently; he'd been one of the few boys to escape and, if money and fame were a measure of success, he'd gone on to achieve greatness. He'd gone from the school on to music college to study opera and then to Brighton Conservatoire, where he'd excelled in his chosen field, graduating as best student in his year. Within months he'd made a sensational public debut by winning the Cardiff Singer of the World competition in front of millions of television viewers. He was immediately signed by top agent Rupert

Dawson, and his career sky-rocketed with a host of international appearances. His New York debut at the Met had warranted a front-page review in the *New York Times*—an unprecedented honour. Evan had embraced his success readily and had never looked back at this small village that had almost swallowed him. Now he was respected, courted and cosseted around the world. Yet he hadn't escaped unscathed. Evan hadn't wanted to marry a village girl. Or any of the other girls he'd been involved with over the years—if you could count casual dating as being 'involved'. Any form of emotional involvement was the one thing he'd steadfastly avoided. Since then, he wanted to be alone, untouched by the pain of love.

He took a pristine white flower from the grave that entombed his devastated mother, his strong, capable father from whom he'd inherited all his God-given talent and his beautiful sister, and he crushed the fragile petals in his hands. What if he'd found someone who made him want to sing Beatles songs with her again—someone like Fern, perhaps—would she, too, be cruelly snatched away from him? How could he ever hold a child of his own in his arms and not shake with terror at what the future might bring? The very thought of it made him go cold. But what was the point of his life, his success, if all of it was to be endured alone? It caused him great anguish to admit it, but he was tired of being isolated in his own life, of being by himself. Wasn't it time he summoned up the courage to open up and share his life with someone else? He knew only too well that loving and losing someone could ruin your life, forcing you into a dark place that left you unable to function at anything more than a primary level. Could he ever risk loving so much again? Was he prepared to put everything else that he'd worked so hard for in his life on the line for that chance? He'd built an impenetrable bubble round himself, and now he longed for someone to come along and pop it, to liberate him. With help, surely he would be able to break free and step back into the real world once more?

He looked at the sky and cried. This village, this tragedy, this loss, was still in his blood, coursing through his veins. To keep the darkness away was a constant effort. That was why he always needed to be in bright, airy apartments with big rooms. Why he needed windows that didn't have curtains to obscure them. Why the noise of jet engines sent a chill arrow of fear into his heart. Why he kept himself healthy with handfuls of vitamins, punished himself with a stringent fitness regime. And it was why, when he was alone at night, he still slept with the light on.

Forty-two

'**W**ho are you?'

I spin round and see my dad standing in the kitchen doorway scratching his head in a confused manner. 'What?'

'Who are you?' he repeats. 'What am I doing here?'

I wolf down my cereal, despite the fact my nervous stomach has decided we don't want to eat. 'I don't have time for this, Dad,' I say, showing him the hand. 'Today is very important for me. This is the first round of the television competition for the *Fame Game,* and I have to have all my wits about me.'

'Tell me your name,' my dad responds as if he's hypnotised. 'Do I know you? Has the war ended?'

Clearly, my dad's wits are nowhere to be seen.

I put down my bowl. 'So what's this? Imaginary amnesia? Is that what you're supposed to have now? Tourette's syndrome not working quickly enough?'

At this point, my aged parent would normally tell me to 'fuck off', but he doesn't.

'Where am I?' He looks round at my kitchen in dazed wonderment.

'Oh, for heaven's sake, snap out of this.' I march through to the lounge and bash my way into the computer, checking Dad's Internet history when it eventually gears up.

Ah. He's been on all the information sites for Alzheimer's disease. So I wasn't too far wrong in my guess at amnesia, but I guess he feels that Alzheimer's will elicit more sympathy. Some hope.

'Alzheimer's?' I say when I'm back in the kitchen. 'Is that the best you can manage?'

'Is this breakfast time?' he asks, gazing vacantly around him. 'What do I like to eat?'

'I hope you like to eat cheap and nasty cereal,' I tell him, 'because that's all we've got.'

Dad sits down at the table, and with much dramatic banging, I pour out a bowl of cereal and put it in front of him.

'Thank you,' he says. 'You're a very nice person.' Dad tucks into his cereal. 'Whoever you are.'

'This won't work,' I advise him. 'This won't work at all. Mum is managing very nicely without you.'

He flinches at that.

'Can't you see this is all a waste of time? Mum doesn't care about you anymore, and I can't say that I blame her when you're putting on this silly display. No wonder she's more interested in Mr Pat—'

Now my dad is wide awake. His eyes have popped out on stalks and his jaw has dropped open. Although, ironically, he does look slightly more catatonic than he did a moment ago.

'I'm going,' I say hastily. 'I don't want to be late for my big chance.'

'What did you just say?' he demands to know—and not in a poor-me-I've-lost-my-memory way.

'Nothing,' I say. 'I can't remember. Perhaps I've got Alzheimer's, too.'

I grab my bag from the chair. I don't have to take anything with me today as they're giving me a complete makeover—hair, clothes, everything. The only thing I had to do was get up at the crack of dawn to make sure that I was in the shower before Dad so that I'd actually have some hot water.

As if to wish me good luck, Squeaky pops out of his bolt-hole and I go over and give him a cornflake. If I didn't think he'd bite me, I'd probably kiss him.

'Leave this mouse alone while I'm out,' I warn my dad in my sternest voice. 'Don't you dare terrorise him.'

Dad looks at me blankly. There's a knock at the door and I know that it's Carl come to give me a lift to the television studios. The *Fame Game* team would have sent along a car to collect me, but—once again—I couldn't bear for anyone to see where I really live, which makes me think that I must try to do something about upgrading my embarrassing accommodation before too long.

I let Carl in and he joins us briefly in the kitchen, while I fuss with tidying away stuff that I really don't need to—putting off the minute when we need to depart.

'Morning, Derek,' Carl says brightly to my dad.

'And who are you?' Dad replies, at which my friend frowns.

'Don't start that again,' I snap over my shoulder.

Carl looks suitably shocked at my outburst.

'He's developed Alzheimer's,' I explain. 'Overnight.'

'Oh,' Carl says. 'I'm sorry to hear that.'

'It's not all bad news,' I tell him. 'Miraculously, the Tourette's syndrome has cleared up.'

'Oh, good.' Carl grins while my dad scowls darkly at both of us. And, despite extreme provocation, there are still no colourful expletives forthcoming from my parent.

Carl rubs his hands together. 'So. How are you feeling?'

'Nervous,' I admit. I haven't done anything yet and my palms are sweating.

'Piece of cake,' he tells me. 'You'll walk it.'

'You'd better get me there in one piece first,' I remind him.

With that Carl hands over a crash helmet. 'We're on the scooter,' he says. 'Put on the skidlid and no arguments.'

I can hardly complain that it will mess up my hair, as I haven't done a thing with it. I'm going to hand myself over to the *Fame Game* stylists and let them do their worst.

'You could wish me good luck,' I say to my dad as we prepare to leave.

'Good luck,' he says grudgingly.

And to think that I'm putting myself through this to try to give my family—including my ungrateful father—a better life. Sometimes I wonder why I bother.

Forty-three

'I wish you'd come in with me.' I'm at the point of begging Carl to stay. He's just dropped me off at the stage door of the main BBC television studios in White City, having skirted the traffic expertly on his little borrowed phutt-phutt.

'You're better on your own,' he assures me.

I'm not sure how he's worked that out, but Carl has become convinced that he is no longer my good luck talisman and is bound to bring me all kinds of bad karma. Frankly, I'd rather have him by my side and take my chances. But my friend is quietly stubborn and, after hugging and kissing me half to death, he leaves me standing there while he walks away, blowing another kiss in my direction as he goes. My heart squeezes as I see him putter away on his scooter. Now I feel truly alone.

There are a few faces I recognise from the last audition, getting out of posh cars and skipping up to the stage door. I don't feel like skipping. I feel like slitting my throat. Once again, they all look so much more 'up for it' than I feel. Why am I so wracked with doubt and insecurities? This is not the way for a potential pop superstar to behave. Carl would be kicking my backside—which is, I guess, what I need him here for. Just ten of us have made it this far. Out of all the thousands of hopefuls, I'm one of the few who got here. I should be proud to be among them. And I should give myself a pep talk: these *Fame Game* people know what they're doing and I haven't got through to the finals by mistake.

Girding my loins, I go through the hideous process of getting past security—which seems to involve signing my life away—and into the BBC building, and then I'm whisked into a vast studio to wait my turn to rehearse. The *Fame Game* folk have asked me to sing 'The First Time Ever I Saw Your Face' again as I did in the auditions, but instead of doing it unaccompanied, I'm going to be backed by the string section of the *Fame Game* orchestra, which is terrifying as I've never been backed by anything or anyone other than my lovely Carl before and I can feel the ante being notched up further and further.

Sitting on the sidelines, I watch as the other acts go through their routines. There's a young guy singing old Glam Rock tunes with gusto; a frighteningly pubescent girl doing the obligatory Britney Spears song; some smarmy boy-next-door soul guy singing Motown classics—and absolutely no one as old as me. But do you know what? I'm as good as them. I know I am. I have what it takes to win this. If I can keep a grip on my nerves, then I could be in with a fighting chance. Only the cutesy boy band singing opera songs has got me terrified. My heart sinks to my boots. If I'd tried very hard, I could have almost forgotten that one of the judges I'm going to have to face is Evan David.

★ ★ ★

Several hours later, I'm polished, preened, plucked within an inch of my life and ready—it is deemed—to face my public. I have my own Hollywood-style mirror and my very own make-up artist, Kirsty. It takes me back to my last evening with Evan David, and I try very hard not to think about it as it will make me want to cry and Kirsty has just spent ten minutes applying layer after layer of mascara and probably wouldn't thank me for it. I am, however, sharing the dressing room with all the other female contestants, so I try to pull myself together.

'I'm finished,' Kirsty announces. She fluffs my hair and leaves me to admire myself.

Even I have to admit that Kirsty has done a wonderful job. She has taken a sow's ear and turned it into the veritable silk purse. I stare into the mirror at this goddess before me and can hardly believe that it's me.

'Do you like it?'

'I love it,' I gasp.

My mad, flyaway hair with a life of its own has been transformed into a mane of glossy curls that frames my face. My stubby barmaid's fingernails are long, graceful talons thanks to the miracle of acrylic. I'm wearing jeans, but designer ones, that cajole everything into the right place, vertiginous heels that make my legs look like those of a giraffe, and I can quite safely say without contradiction that I've never, ever exposed so much cleavage in all my life. And now I'm going to do so on national telly.

A gulp travels down my throat. Oh, my giddy aunt. I look like a pop star. A real pop star, not some poor old girl they've dragged in off the street for the pity vote. The regulars at the

King's Head will never look at me in the same way again. If I don't recognise myself, am I in with a chance that Evan David won't, either? A fat chance, I think is the answer to that. I feel sick with nerves.

The programme has already started, but I can't bear to look at the monitors. I have no desire to see what's waiting for me out on the studio floor. My rehearsal with the orchestra went brilliantly, and I can only hope that my performance will be half as good on the night when it counts. I even saw one of the PR Identikit girls wipe a tear from her eye when I'd finished.

'Ten minutes and then we're ready for you, Fern,' someone with a clipboard and headphones announces.

A tremor starts to shake my whole body and won't stop. I pick up a copy of *Hello!* magazine which is lying next to me and start to flick through it in an effort to distract myself. I get halfway through the magazine, aimlessly scanning the orange faces of the übercelebs when I'm stopped in my tracks. Smiling out at me— well, scowling really—is the face of Evan David, and he's wrapped round a comely dark-haired woman who, the caption tells me, is opera star Lana Rosina. And very glamorous she looks, too. My confidence takes a nosedive. They're going into a hotel foyer and I think I can draw my own conclusions from that. An unreasonable green mist descends on me. I was never anything to Evan David, so why should I feel so damn jealous? And if I was labouring under the illusion that he felt anything for me, then this is evidence enough that he's soon got over me. Closing the magazine, I give an involuntary shudder. Now I want to face him even less.

I'm sure that the headphone-bedecked girl was lying, because she comes back in what seems to be about ten seconds later and tells me that it's time to go.

To a chorus of 'Good luck, Fern,' I follow her through the corridor towards the studio. On stage the young glam rocker is strutting his stuff. He's good. The crowd, all bearing banners emblazoned with his name, are cheering and clapping as he comes to his big finish. And then, out of the corner of my eye, I see Evan David sitting in the middle of the panel of judges at the front of the stage. He's wearing his customary monochrome colours—a black linen suit with a grey silk T-shirt. He looks tanned, healthy, relaxed, and he toys with his pen, tapping it on the desk along with the rhythm of the music. My insides turn to liquid. I don't know if this feeling is love or fear or a potent mix of both, but I'm smashed with a fist of emotion, the strength of which I've never experienced before.

And then I know with absolute certainty that I can't do this. I can cope with the unfamiliar orchestration. I can cope with the live audience and the fact that the programme will be broadcast to over twelve million homes. I can cope with all that. I just can't go out there and face Evan David. Not like this.

My heart is beating too fast. Sweat breaks out on my brow. I turn to the woman with the clipboard. She's deep in concentration, watching the floor manager and the cameramen. The glam rocker finishes his song and rapturous applause breaks out. She starts to mutter something into her headphones to someone unseen, and while she's doing this, I tiptoe silently away.

The minute she realises that I've gone, she spins around. 'Fern!' she barks at my rapidly departing back. But I don't stop. No way. I'm outta here.

My tiptoeing picks up speed and I race along the corridor,

knocking over waiting assistants and some of the other contestants in my ungainly flight. The woman with the clipboard
pursues me. 'Stop her!' she shouts, and several people lunge
for me as I run.

I know that I'm letting people down. At home Joe will be
watching out for me with Nathan who is loads better and out
of hospital now, thank goodness. Mum may be there, too, if
she's not too busy gallivanting with Mr Patel. Carl will die a
thousand deaths when I don't appear on screen and will, of
course, blame himself. All the regulars at the King's Head were
going to tune in and vote for me, too. But I can't think about
that now. I just have to get out of this place.

My athleticism has never been one of my strongest points,
but believe me, I could make the Olympic sprint team with
the time I'm putting in. My breath is coming in heavy pants,
and I can hear my heart pounding to the beat of the footsteps
behind me. It's accelerating alarmingly, rat-tat-tatting against
my chest, and my legs are on fire. I keep on pumping, dashing through the corridors, pursued by a variety of people from
the *Fame Game* shouting my name until I burst out through
the stage door. Ducking under the security barrier, I pass the
bemused guards and then I fly across Wood Lane, dodging the
traffic and leaving my pursuers behind. Someone is waving
their fist. My God, what have I done? I've left the *Fame Game*
firmly in the lurch, that's what.

I have no money for a train ticket, so despite my vertiginous
heels, I vault the ticket machines at the entrance to White City
Underground station and run down onto the platform. Thankfully, no one from London Underground takes up the pursuit,
because running any more would surely kill me. A Tube train

is just departing and I squeeze inside the doors and fling my-self down on one of the seats, puffing outrageously. The train rattles out of the station and I sit back, trying to catch my breath and contemplating the fact that I have just spectacularly, com-pletely and utterly, blown it.

Forty-four

'Would anyone care to offer any explanations?' Pop impresario and producer of the *Fame Game* show Stephen Cauldwell was not a happy man.

His staff shuffled uncomfortably in front of him. The champagne was flowing, but Evan stood on the sidelines with nothing stronger than a glass of sparkling mineral water. They were in the Green Room—the obligatory television hospitality suite—after the conclusion of the first part of the *Fame Game*. Now they all had to hang around for an hour until the phone voting element was complete while they went back into the studio and gave the public the benefit of their wisdom, and then they could finish for the night. Though why he was in a rush to go back to an empty apartment, Evan wasn't quite sure.

The show had been every bit as much of a trial as he'd imagined. Not one of the performers they'd seen had real talent, and the whole thing just seemed to be an ego trip for the other judges. Evan, quite frankly, could have lived without it. Even the operatic boy band had failed to lift his spirits. Tomorrow, he would remind himself to kill Rupert for ever getting him involved with this.

'Where did she go?' Stephen Cauldwell wanted to know. The guy looked as if he was about to stamp his foot. 'Why didn't anyone stop her?'

One of the acts—a duo called Just the Two of Us—had, Evan learned, thought better of appearing on the show and had made a break for it just before they were due to go on air. It had caused complete havoc behind the scenes. The next act had been rushed onto the floor and had appeared nervy and unprepared because of it. The running order went to pot, with the whole programme having to be padded out to fill the resulting gap. It was something that had never happened to the production team before.

'She just bolted,' the woman with the clipboard mumbled. She seemed to be the one in the main firing line. 'No one could catch her.'

'This is terrible,' Stephen Cauldwell continued. 'She was the best damn performer we've ever had on this show and we just *lost* her.'

Everyone looked suitably chastised.

'What do I pay you guys to do?' Stephen Cauldwell snatched up his glass of champagne. 'There will be a post-mortem. And it won't be pretty. Someone's head will be on the block for this.'

The woman with the clipboard looked worried.

'Get out of my sight. The lot of you.'

Stephen's crew shuffled out of the room. The producer pinned the smile back on his face. 'Sorry, Evan,' he smarmed. 'Sorry about that.'

Evan gave him a shrug by way of a reply.

Stephen shook his head. 'Cock-ups happen,' he said, 'but we never made any contingency plans for this. Jeez. Who'd do live television, eh?' The producer gave a strained laugh. 'She was bloody good, too. Bloody good. She had this in the palm of her hand. The prize is a recording contract with my label, but between you, me and the gatepost, I would have signed her up anyway.'

'And what about the bloke?' Evan asked.

'What bloke?'

'I thought the act was a duo. Just the Two of Us?' Not that he was particularly interested, it just seemed polite to make conversation and try to calm Stephen down before the next part of the show. 'Was she the only one with any talent?'

'Oh, yeah,' Stephen said dismissively. 'We blew the bloke out at the audition stage. Good guitarist, but too much of a hippy, if I remember rightly. I don't know why she didn't change the name, or perhaps it was us that forgot to.' Another dark look crossed his face. 'But, yeah. She was the only one with any talent.'

'Shame.'

'Terrible shame. Can't believe she just fucked off.'

Evan thought it sounded like quite a feisty thing to do—not that he'd voice that opinion just at the moment.

Stephen knocked back his champagne and poured himself another glass. He waved the bottle at Evan in invitation, but he declined. The producer ruefully shook his head again. 'I thought Fern was made of sterner stuff.'

Evan David felt the hairs on the back of his neck rise. Despite the stuffy heat of the room, for some reason he'd suddenly developed goosepimples. He was sure that the temperature of his blood dropped a few degrees. 'Fern?'

'Yeah.' Stephen brightened. 'Have you heard of her?'

'I'm not sure,' he heard himself say. Fern? Surely it couldn't be her. She said she only sang at family weddings when she was drunk.

'Great voice. Great arse,' Stephen summarised.

'You don't happen to have a publicity photograph of her, do you?'

'Yeah.' Stephen rummaged through a folder on the nearby table. 'There must be one here somewhere.' After a few moments of searching, he pulled out a photograph and sighed. 'If I wasn't such a nice guy,' he said, 'I'd be really pissed off about this.' He handed the picture to Evan.

Before he looked at it, Evan knew he was right. It was Fern. *His* Fern.

Forty-five

I feel as if I'm in a trance when I finally manage to stagger off the Tube at Oxford Circus station. I don't want to go home, and I'm in such a daze that I pick the first station where I think my legs will support me. Luckily, at the bottom of one of the escalators, I see a guy that Carl and I know who's busking one of our pitches in the Underground. With a bit of chat and schmoozing I manage to blag a fiver from him so that I can buy a Tube ticket and not add getting arrested for fare dodging to the list of stupid things I've done today. Sure enough, I'm sufficiently coherent to sweet-talk one of the guards and pay my legitimate fare from White City without too much pain. And, to be honest, that little bit of interaction seems to sap the last of my strength, as I'm barely able to haul myself out of the Tube and onto the street.

Oxford Street is virtually empty at this time of night; the crowds of shoppers and the pickpockets have long gone. The red, double-decker buses trundle up and down largely unhindered; the normally bustling shops are all shuttered up for the night. The bright lights blur together and I have a post-traumatic stress headache coming on. I sit on a bench next to a very smelly bum and phone Carl on my mobile.

'What happened?' he says immediately, concern thick in his voice. Clearly he noticed that I was conspicuous by my absence on the television show.

'I fucked up,' I tell him tearfully. 'I fucked up big time.'

'Where are you?'

'In Oxford Street. Sitting on a bench outside the huge H&M store.' I start to cry. 'I don't know what to do.'

'Don't move,' he instructs me. 'I'll be there as soon as I can.'

And with that Carl hangs up and I sit there and cry some more. Big self-pitying tears. Eventually, I'm depressing the bum so much that he offers me a swig of his cider to cheer me up. And, this is how low I've sunk, I accept it and drain half of the bottle, which brings a touch of alarm to his eyes. Perhaps he is regretting feeling sorry for such a madwoman. I hand over the change I have from the fiver I blagged to pay my Tube fare as some sort of recompense.

Whether it's minutes or aeons later, I don't know, but soon Carl is beside me and he hoists me up, wrapping me in his arms, shushing my tears and stroking my lovely pop star hair. He rocks me back and forth while I wail like a banshee.

'What on earth went wrong?' he wants to know when I finally pull myself together enough to stop sobbing.

'I just couldn't go through with it,' I croak. 'I saw Evan David sitting there as large as life in the front row and I lost my bottle.' In truth, I thought of all the lies I told him, all the sloping off from work to further my own cause and, quite honestly, I knew I wouldn't be able to look him in the eye—let alone lay my soul on the line before him.

'Oh, Fern,' is all that Carl says.

'I need to be drunk,' I tell him. 'I need to be very drunk. Take me to a terrible pub somewhere and ply me with strong drink until I'm unconscious.'

'We could go to the King's Head. They'll all be worried about you.'

'I want to be among strangers. I couldn't stand anyone asking me difficult questions.' Or any kind of questions.

'Phone Joe,' Carl advises. 'They'll all be worried sick.'

'You ring him,' I plead. 'I don't want to speak to anyone.'

'Not even your brother?'

I shake my head.

With a sigh, Carl finds Joe's number on his mobile phone and in a brief conversation to my nearest and dearest explains that I have messed up and that he is about to take me out to get me completely bladdered.

'He's sorry,' Carl says when he hangs up. 'No one blames you for this, Fern.'

'I blame me,' I say.

I don't know where Carl takes me, but it is, indeed, a terrible pub. We're crushed up into the corner of a place knee-deep with rowdy people and thick with smoke. Every mouthful of my drink follows a tortured route of elbow-jogging until it gets to my mouth, but it isn't hampering my progress much. I can't tell you how much I've had to drink, but I know it's lots. Lots and lots.

But oblivion isn't coming. In fact, reality is hitting home

rather too hard. I keep reliving my pathetic sprint from fame, and I can't get the picture of Evan David's face from out of my brain. Each time I go over it doesn't make it get any better. 'Vodka,' I demand. 'Give me vodka.'

'I think you've had enough,' Carl tells me, sounding rather more sober than I do.

'Nooo,' I slur. 'Need more.'

'I think you don't.'

And, as I slither down the wall, I think Carl might be right.

He hoists me up once more and, arms tight around me, guides me towards the door. Out on the street, the fresh air makes my head reel. Carl risks letting go with one arm while he hails a taxi and while a few, quite sensibly in my opinion, give us a wide berth, one idiot eventually stops. My friend loads me into the back of the cab, where I promptly slide off the seat and onto the floor.

'She'd better not throw up,' the cab driver warns Carl.

'She'll be fine,' Carl assures him, rather recklessly I think, and gives the driver his address, which is only a few minutes away.

My dearest, darling friend picks me up off the floor, physically and metaphorically, and puts me back on the seat. Then he collapses into a heap next to me.

I start crying again. What a wreck. What a useless wreck I am. I've let everyone down. I've let myself down and, more importantly, I've let Carl down. And he so does not deserve this after all that he has done for me. I feel terrible. More terrible than I ever thought I'd feel. Gulping back the tears, I take hold of Carl's hand and say, 'Do you hate me?'

'No, Fern.' Carl exhales a long and unsteady breath. He turns towards me and fixes me with an unwavering gaze. 'I love you.'

Forty-six

Carl lives in a housing association flat behind Euston station, not far from my parents' place. The tiny one-bedroomed digs are in a marginally worse state of repair than mine. His front door looks like a dozen people have tried to kick it in this week. Carl lives here alone apart from about two dozen guitars, an electric keyboard and a bunch of amplifiers in a range of sizes and ear-splitting volumes.

My friend is very tidy for a rock 'n' roll rebel. Whereas my flat could quite easily pass for a student squat, Carl's dishes are always washed and his bathroom sparkles. You do have to clamber over the aforementioned musical equipment though.

'Do you want tea?' Carl asks.

I nod, immediately regretting the violent movement, and he deposits me on the sofa while he goes off to do domesticated things. I'd like to tell you that I managed to sober up in the taxi on the way home, but that would be a lie. Yet another one. How easily they trip off your tongue once you start.

I've kicked off my shoes and have sprawled out on the cushions, but have singularly failed to make the room stop rotating by the time Carl comes back with two steaming hot mugs of tea and a plate of toast.

'I don't suppose you've eaten, either,' my friend says, which makes me cry again.

He sits down next to me and pulls a nice, buttered bit from the toast and feeds it to me. I chew lethargically, but swallow it down obediently until the whole slice is gone. Then he gives me sips of tea until the mug is drained.

'Better?' Carl asks.

And I nod, even though I'm not. My head is still spinning as much as the room is. Carl leans against me, letting his head fall back against the sofa. 'What are we going to do with you?'

Nestling into his shoulder, I say weakly, 'Look after me.'

'Don't I always?' Carl gives me an affectionate squeeze. 'We should get you to bed. You're going to have a thumping headache in the morning. I don't know if I've got any clean sheets though.' He looks worried and chews at his lip.

Whether Carl's sheets are clean or not is the least of my worries.

'I'll bed down on here.' He pats the sofa.

I look up at him. 'Carl...I don't want to be by myself tonight.'

'I'm here for you. You know that.'

'I mean...' I hesitate over the words. 'Stay with me. Tonight.'

'That's too much vodka talking,' Carl says, putting his finger on the end of my nose.

'It's not.' I run my hands over the front of his jacket, fiddling with the Levi's–stamped buttons. 'It's…it's… I want to… I want to…' I want to feel something other than pain and guilt, but I don't know how to say it as my brain is fuddled with alcohol.

'If you're offering to sleep with me, Fern, then that's very nice. But having waited for about seventeen years to consummate our platonic relationship, I'd really rather do it when you're sober.'

'I don't know what you mean,' I say and that's the last thing I remember.

I wake up in Carl's bed. The sheets are very crumpled, but they look perfectly clean to me. I'm worried that both sides of the bed look equally crumpled though. Did Carl and I end up sleeping together?

My vertiginous heels and my jeans have been removed, but when I check my underwear, it's all where it should be. Surely that's a good sign? Lifting my head from the pillow, I realise that it is a bad, bad thing to do. With a superhuman effort, I haul myself out of bed, pull a sheet round me and stagger towards the kitchen. I will never, ever drink again. Never. Ever.

Carl is already in the kitchen. While he scrambles some eggs he's whistling softly, which hurts my ears.

'Hi,' I croak from the doorway, sounding more like gravel-voiced Barry White than is healthy in a woman.

Carl spins round. 'Whoa!' he says, recoiling. 'You look like a spat–out Smartie.'

'I feel like one.'

'Sleep well?'

'I think so.'

'Scrambled eggs?'

I shake my head which is also a bad, bad thing. 'No.'

'Yes,' Carl says. 'It will do you good.'

I sidle into the kitchen, pulling my sheet tighter around me, and lean on Carl's cupboards in order to stay upright. Even in my dull-sensed state I feel that Carl is looking a bit hot this morning. My friend is even more tousled than he normally is and it suits him. He's wearing just his jeans, and somehow the rips seem to be in all the right places—teasing little glimpses of his legs peep out. I haven't seen Carl in such a state of undress for a very long time. His feet are bare as he pads about his kitchen, and that also seems incredibly sexy. Grunge has never looked quite so gorgeous. My eyes drift towards the bedroom. Carl follows my gaze.

I clear my throat and rasp, 'Did we…?'

'Yes,' Carl says. 'It was wild. *You* were wild. I was shocked. I didn't know you did those things. Are they legal?'

I smile at my friend. 'So we didn't?'

'No,' he admits. 'Of course not. Call me strange, but when I have sex with a woman, I kind of like her to be conscious.'

'Oh.'

'I have, however, stored your kind invitation to share your body for future reference. I think that also requires an "oh."'

'Oh,' I oblige.

'Your eggs are ready.'

Taking the plate, I go through to the lounge. Carl follows and sits opposite me on the one armchair.

'Thanks,' I say.

'For the eggs or for not ravishing you?'

'Both,' I admit.

We avoid looking at each other and concentrate on our eggs instead. Among other things that Carl's wonderful at, I now discover he makes great scrambled eggs, too. I balance the plate precariously on my knees, and the heat of it burns through to my skin.

'Want to tell me a bit more about yesterday?'

'Not really,' I sigh.

'In the cold light of day does it still feel as if you did the right thing?'

'No,' I confess with a heavy heart. 'What I should have done was arrange to speak to Evan before the show to clear the air.'

'Maybe they wouldn't have let you do that.'

'I should have at least asked,' I say. 'That would have been the grown-up, sensible thing to do. Then I could have gone on the show and given it my best shot. I can't believe that I blew something that was so important to me. To us.' I want to hang my head in shame. 'Perhaps I just haven't got the right temperament for the big time. Perhaps I'm destined to sing at the King's Head for ever.'

'I don't believe that and neither do you.'

'Thanks for being so bloody reasonable about this, Carl.' I give him a sad smile. 'And thanks for not taking advantage of me when I was…vulnerable.'

'Lashed on vodka, you mean.'

We both laugh.

'Thanks for being my best mate.'

'Is that all I'm ever destined to be?'

I can't answer that, so say nothing.

'You're not likely to offer me your body again, are you?' Carl says, suddenly serious.

'Oh, you never know,' I quip lightly. It's not that I don't adore Carl—I do. But we managed to survive our break-up as teenagers, and I don't think we would if it happened again as adults. I'm scared to become more intimate with Carl because I'm even more scared of losing him as a friend. What if our relationship didn't work out—could we ever salvage our death-defying friendship once again? I don't know that I want to risk it. Plus there's another complication, of course. Despite looking 'hot' in the kitchen just now, Carl doesn't turn my legs to jelly anymore. He did do once, when I was fifteen years old, but I've known him for too long to be turned on like that. I can hardly bear to say this, but my emotions have moved on since then. Evan David, on the other hand, makes me feel exactly like a gauche fifteen-year-old again, and my legs definitely turn to jelly when he's around. Unfortunately, my brain does, too.

'I think I do,' he says in answer to my quip. 'You must love Evan David very much.'

It doesn't lift my spirits to say so, but I blurt out, 'I guess so.'

'But he's just screwed up your life.'

'No,' I say. 'I think we've just established that I managed to do that all by myself.'

My friend stabs at his scrambled egg with his fork. 'You would have won that stupid competition, Fern.'

And Carl's quite possibly right. But that doesn't make me feel any better at all.

Forty-seven

The doorbell rang insistently. 'All right. All right. Keep yer hair on!'

Derek Kendal jumped off the sofa, twitched the curtain and looked out of the lounge window onto the busy morning street. A very posh car was parked outside Fern's door. Derek pursed his lips. 'Who the hell's that?'

It wasn't a visitor for him, that was for sure. He glanced at his watch. Ten o'clock and still no sign of his daughter. He wondered what had happened last night. Hadn't she said that she was supposed to be on that *Fame Game* show? Yet he'd watched virtually all of the programme—apart from the odd minute when the weight of his eyelids had got the better of him—and she hadn't appeared. Since then he hadn't heard a word from her, and that wasn't like Fern. She was a good girl. Now some idiot was dragging him from his sleep when all he wanted to do was avoid thinking about his current predicament.

Derek struggled down the narrow stairs, pulling on his shirt as he went. The doorbell chimed again.

Derek snatched open the door. 'I'm not deaf,' he said.

A tall, smart man stood in front of him. Well-groomed. The posh car was clearly his. The man tapped his foot impatiently.

'I'm looking for Fern Kendal,' he said without any other introduction.

'She's not here.'

'This *is* her house?' The man took in the crumbling doorway rather sceptically.

'Yes.' Derek eyed him with suspicion. 'I'm her dad. Does she owe you money?'

'No, no,' the man said briskly. 'I just need to get in touch with her. Urgently. I've tried her mobile phone, but she's not answering it. Do you know where she is?'

'No,' Derek admitted reluctantly.

'This is very important,' the man continued. 'I want her to contact me. As soon as she can.'

Derek nodded.

'Can I leave a message for her?'

He nodded again.

The man reached into his pocket and pulled out a business card and an expensive-looking pen. He scribbled on the back of the card and then handed it over to Derek. 'You will remember to give it to her?'

'Yes.'

'Thank you. It's really very important.'

'No worries,' Derek said. Did the bloke think he was an idiot?

'I want to see if I can work things out with her,' the man said. 'Can you tell her that?'

Then, glancing anxiously over his shoulder, the man stepped back into the posh car. Pulling smoothly away, it joined the stream of traffic, its gleaming curves standing out like a sore thumb amid the usual rusty white Transit vans that travelled this road.

Derek closed the door and carefully studied the card before sliding it into his trouser pocket as he climbed back up the stairs. He gave a satisfied smile. Wonder what that was all about? Clearly the guy was desperate to see Fern.

So that was Stephen Cauldwell, the man who was the brains behind the *Fame Game.* Looked like he'd made a few bob from it, Derek thought.

Forty-eight

Rupert Dawson clapped Evan on the back. 'How's the voice today?'

'The voice is fine,' Evan said. Which was true. It was just the rest of him that was feeling terrible.

He was having trouble sleeping. Thinking about Fern rushing out of the *Fame Game* show had left him wide awake until the wee small hours. Why had she done it? Could it have been because she'd seen him there? Surely she would have known that he was going to be one of the judges. It was a puzzle. And one that he'd certainly like solved.

'There's something wrong,' his agent said. 'What's troubling *Il Divo* today? You looked great on the *Fame Game* show. You talked a lot more sense than those other idiots, too. You're a natural, darling.'

'No, I won't do another series, Rup.' He could see exactly where his agent's flattery was leading.

Rupert hung his head. 'I think that's a great shame. A waste of a wonderful broadcasting talent.'

'Talk to Stephen Cauldwell about doing a series on the great operas of the world and then I might be interested.'

The pound signs lit up in Rupert's eyes. 'I'll get on the phone to him right away. You'd be a great presenter. I can just see it. Classy production. BBC Two. Nine o'clock slot. Fantastic.'

Evan had to smile. For every inch that Rupert was given, he'd certainly make sure that he worked it up into a mile.

'Let's concentrate on the job in hand,' Evan suggested.

They were in a prestigious recording studio in London's well-heeled area of St John's Wood, and Evan was here to 'lay down some tracks' in modern parlance with one of the new indie-style bands that Rupert was representing. It seemed like an uneasy mix to Evan, but there was no doubt that these guys were the hot ticket at the moment, and beneath their boisterous exterior they were keen to get down to hard work and make their turn in the spotlight count. He'd agreed to record some of their songs with them to broaden his profile and embrace a younger audience—at least, that was how Rupert saw it. His agent was right though—there were only so many times that you could re-record the classics. It was time to find something fresh and new. Evan watched their youthful energy and wondered if some of it might rub off on him, or whether it would simply make him feel old.

The young guys had been warming up, and now they were ready for him.

'You've got everything you need?' Rupert wanted to know. Evan knew that his agent was anxious for this session to go well.

He laid a hand on Rupert's arm and lowered his voice. 'There's one thing you could do for me.'

'Anything.'

'Find Fern for me.'

'Fern?'

'We must have an address for her.'

Rupert shrugged. 'I have a mobile number. I'll call her.'

'She won't speak to me.' He didn't like to tell his agent that he'd been calling her and that her phone had been turned off. There was no way he'd wanted to leave a message on her voicemail. If Fern was given the chance, she'd probably run away from him again.

His agent stifled a sigh. 'What's happened this time?'

'She was due to go on the *Fame Game*. At the last minute, she skedaddled out of there with half of the team chasing her.' He allowed himself a wry smile. That would actually have been a sight to see. 'I'd hate to think it was my fault.'

Rupert gave him a look that said he'd probably agree with that assessment.

'Don't,' Evan said, holding up his hand. 'That just makes me feel worse. I feel so guilty.'

His agent's expression softened. 'So what do you want me to do?'

'Find her.'

'I'll call Stephen Cauldwell, see if the *Fame Game* crew knows where she hangs out.'

'I don't want them to know that I'm involved with her.'

Rupert couldn't hide his surprise. 'And are you?'

'I don't know. But I want a chance to talk to her.'

'Then what do you want me to do?'

'I don't know,' Evan admitted with more than a note of exasperation in his voice. 'Find her. How hard can it be?'

'London is a big city. What if she doesn't want to be found?'

'Get Izak onto it.' His chief of security could always be relied on. 'He must have contacts.'

'You want me to put a tail on her?'

'If necessary.' He felt a surge of joy at the crumb of hope that this offered him. Izak knew what he was doing. He'd get results, Evan was sure. He had to be sure.

Rupert tried hard to keep his face neutral when he said, 'This must be important to you.'

'It is,' Evan confirmed. 'More important than anything.'

Forty-nine

Life is back to normal. Normal in a rather dysfunctional way. My dad is still pretending to have imaginary illnesses in order to win back my mum. My mum, in the meantime, is who knows where, doing who knows what, and she's more than likely doing it with Mr Patel. I'm back at the King's Head doing my barmaid work and singing nightly sets with Carl. I've given up my stupid dreams of fame and fortune. Carl has a sadness to his demeanour that wasn't previously there—but Carl being Carl, he's trying to hide it. I'd like to say that I've been able to watch the *Fame Game* on the telly to see how it's all going, but I haven't been that brave. Carl says that the glam rocker is currently in the lead. And I can't help but think that it could have been me.

The only good thing to have come out of this is that I now have the time to pick up Nathan from school. Joe has gone off to do his great cash job, and even though I've failed miserably in my quest to bring them a wonderful new life, they'll be a few hundred quid better off this week.

My nephew, once again, has made a nigh-on miraculous recovery from his latest asthma attack but I do wonder how long he can keep going on like this, and whether each time that he has one of these periods of illness, does it leave him weaker or permanently damaged in any way. The doctors seem to be able to give us so few answers to address our fears.

I'm waiting outside Nathan's school, and there's a frisson of excitement running through me. I love Nathan so much and, if this feels so great, it makes me think what it would be like to have my own children one day. I try not to think how terrible I'd feel if that never happened. Probably worse than never making it as the new Madonna, I suspect.

There's an unseasonally strong drop of sunshine warming my back, and all the spring flowers are pushing bravely through the hard, cold earth of the roadside verges—the bright yellow heads of daffodils, the lush purple crocuses and the stark white of a few late snowdrops. The sky is clear and blue. The white, fluffy clouds hold no threat of rain. It's a good day. A very good day. And despite my overall despondency, I feel okay. Quite okay. Things could be a lot worse in my world.

More cars arrive to collect their charges, clogging up the road. A gaggle of mums with toddlers in push-chairs congregate by the school gates, chatting together. One day I'd like to belong to their club, too. Maybe I will. As it is, I spend the time tracing the edges of the paving slabs on the pavement with the toe of my shoe.

In the distance, a bell rings and moments later a horde of scruffy, shouting schoolchildren spill out of the school. I twitch impatiently as I wait for Nathan and then I see him at the same time as he spots me. He hoists up his school bag and starts to run towards me, then—perhaps he sees the look of panic on my face—he drops back, slowing his run to a gentle trot. I respond by scooping him up as he gets to me, not caring that he'll probably get a load of stick from his friends tomorrow.

'How's my best boy?'

'Great,' he says. There are dark shadows under Nathan's eyes and his face is pale. His chest sounds wheezy to me. 'Did the teacher give you your inhaler to take today?'

Nathan nods solemnly.

'Good.' I put him down. 'We're going to have tea with Nana. That okay with you?'

'Yeah,' he says and slips his hand into mine.

I ruffle his hair, which he hates, and then we turn to head back towards the bus stop. As we do so, I notice the big black limo taking up half of the street and I know instinctively who it belongs to. My heart leaps up to my mouth and my step falters. Sure enough, Evan is standing on the pavement just ahead of us. He's wearing a black cashmere coat and his hands are pushed deep into his pockets. He looks handsome, sad and more than a little scary. I fight the urge to snatch Nathan up and leg it in the opposite direction.

'Hey,' he says softly.

Nathan and I stand in front of him and I've no idea what to say. My nephew also looks to me for inspiration.

Evan rescues us both. 'So this is one of your many commitments?'

'This is Nathan,' I tell him.

'I'm five,' Nathan adds.

'I'm very pleased to meet you.'

'How did you know I'd be here?' I ask.

'I had my spies looking out for you.' He says it lightly, but I have a feeling that he might be serious.

I don't know what to say, so we stand and look at each other a bit longer. Nathan starts to fidget.

'I guess we'd better be going,' I say.

'Let me give you a lift,' Evan says swiftly. 'I'll take you home.'

I hesitate. Is this a can of worms that I want opened?

'I'd like the chance to talk to you,' he says. 'Please. Let me take you home.'

'Is this your car?' Nathan asks, pointing at the limo.

'Yes.'

Nathan turns pleading eyes at me. And I cave in. How can I deny my nephew what will probably be his only chance of a ride in a vehicle that's the size of a small housing estate?

'We're going to my mum's place near Euston station,' I tell Evan. 'For tea.'

'Then I'll take you there.'

I'm grateful that we're not going back to my digs, but for the first time in my life—and I feel terrible saying this—I'm embarrassed about where my parents live. I don't suppose that Evan David will have ever been anywhere so small and so threadbare and so obviously owned by the council in his entire life. But this is me. The real me. And, quite frankly, he'll have to like that or lump it.

We go over to the car and all bundle inside the back seat. I think Nathan might hyperventilate with excitement and my fingers curl protectively round his inhaler in my pocket just in case.

'Is this really a car?' he breathes.

Evan looks vaguely uncomfortable. 'Yes.'

'I've never been in one like this,' my nephew says. Then he turns to me. 'Have you?'

I decide not to tell Nathan about Jemma MacKenzie's hen night and skip to more recent times. 'I've been in this car before with Mr David.'

'Wow,' he says and settles back into the gargantuan seat.

'Where are we going?' Evan asks.

I reel off the address of Frodsham Court, the driver gives me an acknowledging nod and, silently, the car moves off.

'People will think I'm a prince,' Nathan says and he stares out of the window, transfixed.

I look at Evan David, feeling ridiculously shy.

He shifts, turning to face me. 'Why did you run out of the *Fame Game?*'

I shrug and stare out of the window like Nathan.

Evan clears his throat. 'Was it because of me?'

I want to tell him not to flatter himself, but in my heart, I know that I couldn't carry it off. 'I felt terrible for lying to you,' I admit. 'For as long as I can remember, I've wanted to be a singer.'

I'd expected Evan to look shocked, but he sits there calmly regarding me.

'I *am* a singer,' I correct, giving him a self-deprecating look despite a rare burst of defiant confidence. 'I belt out popular hit tunes every night down at the King's Head public house with my best friend, Carl, on piano.'

'Why didn't you tell me?'

'What's it to you?' My voice comes out sounding more

harsh than I would have liked. 'You must get people telling you that they want to be a singer all the time.'

Evan rubs his chin thoughtfully. 'Actually, I don't.'

'It's probably because they'd be frightened of humiliating themselves.'

'And that's how you felt?'

'Of course it is.' I also felt stupid. And pathetic. And unworthy. And any other negative emotions you'd care to trot out. I turn my attention to Nathan, who is amusing himself by waving at the staring passers-by in the manner of the queen. At least one of us is happy.

'You had a good chance of winning,' Evan says.

I do wish people would stop telling me that.

'The rest of the bunch aren't up to much.'

'So you'd have given me your vote?' I can't help sounding sarcastic.

'I haven't heard you sing,' Evan points out coolly, 'but I would have liked to.'

'You haven't missed much,' I tell him.

'You should have let me be the judge of that.' And we both risk a smile at the irony of his comment. 'I did hear that you're a great runner though.'

I can't help but laugh. 'Don't,' I scold him. 'You're making it worse.'

Evan loses his smile and his voice becomes serious once more. 'Stephen Cauldwell thought you had real talent.'

I sigh. 'None of this is much consolation to me. I've blown it. They're hardly likely to have me back on the show now.'

'No,' Evan agrees.

We pull up outside my parents' shabby block of flats and I

try not to notice the peeling paint and the obscene graffiti. 'We're here,' I say pointlessly.

We sit in silence for a moment before Evan asks, 'So what now?'

'I'm back to pulling pints at the King's Head.' I shrug my assumed indifference. 'What about you?'

His arm slides towards me across the back of the seat. 'Back to an empty apartment to have dinner alone.'

I want to do something. To hold him. To hug him. To make some sort of affectionate gesture. But I am useless at this kind of stuff.

'I won't be in England for much longer,' Evan says. 'Another week or so and then I'm back to San Francisco.'

'I've heard it's nice.' Says she who has never travelled any farther than Ibiza.

'It's beautiful.'

I take Nathan's hand—he's looking distinctly put out that his ride has ended so soon. 'We'd better go,' I say. 'Nana will be waiting.'

Finally, I pluck up the courage to reach across and kiss Evan on the cheek. I might even have tried something a bit more sexy, but I'm blissfully aware that our every move is being observed by my five-year-old nephew.

I shuffle across the seat towards the door. 'Come on, Nath,' I say. 'Thank Mr David for the ride in his car.'

'It was cool,' Nathan says. Evan holds up his hand and my nephew high-fives him.

Nathan gets out of the car and I follow him, standing on the pavement with my hand on the door. This could be the last time that I see Evan, and I don't want to leave him like this.

Despite the luxurious surroundings of his car and his expensive clothes, somehow he looks so alone.

Neither of us say anything, but we look at each other for a moment with what might be longing or regret. And then, before my brain has had time to engage, my mouth says, 'You could come up and have tea with us if you like.'

Fifty

My mum will have a blue fit with her foot in the air. I just hope she's cleaned the flat today, otherwise I'll be for the high jump, inviting home posh strangers without any warning.

There's a playground in the middle of the flats and a group of kids are kicking the crap out of each other, and I wonder why my parents didn't move out of here years ago when the area started to go down the pan. We climb the concrete stairs to my parents' flat—the ones that always bear the faint whiff of stale urine.

'This used to be a nice neighbourhood,' I tell Evan, but I'm not sure that he believes me. 'Years ago.'

I put my key in Mum's door, and when it swings open, I'm relieved to be enveloped in the scents of home-baking and lemon furniture polish. Mum has, indeed, been doing the housework today. We troupe into the hall—Evan lurking self-consciously behind me. I bet he's wishing that he turned down my invitation now.

'I've brought a visitor,' I shout in warning. She's not one for surprises, my mother.

She's in the kitchen, which is shining like a new pin. And, come to think of it, so is my mum. Some of her 'best' clothes have been brought out of mothballs, her hair is tightly curled and there's a hint of make-up in evidence yet again. Looks like she's ready for a wild night out—or in—with Mr Patel. This tea with Nathan arrangement was going to be my big opportunity to pump her for some more information about her secret love life, but with Evan here it looks as if I'm going to have to curb my curiosity for a bit longer.

Nathan rushes to hug his nana—who, of course, spoils him rotten. 'How's my soldier?' she wants to know.

'Okay, Nana.' Having discarded his school bag, he's already stripping off his coat. 'I've been in a *massive* car!'

My mum looks to me for an explanation. 'This is Evan David, Mum,' I say bashfully, only just resisting the urge to shove him forward for inspection. 'He gave us a lift home from Nathan's school.'

'Oh,' my mum says, hand flying to the string of beads at her throat. 'You're better-looking in real life than you are on the telly, aren't you?'

Why do parents stay embarrassing no matter how old you get?

'Thank you,' Evan says graciously. 'It's very nice to meet you, Mrs…'

'Kendal,' I remind him.

'Amy,' my mum replies coquettishly. 'You can call me Amy.'

At least she didn't say 'you can call me Mum.' I should be thankful for small mercies.

Then she edges forward and gives Evan an awkward kiss, which he responds to with equal clumsiness. I grin to myself. Nice to see that his smooth façade can slip occasionally.

'I've asked Evan to stay for his tea,' I confess. 'Hope that's all right.'

'He'll have to take us as he finds us,' my mum answers, as if he's not there. I know that any minute she'll be rooting the best china out of the back of the cupboards. 'Would you like a cup of tea?'

Evan and I nod vigorously in response. 'Let's go through to the lounge.' And I tug him by the arm before he has a chance to disagree. Nathan is already installed in front of the television, any interest in our celebrity visitor long forgotten.

Mum has gone overboard with the furniture polish in here, and a cloud of artificial lemon scent hangs in the air. Which, of course, has started Nathan off with his wheezing. It sounds bad to me.

'You need your nebuliser, young man,' I tell him. As he's just come out of hospital, I don't want him going straight back in. We have to nip any wheezing episodes in the bud, and the nebuliser gives out a steady stream of medication that will get his breathing under control again.

Nathan gives me a resigned look and plods off to get it.

'Sorry about this,' I say to Evan. 'Sit down. Sit down.' I make a fuss of plumping cushions before I realise that I'm turning into my mum and stop. The first thing I would have done with my *Fame Game* winnings would have been to have bought her a new three-piece suite. 'This won't take long.'

Nathan brings the nebuliser back and we fiddle with setting it up. 'Do you want to sit on my lap?' I ask him.

My nephew nods, and I settle into the sofa while he climbs up and nestles across my legs. I hook him up to the nebuliser, putting the clear plastic mask over his mouth and nose, then I cuddle him into me. Nathan closes his eyes, almost instantly drifting off into sleep. He's so used to this routine that it doesn't phase him as it used to.

When I look up to smile at Evan, I can see that he's turned as white as a sheet. Every ounce of blood has drained from his face.

The smile freezes on my face. 'What?'

His expression is of pure horror.

'What's wrong?'

He's so shocked that he can't give me an answer. His mouth opens but nothing comes out.

I look down at Nathan. 'It's an asthma attack,' I say steadily. 'Nothing more. He's only just come out of hospital, and I don't want him going back in. This is just a precautionary measure.'

Still Evan says nothing. And then the penny drops—he thinks he's going to catch something from Nathan that will infect his precious throat. A flash of irritation washes over me. Why does he think that everything has to revolve around protecting his bloody voice? Doesn't he realise that people in the real world have worse problems to contend with than that?

'He's not sick,' I snap. 'He's having an asthma attack. You're not going to catch anything.'

'I have to go,' Evan says. He lurches out of his chair and towards the door.

I'm stunned at his extreme reaction to Nathan's illness. A

bit of wheezing doesn't warrant this. What is wrong with the man? 'Why are you acting like this?' I say, baffled. 'He hasn't got an infectious disease.'

Nathan rouses on my lap and I rock him gently. 'Hush, hush.'

Mum is just coming in with a tray of tea. Evan nearly knocks her over as he bolts for the door.

'Sorry, Mrs Kendal,' he says hurriedly. 'I have to leave. Sorry to dash off.' And with that he's out of the front door, slamming it behind him.

My mum puts down the tray of tea and looks after him, bemused. As I am. 'What was all that about?' she asks.

'I don't know,' I say honestly. I lower my voice to a whisper. 'Nathan's asthma attack seemed to freak him out completely.' I give a nonplussed shrug. 'I can only think that he was frightened of catching something from him. He spends his life fretting about anything that might affect his voice.'

'I suppose that's understandable,' my mum says, but she doesn't really look as if she understands. 'Oh well. I thought you'd dropped on lucky with that one, Fern.'

'He's not a boyfriend, Mum. He's a…' My voice tails off, as I have no idea how to describe my relationship with Evan David.

'How's Nathan?' she asks, giving a nod in the direction of her grandson.

'He'll be all right,' I say. 'I hope. What were you thinking of, using so much furniture polish in here when you know that anything like that can start him off? We need to open some windows in here for a few minutes.'

'Sorry, love. I'd no idea that I'd used too much. My mind is on other things.'

Like Mr Patel? I want to ask.

My mum sneezes—a particularly loud one that wakes Nathan up. She does it again and then grabs a tissue from the box by the sofa and gives her nose a hearty blow.

'Sorry, love. Sorry.'

'Please tell me you're not coming down with a cold, Mum.'

She looks sheepish. 'Do you know, love, I think I might be.'

I give her a dark look.

'My throat has been sore and my nose has been blocked up all day,' she admits. 'That's probably why I couldn't smell how much polish I'd used.'

'You might be infectious,' I say huffily. 'I'd never have brought Nathan round if you'd said you were feeling under the weather.'

'I didn't think, love.' It seems as if my mum isn't thinking about much these days.

I could swing for her. How could she put Nathan at so much risk? And what about Evan David? Here's me assuring him that he isn't in a house full of germs when it seems I might have been completely wrong.

Fifty-one

'How's the voice today?' Rupert asked. There was an anxious note in his question.

'Not great,' Evan confessed. 'I've had a dry, tickly throat all night.' They were due to go to the studio this morning to record another track with the indie band, but it didn't look like that was going to happen. Rupert had swung by the apartment to collect him, but in this state Evan was going nowhere. 'I've had Dermuid mix me some juices high in vitamin C. Hopefully that will help.'

His agent frowned with concern. 'You look very peaky.'

Evan hated to admit it, but he felt very peaky, too. He hadn't been able to get warm in bed, and he was still feeling shivery. His limbs ached and his eyelids felt heavy.

'It's been a long time since you've had a sore throat.'

Evan sneezed.

'Or a cold,' Rupert added.

'This is disastrous.'

'I'll cancel today's recording,' Rup said, reaching for his phone. 'The guys can get on with some other tracks that don't feature you. That's not a problem.'

'Send them my apologies,' Evan said. 'Tell them we'll get the rest of the tracks done before I leave for San Francisco.'

Rupert looked sceptical about the last bit, and Evan had to admit that it was more wishful thinking on his part than a realistic suggestion.

His agent spoke into his phone, altering arrangements, making all the right noises. It was at times like this that Rupert earned his commission. When he turned back to Evan he said, 'Tomorrow is more of a problem.'

The next evening, Evan was scheduled to sing at a big blowsy charity evening in aid of child poverty. Everyone who was anyone had been cajoled, bullied or blackmailed into attending. It was a cause that he felt desperately committed to, and he didn't want to let the organisers down. The evening had been logged in his calendar for more than two years—he couldn't possibly go down with a cold now.

'You'd better call them and warn them that I might be a no-show,' he said with a heavy heart.

'They'll be devastated.'

'Don't you think I know that?'

He could kick himself for catching this bug. After all the precautions he took to protect his voice. Precautions that had served him quite well until now. In all his years as a performer, he'd cancelled only a handful of performances through ill health. He knew that Fern had said that Nathan's condition was not infectious, but he did have his suspicions as to where this sudden cold had come from.

It was almost as though Rupert managed to read his mind. He said, 'You managed to catch up with Fern yesterday?'

Evan nodded.

'Did it go well?'

'At first,' Evan said.

'That doesn't sound like an entirely positive result.'

'She has a child.'

Rupert shrugged. 'That tends to be a fairly common occurrence. Particularly in the females of the population.'

'He's sick.'

'That's what comes from playing with other children.'

'No,' Evan said. 'He's very sick. I went back to her home with her…'

Rupert raised an eyebrow.

'To meet her mother.'

The other eyebrow shot up to join it.

'It's not how it sounds,' Evan assured him.

'Is this where you've picked up this infection?'

'I don't know,' Evan admitted. 'Fern said that he was having an asthma attack, but, jeez, Rup, he looked like he was about to…' He was going to say 'die', but the word wouldn't come out. 'He looked very ill. It freaked me out.'

His agent waited patiently for further explanations.

'I got out of there as quickly as I could. Nearly knocked her mother over in my rush to the door.'

Rupert chuckled.

'It wasn't funny,' Evan said. 'I made a complete arse of myself.'

'No change there then,' Rupert offered, and both men exchanged a wry glance.

'Why did you never have kids, Rup?'

'I've never stayed in one place long enough to get anyone pregnant,' Rupert said, trying to make a joke of the issue. 'It's difficult to make adult relationships when you're constantly on the road. Even worse when you bring kids into the equation. Children aren't conducive to our type of lifestyle. That's why I've never embraced the idea of family life.'

'My own reasons are more complicated,' Evan said, and he stared away into the middle distance thinking about the pain he'd nursed to himself since his sister died. There was no doubt that he wanted to become closer to Fern—there were emotions he felt when he was around her that he assumed had been closed off to him. But could he risk becoming so close to her child? The thought of that filled him with emotions that he *wanted* to keep closed off. He couldn't afford to go spiralling into this paranoid apoplexy every time the boy started to sniffle. How conducive would that be to making a go of a relationship with his mother?

'I know,' Rupert said. He patted Evan on the shoulder. 'I haven't forgotten that.'

'You've given up a lot for me, Rup, haven't you?'

Rupert looked discomfited. 'And you, in turn, have made me a very rich man.'

'Are we rich?' Evan wanted to know. 'Sure, we're wealthy—but is that the same as being rich? I have more money than I can ever spend, cars that I don't drive, houses that I don't live in. But what about the things that really matter in life? Do I have any of those?'

'You have a lot going for you,' Rupert responded with a typical display of fervent loyalty.

'I hate to admit this, but I was frightened of the child—of Nathan. He looked so damn vulnerable. It scared me shitless. And what scared me even more was the closeness of the family. Fern and her mother were both so besotted with him and with each other in a family knockabout way. I've never done that before. My own family was…' Again the words ran out. 'Well, you know.'

Rupert pursed his lips to show that he did know.

'I can stand in front of thousands of people and perform, but that close little unit gave me a severe attack of the jitters. I don't know if I'd be up to the job of taking that on.'

'But you are thinking about it?'

'It's got my head spinning, Rupert.' He raked his hands through his hair. 'Am I too old to be having a midlife crisis?'

'I would say this was the perfect age.'

Evan smiled. 'That's very reassuring.'

'Well,' Rupert said, 'you can spend the whole day thinking about it. Uncle Rupert advises that you go straight back to bed. Don't move. Don't speak. Rest your body. Rest the voice. By tomorrow you might feel very different.'

And by tomorrow he might feel exactly the same—and that worried Evan immensely.

Fifty-two

I need a hot bath and some cold wine. The first might prove to be a problem because I don't have a bath, let alone any hot water, as the boiler's on the blink. The second might be a problem because the fridge has been on the blink again, too. So a cold shower and some warm wine will have to be the solution to all my problems.

Hauling myself up the stairs to my flat, I realise that I've reverted to dragging myself through my life and resolve to do something that will revive my flagging energy levels. Something, of course, that doesn't involve relaxing, as I have no time for that. I'm exhausted from looking after Nathan, even though he's really no trouble, bless him. Joe is having a great time at his job this week, and they've said that they want to give him more work—maybe even something permanent. It does him good to have a break from full-time caring and, of course, the extra money doesn't hurt.

I have tried very hard to stop thinking about Evan David, but it hasn't really worked. Even now, I can't understand why he was so keen to get away from Nathan. Honestly, you'd think that he'd seen a ghost from the way he completely over-reacted. My mind has tossed it around a thousand times, but still I can't rationalise it.

'Who are you?' my dad says as I emerge into the kitchen.

'Leave it out, Dad,' I say. 'I'm not in the mood.'

He gives up and sinks into his chair.

The other thing that I need to address in my life is my parents' continuing separation. If I don't get my bonkers dad out of this flat soon, I'm quite likely to murder him. He seems to have put himself into early retirement and hasn't gone to work since Mum threw him out, which means that he isn't giving me any money to stay here, despite the fact that he eats the entire contents of my cupboards the minute I fill them. As far as I can ascertain, all he is doing is sitting watching *Des and Mel* while snacking, with the occasional foray onto the Internet to look up more illnesses that he can come down with. My bedroom floor is littered with my dad's checked jumpers and other items of clothing that you really don't want to see of your father's. The lounge is a bombsite, as there's a bed permanently made up on my sofa, and my bathroom shelf has been bombarded with shaving foam and spent razor blades. At least he's still washing and shaving, I suppose.

Before I turn round and go back out to the King's Head for tonight's rousing performance, I need to do some laundry. There are a thousand other chores I need to do, too, but they can wait. Having clean clothes is something of a priority. 'Is there anything you need washing, Dad?'

'Just a few bits,' he says. 'I'll go and fetch them.'

I'll get something proper to eat later. Maybe Carl and I will hit the nearest chip shop. My life could not be any more glamorous, could it? Needing a quick snack to stave off the hunger pangs, I root around in my cupboards, but, once again, my dear parent has eaten me out of house and home. The only thing that's left is the cheap and nasty cereal that even Squeaky isn't keen on. Pulling the box out of the cupboard, I stick it on the table while I putter round the kitchen trying to find a bowl that hasn't already been used. When I finally lay my hands on one, I go to pour out some cereal and find that the box is completely empty. What is it about blokes that they can put empty boxes back into the cupboard or the fridge? Why can't they simply throw them out like women do? I shake the box again, but unlike David Blane, I still can't make any cereal materialise out of thin air. I could kill my dad, really I could.

He takes that moment to reappear with a pile of washing.

'Why didn't you think to leave me any food?' I ask.

Taking in the cereal box, he says, 'There's bread.'

I open the bread bin. There isn't.

'I'll get some tomorrow,' he promises. 'If I remember.'

'You better had,' I warn him. 'And while you're at it, it's about time that you remembered you've got a wife. If you're not careful, she'll be starting divorce proceedings while you're pretending to have lost your memory.'

He straightens up a bit at that, but fails to rise to the bait.

I snatch the pile of laundry from him and throw it on the floor in front of the washing machine. Even this washing machine is an ancient hand-me-down from Carl's mum, but it has served me well for the past few years. My dad shuffles to the kitchen table to sit down while I sort out the shirts and pants, wishing I had some of those massive laundry tongs so that I didn't have to touch my father's underwear. There's a pair of trousers, too, and I pull out the pockets in case he's left any loose change in there which will wreck my washing machine as I couldn't cope with any unexpected expense at the moment. The only thing in there is a business card, which I go to hand over and then the name catches my eye. The distinctive *Fame Game* logo looms up at me. Stephen Cauldwell's name is in bold capitals on the front. I wish I had one of Nathan's inhalers to hand, because I can feel myself starting to hyperventilate. Flipping the card over, I see Stephen Cauldwell has scrawled a message on the back. It says, quite simply, *Fern. Call me! Stephen*. My hand starts to shake.

Holding the card out towards my dad, I demand, 'What's this? What's this?'

He has the good grace to go ashen. 'I can't remember. I've got Alzheimer's.'

'Like *fuck* you have!'

My dad frowns at me. 'That's no way to speak to your father.'

'Perhaps I've inherited the Tourette's syndrome that you had last week. Or had you forgotten about that, too?'

Dad stares morosely at the table.

'How did you get this card? Did he come here?' I yell. 'Did Stephen Cauldwell take the trouble to come here and you didn't tell me? You've put this card in your pocket and simply *forgotten?*'

'I *did* forget,' my dad insists.

'And what does that say about you?' I ask. 'I've put up with all this stupid behaviour, and when it comes to something so important to me, you can't get your act together long enough to tell me?'

I feel hysterical. Blood is pounding round my veins, and I'll swear there's a red mist coming down before my eyes. I'm more angry than I've ever been in my life.

'When did he come here?'

'Er…yesterday,' my dad says. 'Or the day before. Not long ago. I really can't remember.'

'What did he say?'

'Nothing much.' My dad sounds very cagey. 'He just said you were to call him.'

'You weren't rude to him? You didn't tell him to fuck off?'

'I don't think so,' Dad says with a wobble in his voice. This is not giving me the utmost confidence in his recollection.

'If I thought you'd done this deliberately, Dad, then I'd never forgive you.'

He looks affronted. 'That's a terrible thing to say.'

'And this is a terrible thing to do. Have you any idea how important this is to me?'

'I'm beginning to realise,' he mutters.

This does nothing to calm me down. 'The *Fame Game* and Stephen Cauldwell could be my only chance to get out of my miserable life, out of this miserable hovel of a home. Don't you want that for me?'

'Yes.' My dad perks up. 'And I've done something today to help with that?'

'What?' I briefly wonder whether he's managed to lever himself off the couch for long enough to have a look at what's wrong with the fridge.

'I got rid of that filthy little mouse.'

My blood turns to ice, and I can feel my jaw drop. 'You did what?'

'I got rid of it. You'd have been overrun with the things if I hadn't. Do you know how much disease they carry?'

'What did you do?' I say. 'What did you do?'

My dad now looks more uncertain. 'I bought a trap.'

'You didn't think to buy a loaf or some milk or some cereal, but you made the effort to go out and buy a mouse trap?'

'I thought you'd be pleased,' Dad protests. 'They carry dirt. There were mouse droppings on the floor.'

'What did you do with him? Did you take him to the park?'

Dad looks very shifty.

'No,' I say. 'No. Tell me that you bought a humane trap?'

My dad's eyes travel towards the swing bin in the corner of the kitchen.

'No,' I say again. 'Please tell me you haven't done what I think you've done.'

'Love,' he says. 'It's for the best.'

I go to the corner and open the swing bin. Sure enough, Squeaky's tiny, crushed body is lying on top of screwed-up kitchen roll, an empty soup tin and last week's copy of the *Mail on Sunday*.

Gently, I pick him up, stroking his broken grey body, and fall to the floor, huddling over him on my knees. I hear myself sobbing loudly and screaming, 'No!' over and over again, but I can't stop myself. It's as if this noise is coming from someone else, not me. I've lost the plot, I know. But the unnecessary death—the needless murder—of Squeaky represents all that has gone wrong in my life. All my failures come crushing down on me, like the cruel trap must have done on Squeaky's scrawny body. If I can't even protect a bloody mouse, then how do I deserve my place on this planet?

I wrap Squeaky's body gently in a piece of the discarded kitchen roll and then lay him on the floor by the back door and weep over him.

Eventually, I feel Dad's hand on my shoulder. 'It's for the best,' he says again. 'I did it for you.'

Standing up, I wheel round. 'It's *not* for the best. And it's *not* for me! All this is about what *you* want!'

My dad takes a step back. He's looking at me as if I'm a gorgon. Perhaps a mass of snakes have sprung out of my head, because I'm certainly hissing and spitting. My arms are whirling wildly. I'd never understood the term blind fury, but I do now. My vision is blurred and I lunge for my dad, catching him on the shoulder. He grabs my hand.

'Don't, love,' he says. 'Don't get yourself worked up for nothing.'

'Nothing? How can you be so fucking dismissive of my pain?'

'What about *my* pain?' Dad retaliates.

And the red mist definitely comes over me now. He still doesn't understand or doesn't care what this means to me. I don't think that my dad is in pain. I think he's insensitive, selfish and a sponger.

Whirling round, I grab the empty cereal box from the table and lash out at him with it. I hit him round the head, resounding thunks, while he tries to fend me off.

'Fern!' he shouts. 'Calm down. Calm down.'

But I don't want to calm down, I want to make him hurt as much as I'm hurting. I want him to know what my pain feels like.

And then he stops fighting me and clutches his chest.

'Try another one, Dad,' I snarl, and whack him again.

This time he falls to his knees, clutching at the table.

'What's this—a feigned heart attack?' I stand over him hands on hips, breathing heavily. 'Well, it won't wash.'

Dad is gasping. Almost convincingly.

'I want you out of here,' I roar. 'I want you out of my life.'

Dad starts crawling towards the door. He's nearly there when he collapses onto his stomach and just lies there.

'Nice try,' I growl furiously. 'You should audition for the local amateur dramatics group. I'm sure they'd love a performer like you. However, I'm less impressed. So, if you don't mind, I'm going to get ready for work.' I go to step over my Dad's inert body. 'Don't you dare touch Squeaky. I'm going to bury him in the park tomorrow.'

Then I notice that Dad's lips have turned blue, and I know that even he can't fake that. I also know from my long experience with Nathan that this is not a good thing.

I bend down and shake him softly. 'Dad?'

If he jumps up in a minute or starts to laugh, then I'm finished with him, really I am. Blood relative or not, I'm washing my hands of him. But my dad doesn't move. His eyes are wide and staring. A gurgle comes from his lips, but it's clear that he can't speak. Then I realise that this is one illness that he isn't faking—in fact, this is *deadly* serious.

'Oh, shit,' I say and bolt for the phone, punching in 999 as fast as my fingers can manage it. I give the emergency services my name and address, begging for an ambulance to arrive within the next few minutes.

I rush back to the kitchen. 'There's an ambulance on its way,' I tell my dad. 'Hang on. Just hang on.'

He doesn't look like he's hanging on. And then some first aid that I learned nearly twenty years ago in the Girl Guides somehow kicks in. My panic abates and a calmness descends on me, and as I prepare to give my dad the kiss of life, I say, 'Neither of us are going to enjoy this.'

Fifty-three

I don't know how they do it, but the paramedics arrive what seems like seconds later. They move me aside and, in a calm and professional way, immediately start to administer CPR to my dad. And I promise that I will never, ever criticise our lovely, overworked National Health Service ever again.

They load Dad onto a stretcher and gently carry him down the stairs to the waiting ambulance. I follow and sombrely sit next to Dad, taking hold of his hand. He gives me a wan attempt at a smile as the paramedics hook him up to a dozen different things.

'He's lucky you were there,' one of the paramedics says to me as we set off for the hospital. 'You've probably saved his life.'

I don't dare to tell him that I was the architect of my father's heart attack. I'm not sure what the prison sentence is for attempted manslaughter of one of your parents, but I'm pretty sure I don't fancy it.

My dad has his eyes closed and looks peaceful, but he's gripping my hand. How fragile we are as human beings. I stroke his hair from his forehead, which is soaked with sweat.

'I'm sorry, Dad,' I say.

'Me, too,' he whispers.

At the hospital, they admit Dad to the Coronary Care Unit, and while they do, I shoot out into the car park to phone Mum and Joe from my mobile.

Mum, it seems, isn't at home and, as usual, her mobile phone is turned off. It's probably sitting next to the kettle in the kitchen where she normally keeps it—fat lot of use that it is there. We're always banging the drum to get her to understand that we want her to use her mobile in case of emergencies. But my mum is the sort of person who doesn't believe in emergencies. Now we've got one, and goodness only knows where she is. Dialling Joe instead, I'm relieved when he answers within three rings. I explain the situation, and he promises to get one of his neighbours to watch Nathan for a couple of hours while he comes down to the hospital.

Then I call Carl and cry into the phone. He utters soothing words, shushes my tears, promises to tell Ken that there's yet another domestic emergency in my life and that I won't be in for work again—I must definitely be in line for the sack by now—and then my darling friend says that he'll also come down to the hospital as soon as he can, making me crumble again.

I go back up to the ward and find my dad settled in a corner bed. A tiny Thai nurse is tucking a clean sheet around him. There's an array of pink stickers attached to his bare chest with wires snaking out through a smattering of white hair. He's hooked up to a drip and a heart monitor and there's a blood-pressure cuff on his arm, but he's looking slightly better. Some of the colour has come back into his face and he's sitting up-right. I get a rush of affection for him and go over and hug him tightly.

'Mind you don't knock off any of these gadgets,' he warns, 'or they'll think that I've croaked it all over again.'

Before she leaves us alone, the nurse clicks her tongue against her teeth and says, 'Your daddy is lucky man.'

He's wired up in a hospital having just had a heart attack, and people keep telling me he's lucky? He doesn't look very lucky from where I'm standing. He looks like a doing-poorly old man. A tear rolls down my cheek.

'Don't cry,' Dad says. 'I'm all right.'

'That was a close call,' I sob.

He pats his heart. 'Plenty of life in the old boy yet,' he says. 'I'll be as right as rain.'

'Oh, Dad.' I wipe away the tears with my sleeve, sinking into the plastic chair by his bedside. 'I couldn't bear it if anything happened to you.'

'I'm going nowhere,' he assures me. Then he looks at me, slightly shamefaced. 'And there'll be no more silliness from now on.'

'I'm glad to hear it,' I say, and we both exchange a sheepish grin. 'Joe's on his way. He'll be here soon, I should think.'

'I don't know how Nathan copes with all this,' he says.

'Me, neither.'

'He's made of sterner stuff than I am.' Dad lies back against his pillow. 'I just want to get out of here and get better.'

'And I want everything to get back to normal.'

He clears his throat. 'Did you call your mum?'

'I did,' I tell him. 'But she's out.'

Dad glances over at the big clock on the wall, and a frown crosses his forehead. 'She never goes out at night. Where can she be at this time?'

I pretend that my attention has wandered off down the ward and avoid answering his question. I daren't tell him where I think my mum is—there's no way I want to be responsible for giving him another heart attack.

Fifty-four

Evan had taken doses of Lemsip, Night Nurse, Benolyn Expectorant and a clutch of Nurofen—an array of drugs that any self-respecting junkie would be proud of. Yet still he felt awful. His head throbbed and his nose ran. The throat doctor had visited earlier this evening, had swabbed his throat and had felt his glands and, finally, had pronounced him unfit to sing. The charity concert was off.

Now he was lying in bed, all alone, feeling sorry for himself. It was a cold, he scolded himself, nothing worse. He was a typical bloke, blowing all illnesses completely out of proportion, but with the added neurosis of an opera singer. It was an irrational train of thought, but he always worried that after a cold he might lose his voice permanently. What would he be if that happened?

Evan felt that he was probably well enough to get through one song, but not a whole concert. Rupert had gone to the concert anyway to apologise for his absence and glad-hand some people. Another tenor, Johan Reiss, had stepped in at the last minute. He was good. He would save the day. But he wasn't another Evan David. Plus Evan hated to think that his image might be tarnished by not appearing. He always worried that the higher his star ascended, then the farther it would be for him to fall. And there were plenty of tabloid newspapers braying for the chance to accelerate his plummet to earth. He'd have to make a huge donation to the charity to make up for it—and with a spirit that wasn't entirely altruistic, get Rupert to leak it to the right places.

Flicking the remote control made a plasma screen drop down from the ceiling to hang at the foot of his bed, and he switched on the television just in time to see the celebrities arriving for the gala event. Evan groaned. There was no way he could bear to watch this, so he flicked through the never-ending range of channels making absolutely sure that there was nothing on worth watching. The novel on his bedside table had failed to grip him and required more concentration than he could currently offer it. Thwarted in his search for worthwhile entertainment, he tossed back the duvet and climbed out of bed. Throwing on his dressing gown, he padded through the apartment, the slap of his bare feet on the wood flooring echoing throughout the place. He'd been trapped indoors for two days now with this wretched cold, and he was starting to get cabin fever.

Evan wandered over to the windows, slid back one of the partitions and stepped out onto his balcony. The evening was pleasantly cool, the breeze soothing against his hot skin. Lights sparkled on the Thames, and the rhythmic lap of water against the building eased his headache. Out there somewhere was Fern. Evan spread his hands on the stainless-steel rail and exhaled heavily. He was missing her. Missing what might have been. And he wondered what she was doing now. She'd probably be getting ready to sing her set at the pub where she worked. Where did she say it was? Wasn't it the King's Head?

Suddenly Evan knew that he needed to go there. More than anything, he needed to find Fern. Before he could think better of it, he strode back inside, threw on some clothes and headed out of the apartment. He'd given Frank the night off, never imagining that he'd be going out into the city night with a raging head cold. He checked his wallet as he left—Rupert always complained that Evan never kept cash on him. Just like the queen, he was continually having to ask minions to settle his bills. Rup followed him around with a wedge of notes on hand for every occasion. Was this how far he'd come from real life? Evan had no idea of the cost of a loaf of bread or a pint of milk—he didn't even know how much he was paying to stay in this place. There was, not surprisingly, a noticeable absence of money in his wallet, so he rifled through the desk until he came on what appeared to be a petty cash box and helped himself to fifty quid—leaving an IOU just in case he forgot to replace it, even though, technically, it was his money.

Evan took the elevator down to the street. He was going to get in touch with real people again. And he was going to start by taking the Tube. Walking in the night air cleared his head, and he descended into the nearest Underground station feeling quite buoyant. The place was deserted, and Evan looked round him, wondering what to do. When was the last time he'd been on public transport? He hadn't always travelled in top-of-the-range stretched limos, but over twenty years had passed since he'd caught a bus or a Tube. The banks of ticket machines looked far too complicated, and it took him a minute or two to search out a ticket office. At least a human being would be able to give him some assistance.

He watched someone else putting their ticket through the barrier and then followed suit. This was ridiculous! He was forty-five years old and incapable of travelling on public transport without help. He only hoped that he was heading in the right direction on his wild-goose chase. One of the few things that he remembered about where Fern worked was that she'd said it wasn't far from her parents' home and he was sure that was near Euston station. He might not use public transport, but he could still recognise a mainline station when he saw one. At least, he thought he could.

No one gave him a second glance as he waited for the Tube train and then boarded it. Not a second glance. No one looked up from their books or newspapers as he passed. No one's mouth gaped open. No one pressed him for an autograph. Everyone minded their own business, and Evan slid, gratefully, into an empty seat. It was refreshing to go unnoticed, to just blend in anonymously with the mass of humanity, and he wondered if he could just slip quietly back into society once again. It was clear that he didn't need a disguise to do it—all he needed was a stinking cold and a bright red nose so that he looked like shite to make him unrecognisable to Joe Public. Somehow, that made him feel much better. No one could understand what it felt like to be on show all the time, unless you'd been in that place.

He settled back into his seat. Things had changed since he

last caught the Underground. This station and the train were clean, shiny and new. Clearly, some money had been pumped into it since he'd been a student in London. It was a pleasure to travel like this—relatively speaking. He closed his eyes and tuned into the thump of his headache as he wondered what he was going to say to Fern.

As he changed to the Northern Line to head up to Euston station, he realised that nothing much had changed at all. Here the stations were old, dirty and crumbling, the trains nearly as rickety. It was busier and he was jostled onto the next train, although still no one gave him the time of day. He had to stand as all the seats were full, swaying alarmingly as the train hurtled through the tunnels. Then the train stopped in another tunnel and they waited in darkness for ten minutes until it moved again. Progress was painful—due to a signalling failure, the driver announced over the crackling intercom. There was nothing he could do but sniff miserably into his handkerchief and wonder whether he should have stayed tucked up in bed. At this rate the King's Head would be closed by the time he got there, if he ever managed to find it.

When he did, eventually, reach Euston station, he realised that he'd had more than enough of real life and wished that he'd dragged Frank away from his evening's television or whatever to get the limo out. He was beginning to appreciate how comfortable and cosseted he was in his privileged world. Having arrived at the station, Evan realised that he was still no closer to knowing where the King's Head might be, so he disappeared into the depths of a filthy underground garage to jump into a cab. Still not quite his limo, but much better than being bounced and battered along in that hideous sardine can they called the Tube.

'I need to find a pub called the King's Head,' Evan told the driver.

'There must be five hundred of them in London, guv,' the cabbie said. 'Can you be a bit more specific?'

'It's round here. Not far from the station, I think. Can we just take a drive?'

'I love you Yanks,' the driver said with a hearty laugh. 'You all think England's the size of a threepenny bit.'

Evan was surprised that the driver didn't recognise his accent as British or Welsh. Was that because his roots were floating somewhere over the mid-Atlantic now?

'Haven't I seen you on the telly?'

'I don't think so.'

'I had that Jude Law in the back of my cab last week. What a star he is! Mark my words, that boy's going places. What did you say the pub was called?'

'The King's Head.'

'Then let's give it a whirl.' To the honks of a dozen impatient horns, the driver pulled out into the traffic.

Despite a lack of coherent directions, within minutes Evan had been deposited outside a faded, typical London backstreet pub called the King's Head. Tipping the cab driver generously for what had been a very brief ride, Evan could only hope that it was the right King's Head.

Fifty-five

Evan stood on the pavement still wondering whether this was a wise idea, but unable to think through the fog of his cold. He'd come this far and had gone through the hell of public transport to get here; there could be no turning back now.

Evan blew his nose and coughed a little before taking his heart in his hand and pushing through the swing door that led into the King's Head. You could have cut the smoke with a knife, and it made him splutter a bit more. The pub was packed with punters jostling for space. He scanned the area around him, but he didn't have to wait long to see whether he'd come to the right place or not. Above the heads of the crowd and on a rather makeshift stage, Fern stood right in front of him.

She was wearing scruffy jeans and a blouse that had probably seen better days, and her hair fell loosely round her shoulders, but she had a presence on the stage. A charisma that could never be taught. Her voice was clear and strong—and completely wasted on this place. Stephen Cauldwell was right, Evan thought. She was good. More than good. Even after a few notes he could tell that. Fern would have walked the *Fame Game* contest, and Evan's heart went out to her. He didn't recognise the song she was just finishing, but the audience clapped enthusiastically—so it was obviously a firm favourite. Sometimes he was so wrapped up in his own music that he had no idea what was big in the current pop culture. Nevertheless, Evan joined in with the applause. Fern nodded in thanks and then walked across to her keyboard player, who started up with the introduction of the next song. It took a lot of courage to do this sort of gig night after night. Evan wasn't sure he could tolerate it. Every night she had to fight for the attention of the audience, over their chatter, the clank of the fruit machines and the noise of the bar. Even when he'd started out, he'd automatically been given a certain respect. Fern had to claw every inch of hers.

When the next song started up, he recognised it instantly. It was a Beatles number, ironically called, 'Can't Buy Me Love'. It had been one of his sister Glenys's favourite tunes, and the memory brought up a huge ball of emotion that blocked his throat and made tears spring to his eyes. They'd given it a modern beat and, expertly, Fern belted it out to the back of the pub. The audience started to dance along to the music as Fern sang boldly about not caring too much about money. Evan realised with a sinking feeling that perhaps he'd spent too much of his life focusing on little else. Slowly, he threaded through the crush of bodies, moving to the front of the crowd. Fern finished her song, once again to frenetic applause.

'Okay,' she said, flicking her hair from her face. There was a sheen of perspiration on her skin and a bold little jut to her chin. She was putting her heart into this, and Evan knew in that moment that he'd lost his for ever. 'Let's slow things down a little.'

The keyboard player struck a chord which hit Evan hard in his stomach and Fern sang the opening words of the timeless Beatles ballad 'Yesterday'. Before he fully appreciated what he was doing, Evan was walking up onto the stage.

As Fern saw him, she rocked back slightly on her heels and stumbled over the haunting words. Around the pub, as people recognised him, a cheer went up. Evan held up a hand in grateful acknowledgement. Fern regained her composure, smiled widely at him and took up her song once more. A reverent hush fell over the audience as he joined her in a duet. The guy on the keyboard cut his accompaniment to a bare minimum. All that could be heard was a blend of their voices, harmonising perfectly. If nothing else, their voices were a marriage made in heaven, Evan thought. He took Fern's hand and folded his fingers around it. She trembled at his touch and he watched a tear slide down her cheek, before he brushed it gently away with his thumb.

It was idiotic to sing while he had a cold—Rupert would have killed him if he'd been here. But his agent wasn't here to stop him and, right now, Evan didn't care. This was a bit different from singing a full concert. He reasoned that one small song did not an aria make. And it was a long time since a woman had made him want to sing Beatles songs with her. He sang for Glenys, for Fern and for himself, loving every minute. In the past he'd performed for President Bush, the pope and the queen on many occasions, but he'd not enjoyed it as much as this. The song finished and he took Fern in his arms, holding her close.

'I can't believe you're here,' she breathed.

'Me, neither,' he said.

Then he held up their hands and they took a low bow to their ecstatic audience. He'd done things wrong, and now perhaps he'd have a chance to put them right. As the song said, he believed in yesterday—but he now also had great hopes for tomorrow.

Fifty-six

Carl turns away from me as I leave the pub with Evan, but I've already seen the expression on his face. My friend's pain nips at me, holding me back, but then Evan takes my arm and steers me through the crowd. And I don't look back. It seems as if Ken the Landlord will have to manage without me, once again.

Out on the street, the cold cuts through me, and I wish I'd thought to pick up my coat en route. Evan holds up his hand and a cab pulls up.

'No limo tonight?' I tease.

He hurries me inside. 'You would not believe what I did to get here,' Evan says with a disbelieving tone in his voice. 'I took public transport.'

I start to laugh. 'Wow! Poor you!'

'I gave Frank the night off,' he explains. 'How could I drag him away from the bosom of his family?'

'You're all heart,' I say.

Evan gives his address to the driver and he speeds off towards the Docklands. In the back of the cab, we stare at each other with lust and longing. Evan slides his arms round me. 'I have a terrible head cold,' he tells me.

'And you brought it to my door?' This is what's commonly known as bluster. I daren't admit that I think he caught it from my dear old mum. 'What a charmer. Thanks.'

'I was supposed to be singing at a charity gala,' he admits, 'but I had to cancel. The doctor wouldn't let me perform.'

Now I feel really terrible.

He takes my hand and grips it tightly. 'I just lay there thinking about you. In the end, I had to get up and find you.'

'You got off your sickbed to look for me?'

Evan nods. 'I wanted to hear you sing.'

I give him a wry look.

'You're very good,' he says.

'Don't tell me that I would have won the *Fame Game* competition or I might have to hurt you.'

'I also wanted to apologise for running out of your parents' flat,' he continues. 'It was very rude of me, and I wanted to explain why.'

'You don't owe me an explanation.'

'It was seeing your son like that…'

My ears prick up. 'Nathan isn't my son.'

Now Evan perks up, too. 'He isn't?'

'He's my nephew. My brother's kid.'

'Oh.' Evan settles back in the cab. He seems relieved. I wonder if he thinks I'm a better proposition if I'm a child-free zone, and a wave of irritation washes over me. I'd love to know what's going through his head.

'I thought he was yours,' he says, and blows his nose.

'You know what "thought" did,' I say briskly. Then I relent. 'I do look after him a lot. His real mum ran out on them when he was still a baby. I'm sort of his unofficial maternal replacement and favourite aunty.'

Evan stays silent.

'I thought you were worried that you'd catch something,' I say.

He gives me a slow smile. 'I *did* catch something.'

'That was from my mum,' I confess. 'She's got a cold.'

'Join the club.' He takes my hand again. 'I *was* worried about his illness, but not in the way you think.'

I wait patiently for the next bit, which I sense is coming with some sort of internal struggle. We bounce through the darkened London streets, snaking through the light evening traffic.

'I had a sister,' Evan says finally. He chews nervously at his lip. 'She was killed when we were young.'

'Oh, Evan,' I say. 'I'm sorry.'

'I've never really got over it.' His voice is gruff, filled with emotion, and he toys with my fingers, not looking at me. 'Since then I've avoided anything to do with children. With relationships. With anything that might involve me in real life.'

'And a sick child completely freaked you out?'

Evan rests his head back on the seat and stares at the roof of the cab, which I take as a yes. 'I wanted to get close to you— I felt we *were* getting close—but the thought of dealing with Nathan's illness scared me.'

'And now?'

'It's ricocheted round my brain like a pinball machine,' he

admits with a wavering sigh. 'But I think it's worth giving it a try.'

'It?'

'This,' he says, leaning towards me. I can hear my heart pounding in my ears as he threads his hands through my hair and draws me close to him.

'I'll catch your cold,' I say.

'Then you'll know how much I'm suffering.'

And Evan kisses me, deep and hard, making me lose all sense of reason. We slide together on the seat as his body covers mine, and I wish that the cab driver had a blind to pull down or something, because this is definitely going to get steamy. My clothes seem to be coming adrift at an alarming rate. I tear at Evan's clothes, ripping all the buttons off his hideously expensive shirt, but he doesn't seem to mind. Actually, he doesn't seem to mind at all. This is a man who has stayed in five-star luxury places all around the world, and we're making out like teenagers in the back of a grotty cab. A low groan escapes his lips. 'I've never wanted anyone so much,' he murmurs.

Then the cab pulls up outside Evan's apartment, which is just as well or we might have been arrested for indecent exposure.

Fifty-seven

We dishevel each other's clothing some more as we ride in the lift up to the top floor. I want this man naked. My hands travel over his smooth, bare chest. His skin is hot and silky beneath my fingers, and my knees go weak with desire. I haven't had sex in a long, long time and, make no mistake, I WANT IT NOW!

Evan struggles to get his key in the lock as we're reluctant to part our lips and his hands are keen to do much more interesting things than unlocking the door.

'I thought the doctor said you weren't fit to perform tonight,' I remind him as he breaks from ravishing me for a moment to concentrate on what he's doing.

'Never trust doctors. They don't know what they're talking about. I'm sure I can still give the performance of my life,' he assures me. 'In fact, I fully intend to.'

I can hardly wait.

And so we stumble into the apartment, hastily tripping over each other as we do. We fall onto Evan's sofa, a tangle of arms and legs, and smother each other in passionate kisses again. Evan's hands find the buckle of my belt, and he eases it undone.

'Wait, wait,' I say. 'Wait.'

We both sit up. 'What's wrong?'

'I need to do things,' I say.

'What things?'

'I need to go to the bathroom.'

'Oh.'

I jump up from the sofa. What I really need is time to think. I want to savour every moment of this, and it seems to be going way too fast. Suddenly the pace of this has upped considerably and, I'm not sure which, but my body or my brain seems to be lagging behind. I need to get one of them up to speed.

Evan kisses me again and I nearly forget that I should take a break. 'I'll open some champagne while you're gone,' he says huskily.

'You don't drink.'

He puts my fingers to his mouth and sucks on them. Knees. Jelly. Again. 'I think this could be classed as a special occasion.'

Before I lose my mind completely, I bolt for the bathroom, gathering my clothes around me as I go. I scrabble round, opening the wrong doors until I find the sanctuary of the bathroom. This is the same room where I found out that I, and I alone, was to go through to the *Fame Game* competition. My body is shaking just as much now as it was then, but for entirely different reasons.

I catch a glimpse of myself in the huge mirrors, and it isn't

a pretty sight. I look suspiciously like I've been recently rav-
ished in the back of a taxi. My hair appears to have been back-
combed by an insane hairdresser. My make-up is all over the
place—lipstick on my nose, that sort of stuff. Toyah Wilcox
somehow managed to carry off this image in the 1980s—but
it *so* doesn't work now. I grab some tissues and dampen them,
rubbing them over my face. Breathing into my hand, I check
my breath. Not good, either—passive beer inhalation. My
God, I can't believe I've snogged Evan David stinking like an
old brewery. Thank goodness he's got a cold and won't be able
to smell it. There's a toothbrush and some toothpaste in a ce-
ramic holder—I'm going to use it. I don't care whose it is, but
I do hope that it's Evan's rather than anyone else's. Bracing myself, I rub the bristles round my teeth and hope that I don't get
any more germs than I've probably already contracted. If Ken
the Landlord hasn't already sacked me—again—then Evan
David won't be the only one who isn't fit to sing this week.

I want to do this in a sexy and sophisticated way. I want our
love to be slow and seductive. There's no way that Evan is used
to wrestling mad-looking women into submission on his sofa.
His conquests are probably more subtle and skilled than this.
That's the kind of man he is. I flush when I think of what we
got up to in that cab—the driver will probably be recounting
that story for weeks. Evan must wonder what on earth he's
brought home. I open up one of the bathroom cabinets and
find a comb, which I pull through my hair and fluff it back
into some semblance of a style.

Undoing a couple of buttons on my blouse, I check to see
if my sophistication level has gone up. No, not a chance. There's
only one other way to tackle this, and that's to go all out for

it. I give my underwear the once-over and bless the fact that I didn't have time to do a second load of washing this week. All my scabby, workaday pants are in the wash, so I'm down to my posh, special occasion knickers and—get this—matching bra! Ha! How often is it the other way round? Find yourself in the arms of a desirable man and you're bound to be wearing greying undies with sagging elastic. But not this time. I grin at myself in the mirror. 'You are going to work this, girl!'

Before I can bottle out, I strip off the rest of my clothes. Thankfully, the thermostat in Evan's apartment is set at about a million degrees to keep his voice cosseted, so there's no danger of my coming down with hypothermia. I stand in front of the mirror and scrutinise my appearance once again. Black lace bra and oh-so-tiny thong. Yay! Legs *and* underarms shaved. Yay! Killer heels. Yay! This would not be a good look with trainers. Bite lip to encourage bloodflow and produce pout, as stupidly left lipstick in handbag back on the sofa. Could definitely do with a drink before my courage deserts me. Looking forward to that champagne immensely.

I give myself one last look. Not bad. Taking a few deep breaths, I psych myself up. 'I can do this. I can do this.'

And so I burst out of the bathroom, put on my catwalk strut and sashay back into the living room to find my man and make his eyeballs rotate. Look out, Evan David, you ain't seen nothin' yet!

Fifty-eight

'Da, da!' I announce as I make my entrance, arms held aloft displaying my rather obvious charms. Evan David's eyeballs, do, as I'd imagined, shoot out on stalks. They almost spin round. His chin nearly hits the floor, too.

But my paramour isn't lounging on the sofa as I'd imagined, champagne in hand. He's standing clutching the bottle, a look of terror frozen on his face.

I drop my arms. 'What?'

He opens his mouth, but before words can come out, his eyes cast a panic-stricken glance to his right. I follow them.

'Hi,' the woman says.

My hands fly to cover my bra, then my pants and then... I give up.

'Lana Rosina,' she purrs. 'You must be...'

Mad, I think. I must be mad.

'Fern,' Evan says tightly. 'This is my friend, Fern.'

Friend? I'm a *friend?* You don't hop into bed—or onto the sofa—with friends.

Lana's carrying a champagne flute, which she hands over to Evan. 'We must celebrate,' she says.

I recognise her now. This is the woman who Evan was snapped with scuttling into that posh Cardiff hotel in the dead of the night. I saw the photograph of them together when I was flicking through *Hello!* or *OK!* or *Stars in Bloody Buggery Awkward Situations* magazine—whichever it was. No wonder he's turned so white. He'd obviously forgotten that he'd already set up tonight's entertainment. I can feel my jaw go rigid with anger and disappointment. No wild night of passion for me then, it seems. Not now. Not ever.

Lana Rosina holds out her hand. There is a sparkling rock the size of a small planet on her finger. I'm almost blinded by its twinkling. 'I am engaged,' she tells me with uncontained glee.

'Congratulations,' I say, when, 'You're welcome to the conniving bastard!' is a mere slip away from my tongue.

'I am so in love!'

Funnily enough, so was I a minute ago. I glare at Evan, but he's clearly in a state of shock at being caught red-handed, as he doesn't even register my best death rays. I hadn't imagined that someone as handsome as Evan David wouldn't have regular company in his bed that he might neglect to mention, but to forget that your fiancée was going to drop by really takes the biscuit.

Why does this sort of thing always happen to me? Do I create drama in my life? Do I attract it like a magnet sucks up iron filings? If I'd kept my clothes on, then I could have explained all this away by saying that I was working a bit of over-time. But then my blood boils. Why should it be down to *me* to get Evan 'Fast-and-Loose-Willy' David out of the mire? No, I'm off. He can sort this one out himself.

And I tell him as much. 'I'm off,' I say.

He's jolted out of his catatonic state. 'F-Fern,' he stammers. 'This isn't what it seems.'

Oh, that old chestnut! 'I'm sure it's exactly what it seems,' I say, galloping away on my high horse.

'No, it isn't,' he says crossly.

Eh? I'm taken aback. He's the one in the wrong here. This is not the time to be a cross-patch with *me*.

'There is no need to leave,' Lana purrs again and gives a care-less shrug. 'I know these things 'appen. We are all grown-up people.'

Well, I'm not that bloody grown up! These things might ''appen' in opera circles, but they don't ''appen' to barmaids from the King's Head. I'd like to give them both a piece of my mind, but I don't want to be responsible for a pair of heart attacks.

'Lana,' Evan says tightly. 'Stay out of this.'

I hold up my hands. 'I'm leaving.'

'Fern…'

'Oh, save your explanations for someone who cares.' I do my best flounce towards the bathroom, even though I feel I'm hanging on to my dignity by a shred. Actually, my dignity pro-bably left a few minutes ago, come to think of it.

'I don't want it to end like this,' Evan says to my back.

I turn round and look at him. His face is drawn and weary-looking. I want to cry. We were having such a nice time. How could he do this to me?

'I do,' I say softly.

Then I hurry into the bathroom, throw on my clothes and brace myself for the walk out of here. I'm dreading having to go back out there and face both of them, together, but I can do this with my head held high. I might have been caught out in my underwear, but at least there were no bottoms bobbing up and down. It was a close call, mind you. But I can, at least, hang on to that thought.

Brushing the tears from beneath my eyes, I push the smudges of mascara back into place. Neither of them will see me cry.

Fully clothed again, but still feeling just as naked and vulnerable, I go back into the vast living room—which suddenly seems to have shrunk considerably in size and is rather crowded with just the three of us in there. Lana is helping herself to champagne and grinning widely. Evan is standing by the windows staring out at the river, even though all he can see is blackness.

I have no idea how my legs are managing to carry me, but they do somehow convey me to the door. Turning, I say in the strongest voice I can muster, 'I hope you'll be very happy together.'

Then before I break down and weep, I'm out of the door—and I make sure that as I leave I give it the most almighty bang.

Fifty-nine

Taking the Tube, I go straight to Carl's flat. It's all in darkness, so I bang on the door, which makes my fist ache and also causes the neighbours to stick their heads out of their front doors to glare at me. One of them hurls a few obscenities in my direction.

'Sorry, sorry,' I mutter and try Carl's mobile instead. No joy there, either. What do I do now? My already deflated spirit sags a bit more. Carl is *never* not around when I need him. It feels as if my own shadow has deserted me. I leave a cheery message. 'Hey, Carlos, it's me. It's late, but I thought you might want to hang out for a while. Call me.'

Not knowing what else to do, I head for home. Back at the flat—I plod up the stairs, peeling off my clothing in a less sedate manner than had previously been the case. This is the one good thing about my dad not being in the flat, I can wander around in my undies and have the bathroom all to myself once more. But you know what? The strange thing is, I actually miss the old bugger. This place is so quiet without him and I wonder how I ever managed to live alone before.

Dumping my handbag, I go into the kitchen. The boiler's gone out again, so the place is freezing. I fiddle with all of its knobs for a good ten minutes until it deigns to ignite again with an alarming hiss and bang. I have to get Ali in to look at this thing—it's a death trap.

Sitting down at the table, I nurse my head in my hands. I miss Squeaky. You'd never think a mouse could be such good company, but he was and now he's gone, too. Never have I felt quite so alone in the world. Evan David is off my Christmas card list, my dad's banged up in a Coronary Care Ward, my mum's turned into a wanton woman, Carl's gone AWOL and my pet mouse is wrapped in a piece of kitchen roll on the floor by the back door.

I think about making myself a cup of tea, but I can't face looking at Squeaky's broken body for a moment longer, so I pick up my clothes and get dressed again. Rummaging in the kitchen drawers, I find a plastic bag to slip Squeaky in. If I'm going to give him a decent burial in the park, I don't want some mangy dog digging him up the very next day. So, for good measure, I put him in yet another plastic bag. Then I take a tablespoon which I slip into my pocket and carry Squeaky down the stairs and outside.

Running the gauntlet of the late-night druggies huddled into doorways, I take a bus up Eversholt Street walk to the Oakley Square which is, thankfully, deserted except for a few harmless bums. I really could do with Carl's help with this. He's the one who always gives me a hoof up over the railings into the park, but I'll just have to manage. Again, I can't really put Squeaky down, or hurl him over the fence before me, so I tie the plastic bag to my wrist and scale the railings unaided.

I haven't got a torch, either, so once I'm away from the glare of the streetlights, I stumble to the back of the park near to the few straggly bushes that survive here. Laying Squeaky down, I fish out my tablespoon and dig in the soft earth until I've made a shallow grave. Not too shallow—but hopefully dog-thwartingly deep. Taking Squeaky's body, I lay him reverently in the hole and then cover him over with the soil. I wish I had a flower or something to mark the spot, but I don't because I hadn't really planned on coming here tonight. Maybe I'll buy Squeaky a rose tomorrow—he'd like that.

Standing up, I gaze at the tiny mound of earth and am close to tears. I want to say a prayer, but it's so long since I've prayed that I wouldn't know what to say or who to address it to. If it's this difficult to say goodbye to a mouse, how hard would it have been to bury my dad? It's unbearable to think that anything could have happened to him. You always assume that your parents are going to be around for ever—it's horrible to suddenly view them as mortal.

I try not to think of Evan, but I can't help wondering what it would feel like to have your sister die so young. I'm sure I'd come apart at the seams if anything happened to Joe or to Nathan. And maybe Evan has. Putting my face in my hands, I slowly massage my eyes. I can't believe what happened tonight. Who would have thought that it would have turned out like that? But, in a twisted way, I'm pleased that things hadn't gone any further. Having just one night with him would have been far worse than not having one at all. This is what I'm going to keep telling myself—over and over—until I actually believe it.

I'm so grateful that I've got the chance to repair my relationship with Dad, and, hopefully, at the same time, steer him and Mum back on track. Family is all that matters and I shouldn't forget that.

Trailing back across the park, I wipe the dirty spoon on my jeans and promise myself that I'll remember to soak it in bleach before I use it again. With much huffing and puffing, I haul myself back over the railings. I wonder where Carl is now? He's been so much like my right arm for the last umpteen years that I've forgotten what it's like to function without him. Maybe I should take more notice of how much he cares for me. Maybe I should forget all notions of my stupid crush on Evan David— that's all it was, after all. A stupid, stupid crush. And maybe I should start looking for love closer to home.

Sixty

'So when's the wedding?' Rupert asked.

'In two months.'

'That woman doesn't hang around when she sets her mind to something,' his agent said. 'You have to hand it to her.'

Evan's mouth was set in a grim line. 'You sure do.'

'I'll put it in the diary now.' Rupert strode towards the desk. 'This is one arrangement you won't be able to wriggle out of.'

'You're telling me.'

'Fail to turn up for *that* gig and you might part with your manhood permanently.' Rupert rubbed his hands together. 'I think I'll write it in blood.'

'Make sure it's your own,' Evan said. 'I'm all out.'

Rupert halted his progress. 'You don't sound too pleased about this, my friend.'

Evan shrugged noncommittally. 'I'm pleased. I'm delighted. I'm thrilled.'

Rupert didn't look convinced.

'What else can I say?' Evan asked moodily.

'You can tell Uncle Rupert why you're looking quite so miserable about this revelation. I thought it would be good news for you.'

Evan scratched distractedly at his stubble. 'Lana turned up and made her announcement just as Fern and I were getting cosy.'

'Fern was here?'

'I went to the pub where she was singing.'

His agent looked aghast. 'Against doctor's orders, you got out of bed and went to the pub?'

'She's very good,' Evan sighed.

Rupert's eyes widened farther. 'At what?'

'At singing.' Evan stared at his friend levelly. 'Lana arrived before we managed to get down to anything else.'

'I'm very glad to hear it,' Rupert said. He returned to the sofa and slumped into it. 'All this is very bad for my heart, darling.'

'You haven't got one, Rup.'

Rupert Dawson clutched at where his heart might be.

'Oh, don't be such a drama queen,' Evan said tiredly. 'I was the one that was very nearly caught with my pants down.'

'And Fern? Where does she fit into the picture now?'

'Nowhere,' Evan replied with a shake of his head. 'It's over.' It pained him to think that it never even actually began. 'I don't need the hassle. When she saw Lana here, she thought…' Evan sighed heavily. 'Well, she thought some pretty awful things.'

'And who can blame her?' Rupert wanted to know.

'She didn't even want to know my side of the story,' Evan persisted. 'She just took everything at face value.'

'Is there any other way to take it?' His agent poured himself a glass of champagne from the half-empty bottle that stood on the coffee table. 'You know that women lack a certain rationale when it comes to matters so close to the heart.'

Rupert sipped his champagne and grimaced at its lack of sparkle. That was exactly how Evan felt—flat and lacking in fizz.

'She's the only person I've ever...' Evan broke off. 'What's the point?'

'Exactly,' Rupert said heartily. 'Learn from it. Move on. We'll be out of here in a few weeks, and she'll be a distant memory.'

'I want you to go and listen to her sing, Rupert. She's great. She could be fantastic.'

'No,' Rupert said. 'This is your nether regions talking.'

'Offer her a contract.'

'I'm a hard-headed businessman, not a charity for discarded lovers.'

'You wait until you hear her,' Evan insisted. 'Then you'll know I'm right. I'll put up the money if necessary. You just do the paperwork.'

'She's a pub singer, for heaven's sake. A crooner. This will never work out.'

'Stephen Cauldwell could snap her up from under your nose,' Evan warned. He'd thrown down the gauntlet and, if he'd gauged it right, he knew that his friend couldn't bear to lose out to another talent-spotter.

Rupert worried at his lip. 'Okay, I'll take a look.'

Evan hid a dry smile. 'She has a nephew,' he continued, 'the one I told you about.'

'I thought it was her son?'

'Another Evan David blunder.'

'You're not going to make a habit of being such a twit, are you?' Rupert wanted to know. 'You used to be such a regular sort of guy. If a bit grumpy.'

'Son, nephew, does it matter? He's ill,' Evan said, 'and I want to pay to make him better. Tell her, whatever it costs, that his medical expenses will all be covered. Whatever he needs, I'll pay. Just tell her. Tell her that.'

It was the only thing he could think of that would go some way to making this up to Fern. Some gesture to let her know that he still cared very much about her. Perhaps it would help to ease some of his own pain, too, if he could do something to save just one sickly kid. Not that it was his main motivation, but in his simple, struggling, stupid bloke way, he hoped that it would be a positive by-product.

'Love is making you behave very strangely.'

'Tell me something I don't know.'

'I'd better put that wedding date in the diary, or be damned.' Rupert stood up and headed towards the desk again. He paused and looked at his friend. 'Are you absolutely sure you know what you're doing?'

'Rupert, quit with the lectures and just do as I ask,' Evan snapped. 'Sometimes you forget that I employ you.'

'Ah,' Rupert smiled and rubbed his hands together. 'Thank goodness. The return of old Grumpy Guts. I was beginning to think I'd lost you, darling. Let's hope the rest of your life soon gets back to normal, too.'

But Evan knew, that whatever else it was, his life was a long way from being normal.

Sixty-one

I call Carl again on the way to the hospital to visit my dad, but still I get a robotic voice telling me to record a voicemail message—which I duly do. 'Hey, Carlos. Have you skipped the country?' I say, trying to sound as cheerful as possible. 'I'm worried about you. Just off to see Mum, then I'm going to the hospital to visit Dad. It's ten o'clock in the morning. Where are you, you lazy bastard?'

And then I set off in the direction of the Euston Road.

Carl could well be in bed. This is not his time of day. I'm not sure what is really. A part of Carl always wants to be horizontal in a hammock. He has some great ideas, but he's generally too lazy to swing his legs to the ground and get on with making them real. The first time I've ever seen him truly motivated was when he came up with the whole *Fame Game* idea. It just goes to show that he has ambition lurking deep within him if he can summon up the effort.

I thought he might have turned up for breakfast this morn-ing—maybe bearing some baked goodies—but Carl has sur-prised me once again with a no-show. I just hope he's okay.

My mum is in the newsagent's shop, serving behind the counter, when I swing by there. I wait patiently until she's chat-ted to all her customers, dished out their change and has rear-ranged her newspapers before I step forward.

'Hello, Fern.' She leans over piles of *Daily Mails* and gives me a brisk kiss on the cheek. My mother adores us all, but she's never been big on soppy displays. 'What brings you here, dar-lin'?'

'I thought you might want an update on Dad.' I still haven't spoken to her about what happened. Frankly, the fewer details she knows about my role in Dad's admittance to the hospital the better, or I'd definitely be in for some flak. All the mes-sages about Dad's heart attack—or 'wobble', as he likes to call it—have been relayed through my brother, Joe.

'Joe says he's doing fine.' She carries on fiddling with her newspapers. Her fingers are black with newsprint, but the rest of her is immaculately groomed.

'He is.' I take a breath. 'Mum, he's asking for you.'

All she does is raise one eyebrow and in a slightly ironic way. I have no idea what that means, but I suspect that it's not good.

'You haven't been near the hospital yet.' My voice sounds more accusatory than it should.

Regarding me levelly, she rests her folded arms on the counter. 'Are you sure that he's not faking it again?'

I shake my head. 'Not this time.'

She looks unconvinced. A stream of customers arrive, and I move aside so that she can serve them. While she's busy, I crane my neck around to get a glimpse into the backroom of the shop to see if Mr Patel is there. When we're alone again, I take up the cause once more.

'He needs you,' I say. 'Just go to visit him. Say hello. That's all I'm asking.'

My mum sighs and moves her folded arms to cover her chest. 'Tell me why I should.'

'He's still your husband,' I point out softly. 'Don't you have any feelings for him at all?'

She rather looks like she doesn't.

'We nearly lost him, Mum. Seriously. How would you feel if that happened and you hadn't seen him?'

Her posture sags a little. I've spotted a slight chink in her armour. 'Joe says he's out of danger.'

'He's better,' I agree, 'but he's not exactly ready for running the London Marathon.'

'There's no need for sarcasm, young lady,' my mum warns.

Now she's on the defensive, which I view as a good thing.

'Go in to see him. Please. Please.' I resort to begging. 'Please. The doctors say that he shouldn't be upset, and there's no doubt that this *is* upsetting him.' The doctors haven't actually said that, but I'm sure they would if they knew the situation. 'Just drop by with some flowers.'

'Flowers?' Mum huffs. 'For that old goat? He doesn't deserve flowers.' She looks like she's warming up for one of her I-hate-your-father rants, which I can't bear to hear. My dad's no angel, but he's not that bad, either.

I hold up my hands. 'Okay. I'm done,' I say. 'If you don't want to see him, then that's up to you. I've tried my best.'

Mum's mouth is set in a grim line. I don't know how she

can be so heartless. To me, it's proof that her affections now lie elsewhere.

'But if anything happens to him, Mum, remember that I tried,' I say. 'Remember that I tried my best.'

Sixty-two

When I finally get to the hospital, I find my dad sitting up in his bed being spoon-fed some sort of porridge concoction by the same petite and pretty Thai nurse who was on duty when he was first admitted. She always seems to be here, and I wonder if some of these staff ever go home.

The only benefit of Dad being in a Coronary Care Ward is that there are no regular visiting hours. The staff turn off the lights at around three o'clock when the patients are all supposed to bed down for a snooze, but other than that you can pretty much come and go as you please. I thought I'd drop in early as my next stop is the King's Head, where I am seriously going to grovel to Ken the Landlord and apologise for all my terrible behaviour recently and for having to keep leaving him in the lurch. But that's the end of it. I will be a model employee from now on. I might even persuade him to instigate a system of reward stars like McDonald's—so I will go from a *Johnny No-Stars* to top, fully loaded *Employee of the Month* within no time. This is my pledge, and I will tell Ken all of this with my hand on my heart. He'd probably prefer it if I put my hands somewhere else, but he can lump that.

As I get closer to Dad's bed, I can see that he's telling the nurse a joke and she, in turn, is giggling furiously. I'm stunned to see that there's flirting going on. My dad—who has just had a major heart attack—is flirting! Jesus, Mary and Joseph, how was I blessed with such parents? Aren't parents supposed to be the well-behaved ones with a set of unruly kids to stress over? There seems to be a bit of role reversal going on here.

When I get to the bed, they both look up at me guiltily. I might not be a trained medical professional, but there doesn't seem to be much wrong with Dad now, in my opinion. In fact, his heart monitor seems to be beeping rather too perkily for my liking.

'Hello, Dad.'

'Hello, love,' Dad says sheepishly.

'You look a lot better.' Even I can hear the edge in my voice.

'I'm feeling grand,' he says.

'I'm glad.' So why don't I sound glad?

'This is Kim.' Dad licks his lips nervously as he nods towards his carer.

She gives a little girly giggle. 'Hello, Fern,' she says. 'I have heard many things about you.'

Oh, really? I give my dad the evil eye.

'I was telling her about the *Fame Game,* love,' he admits. 'And how clever you are.'

Oh, yes. That'll be clever as in 'clever enough to blow my one big chance', then, will it?

'Kim's from Thailand. Bangkok. She's come over here for work. Not been here long.' Dad's gabbling. 'She's got a huge family at home. Sends money to them every month.'

Kim is nodding furiously, her winsome grin widening as he reveals more and more details of her personal life. I can feel a frown coming on. There must have been a lot of cosy chats going on here.

When my dad eventually runs out of steam, we all stare at each other in uncomfortable silence. Whatever Kim's doing, she's certainly giving my dad a tonic.

'All done,' she says, and takes the empty bowl away from him. 'Good boy.'

Boy? My dad—a *boy?*

He certainly gives her a boyish grin.

'I come back later and give you nice new sheets,' she promises him. I half-expect her to peck him on the cheek. Kim gives me a shy smile and scuttles away.

I sit down at his bedside. 'Personal care, eh?'

'She's a lovely young lass.'

'Well, she certainly seems to have put the colour back in your cheeks.' I suppose I shouldn't resent him getting a bit of comfort. I just wish his comfort hadn't come in such a young and pretty form. 'How are you feeling today?'

He nods. 'Better. Much better.'

I give his hand a squeeze. 'Good.'

Dad's eyes turn towards the window. 'No word from your mum?'

'I've just been to see her to give her an update. She's worried about you.' The lie trips easily from my tongue.

'But not worried enough to come and see me?'

My dad may be ill, but he's not stupid. I shake my head word-lessly. Dad sags back against his pillow, and tears fill his eyes.

'I don't know what's going on in her head,' I admit.

'I spent forty years trying to fathom that out,' Dad jokes shakily. 'Your mother will come round in her own time.'

I cast a surreptitious glance at pretty, young Nurse Kim as she bustles about the ward. She turns back and meets my gaze. I just hope that Mum doesn't leave it too late.

Sixty-three

My brother Joe arrives on the Coronary Care Ward at the same time as Carl. I kiss them both.

'How's Nathan?' I ask Joe.

'Good,' he says. 'Missing you.'

'I'm missing him, too. I'll try to come round later,' I promise. Now that I'm not mega-busy trying to forge a pop career and look after Evan David's every whim in between time, I should have some of my life back to myself.

Joe clasps Dad's hand and then takes my place at his bedside.

'Come on,' I say to Carl, 'we can clear off and get something to eat.'

'Bye, Mr Kendal,' Carl says to Dad. 'Glad to see you're looking better.'

'That was a bloody short visit,' Dad complains. 'And where are my grapes?'

Yes, it seems that my dad is making a marvellous recovery. Carl flicks him a good-natured peace sign and we head out towards the hospital café.

'He looks well,' Carl says as we stride down the corridors, the echo of our footsteps bouncing back at us off the walls. 'You must be relieved.'

'Relieved?' I say with a huff. 'He's already trying to get one of the young nurses to give him more than a bed bath.'

Carl chuckles.

'It's not funny,' I tell him. 'Even though he had a quick knock at death's door, it hasn't moved my mum to come and see him. I never imagined that she'd be like this. I thought they'd both forget all their silliness and make it up. It grieves me to say this, Carl, but I don't know that they'll ever get back together now.'

'You worry about them too much.'

'Not for much longer,' I say. 'I'm definitely thinking about trading them both in for better parents.'

'You love them both just as they are,' Carl counters. 'And you know it.'

I give an exasperated sigh. 'It's not good manners to be right all the time.'

With a carefree laugh, Carl swings me through the door to the hospital café. As a further assault to the senses, the café is decorated in shades of red and white. With all the blood and bandages around this place, I would have thought it was a really bad choice of colour scheme, but what do I know?

'I wish I smoked,' I say to Carl as we queue up at the self-service counter. 'I have a craving for some toxins to give me a kick-start.'

Honestly, I could lie down on the counter and go right off to sleep. I'm exhausted, and the only time my brain seems to shut off is when I'm flat out in bed. I wish someone would whisk me off to the Bahamas so that I could lie on a sunbed on the beach for two weeks and recuperate—but, like everything else that I dream of, it's simply not going to happen. Hospital canteen food is set to be my only succour.

'I could give you a cancer stick, or I've got some dope back at the flat,' my friend offers.

'You are *so* rock 'n' roll!' I tease, and we both have a laugh. I don't know why, but I thought there might be some tension between us this morning. Of course, as always, I deeply underestimated Carl's ability to be nice, understanding and utterly accepting.

We opt for a putrid cup of hospital coffee and a bacon roll each, which I buy because I'm feeling guilty. I expect Carl has been taking a lot of flack from Ken the Landlord about my continued absences, but if he has, he's said nothing to me. We find a table without too much rubbish on it, and I wipe it down with a serviette. So much for the improvement in hospital cleanliness. It obviously doesn't extend to the cafeteria. We plonk down on the hard, red plastic seats and spread out our wares.

Glugging down the bitter coffee, I pick at my bacon roll. 'So,' I say to Carl. 'Where did you get to last night?'

'I could ask you the same thing,' he replies.

'Back to Evan David's apartment,' I say, choosing to go first. Wherever Carl went, his experience couldn't have been as disastrous as mine. I pause for dramatic effect. 'Where I was introduced to his fiancée.'

'Oh.' Carl looks suitably taken aback. Imagine if I'd filled him in on the gory details. I daren't tell him about prancing round in my underwear or he'd come over all unnecessary. 'That's a bummer, man.'

'Well said.'

'How do you feel?'

'Stupid.' That pretty much sums it up. I wave my hand dismissively, though my heart twists with pain—and say, 'Well, it's all over now. No more silliness.'

'Shall I give you the plenty-more-fish-in-the-sea speech?'

'Not necessary,' I say. 'My nets will soon be out trawling for a new haddock.' I knock back my coffee with a shudder. 'In fact, I'm going to start interviewing for replacement heartthrobs any day now.' I flutter my eyelashes at Carl, but he doesn't offer his body as he normally would—not even in jest. Instead, he shifts in his seat and pretends to study the plastic menu on the table.

'So,' I say into the gap that Carl leaves. 'I hope your evening was more successful than mine. Where did you get to?'

He still doesn't look at me. 'To a club.'

'A club?' Carl never goes to clubs. He has a congenital aversion to them.

'In Camden.'

'What sort of club?'

Carl shrugs. 'Can't remember the name. It had good live music.'

'Is that the only information I'm going to get?'

'There's not much else to tell.'

'Who did you go with?'

Carl shifts again. 'Some guys from the pub.'

And some girls, too, if I'm any sort of judge of body language. Does this mean that Carl's dating someone? Ooo. That brings up all kinds of emotions, and one of them is definitely jealousy.

He's dated other women while we've been friends—he's hardly a monk. There's no vow of chastity just because I won't leap into bed with him. But normally he tells me all about them, and I know that there's never been anyone special in his life. Is that why he's suddenly being so cagey?

'Come on,' I cajole him. 'Dish the dirt.'

'There's none to dish.'

'I would have given you every detail of my shagfest with Evan David, if I'd had one.' Of course I wouldn't, but Carl isn't to know that.

'That would have been very nice for me.'

'I could come to the club with you,' I offer. 'Whatever it's called. After the pub one night. We haven't spent much time together over the last few weeks. I've had my dad to sort out and my mum. Then there's Joe and Nathan. I can't leave them alone for five minutes…'

'You can't spend your entire time trying to run everyone else's life, Fern,' my friend says crisply. 'With the exception of Nathan, we're all grown-ups. Maybe there are times when we need to make our own decisions and our own mistakes. Just sort *yourself* out.'

I nearly cough up my coffee. Carl has just told me to butt out. For the first time ever. I'm nearly rigid with shock. I wonder if this means he's in love?

Sixty-four

Ken the Landlord is giving me baleful glares and is puffing pointedly whenever he comes near me, but, as he hasn't given me the sack, I assume he's just posturing. Nevertheless, I'm trying to look like the model employee, and I'm polishing glasses as if my life depended on it. The pub is filling up nicely for the evening, and I'm going to be so busy that I won't have time to think—which is fine by me. Thinking is an overrated pastime.

I smile my sweetest smile at Ken, who bares his teeth at me. I polish harder. In the middle of this stand-off, my mum slips into the King's Head and hops onto a bar stool in front of me. 'Hello, darlin',' she says.

I nearly drop a glass. It's months—probably longer—since my mum has popped into the King's Head. In fact, Mum doesn't really do 'popping', so there must be a purpose to this.

I give her a wary kiss. 'To what do I owe this pleasure?'

'You can buy your old mum a gin and tonic,' she says, clasping her handbag to her knees.

Dutifully, I squeeze a single measure of gin from the optic and go heavy on the tonic—I know what my mum's like after one sherry. I hand it over and then wait to find out what this is really about. Perhaps she's finally going to come clean about her fling with Mr Patel. It might be that she's even coming to tell me that they've bought a bungalow in Eastbourne and are going to be moving in together. It doesn't bear thinking about. But Carl's right—they're adults and they have to live their lives as they see fit. If Mum hasn't hightailed it back to Dad's bedside after all this, then maybe nothing will make her take him back now.

She sips her drink. 'Mmm, lovely.'

I can tell that she doesn't want it at all. Two other customers come to the bar, so I move away to serve them, keeping a watch on Mum from the corner of my eye. Viewed dispassionately from a distance, it saddens my heart to see that she's looking older and more frail these days. It's a subtle shift, but some of her feistiness has drained out of her. I wonder when that happened. Is her mysterious double life starting to take its toll on her? Is it the thought of going through a divorce at her time of life? It's never easy at any age, but when you're on the verge of drawing your pension there seems an extra poignancy to the whole proceedings.

I finish serving my customers and move back to her. 'So?'

She sighs before she says, 'How's your dad?'

'He's fine,' I say truthfully. 'According to the doctors, he should be able to go home within the week.'

'Good,' my mum says, but she sounds shaky. She takes a glug

of her gin and I can see that she struggles to swallow it. 'Is he going back to your flat?'

I shrug. 'I guess so.'

When she looks up at me, I can see that there's a tear in her eye. 'Was it really bad?'

'About as bad as it gets,' I tell her flatly. 'We very nearly lost him.'

'Old goat,' she mutters, but there's no venom in the words.

'There's no need for you to worry about him.' Not that she has been, it would appear. 'He's getting great attention in the hospital. There's a really nice, pretty young Thai nurse who's taken a shine to him,' I say with a barb in my tone. 'She's making sure he's all right. I'm going in every day. So is Joe.' *There's only you that's missing from our cosy little line-up, Mum,* is my subtext.

Mum looks tiny perched on her bar stool, a worried frown on her brow. This may not be the right time and it definitely isn't the right place, but I decided to bite the bullet and address the other problem that's tearing our family apart.

I rest my hand on Mum's. 'I know about Mr Patel,' I say. 'I sussed out what was happening ages ago.'

Mum's eyes widen. 'How did you find out?'

'You're my mother,' I say gently. 'I'm not stupid.'

'I didn't want anyone to know,' she admits. 'It was something just for me. Something that no one else knew about.'

'You were a bit obvious.' I laugh softly. 'The make-up. The new hairdo. All your best clothes dragged out of the back of the wardrobe. It didn't take a genius to work out what was going on.'

My mum looks taken aback.

'I understand,' I say as I pat her hand. 'Mr Patel's an attractive man. Who wouldn't be tempted? I just wish you'd be straight with us, Mum. All these idiotic things that Dad's been doing to try to get you back, and he still has no idea that you've found someone else.'

'Someone else?' My mother's voice is a strangled squeak. She slugs back the remains of her gin.

'It's written all over your face.'

My mum nearly splutters out her drink. 'You think I'm having an affair with Mr Patel?'

'You might be my mum,' I say, 'but we are both women of the world.' I give her a knowing wink.

My mum's face turns a thunderous shade of black. 'Is that all women of your generation think about? Sex. Sex. Sex.'

Now it's my turn to be taken aback. I might think a lot about sex, but it doesn't mean that I'm getting any.

'There are other things in life,' she raves on, 'like helping out a friend. Don't you understand the meaning of platonic friendships?'

My mother does not need to lecture me on this. 'I happen to have been having a platonic friendship with Carl for the last seventeen years.'

'Yes,' my mum snaps. 'Shame on you. That boy adores you—it's about time you did the decent thing by him.'

That makes my jaw drop. My mum's never commented on my relationship with Carl.

'Where's that fancy man you brought home now?' Mum wags her finger at me. 'Gone.' She clicks her fingers. 'Gone in a flash.'

Her words stab into my heart.

'Carl's been there for you for most of your life, since you were both scrawny kids.'

'I couldn't manage without Carl. I do love him.' And then the truth of the matter hits me and I feel my insides crumble. 'But not enough.'

'And I love your dad,' Mum snaps back. 'But I don't *like* him very much sometimes.'

We stare at each other for a moment, then I fetch Mum another gin and help myself to one. We knock them back together. 'So what are we going to do?'

'You've got to let Carl go,' she tells me.

'And what about you?'

Mum tries an uncertain smile. 'I've been going ballroom dancing,' she says. 'That's all. I didn't want anyone to know because you'd all make fun of me. Mr Patel's wife's had a hip replacement and she can't dance for six months. I've been partnering Tariq—Mr Patel—instead.'

I shoot her a warning glance. 'That's how these things start.'

'Mrs Patel—Chandra—she comes along, too. On her crutches. She's a lovely woman.'

'I'm pleased to hear it,' I say, shamefaced.

'I feel twenty years young when I'm tripping round that dance floor, light as a feather,' my mum continues, a wistful look in her eye. 'I can forget all my problems. I can forget I've got a grandson who's poorly. I can forget I've got an unhappy son with no wife who struggles to make ends meet. I can forget that my daughter's living in a hovel with all her precious dreams unfulfilled. I can forget that I've got a husband who's never given me so much as a moment's peace throughout our marriage. Most of all, I can forget who I am. I can pretend that

I'm young again without a care in the world. Don't you think I deserve that?'

Mum's close to tears, as am I. 'Why didn't you tell us all this?'

'You'd have all laughed,' she says with a hint of bitterness. 'I've never had time to myself. Never had a hobby. The family have always come before my own needs. Well, this was just for me and for no one else. I wanted it to be my secret. I have dreams, too, Fern.'

I give her a sympathetic look. 'It would have helped if you could have sat down and told Dad.'

'When can you ever tell your father anything?' my mum states—quite rightly. 'He would have made stupid jokes about it. He would have tried everything to stop me going out by myself.'

'He could have gone with you.'

'He'd have embarrassed me. He'd have drunk too much and would have made fun of everyone. You know what he's like, Fern.'

I do.

'He's never been the easiest man to live with,' she says—something of an understatement, I have to admit. 'I'd just had enough.'

'But you've always managed before. Why did you kick him out now, after all this time?'

'I needed time to be myself without always having to think about Derek.'

'And now?'

Mum hangs her head. 'And now I'd better go straight to the hospital and see how he is.'

I lean over the bar and hug my mum. 'I love you.'

'I love you, too, darlin'.'

Mum hops down from her stool. She wipes a tear from under her eye and pulls up her tiny five-foot, two-inch frame to its full height. 'Now what did you say the name of that pretty Thai nurse was?'

'I didn't,' I tell her with a smile, and she gives me one of her death-ray looks, the one that I can copy so well. 'Will you have him back at home, Mum?'

Mum hoists her handbag over her shoulder and straightens her jacket. 'Just let anyone try and stop me,' she says.

Sixty-five

'Another family crisis?' Ken the Landlord asks.

'Sorry, Ken,' I say looking suitably downcast. How can I begin to explain to him that all this heartache stems from my mum's newly developed fetish for ballroom dancing and freedom? I'm not sure that I fully understand it myself. 'This is the end of it. Truly it is. The bar of the King's Head will be my sole priority from now on.'

'The day I believe *that* is the day I believe pigs can fly,' Ken tells me in his best hangdog voice.

At that moment, Carl turns up and comes to my rescue. 'Hey, guys,' he says in his laid-back style. 'What's the matter?'

'Ah,' Ken says as he wanders off. 'Lover Boy here will sort it all out again.'

Carl waits for my explanation, so I launch into it. 'I promised Ken that nothing would come between me and pulling pints, yet I've spent the last half hour trying to sort my mum out.'

He looks at me quizzically.

'She's off to the hospital to see Dad,' I tell him. We both indulge in a relieved sigh. 'I hope this is the start of them getting back together.'

'And Mr Patel?'

'She's his temporary ballroom dancing partner,' I say. 'Nothing more.'

Carl opens his mouth.

'Don't.' I hold up my hand. 'I don't want to think about my family for a moment longer. They give me a headache. Tell me something about you instead.'

Carl hops onto the stool that my mum has just vacated, and I pull him his usual pint of lager and put the money in the till myself. 'Nothing to tell,' my friend says.

'Don't you want to tell me about someone special?' I cock my head on one side and try to look appealing.

Carl flushes and studies the contents of his glass.

'Carlos, we have no secrets between us,' I remind him. 'You should tell me about her or I'll have to hurt you.'

My friend looks up at me and his gorgeous hazel eyes soften. My insides flip as I feel Carl slipping away from me. 'She's in one of the bands at the club I told you about.'

'Does she have a name?'

'Shelly.'

'Great.' She sounds young and pretty and I think I hate her already. 'What does she do?'

'She works in one of the shops in Camden during the day. At night, she fronts the band.'

Ah. Another one of us million wannabes. I want to know if she went along to the *Fame Game* auditions, too, but am scared to ask. Instead I say, 'Are you going to introduce her to me?'

'No,' Carl says. 'You'll scare her off.'

'I'll love her,' I assure him. Or scratch her eyes out.

'I thought you'd be...' Carl runs out of words.

'I'm delighted for you. Come here, you big lummox.' I lean across the bar and hug him. 'I'd come round there and give you a great big kiss, but Ken would lose what little is left of his hair.'

'We wouldn't want that,' Carl agrees. 'Besides, it might make me change my mind.'

'Don't say that. I want you to be happy,' I tell my friend. 'I want you to be settled. I want you to be in love.'

He gives me one of his soulful looks. 'I've been in love for a long time.'

'I mean with someone who isn't such a fucking idiot as me.'

'Well,' he admits, 'I think I've found her.'

Ken the Landlord looms over us. 'Now that you've found love, perhaps you'd like to wander to the stage and sing some bloody songs about it.'

We both take the hint. Carl downs his pint while I take off my apron and then I follow my friend to the stage. It's extraordinary how quickly we've slipped back into our routine. I have a moment of panic as I wonder whether Carl will desert me for Shelly and be her pianist and ace guitarist instead of mine.

'Ken's right,' I murmur to him. 'We should sing some songs about love, it might bring us both good luck.'

We take up our places and I'd like to say a hush falls over the bar, but it doesn't. There is, however, a slight hiatus in the conversation as we launch into a set of standards that has the audience tapping their feet in time to the music. Being on the

Fame Game has, bizarrely, given me a new confidence in myself. I throw back my head and enjoy becoming absorbed in the songs. Carl goes up a gear and the audience is rocking. Ken gives us a nod to carry on, so we trawl out some more favourites about love being the answer to everything. I don't think we've ever done such a great set here. Some of the punters start to dance, and lifted by the mood we increase the tempo. Before long the joint is absolutely jumping. Ken is delighted because beer sales are increasing rapidly along with the thirst of the dancers.

We're having a wild time. I strut about the stage like the rock goddess I should be. Carl is in a frenzy. Never have I heard him play so well. If this is what being loved has done for him, then bring it on, I say. I toss back my hair and give free rein to my voice. I'm loving it. So are the crowd, who cheer for more. We hurl ourselves, full pelt into our final song. For a minute I forget everything—where I am, who I am. I am a superstar on the stage at Wembley Stadium playing to her adoring fans. I even forget about Evan David, until I look up and see that his agent, Rupert Dawson, is standing as still as a stone at the back of the pub.

Sixty-six

After the set, I fly off the stage lifted on the wings of tumultuous applause. But before I can get back to the sanctuary of the bar, Rupert Dawson crosses the room and is in front of me.

'Fern,' he says, staying me with a hand on my arm. 'Nice to see you.'

I can't deal with any pleasantries. 'What are you doing here?'

Rupert, it seems, is slightly thrown by my hostility. 'Evan asked me to come and listen to you sing.'

My face clearly sets into a scowl, because he says hurriedly, 'I like what I hear.'

'Good. I'm pleased.' And then I go to push past him because I really don't know what else to say.

'He wants to help you, Fern,' Rupert says.

'I don't need his help. Thanks all the same.'

'Evan said I'm to give you whatever you need for your nephew.'

'Nathan?' That does stop me in my tracks. 'What's he got to do with anything?'

'Evan wants to pay for his medical expenses—to get him well again. Money's no object. You can have anything. Anything at all.'

I snort with derision. 'My God, does he think he can pay me off by using my nephew? Does the man have no integrity?'

Rupert looks shocked. Perhaps he is used to settling Evan's accounts much more easily than this. Maybe he thinks I'm so desperate for money that I'd sell my story to one of the red-top tabloids that specialise in salacious stories and this is his way of buying my silence. What I wouldn't give for this sort of offer normally—I thought I'd do anything to get the money to help Nathan, but I won't take Evan David's pay-off.

'That's not what it's like, Fern, I can assure you. Evan only has your best interests at heart.'

I laugh out loud. It's a horrible and hollow sound. 'Oh, I'm sure he does.'

'He really does care about you.'

Oh, yes. He cares enough to let you do his dirty work, I think.

'He feels terrible about what happened.'

'He told you?'

Rupert nods. 'I'm his agent. His friend. I know what it would mean to him if you'd let him help you.'

'Well, tell him from me that I don't need his help. He owes me nothing—he can walk away with a clear conscience. I can manage on my own. I don't want Evan David and I certainly don't want his money.'

'Fern,' Rupert implores. 'Think about this.'

'If he's worried about me talking to the newspapers,' I continue, 'then I won't do that, either.'

Rupert shifts uncomfortably. 'I've handled this very badly, Fern. Perhaps you and I could go somewhere and have a coffee or a drink. Let me take you to my club. It's quiet there.' Rupert looks at the shabby surroundings of the King's Head and leans in towards me. 'There's something else I want to talk to you about.'

'I don't have time. I'm sorry,' I say, but I'm not sorry at all. I just want to get away from this creep who doesn't mind doing Evan David's dirty work. My judgement of people is all skewed these days, because previously I'd have told you that Rupert was quite a decent guy. 'I have to get back behind the bar.'

'You haven't spoken to Stephen Cauldwell?' There's genuine concern in Rupert's eyes.

'Stephen Cauldwell? No.' Then I remember that the pop impresario had left a business card with my dad and that this was what had started off the chain of events leading up to Dad's heart attack. What a klutz! How could I keep a guy like that dangling? The knowledge hits me on the head like a hammer. 'I haven't had time to do that, either,' I say briskly, fully appreciating that my time has, once again, passed. 'I'm a very busy person.' How lame does that sound?

'Then I'd like to offer you a contract.'

'What?'

'I'd like to offer you a contract.'

'Fern!' Ken the Landlord shouts. 'You've customers waiting.'

I turn back to Rupert. 'I have to go.'

He pulls some papers out of his jacket pocket and forces

them into my hands. 'Read this,' he says. 'Read it carefully. You have a rare talent. Tonight I've seen it in action. Evan made me promise to come here, but I'm glad that I did. He's right—you're very special. I would never have believed it if I hadn't seen it for myself. There are a thousand women with pretty faces out there who can sing, but none of them have your potential.'

'I don't want anything from you, Rupert, or from Evan David.'

Rupert is going purple with exasperation. 'As well as being special, you're also a very stupid and stubborn woman.'

'It's not the first time I've been told that.' I blurt this out with some sort of pride until I realise what I'm actually saying.

'Forget Evan,' Rupert snaps. 'This has nothing to do with him. It's between the two of us. Do this for me. Do this for yourself.'

I shake my head and I go to hand him the papers back.

'Keep them,' Rupert insists. 'You have two days to call me and change your mind. If I don't hear from you, then I'll take it you've decided to remain a pub singer for the rest of your life.'

That stings and I take a step back.

'Phone me,' he says. 'Don't let me down.'

Then Rupert Dawson spins on his heels and walks out of the pub. The door reverberates on its hinges in his wake, and a shiver goes down my spine as everyone turns to look at me.

Sixty-seven

'Fern!' Ken the Landlord shouts again. 'Could I trouble you to do some work?'

I walk back to the bar with shaking legs and shaking hands. There's a queue of thirsty punters a mile long. Ken is single-handedly pulling pints as if they're going out of fashion.

Carl gives me a slow handclap as I approach. 'Oh, man.'

'What's *your* problem?' I snarl as I push the contract into the depths of my handbag. I might as well rip it up and put it in the bin, but that seems like an empty gesture too far.

'Would you like me to put a gun to the other one?'

I give Carl a puzzled look.

'That was the best case of shooting yourself in the foot that I've ever seen,' he tells me.

All the fight floods out of me. 'Don't,' I say. 'I don't want you on my case as well.'

'He's right, Fern. You're running out of chances to get out of this place.'

'This has Evan David stamped all over it,' I counter. 'I don't want anything to do with him. You, of all people, should be supporting me in that decision.'

'Do you know who that guy is?' Carl asks. He nods his head towards the door where Rupert Dawson has recently departed, taking some of the paintwork with him.

I shrug. 'It's Rupert Dawson. He's Evan David's agent.'

'He also represents Carrion Ten, The Spiel, Culture Clash, Aimee…' Carl reels off a list of the hottest indie bands of the moment. 'Shall I continue?'

I hold up a hand. 'I've heard enough.'

'So, you see, I don't think he'd simply be offering you a contract because your precious Evan David told him to. I think the guy's probably capable of spotting talent all by himself.'

I feel myself gulp. 'I've got two days to call him.'

'Then I suggest you do just that.'

'So do I.' Ken the Landlord is behind me. 'Because you're sacked.'

I look at him open-mouthed.

'You're the worst barmaid in London,' Ken says.

'You d-don't mean that,' I stammer.

'I do,' he says, handing me my coat and handbag. 'Go on. Sling your hook. And you.' By that he means Carl, too.

'Ken. Man…' Carl starts.

'Bog off, the pair of you,' Ken growls, and with that we do as we're told and leave.

Carl buys me a cup of tea in the brightly-lit McDonald's across the road from the King's Head, and I nurse the scalding hot liquid in my hands. Thankfully, I do still have the ability to feel something other than numb.

'This is desperate,' I say with a nervous laugh. 'You don't think Ken's serious?'

'He sounded pretty serious to me.' Carl distractedly unfolds the rim on his paper cup.

'What am I going to do for money now?'

'We'll have to look for another gig. I'll trawl around some pubs tomorrow. Maybe we could get a set at Monsters.'

'Where?'

'The club in Camden where Shelly sings.'

'Oh, right.' I'd forgotten about Shelly. 'Yeah, maybe.' I let the tea burn my throat. 'Perhaps Ken will reconsider if I have a word with him in the morning. Or maybe you should talk to him. He likes you.'

'He likes you, too, Fern,' Carl says, 'but I think it's time that we moved on. We've used up all our lives at the King's Head.'

'I'm becoming a liability for you, Carl. Perhaps we should split up and go our separate ways.'

He laughs. 'You've been a liability for me since we were fifteen. Why spoil the fun now?'

'Jeez,' I say. 'I am such a fuck-up. Why don't you push me under a bus when I've finished my tea and put us both out of our misery.'

'Cheer up,' Carl says gently. 'Things could be worse.'

'I love your optimism,' I tell my friend. 'I can never decide whether you're very spiritual or just as stupid as I am.'

Carl takes my hand and pulls me up. 'We'll go and say good-night to your dad and then I'll take you home.'

I hug Carl to me. 'I love you, you know. You're the nicest man I've ever met.'

'It's too late for all that now,' Carl tells me with a grin. 'I'm already spoken for.'

'She's a lucky woman.' I dig him sharply in the ribs. 'I should have snapped you up when you were hot for me.'

He throws his arm round my shoulder and steers me out into the street. And I'm so pleased that whatever else is going on in my life, when it all comes crashing down around my ears, my relationship with Carl is the one thing that endures.

Sixty-eight

In the Coronary Care Ward the lights are turned down low and the nurses are settling the patients for the night. Over in the corner bed, I can see that my dad has his bedside lamp on. His little area is bathed in a warm glow, and when Carl and I draw closer, I realise that Mum is there. Her chair is pulled up right next to the bedside and she's snuggled up to Dad, her head resting on his arm. Dad's eyes are closed, but the expression on his face is one of contentment.

I stop Carl's progress. 'I don't want to disturb them,' I say.

He urges me forward. 'They'll be pleased to see you.'

Sure enough, they both look up and smile warmly as we arrive.

'I thought you'd still be at the pub,' Dad says.

I give Carl a silencing glance. 'Early night tonight,' I say lightly as I kiss my dad on the forehead. 'How are you feeling?'

'All the better for seeing your mum.' He squeezes her hand as he answers and she looks up at him adoringly.

Now I do feel like we're intruding. 'I just wanted to say goodnight and then we're off.'

'I've spoken to the doctor,' Mum says. 'He says that your dad can come out next week if he keeps getting better.'

'Good.'

'And then he has to take up some gentle exercise. I thought we might go to ballroom dancing classes together.' My mum silently wills me not to say anything.

'Ballroom dancing?' I can feel my eyes twinkling with mischief. My mum owes me one for keeping quiet about this. 'You'll like that, Dad.'

He looks rather sceptical, but rashly says, 'It's what your mum wants.'

The pretty little Thai nurse, Kim, arrives at the bedside. 'Time to go to sleep, Derek,' she coos. 'We don't want you overtired.' She starts to tuck in his bedclothes.

Mum jumps up. 'I'll do that,' she says briskly. 'I'm his wife. I've been tucking this man up for longer than you've been on this planet. I'm sure you've got lots of other patients to attend to.'

I roll my eyes at Carl and stifle a smile. There's nothing like a visit from the green-eyed monster to get love all stirred up again, it seems. Kim, trying not to look put out, bustles away but not before saying, 'You call me, Derek, if you need me. Just press the buzzer.'

'I thought they were supposed to be overworked,' my mum says with an impatient tut to her retreating back.

My dad, of course, like all males is lapping up the attention.

'Shall we wait for you, Mum, and see you home?'

'No,' she says. 'I'll stay here a little longer. Your dad and I have a bit more to talk about. Give me a ring in the morning.'

'Okay.' I kiss them both warmly and Carl gives them both a peace sign. My mother gives him a fuck-off sign in return, but we don't bother to correct her.

Out on the street we jump on a passing bus, even though we've only got a few stops to go before we reach my skanky flat. It's great to see that my parents are finally making up, but I feel as if I've had all of the stuffing knocked out of me today.

The late-night bus is empty so Carl and I sit on the top deck like we used to do when we were kids. I hate the thought that the council is going to do away with the double-deckers and replace them with these new-fangled bendy Eurobuses— overlong, single-storey snakes. The red double-decker is part of London, part of my life. Tourists aren't going to come and marvel at the new ones. I snuggle against Carl and rest my heavy head on his shoulder, relaxing into the jogging motion of the bus.

'I need my bed,' I say. 'I'm absolutely knackered.'

'Me, too,' Carl agrees.

'Do you think we'll ever manage to keep a relationship going for forty years?'

'I'm not planning to live that long,' Carl says. 'I'm a rock 'n' roller. We live fast and die young.'

'Oh, yes. I keep forgetting.'

'Plus you've got to find someone that you can stay in a relationship with for more than ten minutes.'

'Hey,' I say. 'Your track record isn't much better.'

'I can blame my lack of success on extenuating circumstances,' my friend tells me. 'What's your excuse?'

I look up at him. 'That I can't recognise a decent bloke when one pokes me in the eye.'

Carl pokes me in the eye.

'Ouch!'

'Come on, rat bag,' he says. 'This is our stop.'

The night air's sharp and I wish I had a warmer coat. I'm going to have to drop by ye olde charity shop tomorrow and see if I can pick up something cheap that doesn't look like it comes with its own fleas.

We stroll along as if we're walking on a balmy evening by the Seine or something and then when we reach the top of my street I see a sight that takes my breath away.

'Oh, no,' I say. 'Oh, no.'

Carl follows my gaze and breathes, 'Shit.'

All thoughts of strolling gone, we break into a run. Carl outsprints me and reaches the scene first, but I'm hot on his heels—if that isn't a bad phrase to use.

Then we stand speechless, hands entwined, and watch as the flames leap out of the space where my flat used to be. Orange tongues lick at the sky while two firefighters at the top of ladders spray them ineffectually with gallons of water. On the ground their colleagues fight the flames that are spreading to The Spice Emporium restaurant below. I can't even find the wherewithal to say, 'That's my flat'.

I feel a tug at my sleeve and turn to see the blackened face of Ali, my landlord. He coughs dramatically, clearly suffering the effects of smoke inhalation.

'My God, Ali,' I manage. 'Are you all right? What happened?'

'I think it was your boiler, Fern,' he croaks. 'We heard a boom from upstairs. Shook all the pictures off the walls in the restaurant. A minute later the whole place was on fire.' He looks like he's about to collapse on the pavement. Carl puts his arm round Ali and hoists him up. 'I'd been meaning to fix that boiler for ages. Thank goodness you weren't in there, Fern.'

The thought makes me go weak at the knees, too, but as Carl's arms are already full, I lean against a nearby car. I think I'd like to cry, but tears won't come. Perhaps they're too stunned to make an appearance.

'Mate,' one of the firemen calls over to Ali. 'We need a word.'

Ali looks gratefully at both of us. 'I'm sorry, Fern. Really sorry.' Then he's gone, being led away by a burly bloke in a fluorescent yellow jacket.

Carl joins me, leaning against the car to watch my home burn down.

'What do I do now?' I ask him. 'I've no job and nowhere to live.'

My friend slips his arm around my shoulders and pulls me to him. 'Looks like it's Super Carl to the rescue once again.'

Sixty-nine

I don't know how we get to Carl's flat—we might have walked or taken a cab, I simply don't know. My mind must have gone into shut-down mode, because the next thing I know I'm being ushered through his front door and the kettle is on and Carl is muttering to himself about clean sheets and kipping on the sofa for the second time. He's in the process of plumping his cushions, which is *so* not rock 'n' roll.

'Stop,' I say.

My friend stops dead and looks up at me. I take the cushion from him and throw it back on the sofa with a certain cavalier action, then I pull him to me and kiss him softly on the lips. He steps back from me, hands on my shoulders and gives me a quizzical look. I pull him to me again and kiss him once more. This time he doesn't question it and responds to my kiss with a passion that leaves me reeling.

I take his hand and we walk to the bedroom. Without words,

gently and carefully, Carl undresses me, touching me as if I'm a beautiful sculpture, letting his hands savour my curves. And then, when I'm naked, I undress him, too, slowly, my mouth travelling over his body as I strip him of his shirt and his jeans, making him gasp and shiver. He lowers me to the bed and we make love, tenderly and with a tantalising languidness that leaves me breathless with desire. His body feels so familiar, and yet this is a wonderful new experience, as if I'm unwrapping a present when I already know the delights it holds inside. When Carl breathes my name, I feel my soul sigh. Hours later we fall asleep in each other's arms, and I wonder why it has taken us so long to come to this point. I could have died in that flat. I could have died and never have experienced this.

I wake up early and lie watching Carl as he sleeps. Then I switch onto my back and stare at the ceiling, considering my homeless, jobless state. My friend's curtains have a terrible swirly pattern, but the sun struggles through them, bringing a warm pink glow to the room. It's cosy in here and it's a long time since I slept with a hot, male body next to me. I slide across the bed to fit into Carl's shape, relishing the feeling.

After a while, Carl starts to rouse, too. He stretches in his state of half-sleep and reaches out, throwing his arm across me. I plant a kiss on his forehead and his eyes open wide. 'Do you know,' he says, 'I thought I was dreaming.'

I turn towards him and we snuggle down nose-to-nose. Carl brushes my hair from my forehead and gently tucks it behind my ear. I thought that maybe we'd be awkward with each other this morning, but it looks like the event has passed without too much fallout.

'Are we still friends?' I ask him.

'I should think so,' he says.

'I enjoyed last night.'

'Me, too.' He moves closer to me. 'I can't believe we waited all those years to do this.'

'Was it worth it?'

'Almost,' he teases.

I kick him in the shins for his cheek.

'So what happens now?' I want to know.

'You could fall in love with me,' Carl suggests. 'That would make everything that bit easier.'

Perhaps I hesitate for a moment too long, as Carl's eyes darken slightly.

'Or,' he carries on a touch too brightly, 'you could continue your futile quest to make Evan David love you while I resume my search for someone who can begin to compete with the impossibly high standards you've set.'

'I think we should try to sort out our current financial embarrassment and accommodation crisis before we worry about our relationship.' Which nimbly avoids the situation, I believe.

'It's in your hands, Fern,' Carl reminds me with a sage tone. 'You have a big, fat contract from one of the music industry's top players in your handbag.'

'We don't know that it's a big, fat contract.'

Carl slips out of the bed, pulls on his jeans and pads into the living room. He retrieves the aforementioned handbag and hands it to me.

With a mounting feeling of trepidation, I pull out the sheaf of papers and flick through them. Reading them makes my eyes pop out on stalks and I hand the bundle over to Carl, who also scans them with ever-dilating pupils.

We look at each other. 'It's a big, fat contract,' we say in unison.

I take the papers off Carl again. 'This can't be true, can it?' He shrugs. 'It looks like it.'

'This amount of money solves an awful lot of problems,' I tell Carl needlessly.

'I don't know why you're hesitating,' my friend says.

'Neither do I.' I search deeper into my handbag and dredge up my mobile phone. There's barely enough credit on it left to make a phone call, and I know that I have less than a fiver in my purse. These are all my worldly goods, and yet I'm holding a piece of paper in my hand with more noughts on it than I ever thought possible.

I stare at my phone and then look to Carl for reassurance. 'Are you sure I should do this?'

'Absolutely,' he says with a nod.

I tap in Rupert Dawson's phone number, and while I listen to it ringing, I say to Carl, 'There's no way that I'm doing this without you. This time it's the two of us or not at all.'

Carl holds his head in his hands. Clearly he thinks I could still blow it.

Then the phone is answered.

'Rupert?' My voice is shaking. This feels like the right thing to do. I guess only time will tell. Carl wraps his fingers round mine and squeezes them as I say, 'It's Fern. I want to accept your contract.'

Seventy

I'm to be known as Fern now. Just Fern. Nothing else. I know that I've made it as I'm reduced to one name. Fern Leanne Kendal is dead. Long live Fern.

A lot happens very quickly. Carl and I sit in front of Rupert Dawson in his swish, modern offices just off Tottenham Court Road. I put down the pen and push the contract back towards him. Our agent rubs his hands together, indicating a degree of satisfaction. A contented beam spreads across his face. 'Welcome on board.'

He shakes my hand and then Carl's. We both sit in stunned silence. Rupert has already set us up with a 'major recording deal'—as reported in the press—with a huge record company. Apparently, he'd already set the wheels in motion as soon as he left the King's Head, which I find amazing. Rupert says that he knew I'd phone him, and I have to admire his confidence because I was absolutely sure that I wouldn't phone him at all.

If miracles can happen, then this surely must be one. It's as if someone has shaken up my life and rolled me out again with a full set of sixes. Things simply can't get any better. Rupert Dawson has turned out to be the knight in shining armour I've always wished for; he has transformed me from a homeless, jobless, futureless damsel-in-distress to a hot new pop star with one wave of his twenty-four-carat gold pen. If this was the Lotto, I'd have just won The Big One.

Carl is one hundred percent involved this time and is in the process of putting a band together. We've already swapped the London Underground as our favoured mode of transport in exchange for chauffeur-driven limousines, and Rupert has given me some money upfront from my advance to buy a house. A big, bollocky house! I can hardly believe this is me saying this.

Rupert sits back in his chair, feet up on his frosted-glass desk. Pictures of the rich and famous smile down at us from every wall. I only wish there weren't quite so many of Evan David. My stomach lurches just to look at them, so I try to keep my eyes staring straight ahead.

'Evan doesn't know about this,' Rupert says as if reading my mind.

Carl's hand creeps across to mine and he holds it tightly.

'Then I'd like to keep it that way.'

'It may not be possible for very long, darling. You've hidden your light under a bushel for too long. I want you to be big. Very big.' Rupert looks as if he wants to say more, but he glances at my hand in Carl's and clearly can't read what the situation is between us, so it seems he decides to stay quiet.

Instead he breezes on, 'You have appointments with the stylists and photographers this afternoon. I'll be over there later

to check on everything.' Rupert consults his diary. 'We want
to get a single out quickly, so I've booked some studio time
and then we need to put some material together for the first
album.'

Carl and I, more than dazed, nod in unison.

Rupert reels off a list of people we'll be working with—
names that I've only ever seen on other people's records. I give
myself a firm pinch. Yep, I'm awake.

'Anything else you need, just call me,' Rupert says. 'I mean
that. This should be an experience that you enjoy. Leave any
problems to me.'

Carl and I stand.

'See you later,' Rupert says.

I go round to his side of the desk and hug him. Rupert
flushes, but relaxes into my embrace. 'Thank you,' I say, my
voice choked with emotion. 'Thank you so much.'

Outside, our driver is waiting for us and we slide into our
limo, slipping on shades. Inside, Carl and I burst out laughing.

'Is this really happening?' Carl asks.

'I think so.'

'Shit,' he says. 'Who'd have thought?'

'Not me. That's for sure.'

Carl turns to me. 'I dropped into the King's Head yesterday.'

'Is it still struggling on without us?'

'You know that Ken the Landlord sacked you because he
thought you were going to mess up another big break?'

'Did he?' I can't hide my surprise. 'The old bastard.'

'Shelly's band is playing there now.'

We don't talk about Shelly, and I feel bad that Carl's relationship with her never got much beyond first base. He doesn't seem to be holding it against me.

'When we're rich and famous, we should go back there and play a gig for Ken,' I joke. 'That would make his eyes pop out.'

'We're already rich,' Carl says. 'We just need the fame to follow.'

Now our fate is in the hands of others, all we have to do is the same thing we've always been doing—sing well and graft hard.

'Let's go home,' I say. 'Joe and Nathan are moving in with me today, and I want to be there to help them.'

Home for the moment is a vast Georgian house with views over Regent's Park that I'm renting for some astronomical, telephone-number sum of money that makes me shake with terror when I see it. When I have time, I'm going to look for a place to buy as an investment and maybe somewhere in the country to get Nathan out of the city smoke on a regular basis. I'm only too well aware that the clock could already be ticking on my fifteen minutes of fame and I could be nothing more than a one-hit wonder, so I want to make sure that as well as enjoying my money, I have some security to show from my time in the spotlight, however brief it might be. But I'm also going to make the most of this and do everything in my power to ensure that I'm not featuring in *Where Are They Now?* shows in a few years time.

Currently, though, I'm basking in the golden glow of glory. I have more rooms than I have fingers to count them on, and the best thing about it all is that my lovely brother and my beautiful nephew are going to move in with me. With my first flush of success, I've already achieved more than I could ever have dreamed of—Joe and Nathan are moving out of that terrible damp flat and into this wonderful, airy home with floor-to-ceiling windows and oak floors in every room. This record deal means that I can give them all that they need—in physical terms, at least. I just hope that we'll see an improvement in Nathan's condition and that he'll be able to live a normal life. I couldn't want for anything more.

There's a vast self-contained apartment at the top with two bedrooms, a bath that would hold a team of rugby players and a private roof terrace which I'm going to claim as mine. Joe and Nathan will have the run of the rest of the house. I'm also trying to persuade my mum and dad to move in as well, but they're currently convinced that this is all a big misunderstanding and that any time now the debt collectors are going to be banging at the door and the men in white coats will arrive to cart me off to the funny farm. Carl has also chosen to stay in his own flat—he too is having trouble dealing with the reality of our changed circumstances and wants to take it a step at a time. Though he does spend more time hanging out at my place than at his own. He can't quite come to terms with the fact that he is now a wealthy man, although he has given up claiming government benefits.

We're still sort of an item following our unexpected night of passion, but we've slipped back more to our old platonic ways and, strangely, I'm quite glad of that. I know that we need to discuss what's going to happen in the future, but frankly we're so caught up in the mad whirl that has become our lives that it's been relatively easy to avoid it. Carl is wonderful, as always, and I hate to admit this—even to myself—but there's still an ache inside me for someone else. And that's less easy to ignore.

Seventy-one

A couple of heavies lift the boxes containing Joe and Nathan's meagre possessions from the removals van and place them in the huge rooms I've earmarked for them.

'This is fabulous, sis,' Joe says as he walks round the place wide-eyed. 'Are you sure it's yours?'

'Amazingly, it is.'

Nathan clings to my waist. 'Are we really going to live with you, Aunty Fern?'

'Yes.' I hug him to me. 'Is that okay with you?'

'Cool.' Nathan high-fives me.

'I'm going to be away a lot, but you and your dad will look after the house for me while I'm gone.'

'This is a nice house.' My nephew spins round, gazing at the ceiling. 'It looks like a house where the queen would live.'

The doorbell rings and I check my watch. 'There's one more thing I meant to tell you, Joe.' I head towards the front door. 'You're going to have some help, so if you want to go back to work, you'll be able to.'

'Fern. This is too much...'

'No arguments. Wait until you see her.'

I open the door and let in the total babe who's standing there. 'Hello,' she says in heavily accented English.

'Hi, Alina. Come on in.' I steer her into the living room. My brother's jaw hits the oak flooring and a beetroot flush suffuses his face. Hmm. Think I might have made the right choice here. 'Guys, meet the latest addition to our little team. This is Alina and she's from Poland. And I hope you're going to agree that she can come and live with us, too.'

I spent ages interviewing potential candidates until I found someone that I thought would be just right. Not only is Alina a babe, but she comes with great references and a wealth of experience when it comes to looking after kids. The fact that she's single and a looker and might well prove to be suitable girl-friend material for my darling brother were only minor considerations. Honestly.

The doorbell rings again. 'Why don't you guys show Alina round the house and then you can get to know each other a little better.'

Nathan takes Alina's hand. 'I'll show you my dinosaur collection first,' he says, leading her up the stairs. 'That's the best thing.'

Joe turns to me and mouths. 'She's a fox!'

Which I assume means that he's happy for her to take charge of his son's welfare. I smile to myself and go to the door once again.

This time it's my mum and dad, who hover at the door as

if they're not supposed to be in such a grand place. They both kiss me while looking round furtively.

'Take your shoes off, Derek,' my mum instructs.

'It isn't necessary, Mum.'

Ignoring me, she pulls two pairs of well-worn slippers out of her voluminous handbag and hands a pair to my dad, who does as he's told.

'You can't be walking on floors like this in outdoors shoes,' she admonishes me, while taking off her own heels and replacing them with pink fur-trimmed beddies. My trainers—even though they're new—earn a scowl.

'I just want you to be comfortable here,' I tell her. 'Whatever that takes.'

'How can I be comfortable here?' she says tetchily. 'It's posher than Buckingham Palace.'

I link my arm through my dad's. 'How are you feeling? Getting better?'

'Champion,' Dad says. 'Mustn't complain. We've just come from our ballroom dancing lesson.' He rolls his eyes at me behind Mum's back.

'He's got to watch his weight, too,' Mum pipes up. 'So no more booze or bacon sarnies.'

'There'll be no pleasure left in my life at all if your mum has her way,' he whispers to me.

I'd love to say that having got back together, my parents had found a renewed strength of love in their relationship, but after forty years, I guess it's hard to completely dispense with the familiarity that breeds a certain amount of contempt. The best I can offer is that they're rubbing along as well as they ever did. But they do go ballroom dancing together now.

'I don't suppose there's a kettle here?' Mum says.

'Of course there is. Come through to the kitchen.'

Warily, she follows me into the massive room, which over-looks the mature garden filled with roses and honeysuckle. 'We came to see how Joe and Nathan are settling in.'

I hear laughter and giggling coming from upstairs and allow myself a satisfied smile. It's good to hear Joe sounding so care-free for once. 'Oh, I think they're going to enjoy living here.'

'We might move in while you're away,' Mum says as if she's doing me a favour. 'Just so we can look after the place. That garden will be overgrown in five minutes if someone doesn't look after it.'

I don't tell her that I now have a full-time gardener. He's a really nice old boy and I'm sure he'll let her help him.

'I'll make a pot of tea, then we can all sit out there and enjoy the sun for a few minutes before Carl and I have to go off for our photo shoot.'

'Get *you*, madam!' my mum says, giving me a sideways glance.

I set up a tray with mugs and a heap of chocolate biscuits—bought from Harrods. Gone are the cheap and nasty own-brand custard creams.

'Where is Carl?'

'He's upstairs,' I reply. 'He's set up a room with his piano and guitars so that we can do some writing together.'

She gives me another one of her prize looks. 'And is Carl going to be moving in here, too?'

'He hasn't decided yet.' I make the tea to avoid getting fur-ther into this discussion because I'm not sure that it's Carl who hasn't decided yet. I actually think it's me.

'You're not still hankering after that Evan David chap, are you?' Trust my mum to get straight to the crux of the matter.

I hold up a hand. 'I don't even want to talk about this. I have so much going on at the moment that I can't think straight.'

My mum raises her eyebrows. 'Sounds to me like you've got unfinished business, lady.'

I hear a soft chord being struck behind me and turn to see Carl lounging in the doorway, guitar slung low round his body. His expression is guarded, and I can't read what's behind his eyes. 'It does to me, too,' he says.

Seventy-two

Evan David sat on the roof terrace of his home in San Francisco, reclining in a sun lounger, sipping iced tea and enjoying the view over the distinctive skyline of the city. The Golden Gate Bridge stood proud in the distance, for once, not shrouded in mist, as they were enjoying a heatwave this summer, with temperatures soaring to well over one hundred degrees, which was helping to burn off the regular sea frets that engulfed the Bay. Today, the sky was the sort of heartbreakingly pure blue that only California could do. A gentle breeze ruffled the potted palm trees on the terrace, the hot scent of flowers floated on the air. Evan sighed and closed his eyes. This was the closest he was ever going to get to relaxing.

Then the hammering started up again. Down in the garden, workmen shouted across to each other. Above their noise, the wedding planner shrieked instructions into her cell phone. Goodness only knew why he'd let Lana talk him into holding the wedding here, at his home. She knew that he valued his privacy above anything, and now she was turning this place into a cross between a circus and Grand Central Station. His assistant, Erin, had been purloined to help with the arrangements, too, and she wasn't enjoying one minute of working so closely with Lana. Evan suspected that she'd rather go down with the chicken pox again. Without telling him, *La Diva* had already sold the coverage rights to a raft of glossy gossip-pushers across the globe; hordes of photographers would be arriving to record the event for her adoring fans. He didn't know why he hadn't put his foot down and pulled the plug on this weeks ago. This place was his sanctuary. It had been his home now for many years, the place he returned to most often when his spirit was in need of an uplift. The house had been a former archbishop's mansion at the turn of the century, and in need of serious renovation when Evan bought it as a bolt-hole. Its rooms were vast and grand. Original stained-glass windows let scattered shards of light flood into the hallways, sprinkling the hand-carved oak staircase with a confetti of colour. Lana had already earmarked this spot as suitable for wedding photographs. It was only due to the fact that he couldn't face her wrath that he was allowing this fiasco to continue.

Some sort of giant rose arbour had been constructed in the middle of the lawn where the wedding was to take place. A vast marquee had been tacked onto the house to hold all two hundred of the guests that Lana had invited. At least he did actually know most of them, which would, no doubt, provide a welcome distraction on the day. Flowers were already arriving by the crateload. Somewhere a rainforest had been decimated to provide an abundance of glossy foliage. Evan shuddered to think of it. This was Lana's idea of an 'intimate' affair. It was his idea of hell. At least the white chiffon and frilled monstrosity was self-contained, so he wouldn't have a slew of unwanted guests trailing through his home, squashing canapés into his antique carpets, putting fingerprints all over his Baccarat crystal. He would be glad when it was all over and his life could get back on track.

Rupert chose that moment to open the terrace doors and step into the sunshine. 'Bloody hell, it's hot today, darling,' his agent muttered.

Evan clasped him by his hand. 'It's been ages, you old rogue. Good to see you.'

For the last few months Evan had been back in San Francisco, heavily involved in the new season of productions here at the California Opera House. He'd thrown himself into his work—which was never difficult. If he tried very hard, it nearly blotted out his real life.

He and Lana were performing together again, starring in *Turandot*. There was no doubt that it was placing a strain on their relationship. Lana was singing the lead role of Turandot—a tyrannical Chinese princess known for slaughtering men who were foolish enough to try for her hand in marriage—an irony that wasn't lost on Evan. He, of course, was taking the role of Calaf, the hapless lover trying to save her from herself. But somehow they never had reached the emotional heights as they did back in Wales with *La Traviata*. Lacklustre reviews of her performance reflected the fact that Lana was too caught up with making arrangements for her big day to be fully focused on her work. Working with Lana was difficult at the best of times, but things were even more tricky now. Maybe it was time to call it a day on their working partnership and move on. It wasn't an issue he felt able to tackle at the moment. Tonight was the final night and, frankly, it couldn't come soon enough for Evan.

With the impending wedding looming large, Lana's famous Italian temper was rather more on display than normal. He'd missed his agent's steadying influence and was glad to see that Rupert had turned up in time for the nuptials. Not that he would have been allowed to miss it. Lana had decreed that he should be there, and be there he would. 'What's been keeping you so busy in London?'

'This and that.' Rupert threw a CD onto Evan's lounger. It was the result of his collaboration with the indie bands in London, which, miraculously, they'd been able to finish on time. The publishing company had rushed it out to catch the crest of the wave, and it certainly seemed to be working. 'It's going great guns,' his agent said. 'It'll be number one next week, with good luck and a following wind.'

'If you're going to tell me that I should be heading back to London to promote it, then don't bother,' Evan said. 'There's no way that's going to happen.'

'You have an hour-long Christmas special with the BBC. You're going to have to go back sometime.'

'I could pull out of it,' Evan threatened.

Rupert looked crestfallen. Well, his agent would have to live with it, Evan thought. The farther away from London he was, the better; that way it might just stop him from thinking about Fern. Something that he was doing far too much of. Several times in the last few months he'd gone to pick up his phone to call her, simply to see how she was and to try and explain what had happened on their last evening together. Needless to say, he'd never managed to make the call. In the cold light of day, any relationship between them would have been far too complicated. There were too many obstacles to overcome. Too many differences between them. His brain could rationalise all of that, but it didn't seem to make his heart any lighter.

'When this is all over, I'm going to take a few months off,' he said now. 'I might head out to Tuscany, take some R and R.'

Rupert peered over the balcony, trepidation written large on his face. The sight made him grimace. 'How's it all going?'

'Terrible.' Evan shook his head impatiently. 'Why on earth I let that woman talk me into all this, goodness only knows.'

'It will all be over in a few days.'

'If only,' Evan said. 'Did you book a wedding singer to perform the opening number at the ceremony? Lana would kill me if I forgot to do it.'

'If *I* forgot to do it, darling,' Rupert corrected. 'And, yes, I've booked someone great.'

'Someone I know?'

'It's going to be very expensive.'

'I don't care about that, so long as Lana is happy. Who is it?'

Rupert fussed with pouring himself some iced tea and then looked at the glass disdainfully. 'What is this stuff? Why can't they drink proper tea over here?'

'Rup, who did you book?'

'It's a surprise.' Rupert avoided his gaze. 'My surprise. Trust me, you'll be blown away.'

'Is that good "blown away" or bad "blown away"?'

Rupert tapped the side of his nose and winked. 'You'll just have to wait and see.'

Seventy-three

Get this. I'm flying into the USA on a private jet. I look out of the window to give myself a reality check. Yep. That's right. Li'l ol' me is travellin' in big style!

Carl reaches over and gives my knee a squeeze. 'Feeling okay?'

'Yes,' I say. 'Feeling great.'

The steward comes to ask us to put on our seat belts as we're on our final approach to the airport at San Francisco, so I settle back into my seat and close my eyes. It's amazing how quickly I've grown accustomed to all this luxury. And, no, I'm not going to wake up in a minute and find out that it's all been a dream and I'm still without a job and back in Carl's flat having been unceremoniously burned out of my own. At least I hope not.

The rest of the band is with us. Carl managed to pull it all together at short notice by purloining Shelly and her band to back us, leaving Ken the Landlord without a headline act again. It's a tribute to Carl's personality that he manages to stay best mates with all of his ex-girlfriends. However, I have noticed one or two lingering looks between my ace guitarist and my new back-up singer and I'm not sure how I feel about that.

Life continues to be amazing. Our first single has been released and is topping the charts. It's a song that Carl and I penned together, sitting in my lounge when we dreamed about all this sort of stuff happening and assumed that it would, but to people other than us. Thankfully, it's had great reviews—I was even hailed as the new Madonna—and, as a result of all the attention, hordes of paparazzi have been camping out on my doorstep, so that I really know that I've made it. My mum keeps them sweet by taking them out trays of tea and biscuits at regular intervals—which I'm sure will end as soon as they print some scuzzy picture of me in the *Mirror* with my arse hanging out of my jeans or an up-skirt photo or some such. I've also had to employ a bodyguard to take Nathan to school, which he thinks is cool and has given him a certain amount of street cred with his friends. Kids are so shallow, but no longer is Nathan standing on the sidelines while they play without him.

I've been in so many magazines that I've lost count. My mother started a cuttings file to show all her neighbours, but gave up when she'd filled three plastic W. H. Smith ringbinders in the first two weeks. My stylists have turned me into a permanent rock goddess with judicious application of acrylic, highlights and hair extensions. I've been given a sort of Boho look—which I love—and it seems that I'll never have to trouble myself with choosing my own clothes ever again. Carl was deemed to be cool, the stylists loving his retro-grunge look. Just goes to show how fickle this industry can be when the *Fame Game* show bounced him for exactly the same reasons. So Carl still looks pretty much like good old Carl, except he now pays a hairdresser ten times more than he used to, simply to cut a millimetre from the length of his hair. No more the three-quid knife and fork cut for Carl. The stylists seem to think it makes all the difference. And I'm sure it does.

We're heading to San Francisco, where I'm going to sing at a special private gig that Rupert has particularly requested us to do, and then we're flying down to Los Angeles to play at the world-renowned Staples Centre in a summer charity concert where Bruce Springsteen and the Red Hot Chilli Peppers, among others, are headlining. We're way down the list, but we have been given a set of three songs and I still view that as a big step up from top-billing at the King's Head Public House for the Terminally Inebriated.

The plane touches down and Carl and I disembark, waving goodbye to the rest of our party. The other members of the band are staying on board to head straight for L.A. to settle into the hotel and do the sound checks for the gig. We'll join them tomorrow as soon as we're finished here, getting there just in time for the concert. This is the first time that I'll have played before such a big crowd and I'm waiting for the anxiety to kick in, but it hasn't yet. I might not be anywhere near as famous as some of the folk on the bill, but I feel I've earned my stripes through sheer toil and determination.

Carl and I head straight for a stretch limo that whisks us into the terminal. No longer the sardine treatment on a squashed airport bus. We sail painlessly through immigration and, after we pass through a smattering of photographers who seem to be snapping frantically at anything that moves, are relieved to find Rupert Dawson waiting for us.

Our agent hugs me warmly and slaps Carl on the back. 'Welcome to San Francisco. I have a car waiting outside.' And before we know it, we're bundled into another limo and are speeding away from the airport.

On the journey, Carl and I peer out of the blacked-out windows as we wind our way through the streets, taking in some of the vertiginous hills for which San Francisco is famous. We pass a cable car on Powell Street which has a dozen tourists hanging on the outside of it. Then we pass by the California Opera House and I see bright red banners bearing Evan David's name plastered all over the front of its imposing facade. The knowledge takes my breath away.

He's here, in this city, at this very moment, performing in *Turandot*. I could buy a ticket and go to see him tonight. I could sit in my plush velvet seat and drink in my fill of him without him ever knowing that I was there. My heart doesn't know whether to soar or sink. My stomach aches with missing him. Everywhere I go, there seem to be constant reminders, and I wonder will my emotions ever manage to break free from this man? Then I see that beneath his name, written nearly as large, is Lana Rosina's. I feel sick inside. They're here performing together, and I wish that we'd taken a different route and I could have remained in blissful ignorance. I've deliberately avoided surfing the Web to see where Evan is performing. Tailing him round the world like a virtual stalker would have been too, too sad. And now he's here. We're in the same city once more, separated by a few miles, a few streets, a few steps. I feel the colour draining from my face and suddenly the air-conditioning doesn't seem to be working properly. I fumble for the switch to open the window and let a stream of fresh air blow into the car, gulping it down.

Carl swivels in his seat. The lines round his eyes crease in concern. 'Okay?'

I nod, unable to find my voice.

'It's probably jet lag,' Carl says, and I wonder whether he really didn't see Evan David's name in six-foot-high letters.

I nod my agreement again.

Rupert also registers my discomfort, opens a minibar in the limo and smoothly hands me a glass of water as he carries on with his chatter about the sights of the city. But I can tell that he keeps a worried eye on me. I don't suppose he'd be happy if his new protégée showed signs of having regular attacks of the vapours.

Eventually, we pull up outside a plush hotel on Nob Hill—so called Rupert tells us, because of all the 'nobs', or well-off people, who once lived here. This is the sort of place that pop stars stay in, the sort of place I could only ever have dreamed of staying in just a few short months ago.

Carl helps me from the car and then we check in, hanging around in the ridiculously opulent reception while our bags are brought from the limo. This gives me time to calm down and get my emotions back on track. Then we're whisked up to a penthouse suite, which means that basically we have the whole of the twenty-fifth floor to ourselves. The heavy velvets and damasks of the lobby have given way to a more contemporary style, which I'm relieved about. It feels less like staying in a museum.

Rupert tips the bellboy generously and then shows us round the rooms. There are two bedrooms and two bathrooms, both with vast Jacuzzi baths. A glass dining room with the most amazing views takes up the corner of the suite. There's a massive lounge, all decorated in black and white, with a view that takes in the awesome sight of the Golden Gate Bridge.

'I'll leave you to it,' Rupert says. 'I have a function to attend tonight. Can you kids take care of yourselves for the day?'

We tell him that we can.

'You need to be ready by around eleven-thirty tomorrow morning. I'll have a car pick you up.' Rupert checks his diary. 'The stylist and hairdresser will be here at nine-thirty.'

'Two hours to get ready?'

Rupert shifts from foot to foot, looking uncomfortable. 'This is important, Fern. It will be worth it.'

I realise that gone are the days when I could get up and be out of the flat two minutes later. Rupert has been very reluctant to give us any information about tomorrow's event and I don't know why, but I decide not to push it.

'I've ordered breakfast to be served in your room,' he goes on, 'you just need to let them know what you want to eat.' Then Rupert kisses me on the cheek, slaps Carl on the back and heads for the door. 'Have a great afternoon in San Francisco.' He waves at us over his shoulder and is gone.

'Wow,' I say when Carl and I are alone. 'What do you reckon to this?'

'Cool,' Carl says. 'I'm enjoying being a rock god.' He slips his arm round my shoulder and gives me a squeeze. 'I always knew that, one day, you'd keep me in the style I intend to become accustomed to.'

'Well, let's make the most of it,' I chirp, 'and go and paint this town red.'

'I'm going to have a shower first,' my friend says as he moves to pick up his bag. 'I think I'll take this bedroom—if that's okay with you.'

'That's fine.' I don't know why, but I'm relieved that Carl doesn't assume that we'll be sharing a bed. He is so aware of my needs and my feelings and is so careful to respect them that I love him all the more for it.

Then Carl turns back to me and his dark eyes are clouded. 'Are you going to see him while you're here?'

I fold my arms across my chest, hugging myself. 'Who?'

Carl gives me a don't-fuck-with-me-Fern look. Clearly he did see the Evan David posters. I suppose he would have had to be blind to miss them.

'No. I, er…' I'm babbling so settle on, 'We don't have time.'

'If it's important to you—and I think it is—then we can make time. Rupert must know where he is.'

I shake my head. What good would it do to find Evan and talk to him? He's engaged to be married to someone else. What would there be to say? I do admit that to torture myself a little bit more, I've scoured the gossip mags over the last few months for any details of his impending marriage, but I've found nothing and I probably should be glad about that. I can't believe that Lana Rosina has managed to keep this a secret from the media—she's probably sold the rights to 'expose' it for millions. 'I've no wish to bother Rupert with this. I want nothing more to do with Evan David.'

Carl looks as if he doesn't believe me.

'Really,' I insist. 'It's something that I just have to get over.'

'But it's not proving that easy, is it, Fern?'

I don't have to answer as Carl turns away from me and heads for his bedroom. Wandering over to the window, I gaze out at the spectacular view. Somewhere in this city Evan David is going about his daily business. He's doing it with someone else and not with me. And, as hard as it may be, I just have to live with it.

Seventy-four

Yesterday, Lana had ripped up all her costumes, saying that they made her look fat. The temper tantrum had left *La Diva Assoluta* sobbing with exhaustion and the rest of the cast giving her a very wide berth. Evan, who had seen it all before, no longer allowed himself to be distracted by his leading lady. The hard-pressed and ultrapatient folk in the wardrobe department, on the other hand, had stayed up all night to remake the costumes.

Now Lana appeared before him in his dressing room looking radiant in a stunning, tight-fitting black sheath of a dress made in a flattering Chinese style, which certainly emphasised all her womanly curves, but Evan had no idea how she would breathe in it, let alone sing. He hated to admit it, but Lana had been right. This sexy costume was much more to her style than the previous sombre outfits—it was just her timing that was completely off. Why she hadn't taken exception to her costumes during the previous six weeks of tense rehearsals—when she'd taken exception to virtually everything else—was a mystery to him. This season of productions had been fraught with problems and Evan was weary. He was glad that the end was in sight. Thankfully, today Lana looked to be bursting with happiness, which meant that another crisis had been averted. Tonight's performance would, once again, go ahead with Lana Rosina starring as Turandot.

'*Ciao,* darling.' She kissed Evan warmly. 'How are you today?'

Evan shrugged. 'Fine.' His elaborate make-up was completed, his costume already weighing him down and now he was sitting alone waiting for his five-minute call and thinking about Fern when he knew he shouldn't be.

'All the Calla lilies have been delivered for tomorrow,' Lana told him, interrupting his thoughts. 'They are truly divine.' She made an exclamation of joy.

Evan's home had already been turned into a giant florist's and he wondered where they might possibly find room for any more blooms. But if it kept Lana sweet, then who was he to complain? It would all be over soon enough. He only hoped that everything went smoothly or who could tell what kind of sparks might fly. Someone could end up wearing the wedding cake.

'The caterers are starting to arrive. The marquee is looking like a wonderland.' Lana clapped her hands in glee.

Evan tried to drag her attention back from the wedding arrangements—which he had heard more than enough about over the last few months—to the job in hand. 'All set for tonight?'

His leading lady waved her hand dismissively. 'Tomorrow is

my big performance,' she announced airily. 'I am saving all my
energy for that. Tomorrow I will be the happiest woman in
the world.'

Evan took her hand. 'I'm pleased to hear it.'

Lana's tantrums were disrupting everything lately, and he sincerely hoped that after the wedding she'd settle down to being
a minor whirlwind instead of the tornado she'd become. Lana
was one of the most acclaimed sopranos of her generation and
yet, despite her outward appearance of arrogance, she still was
deeply insecure about her talent. It wouldn't do for her to see
the reviews from her last performance or she'd be thrown into
a blue funk again. Evan surreptitiously moved the pile of newspapers farther under the dressing table with his foot. At best
she'd been called 'distracted' and 'lacklustre'. Evan knew that
she'd be mortified to read the critics' remarks, and her publi-
cist had done a great job in keeping her well away from them.
He, on the other hand, had been praised for his 'heroic physical appearance'—which made him smile—and for his 'un-
quenchable vitality'. Which was nice because his vitality had
never felt more quenched.

Lana leaned against his make-up mirror. 'This is important
to me,' she said with a pout. 'I don't want to spend the rest of
my life alone. Look at Callas.' She tossed back her hair. 'She
died alone and friendless, her voice all but gone. Who wants
that?'

Who, indeed? Evan thought. Maria Callas was the icon of
her generation, revered by everyone who met her, yet she'd
ended her life a virtual recluse living on a cocktail of pills and
tortured by doubts, believing she'd failed to make her mark on
the world. Evan knew that Lana was tortured by the same fears,

and he was aware that this forthcoming marriage meant a lot to her.

'There is more to me than my voice,' she continued petulantly. 'I want to make bambini. I want a family.' Lana hugged her arms around herself. 'That will be my legacy. Dozens of little Rosinas running around.'

The thought of that, quite frankly, terrified Evan. One of her was more than enough to cope with.

'Don't you want that, too?' she enquired sweetly.

Evan sighed inwardly. What he wanted from life seemed to be infinitely more complex.

'It may mean that I have to work less,' Lana said. Evan thought that he'd believe that when he saw it. Would Lana really find that the demands of a young family held the same appeal as crowds of adoring fans? 'You do understand that, don't you, darling?'

Evan nodded. 'I understand.'

'And you still love me?'

'I adore you,' Evan answered glibly.

'And you always will?'

'Until the seas run dry.'

Lana gave him a wry glance. 'This will make me very happy.'

'Then it's the right thing to do, Lana.'

His leading lady slid onto his knee and put her arms round his neck. The five minute announcement came over the intercom: the performance was about to begin. Lana looked deep into his eyes. 'And what will make *you* happy, my darling Evan?'

Evan averted his gaze and stared into the mirror instead. Now there was a question that he'd like to know the answer to.

Seventy-five

Carl and I have a wonderful afternoon taking in the sights of San Francisco. We walk the streets hand in hand, visiting Fisherman's Wharf to sample all the seafood on offer at the rows of stalls, and then we wander along to Pier 39, along with all the other tourists and families, to watch the range of mad entertainers who perform there. I buy postcards—a serious one for Joe and Nathan; a picturesque one for my mum and dad; a rude one for Ken the Landlord. We sit on a bench and eat home-made ice cream while I write them and then we watch the boats in the Bay bob out to Alcatraz and beyond, mesmerised by the constant bustle on the water and on the seafront. But still nothing makes our heads whirl as much as how far we've come in such a short time. I lean against Carl and let my head drop on his shoulder. I'm tired, but happily so. He strokes my hair and I hear him sigh. And I wonder again if I can love him as much as he deserves.

When darkness starts to fall, we take a cab up to Haight Ashbury and stroll along the streets made famous by the Summer of Love in the 1960s. This is the place where 'flower power' first arrived and never went away. The tiny boutiques that line Haight Street are filled with vintage silk dresses and tie-dyed clothes from Thailand and India. Incense oozes out of every doorway. There are shops selling bondage gear, Grateful Dead memorabilia, palm-readers abound and, if you're a vegan, this place must be heaven as there seems to be a huge choice in extreme food cafés. All tastes catered for.

Beggars in Gothic clothing grace every corner, and a woman cycles past us on a bike covered in plastic flowers. Some of the hippies, it seems, haven't realised that it's all over. There are too many people with tattoos and green Mohawk hairdos and too many tourists in preppy clothes with video cameras and dropping jaws.

'I could live here,' Carl says with a wistful air. 'Are we planning to conquer America?'

'I'm sure that Rup won't miss an opportunity,' I reassure him.

'Are you having a good time?'

I kiss him on the cheek. 'I'm having a great time.'

Carl pulls me into a second-hand record shop the size of an airline hangar and we spend hours browsing through old favourites, relaxed by the *clack-clack-clack* of people rifling through the acres of cut-price CDs; it sounds like the movement of prayer beads. Even though there's nothing costing more than ten dollars in this place, I can't believe how much I've spent when we stagger out later with armfuls of booty.

'One day,' I say to Carl, 'our records will be in here, too.'

And I think this area is definitely getting to him because my friend replies, 'This is a weird trip, man.'

We laugh and move off down the street, loaded down with bags.

'Let's eat,' I suggest. 'All that shopping has made me hungry.'

We find a lively Mexican restaurant on the corner of the intersection of Haight and Ashbury, the streets that give the area its name. Latin-American music pounds out into the street and we slip inside. The decor is as eclectic as its clientele. We make ourselves comfortable in a black leather booth and marvel at the shrines that decorate the walls featuring crutches covered in sea shells, slinkies, car springs, decapitated dolls and plastic tropical fruit among the pictures of Christ and the Madonna— a sort of blend of religion and cannibalism. There's a plastic pineapple on the bright blue tablecloth at our table and it's filled with fresh orchids.

Carl selects one from the bad-taste vase. 'If you come to San Francisco you've got to wear flowers in your hair. Isn't that what the song said?' He tucks the flower gently behind my ear.

I blush and then fuss with the menu. We order a pitcher of sangria, which is strong and sharp enough to strip the skin from the roof of our mouths. It slides down in a moment, so we order another, chasing it with appetizers of spiced shrimps and fried plantains that we feed each other with our fingers.

I choose a particularly succulent prawn for Carl, peel it with tender, loving care and hold the juicy morsel to his lips. Carl circles my wrist with his hand and holds it tight as he eats my offering.

'I don't ever want to forget what it feels like to have days like today,' he says when he's finished, and there's a catch in his voice. 'It's been wonderful, just the two of us. I'm feeling already that we're caught up in a raging whirlpool and I don't want to be sucked in. I never want to forget what it feels like to enjoy the simple things in life. All this is fun.' He swipes a hand at the decor, but I know what he's really talking about. 'It makes you realise what's important, too. When all this ends—and it will—I don't want to be left without anything in my life. I want the good things still to be there.'

'They will be,' I say softly. 'We'll make sure they are.'

'You could make an honest man of me, Fern Kendal.'

And I don't know if it's the sangria talking or whether I've had some blinding flash of realisation or have come to terms with the fact that Evan David is completely unattainable or what, but I look at Carl and it suddenly doesn't seem like such a bad idea.

'Do you know,' I say, 'I think I could.'

Seventy-six

Last night's performance had been a great success and now
Evan was getting ready for his next one. He lay in bed, arms
behind his head, and studied the ornate ceiling while trying to
summon up his strength to face the day.

Lana had been up and about directing the household since
dawn—he could hear her voice echoing through the house,
bossing everyone around. Evan sighed to himself. He had no
idea where the woman got all her energy from. Perhaps she
was buoyed up on a tide of love. Evan only wished he could
say the same thing himself. He hadn't even been able to face
the obligatory final-night party for the cast after the performance last night. Normally, he hosted them at his own home,
but Lana's current hijacking had put paid to that. There was
no way she would have tolerated a rival celebration in the
house. The rest of the cast had decamped instead to a trendy
restaurant for their merriment—Absynthe or Jardiniere, Evan

couldn't remember which. All he'd done was sign a few auto-graphs at the stage door and then, exhausted, had headed for home. Lana followed shortly afterwards.

On cue she now burst in through the bedroom door. Her dark hair was piled high on her head and was threaded with pearls. Even at this hour, her make-up was meticulously ap-plied. She was wearing a white silk dressing gown and white marabou-trimmed mules. 'Why are you not ready, darling?'

Evan checked his watch. 'There are hours to go yet, Lana.'

'And you have a lot to do.'

'Isn't it bad luck for anyone to see the bride before the wed-ding?'

'I make an exception for you. Get up, get up,' Lana bullied. 'I need you to be ready.'

Then she dashed out again.

Evan sighed as he switched off his bedside light and hauled himself out of bed and into the shower. He turned the head to a massage setting and let the hot needles of water bite at his body, nipping away the tiredness.

Back in the bedroom, Lana had been in again and had laid out his clothes—a black morning suit with a white wing-collared shirt, a cream brocade waistcoat and matching cravat. Dermuid the chef had obviously been in, too, and had deliv-ered him a glass of fresh juice. It was green and Evan hoped that it contained lots of spinach as, like Popeye, he thought he could do with an extra boost today. Wisely, he downed it be-fore dressing. If he spilled it on his white shirt, then he would be the first casualty of the wedding day.

Evan went to the French windows and threw open the doors, stepping out onto his balcony. The hammering and banging had stopped now and the teams of workmen had disappeared, leaving his garden transformed into a tropical paradise with hundreds of white flowers. The huge marquee dominated the lawn and there was a bower framed with dozens of white roses under which the vows would be said. The only thing that hadn't changed was that the wedding planner was still there, screeching into her cell phone. Erin was trailing around after her, and Evan wondered whether his assistant would ever forgive him for this.

Back inside, Evan finished towelling himself down and then started to get dressed.

He was going to sing a wonderful song called 'The Prayer' today—one of Lana's favourite tracks from his last album. A fitting song for a fitting occasion. He started to warm up his voice and then stopped, thinking of the night that he'd gone up on stage with Fern at that terrible pub and had performed a song by the Beatles for the first time in years. The night when things had all gone so very wrong. His heart still contracted with pain to think of it, even though months had passed and he'd found more than enough to occupy his mind since then. He still couldn't get Fern out of his head. Evan wondered how she was now, and he was sure that she'd be fine. If there was one thing he could say about her, it was that she was resilient. He'd offered to help her out financially, but Rupert said that she'd refused everything. Well, that pretty much told him where he stood.

Evan regarded himself in the mirror, smoothing down his waistcoat. The suit was a good fit and so it should be; Lana had marched him to enough damn fittings for it. He looked so sombre—as if he were going to a funeral, not a wedding.

Evan tried a smile, but somehow he just couldn't make it fit. Rupert would be here soon, that would cheer him up. He'd make his agent tell him some dumb jokes or something. Anything to get him out of this black mood. Perhaps it was all this talk of weddings that was making him feel so melancholy. Maybe when the wedding was over, he'd feel differently. He certainly hoped so.

Seventy-seven

Carl and I spent the night together in my bed, but there was no more reference to our momentous conversation. As I lie in Carl's arms I'm not sure whether he seriously proposed to me or whether I seriously accepted.

Our breakfast arrives and we get up, sit in our sumptuous dining room with the whole of San Francisco spread before us and feast on pancakes laden with fat blueberries and heaps of maple syrup and double cream. Rupert has sent up champagne and orange juice, and we duly oblige him by downing it all. The sun beats down from an unbroken sky and, at this moment, I am the nearest I've come to happiness since Evan David went out of my life. Carl takes my hand and I push away the pangs of doubt that pinch at me. He looks like a man who's very much in love.

When the stylists arrive, I'm feeling very mellow and am more than happy to comply when they choose a white floaty dress for me. They give me white, hippy-chick mules adorned with charms and jewels, and armfuls of silver ethnic bangles. Then—I'm becoming accustomed to this—they puff and preen and polish me to within an inch of my life until I'm looking fabulous.

'Man,' Carl says with a note of awe in his voice, 'you look like you're about to get hitched.'

'Not just yet,' I mumble.

He comes over and kisses me. 'You look great,' he says. 'How could I not be in love with you? How could anyone not?'

Then he flushes when he realises that his statement hits a nerve, but we're both saved from further embarrassment by the swarming stylists whisking him away to choose from their rail of clothes.

Carl gets a loose white linen shirt and jeans with designer re-paired rips all over them because he's rock 'n' roll and can get away with it. We're singing Roberta Flack's song 'The First Time Ever I Saw Your Face' again, and this time I have my security blanket, Carl, backing me on acoustic guitar. Rupert has said nothing except that the gig is for a small, personal gathering. He must have his reasons and, no doubt, we'll soon find out what they are.

Carl takes two minutes to get ready and so he runs through the song, letting me warm up and calming the flutter of nerves that has started in my stomach. The two stylists have a tear in their eyes by the time we have finished and I love the way that this song seems to move everyone who hears it. Then Rupert turns up. He's all smiles and, after raving about my outfit, too, we hop into yet another limousine and are whisked through the streets of San Francisco once more.

Minutes later we pull up at a sumptuous mansion house somewhere in the heart of the city, which seems to take up half a block. There's a lush park opposite where people are walking dogs and a small group of elderly Chinese folks are practising Tai Chi. A row of picturesque painted clapboard houses lines the other flank of the green space, beyond which peeps the magnificent modern skyline.

'Wow,' I say. 'This is an amazing place.'

A white ribbon arch spans the gateway of the house intertwined with heavy white rose blooms, and a host of white balloons flutter in the breeze. Carl and I pile out of the limo.

'Come on inside,' Rupert says and hurries us to the door.

'You didn't tell us that this gig was a wedding.' I've been flown here in a private jet and have been paid an absolute fortune to sing just one song. The penthouse suite we're staying in is more than ten thousand dollars a night, and I wonder who on earth has the sort of money to be so lavish. It makes my recent good fortune pale into insignificance.

'Didn't I?' For some reason Rupert looks agitated.

I turn to Carl and a worried frown creases my brow. Does my friend know something that I don't? I look down at my dress. It's very bridal and I do hope that he's not trying to spring some awful surprise on me. And the truth of what I agreed to last night suddenly hits me.

'What?' Carl says when he sees me looking across at him.

'Is something going on here, Carlos?'

He shrugs. 'Not that I know.' And I have to say that he does look completely guileless. After all this time I'd know if Carl was lying to me.

Inside, the magnificent house is similarly decorated with bowers of white flowers. 'My God,' I whisper. 'Who owns this place?'

Carl gives me another bemused shrug. Who's the richest man on earth? It must belong to Bill Gates, I'm sure.

Rupert motions for us to go into a small drawing room—small being a relative word. 'We'll wait here until they're ready for you,' he says. 'Are you all set?'

Carl, who's tuning his guitar, and I nod. Rupert looks more nervous than the pair of us. I go over to the French windows and look out into the palatial gardens. 'This is one high-show wedding,' I say in amazement.

'Do you want some more champagne?' Rupert proffers a full glass of fizz, which I grab and throw down my neck. I'm going to be roaring drunk at this rate before I've even sung a note.

And then I get a funny feeling, a shiver as if someone has walked over my grave. I'm *not* mistaken. There's definitely something afoot here. The hairs on the back of my neck are prickling—just like they do when there's a thunderstorm due. I put my hand on my hip and try to look threatening. 'Would someone mind telling me exactly what is going on here?'

Rupert flushes. 'I don't know how you're going to feel about this…' he says, nervously licking his lips.

A shard of terror strikes at my poor beleaguered heart. 'About what?'

Then a stressed-looking woman in a silk suit puts her head around the door. 'We're ready for you now,' she says. 'Would you like to come this way?'

'About what, Rupert?'

But my agent stands there looking like a fish out of water and simply says, 'All will become clear later, darling.'

Thoughts of explanations evaporate into thin air as we're whisked out of the drawing room and into the garden.

Seventy-eight

There are hundreds of guests at this wedding, and they're already seated in rows of dainty white chairs, all threaded with ribbons and flowers. The scent is heady and exotic. There's a piano playing and the gentle hum of pleasant conversation fills the air. Carl and I are escorted down the side of the garden among the trees, skirting the assembled throng, and guided towards a large bower that's been constructed in the centre of the lawn. Progress is slow as the heels of my lovely mules keep sinking into the grass.

He takes my hand. 'Nervous?'

'Yes.' For some reason, my heart is jumping all over the place.

Our escort stops when we reach the back of the low stage. 'If you could just wait here a moment please, and I'll let you know when to go.'

I nod to her and take the time while we wait to let my gaze

wander over the audience. What a spruce bunch they are—
I've never seen so many designer labels in one place. If I crane
my neck I could perhaps get a glimpse of the lucky—and
loaded—groom. I inch to the side and peer round a dozen
white roses, and that's when I see him. I see Evan David and
his best man standing in the front row grinning like a pair of
loons and looking as proud as punch. He has never looked
more handsome than he does in his morning suit. Evan's head
swivels in my direction, but he doesn't see me. His eyes just
look straight through me. I stagger backwards and Carl catches
me.

'What?' he says with a note of panic in his voice. 'What's
wrong?'

I can't speak and I feel as if I'm hyperventilating. My breath
is high and ragged in my chest. I am here at the wedding of
the one I love and the pain is indescribable.

'What?' Carl is filled with anxiety. 'Tell me what's wrong.'

But I can't. I simply point, and Carl's gaze follows my finger.

'Oh, Jeez,' he breathes when his eyes eventually alight on
Evan David. 'This is Evan David's wedding?' He slaps his forehead. 'What the hell was Rupert thinking of? Why didn't he
tell you? He knows that you love—' And then he runs out of
words abruptly.

I've started trembling violently, as if I've just been struck
down by flu, and I can't stop. This is the nightmare to end all
nightmares. I beg to some unseen God to please let me wake
up and still be in my bed at my flat before it burned down and
before we became pop stars and before everything that brought
me to this point. I would give it all up not to be here right now.

'Fern.' Carl has gripped me by the shoulders and is shaking me ferociously. I can feel my eyeballs rotate. 'Fern, you've got to snap out of this.'

I have to get out of this place. There's no way I'm going to be able to sing for him. I turn and try to run, but my damn heels stick in the lawn, making me stumble again.

Carl grabs my hand and holds me firm. 'Oh, no, you don't,' he says. 'There'll be no running away from this one.'

Now that I'm coming out of shock, I'm ready to blub. 'I can't do this,' I gasp. 'I can't do it.'

Carl looks sternly at me. 'You can,' he insists. 'You *will* do this.'

'I can't.' I can barely manage to speak, let alone sing. My world feels as if it has crashed around my ears.

'Fern.' Carl is looking very fierce. 'You will *not* let me down. You are a professional singer. We've been paid a lot of money for this. You will dig deep and find whatever you need to get on that stage and sing.'

Who has paid for all this? The private jet, the penthouse suite. Evan can't have requested that I sing at his wedding— that would be too, too cruel. And I can't imagine that Lana Rosina would want me here for her big day, either. My head is spinning, and all I want to do is lie down and die. 'I can't.'

'This is not the time for female histrionics.'

Female histrionics? If I wasn't so distraught, I might just punch Carl.

'Whenever you're ready,' the organiser says. If she's taken aback by my appearance, she doesn't say so, but she gives Carl an anxious glance. 'Take a moment if you need to.'

'We'll be set to go in one minute,' Carl tells her crisply.

In his dreams.

When she's gone, Carl takes the hem of my lovely floaty white dress and turns the fabric inside out, using it to wipe the tears from my eyes. 'Get through this, Fern, and you can get through anything.'

I nod blindly, my vision still blurry.

'I'll be with you,' Carl promises. 'Have I ever let you down?'

I shake my head.

'And I'll get you the biggest glass of champagne that I can find when you've finished.' He takes my hand. 'Ready?'

'Yes.' My voice sounds like a strangled croak, which is not what I was aiming for.

My dearest Carl tenderly helps me up onto the stage, and I walk to the microphone like a blind person. I try not to look at Evan, but I can't help it, and when I catch his eye, I see that his face is lit up with joy. He smiles widely at me, that most beautiful and rarest of smiles. I feel as if I could faint as I prepare to start my song. And I wonder what is going through his head right now and am very glad that he can't see what's going through mine.

At my elbow, Carl strikes up with the introductory chords to our number. I close my eyes and try to pretend that I'm somewhere else. It amazes me when my voice comes out clear and loud. I get a sudden surge out of nowhere that tells me that I can, indeed, get through this. I should try to block the lyrics from going through my mind, but I can't and I let the moving, haunting words flow over me. The words form colours and textures in my brain and I feel almost as if I'm hallucinating. I can barely hear Carl, but I know—as always—that he's there for me.

The song, mercifully, comes to an end and I open my eyes. Tears are streaming down my face, and when I look up I see that tears are streaming down the faces of most of the guests. Evan's face is wet, too, and before I can turn away our eyes meet and I feel like he gets a glimpse into my soul. I step away from the microphone, my legs feeling like jelly, and a wave of nausea washes over me.

Then the familiar music of the 'Arrival of the Queen of Sheba' by Handel strikes up—a very appropriate wedding march in my view—and the vision of Lana Rosina appears at the top of the aisle. She's wearing possibly the slinkiest wedding dress known to man—a sheath of white raw silk that hugs her every curve and is probably a couture number by Vera Wang or someone swanky. Her mane of dark hair is piled on top of her head, threaded with pearls and held in place with a pearl tiara. A long veil stretches out for miles behind her—no demure covering her face for Lana Rosina. She's carrying a bouquet of white Calla lilies. Truly, she has to be the most stunning bride I've ever seen. My insides are chewed up with jealousy. If I had a machine gun, I'd gladly use it.

The assembled guests stand and all heads turn in her direction. Evan David and his best man also stand, and it seems as if Evan is unwilling to look away from me. He mouths something to me that I can't understand and then he does turn his head to watch Lana as she sashays down the aisle. I think my heart may rip open with the pain.

I can stand this no longer. 'Come on,' I whisper to Carl. 'I've done my bit. Let's get out of here.' And I'm off the stage in a flash.

'We have to see this through,' Carl whispers back me. 'We can't leave now, Fern.'

But I'm already striding back up the garden. I see Rupert watching us with a worried frown, but that's his problem. I keep my eyes facing forward as I don't even want to look at what's going on.

'We should stay until the end,' Carl hisses at me. 'It would be rude not to.'

'Do I look like I give a fuck?' I snap. 'We're going straight to the airport to get on that bloody plane out of here.'

We're already at the door of the limo when Rupert catches up with us. 'You're leaving?' he gasps between breaths.

I get into the car. I'm so angry, so distraught, so fucking splattered all over the place that I don't even want to talk to him. He should have told me about this. He should have warned me. But then if he'd told me, I wouldn't have been here at all.

'We're going straight back to the airport,' I hear Carl say. Then he lowers his voice, but I can still make out his words. 'This has been a big shock for Fern. She just wants to get away.'

'Why?' Rupert is very concerned.

'Let's go!' I shout.

'You know how she feels about him, Rup.' Carl spreads his hands and glances anxiously back towards the garden. 'I don't think she ever expected that she'd be singing at his wedding.'

That's a typical Carl understatement.

'Evan David's wedding?' Rupert says.

'Can we just leave?' I'm sounding petulant and I hate myself.

Carl shrugs and slides in beside me, then the limo pulls smoothly away, leaving Rupert looking suitably dumbfounded on the pavement.

Seventy-nine

The ceremony seemed to go on for an interminable amount of time. It couldn't pass quickly enough for Evan—and not for the reasons that he'd already logged. All he wanted to do was get through this and then find Fern. He'd had no idea that she would be here today, and he knew that was why Rupert had decided on keeping the identity of the opening singer a secret from him. The way that Lana was smirking smugly at him seemed to indicate that she was in on the secret, too. Plus there was no way that she'd leave something like that to chance after everything else had been organised with such military precision. Just wait, he'd have a word with the scheming pair later even though he was overjoyed that they'd brought Fern back into his life. They must have known that he was going through agonies without her but was too damn stubborn to be able to fix it for himself. Sometimes it paid to have good friends on board.

424					*Carole Matthews*

Evan did his duty with the rings for Lana and her new hus-band, Christophe Vouray, an up-and-coming tenor from Paris with whom Evan had sung a few times in the past. And, it was true to say that he was honoured that the couple had chosen him to be Christophe's best man even though her fiancé was aware that Evan and Lana had history. Lana looked ecstatic with joy, Christophe, too. For now. It had been a short and stormy court-ship that, Evan suspected, would be followed by an equally short and stormy marriage. With two such huge egos circling in close proximity, their married life would be like the Clash of the Ti-tans. It would take a special kind of man to handle Lana Rosina on a permanent basis, as Evan knew all too well. He'd tried, al-beit briefly and with a certain amount of halfheartedness. Still, it was churlish to be thinking negative thoughts at their wedding and, in his heart, he did wish them both the very best of luck.

The exchanging of the rings complete, Evan took to the stage while the register was signed by the happy couple and sang 'The Prayer' with a new verve in his voice. He added his own silent prayer that Fern would be waiting for him with open arms when this was all over. If she'd agreed to be here, then that surely meant she was considering a reconciliation.

Finally, the strains of the overture from the *The Marriage of Figaro* flooded the garden—the opera on which Lana and Christophe met while performing together in Germany—and the important part of the proceedings was concluded.

Evan shook Christophe's hand and clapped him on the back.

Lana turned to him and kissed him on the cheek. 'Thank you, Evan, for all this,' she said, gesturing around the garden. 'It wouldn't have been the same without you.'

'Congratulations,' he said, and returned the kiss.

'I thought you and I might have made it this far—' she shrugged '—once upon a time.'

'You're much better off with Christophe. He'll be more than a match for you.'

Lana laughed as she raised an eyebrow. 'Maybe it will be your turn next?'

'Maybe,' he said, and he certainly hoped so if he could slay his demons once and for all. 'I take it you knew that Fern would be here?'

'Of course,' Lana said. 'Now you can go and find her.'

'That's just what I had in mind.'

He kissed her again and, as Lana and Christophe made their way back down the aisle, accepting the congratulations of families and friends, he slipped away from the throng to go in search of Fern.

Rupert was pacing up and down on the terrace. He looked pale and was barking into his mobile phone while clutching a glass of champagne with the other hand. When he saw Evan, he terminated his conversation.

Evan took the steps up to the terrace two at a time, suddenly finding the energy that had been missing for so long. 'You old dog,' he said to Rupert as he approached him. 'I didn't know you were such a schemer.'

Rupert's eyes failed to meet his.

'She's good, isn't she?' Evan knew that he was grinning stupidly. 'I told you she was.'

'I signed her a few months ago,' Rupert admitted. 'She's something else.'

'You sly old bastard, why didn't you tell me?'

Rupert still avoided looking at him.

'Well?' Evan wanted to know. 'Where is she?'

Rupert shuffled from foot to foot like a schoolboy caught smoking by the headmaster.

Evan's mood darkened. 'Are there any more secrets that I need to know?'

His agent nibbled his lip nervously. 'I think I might have made a horrible mistake.'

'What? Why?' Evan looked around. 'Where's Fern?'

He saw Rupert gulp. 'She's left.'

Evan was taken aback. 'Already?' Perhaps he'd read this situation all wrong. 'What exactly have you been up to, Rupert? She did know that I was going to be here?'

'I might have forgotten to mention that.'

Evan lowered himself into a nearby chair. 'So she didn't want to see me?'

His agent pulled another terrible face. 'That might not be the entire problem.'

'She's not hooked up with that Carl guy?' He didn't think he could bear it if Fern was now with someone else.

'That doesn't quite cover it, either.'

'Then what?

'I think Fern thought that this was actually your wedding to Lana,' Rupert confessed. 'And I don't think I told her that it wasn't.'

Eighty

'That is possibly the most hare-brained plan I've ever heard.' Evan raked his hands through his hair. 'I ought to sack you for this cock-up.'

There was panic in Rupert's eyes. 'I'm sure we can sort something out.'

'How could you fail to tell her that it was Lana's wedding but not mine?'

'I didn't think she'd come if she knew you were here at all. You're both as stubborn as each other. But I didn't think she'd assume it was you getting married. Why would she think that?'

'For the same reason she assumed that I was engaged to Lana.'

'There seems to be a distinct lack of communication between you two, if you don't mind me saying.'

'Well.' Evan strode out into the street. 'We'd better follow her so that we *can* start talking. I need to get this ironed out once and for all.' He broke into a run and dashed to the front of his home while Rupert followed at a pained trot.

'What about the photographs?' his agent wanted to know. 'Lana will go spare.'

His agent, still muttering, picked up his stride in an attempt to keep pace.

'I've done enough for Lana,' Evan shouted back over his shoulder. 'Now I have to do what's right for me.'

A line of limos waited outside Evan's home, but there wasn't a chauffeur in sight. He paced along the pavement. 'Where are all the goddamn drivers?'

'I'll go and find one,' Rupert said and started to scuttle off.

'Don't you go anywhere,' Evan warned. He wrenched open the door of the nearest limo—a stretch one that could hold about twenty people in comfort. 'Can you drive?'

Rupert looked at him in abject horror. 'Darling, I've lived in London all of my life. Why would I need to be able to drive?'

'Get in. Come on.' Evan slid into the driving seat and looked blankly at the controls.

Reluctantly Rupert got in beside him. 'I didn't know that you could drive.'

'It's been a while,' Evan said through clenched teeth as he looked at the array of dials and switches. How car dashboards had changed since then.

Rupert's hand shook as he buckled his seat belt. 'Exactly how long?'

'I don't know, Rupert.' And it was true. He'd been driven everywhere for as long as he could remember. Evan didn't think he'd been at the wheel of a car since he was a callow youth. 'For heaven's sake stop interrogating me and help. How do we get this damn thing started?'

'You turn the key,' Rupert pointed out.

Evan turned the key and the car lurched forward, smashing into the limo parked in front of them.

Rupert unbuckled his belt and started to get out.

'Stay where you are,' Evan ordered.

'It will be a lot quicker if I just go and find a driver. A qualified driver. One with a driving licence. One who won't get us killed.'

'How hard can this be? It must be like riding a bike. Give me a minute and it will all come back.'

Evan pressed the gas and the car lurched back again, this time smashing into the limo behind them.

Rupert put his head in his hands.

'I'm not used to the automatic gear shift,' Evan said. He stamped the accelerator again and lurched out into the street. 'See? Nothing to it.' And he smiled at his agent as they kangarooed down Fulton Street in pursuit of Fern.

Eighty-one

Even though we arrive ahead of schedule, the plane is ready for us in no time and I board gratefully. This is the unmitigated joy of having your own private plane and not having to wait in the departure lounge for a scheduled flight with hordes of tourists. I could never have imagined in my lifetime that I would be experiencing such luxury. Hopefully, it will make up for the shortcomings in other areas of my life.

Within minutes of boarding we're already in the air for the short flight to Los Angeles. When we reach cruising height, the steward comes to offer us drinks. I choose some orange juice in the hope that it will quell my thumping headache. Carl orders a bottle of beer, and when it arrives the glass has been frozen and is so cold that he can barely hold it.

'What I wouldn't give for a nice warm pint of British beer,' he says.

I raise a smile. 'Do you think Ken the Landlord is missing us?'

'No. He'll be dining out on the story of your success for the rest of his life. He'll be the man who gave the world-famous Fern her first break.'

I laugh. 'I can just see the headlines now.'

Because Carl and I are the only passengers, we stretch out in our seats and I kick off my mules with a deep and heartfelt sigh. Carl takes my hand and toys with my fingers. 'Feeling okay now?'

'A bit better.'

'You did very well to cope back there,' Carl assures me.

'Did I?' I take a sip of my OJ. 'I feel terrible for snapping at Rupert.'

'It was a pretty stupid thing for him to do.'

'He's done so much for us,' I say. 'I should apologise to him.'

'And he should apologise to you for putting you in that situation.'

'Maybe he didn't realise how much I still felt...' My sentence peters out.

'For Evan?'

I nod. What else can I do?

'How do you feel now?'

'Stupid,' I say. 'I should move on with my life. So many things are finally starting to go our way. I should be counting my blessings.' *Not wasting time pining for someone I can't have,* I add silently. I go for a bit of overenthusiastic bluster. 'Look at all the great things that are happening for us. We're playing a major concert this evening in front of thousands of people. We should be so proud of what we've achieved.'

'And you've always got me,' Carl says. 'Even though you may not want me.'

'Oh, Carl,' I sigh. 'How could I ever manage without you? You're my rock.'

'Don't forget it,' he reminds me. 'Behind every successful woman is a faithful man in a dodgy denim jacket.'

'Thank you,' I say as I kiss his fingers to my lips. 'Thank you for being you.'

Carl looks out of the window. 'Do you still love him?'

'There's no point in having this discussion, Carl. It's over. That chapter of my life has ended. He's married. I've got to get over him. What else can I do?'

My friend looks into my eyes. 'You didn't say no.'

I didn't, did I? 'My mind's such a jumble right now,' I say honestly. 'Just be patient with me.'

Looking over Carl's shoulder, I watch as the city grows tiny in our wake. Somewhere back there, the celebrations for Evan's wedding will be in full swing. He and Lana will be laughing and all loved-up and I can't even stand the pain of thinking about that.

There's nothing else for me to do—I just have to forget about Evan David. Move on. Put him right out of my mind. Right out of it. From now on my career will be my sole focus. Men—particularly opera singers—will come a paltry second to my single-minded pursuit of fame. I might have left my heart in San Francisco, but there's absolutely no need for me to leave my brain there, too.

Eighty-two

Evan had lost count of how many people had honked their horn at him. Or how many times he'd gesticulated back. Rupert was slumped down in his seat, peering at the road through gaps in his fingers and uttering intermittent howls of terror.

'Shut up, Rup,' Evan said. 'We're nearly there.'

They were still careening their way to the airport. The kangarooing had subsided to a violent lurch, and Evan was almost managing to keep within the lines of the lanes on the highway. The hills of San Francisco had proved trickier. They'd bottomed the stretch limo three times and had hit two parked cars. Rupert had jumped out to put his business card under the windscreen wipers, so no doubt they'd be picking up the bills for repairs in due course. They looked like junkers, so maybe Evan would just buy the owners new cars to appease them.

'What time did you say this charity concert was?'

'She's due on in just a few hours. Timing is very tight.'

Evan frowned. 'You're telling me.'

He pressed the accelerator farther to the floor, ignoring the speed limit. The limo whizzed into the airport slip road, clipping the kerb as it did before Evan slewed it sideways into a parking space right by the terminal building.

Rupert blessed himself with the sign of the cross. 'My whole life flew before my eyes,' he said.

'Was it good?'

'Yes,' Rupert said thoughtfully. 'I've had quite a nice time.'

'Come on,' Evan urged. 'Let's find Fern.'

'And I would like my life to continue. So I won't be getting into another car with you for a while.'

'Don't worry,' Evan said. 'I'll be sticking to singing from now on. I know where my talents lie.' Driving, it seemed, wasn't one of them, and yet he was sure that he had once been quite good at it.

Evan raced into the terminal building, Rupert trailing behind him panting heavily. 'Scheduled or private?' Evan shouted back to his agent.

'Private,' Rupert puffed.

Evan swung towards the VIP area and was instantly recognised as a regular flyer by the stewardess at the desk. 'Good afternoon, Mr David. How can I help?'

'I'm looking for a young woman called Fern Kendal. She's due to fly out to L.A. today.'

The woman looked at her computer screen. 'I shouldn't really give out this information,' she said, giving a coy smile, 'but for you…'

Evan waited, tapping his foot impatiently while he did so. If this was a romantic comedy film the hero would always just catch the plane and there'd be a dizzying reunion where he swung the heroine around in his arms.

The woman continued to tap down her list of departures. Eventually, she looked up apologetically. 'I'm sorry, but you've already missed her. Ms Kendal's plane took off a few moments ago.'

But this was the real world and he'd arrived just too late. Evan felt his heart sink. Rupert came up behind him, panting heavily. 'Good news?'

Evan shook his head. 'No. She's gone.'

They crossed to the window and saw the tail of a plane heading into the distance. Evan wondered whether Fern was on it.

'You need to get my jet ready,' Evan said.

'It's your jet that Fern's on,' his agent admitted.

Evan's face darkened. 'Then hire me another one. Or *buy* me another one. Book me a goddamn commercial airline. Tie me to a carrier pigeon. I don't care, Rup. Do whatever it takes. I have to be in L.A. tonight.' Evan grasped his agent by the shoulders. 'I can't let her get away this time.'

Eighty-three

The Staples Center arena in Los Angeles is full to capacity. I'm lurking in the wings watching the band currently on the vast stage, feeling nervous and faintly bilious. How can they look so cool when I feel so terrified? They're an upcoming American indie band called Craze that I've never heard of, but they sound great. I'm going to have to swot up on my music knowledge now that I'm in the biz. They've certainly got the place rocking.

The crowd is moving as one mass. Girls in skimpy bikini tops sway on the shoulders of burly men as they sing along with the performers on stage. It reminds me of the Live8 Concert in Hyde Park a few years ago, which Carl and I could only go to because we managed to get our hands on a couple of tickets which were dished out for free. This gig is in aid of an outfit called *No Strings* who use puppets to provide information for kids in war-torn areas about the dangers of landmines, and it sounds like a damn fine cause to me.

Carl is beside me with his guitar slung over his shoulder. He's slipped into this world very comfortably and I smile to myself. 'I can't believe we're here, Carlos.'

'You'd better believe it. We're on next.'

'What are you supposed to say to rock gods before they go on stage?' I ask him. 'Good luck seems so lame, and I think break a leg is just for actors.'

'We don't need luck,' Carl says. 'We just need to be great.'

The rest of the band are loitering behind us. They're proving to be a good team; they did the sound checks and got everything sorted out for us this morning. We've all really gelled considering that we've been together for such a short amount of time. I hope that this bodes well for the future.

I've been kitted out in a green chiffon strappy ethnic top covered in beads with denim cropped jeans and high-heeled sandals courtesy of Jimmy Choo. Shelly sidles up beside me. As my backup singer, she's been decked out in coordinating clothing and looks very cute. And I don't think it's escaped Carl's attention. I've also noticed that Shelly's been talking to my dear friend nonstop since we arrived. Whatever there was between them, it clearly isn't over for her, and I can *so* empathise with that situation. It only goes to prove the old adage that you can't choose who you love.

I practise some deep breathing. We're going to be performing our new single and two tracks from the album, which is due for release when we get home, so I run through the lyrics under my breath. My palms are sweating, but I also can't wait to get on there. It's just such a shame that the folks back in England—Joe, Nathan, my mum and dad—can't be here with me, but I know they'll be watching the concert with bated breath as it's going out live on MTV.

Craze finish their set to rapturous applause, take their bow and bounce boyishly off the stage.

'Ready, guys?' I ask. My band punch the air.

Carl pulls me to him and presses his lips to mine. 'You've made it,' he says with tears in his eyes. 'You've bloody well made it.'

And now it's our turn. This is it. This is my moment.

Evan ran through the backstage area at the Staples Center— a place he knew well as he'd performed concerts here a dozen or more times over the years. He'd had no trouble talking his way through the security checks because of who he was. Sometimes being famous had distinct advantages, although his wedding attire was raising some curious eyebrows.

Rupert had hired him a jet to take him to L.A. and he'd got into the air with only a short delay. It seemed he was here just in time to hear Fern's set as the backstage manager told him she was about to go on. He pushed through the crush of musicians and performers as he made his way to the wings, hoping that he might be able to watch from there.

As he approached, he heard the announcement.

'Ladies and gentlemen,' the compère said, 'put your hands together in a big stateside welcome. All the way from London, England—this is *Fern!*'

Out in the stadium, the crowd screamed the place down. He saw Fern clasp her hands in prayer and then run onto the stage. The band followed and Evan recognised Carl as the guy standing at the back. Before he went on stage, Fern's friend turned and then froze as he saw Evan waiting there.

'What are you doing here?' Carl demanded.

'I had to come. I had to see Fern,' Evan said. 'It wasn't my wedding.' He saw Carl take in his clothes. 'I was the best man.'

'So you've followed her here?'

'I love her,' Evan said.

'So do I,' Carl answered bleakly.

'Does she love you?' Evan had to know. If she did, then he would turn around, walk away and try to forget all about her.

Carl's shoulders sagged, and Evan could see his eyes fill with tears. 'Yes.'

Evan felt as if all the breath had been punched out of his body.

Then Carl shook his head sadly. 'But not like she loves you.'

'Then where do I go from here?'

'Remember the night at the King's Head?'

Evan nodded.

A slow smile spread over Carl's face. 'Then let's go for it.'

'It will certainly make Fern's first performance in the USA memorable,' Evan said. Then he clasped Carl's hand. 'Thank you. Thank you so much.'

'If you ever hurt her, I'll kill you,' Carl warned him and then he ran onto the stage.

Our first two songs go down a storm. The audience are really motoring now and give us a great response. I skip about the stage, whipping them into a frenzy, never realising that I could exert this power over a crowd. This is the biggest adrenaline kick I've ever had. I'm just sorry that we only have one more song to go, as I could quite happily stay out here all night. If this has to be my life without Evan David, then it won't be a bad one at all.

I'm ready to launch into our last number when Carl catches my eye. He signals that we're going to slow the pace down, and I'm panicked as I don't know what he's doing and I have no desire to fall flat on my face in front of a capacity crowd at the Staples Center. The rest of the band stop playing, and now I'm really confused. Carl comes to the front of the stage with his acoustic guitar and sits down right on the edge by the footlights. I begin to wonder if he's lost his mind. As he starts to strum, I recognise the chords of the Beatles song 'Yesterday'—the one that I sang with Evan that fateful night at the King's Head before I found out he was engaged to Lana Rosina. What is my mad little friend doing? This is going to break my heart.

I'm blinded by the lights, and then out of the wings I see Evan walk onto the stage. The crowd recognise him in an instant and go absolutely berserk, and all that I feel is that I'm a centre of calm in the middle of a storm. I can't move. My limbs have gone numb, and somewhere inside me there's a sense of acceptance. He's still wearing his wedding clothes and I've no idea what must have happened after Carl and I left the celebration, but if this is what's meant to be and Evan has come here to be with me, then we can work out all the details afterwards.

Evan takes my hand and looks deep into my eyes. 'It wasn't my wedding,' he says quietly to me.

Before I can ask for any further explanations, the screaming dies down and Evan starts to sing 'Yesterday' in that fabulous, rich voice that sends shivers down my spine. This is Evan's apology to me, and the lyrics pierce my soul. I thought I could live without this man, but I now know that I can't.

After the first verse I join in, and we lose ourselves in each other and in the music. Tears stream down our faces as we finish the song. I see that Carl is crying, too. He stands up and goes to Shelly, who throws her arms around him. Somehow my best friend has made this happen for me, and I've never cared for him more than I do now.

Evan leads me to the front of the stage, and he lifts my hand to his lips and kisses it. 'I love you,' he says. The crowd screams their approval.

We take our bow hand in hand, and the audience's cheer reach a crescendo. The whole stadium is on its feet shouting for us. I feel as if the future is stretched out before me, full of wonderful things just waiting to happen. I pinch myself to check that this is, indeed, the real world, and then I fold myself into Evan's arms feeling the power of his strong embrace…and I never want this moment to end.